4 Week Loan

This book is due for return on or before the last date shown
below

4. 8. 14 7. 9. 15		

University of Cumbria

Theatre Noise:
The Sound of Performance

Edited by

Lynne Kendrick and David Roesner

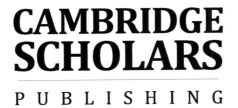

**CAMBRIDGE
SCHOLARS**
P U B L I S H I N G

Theatre Noise: The Sound of Performance,
Edited by Lynne Kendrick and David Roesner

This book first published 2011

Cambridge Scholars Publishing

12 Back Chapman Street, Newcastle upon Tyne, NE6 2XX, UK

British Library Cataloguing in Publication Data
A catalogue record for this book is available from the British Library

ISBN (10): 1-4438-3440-8, ISBN (13): 978-1-4438-3440-7

TABLE OF CONTENTS

LIST OF ILLUSTRATIONS

Figure 3-1: The Wooster Group *To You, The Birdie!* Photograph by Paula Court

Figure 4-1: Still from Anthony Minghella's film adaptation of Beckett's *Play,* Blue Angel Films 2001. Courtesy of Parallel Films

Figure 11-1: "Entr'acte" by Germaine Albert-Birot

Figure 11-2: Untitled incidental music by Germaine Albert-Birot

Figure 13-1: Heiner Goebbels' *Stifter's Things* (2007). Photograph by Mario Del Curto

Figure 13-2: Pat Metheny's *Orchestrion* Tour. Photograph by Ralf Dombrowski

Figure 13-3: Advertisement for an Orchestrion built for the Chicago World's Fair, in 1893. Courtesy of the Tim Trager Archives

Figure 15-1: Graeae Theatre Company's *Reasons to be Cheerful.* Photograph by Patrick Baldwin

Figure 16-1: *Quelqu'un va venir [Someone will come],* a play by Jon Fosse, created by Claude Régy. Théâtre de Nanterre-Amandiers, 1999. Photograph by Michel Jacquelin

Figure 18-1: Paul Savoie in Denis Marleau's *Les Aveugles* (2002). Photograph by Richard-Max Tremblay

Acknowledgements

The editors would like to thank the Central School of Speech and Drama, University of London and the Department of Drama, University of Exeter, for their support for this project. Particular thanks go to:

Caitlin Adams, Joel Anderson, Colette Bowe, Sarah Evans, Stephen Farrier, Carissa Hope-Lynch, Andy Lavender, Dan McGowan, Robin Nelson, Jenny Sealey and James Snodgrass.

We'd also like to thank all photographers who gave us permission to use their images.

PREFACE

PATRICE PAVIS

Are we currently discovering sound? Sound in the theatre, sound in our lives, sound and what distinguishes it from noise, from speech, from silence? *Mise en scène, mise en son, mise en songe?* Staging, sounding, sounding out? At every historical moment—and these come around more and more frequently—we reach a new phase in the performing arts; an original way of conceiving of theatre, and of theorising it, is being sketched out.

Is it sound's turn? Can sound and noise be designed? Can one grasp its hidden designs? The sound design(er) thinks so. But 'sound design' precisely consists of seeing sound as something other than one more piece of design, one more visual trace. The point is to go beyond (or at least to make complete) our vision of theatre as visual *mise en scène* by way of a sonic, auditive, and musical conception of a performance: *aurality*, the counterpart and complement of visuality.

We spend our lives faced with images: they stand in our way, they guide us, and they absorb us. But we live inside the world of sound: it encompasses us, mothers us, feeds and greets us with sound and meaning—it has terrified us since we were little. It is thanks to noise and sounds that we find our position in the world, and we link sound cues with the things, places, and images that appear to us throughout our lives.

But art delights in deconstructing this patiently constructed world, dissociating image and sound: hence a glass that meows as it breaks, lips that explode as they kiss, a person's familiar voice creaking like a door, and all that is now possible on our stages! Even surrealist images never fazed us quite like this.

The discovery of the possibilities of sound in the theatre is almost unheard of; it is unexpected, since theatre was previously understood to be visual (not merely literary and destined to end up in a book, as Mallarmé thought): *mise en scène*, considered the culmination of Western theatricality, is surely visual. So why, then, after the turn of the millennium, does sound cause us to prick up our ears, like a horse ready to gallop away? Beyond hoping for a general semiological explanation of performance, beyond an embodied and physical understanding of the actor in front of us and within us, and beyond the visuality of the world (as promoted by *visual studies;* visuality by way of the eye as well as by way of movement), what else might we find?

We had learned how *mise en scène* groups, hierarchises, or combines its signs—the building materials of an organised world. The sonic aspect certainly always had its place, but it tended to *serve* the visual arrangement, or the design (meaning the sketch and also the intention). But this conception did not take into account the unexpected and necessary resistance emerging from the world of sound, nor did it recognise a phenomenology of listening. This world of organised sound, in fact, as redesigned by theatre practitioners, 'overwhelms' the world of music, passes it on all sides, and drowns it out. Unlike music at a concert, where the musicians and the listeners focus their attention, it is not isolated or capable of being taken in isolation. The world of sound, when it is confronted and combined with the visual and the visible, consciously and unconsciously plays with visuality, as if the better to promote its own uncontrollable subjectivity.

In the theatre, sound is never pure music. Rather, and to its great credit, it is impure music. It is still steeped in what its public embodiment precisely seeks to conceal: the physicality of the performers, the unforeseeable circumstances of the performance, the listeners' more or less noisy and physical attention. To this must be added everything else: the visual setup, the acting, the improbable ballet of bodies in motion. This fortuitous symphony of bodies, of shapes, colours and lines gives sound its colour and its identity; it welcomes all sounds, all noises, and shows them around, an air that was not *(be)foreseen,* nourishing it and causing it to penetrate, as if breaking and entering, the fictional and personal universe of each viewer.

The presence of ever more sensitive sound and soundscapes in a performance coincides with another recent phenomenon of staging: relative dematerialisation. The contemporary stage, in fact, is no longer the realistic illustration of a place or a text, but at most its evocation by way of conventions. It has nothing to do with autonomous stage languages with strong visual metaphors, as seen in the 1970s and 1980s. Sometimes actors, long considered the *sine qua non* of the theatre, are no longer actually visible; they cannot even be reached with the aid of a camcorder, telephone or prerecorded video footage. The rather abstract and immaterial language of sound is thus more readily integrated into the visual representation. The dematerialisation, miniaturisation, and virtualisation of visual or gestural elements facilitate the marriage of sound and image: in fact, they have yet to tie the knot, and lack any absolute hierarchy or definitive contract—either partner might take off at any point ...

All kinds of sounds—from unpleasant noises to the most refined melodies—are reference points in our everyday lives. They allow us to travel all around the world and appreciate its beauty, danger, or consolations. They penetrate our inner life, and mark our social existence. They disappear without a trace, or on the contrary introduce us to other sounds, other imaginary worlds. We endlessly combine them with images, bodily attitudes, and gestures. All the more, since the art of the stage, or that of music theatre, manages to combine visuality and aurality, not as the accumulation or integration of signs in a single, common spatial or sonic volume, but as a confrontation between the two structures, prompting sound and image to see or to hear each other differently. Everything depends on the artistic interactions and interstices of media that have been foreseen (or 'fore-heard') by the *mise en scène*. The art of sound design is *not* to separate the sounds from their spatial situation, *not* to separate them from the body, gesture and the spatial arrangement of the actors. Sound and music no longer have an ancillary function as regards the text or image; indeed, they are independent of them, they force them to take root in the immateriality of the sonic universe.

With this collection of studies on noise in the theatre, a sketched outline for a phenomenology of listening, the foundations of a new discipline (objective and subjective), on sounds and *aurality* (a new notion that the book's chapters seek to establish) are clearly set out. The challenge and charm of this foundational work consists in imagining how far such a shift of sight, hearing, and body might take us. This, in any case, is the objective of this work, the first book tackling the subject: to lay a milestone for research on sound, and indeed for research on dramaturgy and staging as they are still able to function today. By giving sound (and the thousand ways in which it is articulated) a chance, sonic dramaturgy gives theatre, and not just music theatre, a new beginning. By granting noise a place, as the 'other' of organised sound (music and speech), it explodes the traditional boundaries between the different arts of performance and the stage. It lends the work a sonic and rhythmical depth that stage writing once reserved for visuality.

If music stays 'in me', then the sound attached to the visuality and the stage gestures 'enters me', only to 'come out' and 'circulate' inside all that I perceive onstage and in the world, thus enabling me to travel within these musical spaces, places that are both real and imaginary. It is up to me to understand what the sound material is telling me beyond its textual dramaturgy.

The spectator-listener becomes the hero of the day, without whom nothing is possible, irrespective of the noises this chronic troublemaker unfailingly produces, to the great chagrin of other spectators and sometimes the actors. Sometimes the noisy spectator seems to have the task of injecting some noise—but also some meaning—into the show (at points chosen by the spectator, or by the performers). In Korean *Pansori* opera, the spectator, in the course of the performance, has the possibility of making brief interjections, compliments or commentaries. Such *Ch'uimsae*, if correctly placed by a connoisseur spectator—at the right moment, and with the right energy and tone—do not interfere with the dynamics of the singing and playing, and actually strengthen and help the singer. Far from being reduced to annoying noise within the system of communication, *Ch'uimsae* form part of the sonic and visual stage event: the spectators are not abstractions and recorders, but living beings, accompanying and protecting the performance as it unfolds.

This book sketches out and creates the prototype for a new dramaturgy of sound. This will help us rethink the dramaturgy of the performance overall, the better to understand how we experience the performance: by seeing it, hearing it, and embodying it, without always being able to distinguish between these perceptions. Thus we must consider not only the 'listening eye' (Paul Claudel), but also the seeing ear, which discovers the visible and invisible worlds that sound endlessly creates or suggests.

Such is the miracle of a dramaturgy of sound: sonic writing continues to develop; sounds, words, noises, images, and gestures come together, unite, and invite us to feel (to experience) works in the making and our world in motion.

Translated from French by Joel Anderson

INTRODUCTION

LYNNE KENDRICK AND DAVID ROESNER

1. Premises

Theatre and performance studies: why so silent?

A theatrical situation, as John Cage put it in 1968, consists of "things to hear and things to see" (Cage in Kostelanetz 1970, 51). While the latter, the 'spectacle' of theatre or the visual stage has dominated the discourses on theatre histories and performance analyses, the former, the sound of performance or the acoustic stage, still deserves to be listened to more carefully. From Ancient Greece, which built theatres with optimal *acoustic* qualities, the etymology of 'persona', which refers to the actor's 'sounding through' (*personare*) the mask, to the proclamation of an "acoustic turn" 2500 years later by Petra Maria Meyer (2008), there are many phenomena that strongly suggest a closer investigation of the sonic aspects of theatre and performance.

This book is a timely contribution to this emerging field and looks in particular at the interrogation and problematisation of theatre sound(s). Both approaches are represented in the idea of 'noise' which we understand both as a concrete sonic entity and a metaphor or theoretical (sometimes even ideological) thrust. The contributions to this edited volume are indebted to a range of recent research from a number of disciplines: as there are almost no theories of theatre sound to speak of,[1] the authors have drawn upon and contextualised their work in a web of references to musicology (e.g. Attali 1985; Cox/Warner 2004; Hegarty 2007), film sound (e.g. Chion 1994; Beck and Grajeda 2008), philosophical and sociological theories of sound and/or voice (e.g. Schafer 1994; Serres 1995; Kahn 1999; Bull and Back 2003; Dolar 2006; Birdsall

---

[1] Ross Brown (2010) provides the first in-depth *critical* approach to sound in theatre, but most of the literature on theatre sound consists of books which either explain the historical development and current usage of sound in the theatre, or suggest ways in which to create sound for the theatre. See for example: Kaye and LeBrecht 1992; Bracewell 1993; Leonard 2001.

and Enns 2008), and phenomenologies of listening and silence (e.g. Cage 1987; Erlmann 2004; Schmitz 2008; Voegelin 2010). Noise has proven to be a truly interdisciplinary phenomenon, which has resonances and echoes in the sciences and humanities, but whose impact on and implications for live (theatrical) performance need further 'sounding out'. *Theatre Noise: The Sound of Performance* will be a first step.

What is theatre noise?

Theatre provides a unique habitat for noise. It is a place where friction can be thematised, explored playfully, even indulged in: friction between signal and receiver, between sound and meaning, between eye and ear, between silence and utterance, between hearing and listening. In an aesthetic world dominated by aesthetic redundancy and 'aerodynamic' signs, theatre noise recalls the aesthetic and political power of the grain of performance.

For us, 'theatre noise' is a new term which captures an agitatory acoustic aesthetic. It expresses the innate theatricality of sound design and performance, articulates the reach of auditory spaces, the art of vocality, the complexity of acts of audience, the political in produced noises. Indeed, one of the key contentions of this book is that noise, in most cases, is to be understood as a plural, as a composite of different noises, as layers or waves of noises. Facing a plethora of possible noises in performance and theatre we sought to collocate a wide range of notions of and approaches to 'noise' in this book—by no means an exhaustive list of possible readings and understandings, but a starting point from which scholarship, like sound, could travel in many directions.

There is a departure from the everyday notion of noise purely as nuisance and disturbance as well as its usual narrow definition *ex negativo,* as not sound, not music, not intelligible signal. Jacques Attali has thus defined noise as "the term for a signal that interferes with the reception of a message by a receiver, even if the interfering signal itself has a meaning for the receiver" (Attali 1985, 27).[2] If noises are "the sounds we have learned to ignore" (Schafer 2004, 34) in order to avoid its interference, then this books deals with noise(s) that cannot or should not be ignored, that raise questions, render the production and reception of acoustic signals problematic as intervention or friction and thus force us to reflect on the preconceived distinctions of signal and noise. The theories and case studies presented here investigate how theatre, as a place, an event or a

---

[2] See also Gareth White's chapter in this book (chapter XVII).

communicative convention, (re-)negotiates certain aspects of noise including those that might be excessive, unwanted or unintended, not meant or not meaningful. They examine how theatre makes the distraction or distress of noise productive, and affords experiences of materiality as well as abstraction, of subjectifying immersion as well as objectifying de-familiarisation.

This book and its contributors thus propose a radical re-think of noise, not just in relation to the perception or production of, but in our understanding of theatre. The *ex negativo* of noise is not only refuted but reversed. In theatre and performance, noise becomes effective and even productive. Moreover, theatre has the capacity to challenge and alter our understanding of noise and its place in the theatrical soundscape. As Ross Brown (chapter I) proposes,

> theatre should feature prominently as the artform whose self-contained microcosmic scope, whose intermediality and whose governing conventions, whether adhered to or departed from, expose and make play of the interactions between noise, signal, silence and the corporeal subject more than any other.

The notion of noise in theatre as interference is relatively new, as Jean-Marc Larrue (chapter II) points out, prior to the advent of sound mediation, noise was an intrinsic part of "performance's sound universe." Indeed it is theatre's subsequent resistance to sound reproduction technologies as a form of noise that drowns out the "consecrated" (Larrue) place of theatre, that this book sets out to refute.

Theatre Noise: The Sound of Performance owes its title and initial concept to both a seminar and subsequent conference organised by the Central School of Speech and Drama (London) in 2009.[3] Following these events we have curated and strategically invited for this book a range of developed ideas and positions from theatre directors, performers, sound designers, musicians and academics from different disciplines who engage in practice professionally as well as a form of research. These map out the field of theatre noise and will hopefully stimulate further and even more far-reaching discussions about its relevance for theatre and performance aesthetics, processes and histories.

---

[3] In November 2003 Ross Brown convened a seminar entitled 'Theatre Noise' for the London Theatre Seminar series. See http://www.theatrenoise.org.uk/index.html (accessed April 5, 2011).

How to read this book

For the organisation and dramaturgy of *Theatre Noise: The Sound of Performance* we thought of two metaphors from the world of sounds: the audio patch bay where a diverse range of inputs and outputs are interconnected in multiple ways with coloured cable, or alternatively the emerging webs of connections that websites like *last fm*, or software like *iTunes* with its 'genius' function, create between songs because they have something in common: a genre, style or musician.

So while this book *can* be read from beginning to end, it is actually not constructed as a linear narrative, nor organised in larger units or parts (which again would have prioritised some interrelations over others) but instead seeks to 'patch' multiple connections between single chapters, and find 'genius' type correlations. Some of these we will draw out and develop in the following section, others may emerge individually for the reader. The experience may be similar to the often described 'cocktail party effect'—a psychoacoustic phenomenon described elsewhere in the book[4], which describes our ability in 'noisy' surroundings, to 'tune into' different conversations around us and foreground them while suppressing and filtering out others.

2. Patches and Correlations

There are a number of connecting themes and resonances between the following chapters. You will find, for example, that many chapters approach theatre noise from historical and philosophical perspectives. In addition, echoes can be perceived between different ways in which sound and noise become central aspects or entry points for the analysis of performances. And finally, there are those connections which foreground the experiential aspects of theatre noise with a particular interest in audience(s): some of the pervasive themes here are: sound and immersion, sonic interactions between stage and auditorium and the variety of ways of listening that come into play in the theatre.

We will now tease out in more detail the implicit and explicit dialogues in this book based on the following correlations and patches, or through-lines and territories of theatre noise. Commencing with the beginning and end of all sound in *silence*, next we trace the connection of theatre noise with bodies and materials by drawing together adumbrations around

---

[4] See also Ross Brown's chapter in this book as well as Barry Arons "Review of the Cocktail Party Effect" at http://xenia.media.mit.edu/~barons/html/cocktail. html (accessed March 15, 2011).

embodiment, the bruiteur/Foley artist, materiality, and *vocality.* We then focus on structural and semiotic aspects of theatre noise under themes of *musicalisation* and *production of meaning,* explore its relation to sight and site in *sound and vision* and *space,* and turn to theatre noise and audiences in *immersion, interaction,* and *listening.*

Silence

All sound, noise, music and utterance begin and end with silence. Silence is the continuous counterpoint, the defining 'other' to theatre noise, sometimes as a manifest absence of sound, sometimes more philosophically as an idea and ideal. Particularly after John Cage's famous observation that there can be no absolute silence, Brown speaks about the "anxiety of silence" (chapter I)—the anticipatory quietness of a large audience—and questions whether the widely accepted convention for a silent and seemingly undistracted audience, is really what the theatre needs and speaks of an "unhealthy phobia" expressed by the strict conventions for silent auditoria.

This assumed correlation between silence and compliance is dispelled by John Collins, who shifts the emphasis from the innate capacity of silence for meaning, to its *theatrical* potential and effectiveness. He describes Elevator Repair Service's experiments with "super-charged silence[s]" (chapter III) as a vehicle for sonic anticipation and discusses how various pieces have successfully exploited the power of silence in performance. Danijela Kulezic-Wilson discusses in particular the *dramatic* and *musical* purposes of silence in Samuel Beckett's plays and in *Play.* Here, multiple silences shape our experience of passing time and help to rhythmically organise the performance: "the function of silences in this play is more structural than expressive" (chapter IV). Where Kulezic-Wilson draws out attention to silence as an instrument in guiding our diachronic reception, Katharina Rost adds a focus on its *synchronic impact:* she describes how silence as a relative experience in contrast to the loud sounds of smashing bottles against a wall in Luk Perceval's *Andromache* brings different sonic layers to our attention and exposes more silent noises in a kind of "acoustic close-up" (chapter V). Silence thus becomes an integral part of her phenomenology of noise. Conversely, for Alice Lagaay it is the "intrinsic relation to the possibility of silence" which "distinguishes voice from noise" (chapter VI). Her "(negative) philosophy of voice" claims that voice cannot sufficiently be defined by activity—silence for her is not the absence of utterance, but the moment of *potentiality* of utterance. In articulating this threshold of silence, Lagaay also reminds us of how loudly the absence of sound can "speak".

Embodiment

Rost also reminds us of the etymological connection of 'noise' to the *body*: "the word 'noise' has derived from the Latin word *nausea*, meaning seasickness" (chapter V). Throughout the book authors make striking observations on the physicality of sound and noise, countering the naïve assumption that sound is invisible and intangible. Misha Myers, for example, analyses the relationship between listening and touch through Roland Barthes' suggestion of "a return to the tactility or embodiment of hearing" (chapter VII). Pieter Verstraete adds to this interpersonal physicality of sound the dimension of spatial embodiment: "By placing the sounds we relate to them through our bodies and confirm our own positions. Hence, any disembodied voice calls for an embodiment with which we try to solve the auditory distress" (chapter VIII). He follows Steven Connor's assertion that "sounds are always embodied, though not always in the kind of bodies made known to vision" (Connor 2005: 54). George Home-Cook draws our attention to the idea that attention itself is,

> fundamentally, a dynamic act of embodiment [...]. The word 'attention' derives from the Latin compound adtendere, meaning, 'to stretch.' Hence, at the very core of the notion of attention is the idea of a kind of embodiment that entails a dynamic movement through space. This movement is not only imaginal but actual (chapter IX).

Theatre noise is a physical phenomenon. Where the visual conventions of theatre are often designed to make audiences forget about their own physical co-presence with the performance, it is almost inevitable that the acoustic sphere will remind them of their proximity: the (physical) distress felt by excessive noise or the inability to hear and the many noises that can be read as intrusive (the air conditioning, the whispering audience neighbour etc.).[5] But it is not only the audience members' bodies that are

---

[5] It is probably not by accident that two iconic German theatre productions which started in silence, Michael Thalheimer's *Liliom* (Hamburg 2000) and Einar Schleef's *Salome* (Düsseldorf 1997), were often greeted by audience members offering sarcastic or openly angry shouts of "Lauter!" [Louder!/Volume!] and by a quickly increasing volume of the audience's own 'noises' (murmuring, coughing, rustling, shifting etc.). Interestingly the effect was the opposite in Danny Boyle's National Theatre production of *Frankenstein* (2011) where, for several minutes the main and only character onstage, Frankenstein's monster, learnt how to stand and

brought into focus through theatre noise. There is also a parallel, we would argue, between Cage's re-evaluation of noise in music and, for example, composer Harry Partch's enhancing of the status of the body and the musician's corporeality in (performing) music and the theatricality this affords. In both cases there is a traditional discrimination between what is considered an interference with the 'actual', 'pure' signal, which both Cage and Partch challenge in different ways, as Tim White explores in detail (chapter X). Theatre noise, as a consequence, is not only concerned with the sound of performance, but also with the performance of sound, and the theatrical implications of noise's intrinsic relation to embodiment.

The *bruiteur*/Foley artist

Historically, theatre sound and noise are not only embodied but also personified and a key example of this is the *bruiteur*—'noise-maker'—or 'Foley artist.'[6] An interloper from silent cinema, this pianist's side-show accompaniment provides illustrative sound effects equipped with an array of rudimentary props which, as Adrian Curtin points out, provided irresistible opportunities for comic performance, including "'punning' or 'kidding' the film in the manner of a vaudeville drummer who would call attention to himself and to the whole apparatus of sonic accompaniment as part of the show, as another potential attraction" (chapter XI). Situated adjacent to—and crucially outside the performance event (whether film or theatre)—this creator of sound effects had much potential as a foil for the form of theatre. Brought onstage, the *bruiteur* blatantly reveals the actuality of sound effects' production, a sort of sonic diegesis, and in doing so gains a strategic amount of theatrical and dramaturgical control. Apollinaire's maverick, one-man "People of Zanzibar", Curtin suggests, disrupts the visual 'reality' of the performance, by dint of remaining 'outside' the drama and yet visually present amidst the action and as such, "the thing seen and the thing heard are disjointed as the aural and visual registers vie with one another" (chapter XI).

Collins describes his early career as a sound designer as a "real-time Foley artist" (chapter III), typified by his efforts to source re-purposed

---

walk in silence, merely grunting attempts. The contrast may be explained by the heightened respect the British audience grants to (celebrity) actors (Benedict Cumberbatch and Johnny Lee Miller), but we would argue that it was nonetheless the extended relative silence that made for a particularly captivating and memorable beginning of this show.

[6] Jack Foley inaugurated the art of creating everyday sound effects for Universal Studios in 1927.

sounds to illustrate the live action on stage and timing these to create moments of "slapstick synthesis". Yet Collins' *bruiteur* is interactive, a mistimed effect can incur a wrathful exchange with the performer calling attention to the live production of the theatre event, which Collins describes as "a truth within the artificial reality of the production." Such clowning with unwanted, misplaced sounds is an engagement in the extraneousness of theatre production; a utilisation of noise. As his role developed, Collins delved into noise, incorporating the groaning "noisy behemoth" that was The Wooster Group's set, and later as director, sampling the noisy soundscapes surrounding performance spaces, an act aimed to "gain control of that noise" but which was more overtly a reclamation of it, "the real aural environment."

Both Collins and Curtin assert the function of performance; that the theatrical *bruiteur* and the interactive sound designer operate as a performer, a player in the sound of performance. Indeed the *bruiteur*/Foley artist is an exemplar of the redefinition of sound related roles in theatre production. As Eric Vautrin points out, the complexity of technological advances in sound design mean that the sound artist is no longer "'just' a performer, an engineer, or even a composer, but all three at once" (chapter XII).

Materiality

The notion of embodiment and the figure of the *bruiteur* suggest a strong personal and human dimension of sound and noise. Theatre noise is certainly physical but not only in a bodily sense. It is also a phenomenon strongly embedded in a history and aesthetic of materiality and technology. As a medium it has both resisted and innovated aspects of its acoustic dimension and has explored material as noise and noise as material. Vautrin, for example, provides a concise history of sound production and amplification in the theatre and points us to the fact that,

> sound does not exist outside of that which creates it, be it the performer or speakers. Sound matter can essentially be defined as a series of resistances—between the instrument and sounds; between the performer and the gestures they know only too well; between the flow of sound and the space it meets, speakers and resonances in space, resistances which modulate the electric flow etc.—a resistance to reducing sound to a representation, paradoxically (chapter XII).

This resistance indicates the material nature of the theatre event, its liveness, the human and mechanical effort and process it takes, the creaking of the theatre machine. Whereas Larrue discusses materiality in the context of intermediality and interartiality,[7] Rost chooses a phenomenological approach. In her attempt to describe and analyse the sound of breaking glass in Perceval's *Andromache*, she talks about "sound materiality that consists of timbre patterns" and suggests how timbre might be captured in analysing the sound of performance (chapter V). David Roesner (chapter XIII) and Tim White (chapter X) shift the emphasis again by looking not only at the materiality of sound, but of sound *production*: with respect to different performance practices (those of Heiner Goebbels, Pat Metheny and Harry Partch) they investigate the 'noise' of making music and the physical, technical and material efforts of sound production. Noise here becomes part of the paradigm of self-reflexivity that characterises the postmodern: by exhibiting the materiality of sound performance and using the irritations and friction caused by toying with conventional expectations, these artists remind the audience of the fabricated and material condition of the kind of performance of which they are part.

Lagaay (chapter VI) and Zachary Dunbar (chapter XIV) discuss the materiality of vocality and here, specifically, aspects of how voice as material interrelates with the production of meaning and musicalisation (see also *Vocality*). Lagaay argues that,

> any thematisation of voice implies an attunement to the manner in which the voice is not just a transparent medium for language, insignificant in itself, but that in its very materiality a voice may clash with—i.e. disrupt, undermine, or comment on—the main propositional content of what a speaking person is saying (chapter VI).

Dunbar further describes how the departure from the propositional content of utterance may lead to a musical appreciation of vocal sound and cites Andrew Gibson in saying, "to deal with the voice *per se* in drama would be to deal with [...] material questions of timbre, cadence, emphasis, and vocal nuance" (Gibson 2001, 711-12).

Vocality

The theatrical potentiality of voice material is one reason why the term 'voice'—which suggests the transmission of signal, a certainty of sound—is jettisoned in favour of a more appropriate keyword for this book, 'vocality': this encompasses the plurality of matter and utterance, body and grain, sounds and silences, and noises that might constitute the production of and audience to 'voice'. Contributors focus on aspects of

---

[7] Larrue uses this term following Moser 2007.

vocality, including vocalisation and utterance in order to problematise the primacy of voice; its semantics, semiotics and ethics become questionable.

The arrival of theatre sound technology was—and continues to be— considered an attack on voice. Larrue's history of mediatic resistance captures the essence of the problem caused by mediatised sound as an "assault on the actor's 'presence', which is so deeply connected to the theatre's episteme" (chapter II). The plethora of ways in which sound was mediated—considered in this book as mediatised, remediatised, dematerialised, disembodied and acousmatic—disrupted the primacy of the actor's dramatic voice by, as Larrue asserts "causing [in theatre] the first historic split between the voice and the body." The relegation of voice makes way for vocality as a part of the *material* of theatre. Specific chapters consider its material functionality, whether voice *as* material (Dunbar, Kulezic-Wilson and Kendrick), or the act of *making* voice material (Verstraete) (see also *Materiality*). Furthermore, the decentralisation of dramatic voice in turn provides a refocus on a vocality that functions theatrically, as a medium (Lagaay and Myers) whereby voice is considered an intersubjective, performative phenomenon, somewhere between the material body and the immateriality of sound.

Material vocality is predicated on the multitude of shifts in theatre genre, most recently in the emergence of the postdramatic which, as Dunbar explains, requires a structured approach, a particular "praxis [...] of musicality" in which "the intonation of speaking might veer between intentionality and objectivity, naturalism and melodrama, phonetic utterance and semantic conceptualisation" (chapter XIV). Rost's analysis of Perceval's *Andromache* finds vocality is not a "culturally coded signified like vocal speech" (chapter V) but one component of the material sounds against which the central sound event of intrusive noises is played out. Vocal sounds are amplified and audible but merely a part of a range of body noises. Similarly Lynne Kendrick (chapter XV) investigates the materiality of the deaf actor's production of voice as entirely embodied, subjectively generative, a component of the material of the aural placing of sound.

Verstraete also explores the making of voice material, and claims that the aforementioned emphasis on embodiment is a strategy for the auditory realisation of the disembodied voice, which requires a "voice-body" (chapter VIII) as a means of coping with auditory distress (see also *Embodiment*). Thus there is an intrinsic link between vocality and the body. Similarly, Myers asserts that "the voice has an embodying power to produce bodies" (chapter VII). For Myers, in the audiowalk, the voice (whether live or recorded) is the material of the event but one which speaks "from within the listener's own body" (Stankievech in chapter VII). The artist's voice is atopic, "sonically displaced" and reposited in the percipient, emerging as "the sound of inner speech" but not that of the receiver, dialogically it entangles with the percipient's own "inner monologue". The making material of voice is an interiority of vocality, developed by Lagaay whose version of the inner voice is distinct from thought, carries a moral and ethical authority which invokes and cannot be ignored. It is a particular phenomenon of a "sound that lacks acoustic resonance" (chapter VI).

Noise impacts upon and/or emerges in these diverse approaches to vocality. For instance, intrusive noise designates vocality to its material function as sound (Kulezic-Wilson); noise feeds forms of postdramatic speech as "a continuum between a theatre noise and a concert song" (Dunbar), and noise is the vocal discourse of intersubjectivity (Kendrick).

Musicalisation

One aspect several authors identify and investigate is that the attention to sound and noise brings not only the acoustic but also more specifically the *musical* aspects of theatre into earshot. Thus, musicalisation as a range of strategies for the organisation and disorganisation of theatrical media, of exploring and exploiting the sensual, formal, rhythmic and melodic qualities of all elements of theatre, becomes another through-line of this book. Several authors explore music, sound and noise as key materials, symbolic strategies and working principles in creating performances (composing, devising, choreographing, writing etc.) and discuss instances of theatre striving to become music and—the implicit alternative—to become noise.

Kulezic-Wilson, for example, suggests that Samuel Beckett's work, particularly his experiments with language and form, led to "its musicalisation on a number of levels, subverting the primarily semiotic function of language in theatre and inviting alternative modes of perception" (chapter X) and goes on to analyse how film-director Anthony Minghella transformed "the metaphor of music as a model for language into actuality and extend[ed] the process of musicalisation to screen."

Verstraete extends the notion of musicalisation to the "postdramatic stage" and sees it as an attempt "to break free from certain confinements of the text, as an authoritative voice in the theatrical construct" (chapter VIII) and also argues, in contrast to Hans-Thies Lehmann who "stresses the instrumentalisation and control of sound", that "musicalisation brings a great deal of uncontrollability by means of the interventions of sound and the auditory distress it creates". Musicalisation, therefore, should not simply be seen as an attempt to replace one system of coherence (language, character, narration) with another (rhythm, melody, form), but a shift of emphasis of how meaning is created (and veiled) and how the spectrum of theatrical creation and reception is widened. Dunbar further historicises these aspects of musicalisation, particularly with respect to a long lineage of music-word relationships. He cites Roesner who argues that "musicalisation re-introduces a 'full range of textual potential: as rhythmical, gesticulatory, melodic, spatial and sounding phenomenon *as well as* a carrier of meaning' (Roesner 2008, 3)" (chapter XIV).

Production of meaning

In the production of meaning, sound, silence, aurality, vocality, musicality and noise all agitate received ideas of ocularcentric theatre semiosis. Myers clarifies this potential by demonstrating how a "theatre of sound [...] challenges prevalent conceptions of meaning" (chapter VII). Contributors remind us that meaning is multiple (Dunbar), but that this multiplicity is contingent on the sonic; meaning is musically denotative (Kulezic-Wilson, Roesner, Tim White) noisy (Kendrick, Verstraete) and derived from noise (Brown). Indeed, noise is often referred to as the basis of meaning beyond or anterior to signal and logos, as Serres asserts that ceaseless background noise "may well be the ground of our being" (Serres 1995, 13). Brown elaborates, "noise [is valued] not as an antithesis to reason, but as the necessary condition within which meaning manifests, the entropic state from which and to which all returns if left unchecked" (chapter I).

Theatre noise, on the other hand, is more overt than the embryonic background or residual matter of meaning. Its agitatory affect disrupts and repositions meaning. For Rost, the intrusive sonic effect, like noise, arrests the listener "it has or obtains the power [...] to capture the audience's attention, with or against their will" which has an impact upon "how meaning is constituted within that performance" (chapter V). This direct relation between noise and the production of meaning is also characterised by an excess of noise which can abandon the audience in its midst. Curtin concludes that Apollinaire's aesthetic of visual and acoustic noises creates a "noisy surplus" in which "meaning is a structured free-for-all" (chapter XI). Verstraete's concept of "auditory distress" captures this effect of vocal excess and its disruption of meaning; it is "an austere metaphor that corresponds to the act of response in the spectator, in order to relate to the impulse of auditory intensities by means of meaning making" (chapter VIII).

Myers and Verstraete also assert the function of audience in the production of meaning. Through "earpoints" not "viewpoints" Myers' "percipient" is the "locus of meaning creation" (chapter VII). Verstraete adds that "meaning making is necessarily an embodied effect" (chapter VIII): the audience's act of making sense out of noise. Yet, such embodied, actualised responses to noise should not divert attention from the fakery of theatre and the function of sound in its illusion. Collins' captivation with sounding differing spaces by sampling, amplifying and incorporating extraneous noise is driven by a fascination with disturbing what is and isn't 'real' in theatre production, the result of which is "a charged ambiguity neither provable as real-world fact nor dismissible as mere design" (chapter III). This has nothing to do with realism, but its opposite, the fabric and fundamental fakery of theatre in which any meaning is entirely manufactured. Collins argues that sound, above all elements of theatre, in its capacity to extend, exceed and exist entirely exterior to the limiting physical properties of theatre, is in truth "the best liar" (chapter III).

Sound and vision

Collins' chapter is one of several contributions in which the relationships between the acoustic and the visual stages play an important role. These chapters look at the often polyphonic and contrapuntal tensions between "the thing seen and the thing heard"[8] (Heiner Goebbels) and the separations, collisions and interferences of meanings. Theatre noise is also about how the acoustic and the visual sphere bleed into each other and how effacing the separation can be made productive, both creatively and analytically. For example Curtin and others discuss the consequences of a 'noises on' practice, which makes the traditionally hidden sound production visible and puts a face to the noise (see also *The bruiteur/Foley artist*). In the case of Apollinaire's play *Les Mamelles de Tirésias,* which Curtin analyses, this practice subverts "the supposed normality and logicality of sound making" and calls attention to "to the conventionality of sonic mimesis" (chapter XI). Here, the productive friction results from relating a sound (thunder) to the vision not of its imagined source (dark clouds) but of a man with a sheet of metal.

---

[8] This was the title of Heiner Goebbels' keynote at the Theatre Noise conference at CSSD, April 2009. See http://www.theatrenoise.org.uk/pages/keynotes.html #heiner (accessed April 6, 2011).

In contrast, Collins reflects on his sound practice with Elevator Repair Service and The Wooster Group (chapter III) and describes the theatrical effects of separating sound and vision artificially and stimulating confusion by reproducing the sound that the audience expect from the onstage action *offstage instead*. In doing so he plays with the inevitable discrepancies and synchronisation problems, not least for comical effect.

In her "(negative) philosophy of voice" (see also *Vocality*), Lagaay develops the idea further that sound and vision have more than a dialectic relationship, that theatre can actually facilitate a use of "eyes *as* ears, ears *as* eyes" (chapter VI). She concludes that the "enigma of voice in fact suggests [...] that a real challenge of theory/theatre is precisely to understand, grasp and bring to expression the intrinsic, chiasmic interrelation of these various dimensions". This resonates with Home-Cook's observations that seeing and hearing are not dialectical and dichotomic, but engage in complex interplay. He cites Tim Ingold's assertion that looking is not the enemy of listening but its facilitator: "it is the very incorporation of vision into the process of auditory perception that transforms passive hearing into active hearing" (2000, 277). This form of attention also has spatial implications, to which we will now turn.

Space

"The *there*ness of sound, its "outside quality", is a matter of time and space. What you are hearing, in fact, *is* time and space" (Smith 1999, 7). Bruce R. Smith's theory of sound is that it is manifest through time (frequency), and space (amplitude). Smith's phenomenology of sound, its "*here*ness", is in the ear, where "the physical facts of time and space become the psychological experience" (Smith 1999, 8). In concurrence contributors to this book suggest that theatre sound is fundamentally spatial, it designates and even creates theatre space, yet this spatiality is not the arbitrary property of sound but is designed and directed, it produces the space(s) of performance. As such, the distinction between the production and reception of sound, which Smith argues to be an unhelpful difference of sound ontology and the phenomenology of its experience, is somewhat mixed in theatre practice.

Brown's 'aural paradox' draws attention to the assumption that a sound is first created and subsequently resounded in space. Sound is *of* space, as Brown points out, the initiation of sound—for instance the bell chime—is not the sound itself but its origin, its cause. The actual sound is "spatial, and these spatial qualities are part of the environment within which the conceptualised event-object of the bell figures" (chapter I). Ontologically sound necessitates space "because the spatial characteristics of a sound (its reverberation and resonance) are *not* separate to the sound, they *are* the sound". The experience of it is also its ontology. On a similar note Marie-Madeleine Mervant-Roux explores a "quasi spatial sonosphere" exemplified by the phenomenon of audience to the act of listening in Castellucci's *Inferno* as a form of "hearing of hearing" (chapter XVI). In accordance with Brown, Mervant-Roux stresses that theatre sound is not an object to be perceived, but a tangible spatial event. Sound is not an illustration of, but is constitutional of the theatrical space. Home-Cook goes as far as to suggest that the act of listening is a formation, or even a transcendence of, space. Listening in the theatre is a particular "phenomen[on] of felt space" in which,

> we experience sound to be located neither at a fixed source nor at our ears; neither out there nor in here, but rather, we experience both ourselves and the sound we perceive within a heterotopic zone, a no-space which is constantly *on the move* (chapter VIII).

Outside the theatre walls, in other spaces, sound is the means by which performance spaces are designated. Gareth White demonstrates how the participatory, 'relational' territories of site-specific theatre are created and maintained by the producer's auditory control. Spaces are initially sonically configured—soundscapes for instance enforce mute meandering or alternatively invite specific vocal interaction—and are frequently deterritorialised by means of sonic assaults, a form of "noise as [...] a coup de théâtre" (chapter XVII). Furthermore sound can be the very means by which the performance space is created. Myers inverts the notion of the sound of theatre to "a theatre of sound" (chapter VII). A "theatrical auditory space" which displaces that basic element ordinarily assumed essential to the inauguration of theatre—the co-presence of actor/audience. At another extreme, in music theatre, sound populates the entire stage space, materially and aesthetically, becoming the sonic, visual and theatrical elements of the performance, even interpolating the role of the performer. As Roesner demonstrates, Goebbels' colossal musical machinery and Metheny's sonic cyclorama "exploit the sheer space [they take] and the spectacle produced by the both intricate and enormous apparatuses by using them as theatrical set design" (chapter XIII). This sonic occupation of space is far from static; as Roesner suggests, such a scale of "musicking" mimics the properties of the stage and dramatic space[9] including "theatrical dramaturgies of expectation, entrance and revelation."

Liberated from signal or object, these theories of the spatiality of sound find noise within their circumference. Noise permeates the audio-walk (Myers) in ways not permitted in the sound-proofed, sterile, "ashamed" (Brown) theatrical space. Moreover, noise is a necessary element of the theatre soundscape. For instance, though Gareth White makes the point that actual noise—of the audience and the performance— is organised, he makes the intriguing argument that its incorporation is an essential element of the relational aesthetic; the potential disruption this invokes. "There is something reciprocal about the invitation of noise—unsettling the audience through participation also brings chaos into the work itself" (chapter XVII).

Immersion

The idea of immersion in relation to sound is, according to Jeanne Bovet, "considered a given fact of 'natural' auditory perception" (chapter XVIII) but shouldn't be confused with any undiscriminating passive mode of perception. Bovet adds: "Immersed in the theatrical sound event, the audience member hears everything, but listens selectively". Brown argues along similar lines when he suggests: "The phrase 'immersed in sound' evokes some kind of ethereal trip or amniotic ambience but my experience of aural immersion consists in the uneasy relationship between listening and hearing" (chapter I). He calls this mode of perception an "anxious dialectic between engagement and distraction" and thus points us to the kind of oscillating experiences that sound and noise afford the audience.

Analytically, it is the potential of sound and noise to be both omni-directional and simultaneous that is challenging. Bovet (chapter XVIII) reminds us of Walter Ong's observation that "sound immersion makes the hearer intimately aware of a great many goings-on which it lets [him/her] know are simultaneous but which [s/he] cannot possibly view simultaneously and thus [has] difficulty in dissecting or analyzing, and consequently of managing (Ong 1981, 129-30)."

---

[9] The terms 'stage space' and 'dramatic space' are used to specify different manifestations of space in theatre. The stage space is the actual stage area, the dramatic space that which is read by the audience as well as the stage and its inhabitants. The dramatic space is a place of convention as well as the production of meaning. For example see Ann Ubersfeld's theory of spatial function in McAuley, 2000, 18.

Both Bovet's and Gareth White's performance analyses demonstrate the importance of sound and noise with regard to the shifting "micro-politics" with which immersive strategies create "imbalances in the audience-performer relationship of the conventional model of theatregoing: the performers retain authority over the action, while the spectators retain the right to stay out of the action, to watch and hear it" (chapter XVII). Immersion is thus not only a specific spatial-temporal exploration of what sound *can* do, but also a factor in performer-audience relationships and interactions.

Interaction

Consequently, quite a few authors show particular interest in the question as to what role noise plays in the interaction between stage and audience. Mervant-Roux (chapter XVI) interrogates the "artificial partition of space" where supposedly one part, the auditorium, is silent (see also *Space*). In her study of audience noises she discovers the importance, variety and function of the auditorium as a soundscape in its own right and how the audience's "sound of listening" forms a vital part of the co-presence and interaction that distinguishes theatre from other art forms.

Gareth White (chapter XVII) investigates more normative concepts of where and when audiences are *meant* to interact by means of sounds—laughter, applause, stomping etc.—and then develops, with Nicolas Bourriaud's notion of relational aesthetics, concepts of interaction particularly in immersive theatre production such as those by *Punchdrunk* or *Shunt* and the risks and benefits they contain (see also *Space*). Brown echoes and historicises the notion of audiences that interact not least by breaking the perceived "needs [of theatre] to police the silence of its audiences and criminalise those who offend against its conventions" (chapter I).

Kendrick adds a further dimension to this when discussing the aesthetics of access facilitated by the aural strategies of Graeae Theatre Company. Interaction with the audience here escapes precisely through the discursive use of noise, which provides access *and* critiques the "banality of accessibility" (chapter XV).

Interaction, however, is not restricted to the relationship between performer and audience, but also between actors and instruments (Tim White, Roesner) or other sound sources (Vautrin, Collins) or different voices (Kendrick, Lagaay, Myers) and can be said to amount to a theatrical quality, that is uniquely due to the *sonic* circumstances and choices of the individual performances.

Listening

Listening is not the same as hearing. Jean-Luc Nancy (2007) has argued that hearing is an engagement in meaning whereas listening is an act of openness to sonority, a "straining toward a possible meaning and consequently one that is not immediately accessible" (Nancy 2007, 6). Attending forms of theatre that do not disclose meaning in a linear, realistic fashion demand different modes of listening. In this book listening occurs in different places as well as in ephemeral ways. The act of audience may be an auditorium, a collective listening body (Mervant-Roux); an individual discriminatory ear (Bovet); mobilised by the body and sensed through one's feet (Myers); or by means of mediatisation, an entirely aural experience, one which is severed from the visual (Larrue). Or the audience is caught in a process of attendance, stretching towards (Home-Cook) or immersed entirely within the matter of sound to the point where one ceases to hear (Vautrin).

Mervant-Roux reconsiders the theatre as a listening space, where the act of audience can be heard. But the noise of the audience is not merely a response, rather "the audience is always producing a permanent acoustical modulation of the scenic action, a true modulation of *acoustics*. What we may call 'the sound of hearing'" (chapter XVI) and it is this that constitutes theatre *as* theatre. Furthermore, Bovet argues that in the auditorium the act of listening is not all encompassing, (chapter XVIII, see also *Immersion*), that the theatre audience is actually engaged in auditory focus, a tuning in to sound, a specificity normally only associated with directional vision. Vautrin's approach to the concept of directed listening is to consider sound as diegetic, not "distinct from its diffusion" and as such it is "matter and gesture [...] an experience" and one which can be 'marked' by the composer in order to demand a listening which is not "just getting pleasure from a sound, but rather an exploration of something like the thickness of sound; as though listening was hearing without hearing, hearing something which cannot be heard and cannot be expressed" (chapter XII).

For Myers audio-perception is the "primary mediating sense" (chapter VII) in the audiowalk, yet the motion of the walk coupled with the sensorial experience, intimacy and interiority of the re-embodied voice produces a form of "listening that speaks" which in turn conjures the presence of the absent artist to the extent that "it is not enough to say that the performer is not present" in the audio event. Similarly the quasi-acousmatic separation between the presence of the actor's body and the mediation of the actor's voice presents Home-Cook with an aural/visual conundrum in which the thing heard becomes temporarily disassociated with the thing seen, as "our ears often get it wrong" (chapter VIII). At this point listening comes into play as a range of attentional manoeuvres, which de-acousmatize the vocal sound with its source and in doing so implicates the listener, the body (see also *Embodiment*) and the auditory space (see also *Space*). Home-Cook argues for a phenomenology of theatrical listening; one which asks *how* we hear, explores its "co-option" with vision (Ingold 2000, 278), and plunges the listener into a multi-layered attentional process of "sonic/aural juggling" (chapter VIII).

Listening is not merely reception but is active perception, and one which Frances Dyson claims is ignored in Western metaphysics and culture because of its suffuse quality, its ephemeral incorporation of self, sense, vocality, body and place:

> In listening, one is engaged in a synergy with the world and the senses, a hearing/touch that is the essence of what we mean by gut reaction—a response that is simultaneously physiological and psychological, body and mind (Dyson 2009, 4).

This all-encompassing act elucidates how theatre is realised in the act of audience, as listening situates the self within the sound of performance—whether we might call this immersion, focus, attention, engagement, embodiment or distraction—the act of listening, as Home-Cook reminds us, "is inherently theatrical" (chapter VIII).

This concludes our selection of keywords, through-lines or audio patches—they are not meant in any way to exhaust the list of possible correlations (and conscious contradictions) in this book, but merely offer entry points into a multi-layered and 'polyphonic' topic; one which, as Douglas Kahn has it, ultimately escapes any attempt of definite treatment: "Noise does indeed exist, and trying to define it in a unifying manner across the range of contexts will only invite noise on itself." (Kahn 1999, 21). But there is one certainty, we feel, with regard to all this: however our notions, theories and methods are going to develop, theatre noise as a concept is here to stay: theatre performance will always have an acoustic dimension and will always need to creatively engage with the 'noise' inevitably created by its liveness and situatedness. Our book, *Theatre Noise: The Sound of Performance* draws attention to a wide range of the issues this raises and addresses the implications this has.

References

Arvidson, P. Sven. 2006. *The Sphere of Attention: Context and Margin.* Dordrecht: Springer Press.

Attali, Jacques. 1985. *Noise: The Political Economy of Music* translated by Brian Massumi. Minneapolis: University of Minnesota Press.

Barthes, Roland. 1991. The Responsibility of forms: critical essays on music, art and representation. Berkeley, CA: University of California Press.

Beck, Jay / Grajeda, Tony. 2008. *Lowering the Boom: Critical Studies in Film Sound.* Urbana and Chicago: University of Illinois Press.

Birdsall, Carolyn / Enns, Anthony. 2008. *Sonic Mediations: Body, Sound, Technology.* Newcastle: Cambridge Scholars Publishing.

Bull, Michael / Back, Les. 2003. *The Auditory Culture Reader (Sensory Formations),* Oxford: Berg Publishers.

Bracewell, John L. 1993. *Sound Design in the Theatre.* Englewood Cliffs (NJ): Prentice Hall.

Brown, Ross. 2010. *Sound: A Reader in Theatre Practice,* Houndmills: Palgrave.

Cage, John. 1987 (1961). *Silence,* Middletown (Connecticut): Wesleyan University Press.

Chion, Michel. 1994. *Audio-Vision. Sounds on Screen*, New York: Columbia University Press.

Collison, David. 2008. *The Sound of Theatre: a History,* Eastbourne: PLASA.

Connor, Steven. 2005. Ears Have Walls: On Hearing Art, lecture given in the series *Bodily Knowledges: Challenging Ocularcentricity*, Tate Modern, 21 February 2003, *FO(A)RM* 4, Topography: 48–57.

Cox, Christoph / Warner, Daniel. 2004. *Audio Culture: Readings in Modern Music,* London: Continuum International Publishing;

Dyson, Frances. 2009. *Sounding New Media: Immersion and Embodiment in the Arts and Culture.* Berkeley, Los Angeles and London: University of California Press.

Erlmann, Veit, ed. 2004. *Hearing Cultures. Essays on Sound, Listening and Modernity.* Oxford / New York: Berg.

Gibson, Andrew. 2001. Commentary: Silence of the Voice. *New Literary History* vol. 32: 711-13.

Hegarty, Paul. 2007. *Noise/Music: A History,* London, Continuum International Publishing Group;

Ingold, Tim. 2000. *The Perception of the Environment: Essays in Livelihood, Dwelling & Skill.* London and New York: Routledge.

Kahn, Douglas. 1999. *Noise Water Meat. A History of Sound In the Arts,* Cambridge (MA) and London, The MIT Press;

Kaye, Deena / LeBrecht, James. 1992. *Sound and Music for the Theatre.* New York: Back Stage Books.

Kostelanetz, Richard. 1970. Conversation with John Cage (1968). In *The Theatre of Mixed Means,* edited by Kostelanetz, Richard, 50-63. London: Pitman.

Leonard, John A. 2001. *Theatre Sound.* New York / London: Routledge.

McAuley, Gay. 2000. *Space in Performance: Making Meaning in Theatre.* Michigan: University of Michigan Press.

Meyer, Petra Maria. 2008. *Acoustic Turn,* Tübingen, Fink.

Moser, Walter. 2007. L'interartialité: pour une archéologie de l'intermédialité. In *Intermédialité et socialite—Histoire et géographie d'un concept,* edited by Marion Froger and Jürgen Müller, 69-92. Münster: Nodus Publikationen.

Nancy, Jean-Luc. 2007. *Listening,* translated by Charlotte Mandell. New York: Fordham University Press.

Ong, Walter J. 1981 [1967]. *The Presence of the Word: Some Prolegomena for Cultural and Religious History.* Minneapolis: University of Minnesota Press.

Roesner, David. 2008. The Politics of the Polyphony of Performance: Musicalization in Contemporary German Theatre. *Contemporary Theatre Review* 18.1: 44-55.

Schafer, R. Murray. 1994. *The Soundscape: Our Sonic Environment and the Tuning of the World,* Rochester, Vt.: Destiny Books.

Schafer, R. Murray. 2004. The Music of the Environment. In *Audio Culture: Readings in Modern Music,* ed. Christoph Cox and Daniel Warner. New York and London: Continuum, 29-39.

Schmitz, Hermann. 2008. Leibliche Kommunikation im Medium des Schalls. In *Acoustic Turn,* ed. Petra Maria Meyer. München: Fink Verlag.

Serres, Michel. 1995. *Genesis.* Trans. G. James and J. Nielson. Ann Arbor: University of Michigan Press.

Smith, Bruce R. 1999. *The Acoustic World of Early Modern England: attending the O-factor.* Chicago: University of Chicago Press.

Stankievech, Charles. 2006. "Get Out of the Room, Get into the Head: Headphones and Acoustic Phenomenology". In *Responsive Architectures,* edited by Philip Beesley et al., 93-95. Cambridge, Ontario: Riverside Architectural Press.

Verstraete, Pieter. 2009. *The Frequency of Imagination: Auditory Distress and Aurality in Contemporary Music Theatre,*

Bruce R. Smith (1999, *passim*) has demonstrated how the acoustemology of early modern England shaped Shakespearean drama. Sound is also found as a *trope* in many world religions and belief systems and ontological philosophies, which perhaps contribute to a general aura of something mystical or spiritual around the subject of sound.

In 'Western' culture, for example, Boethius' sixth century Pythagorean theories of *musica mundana* and *musica humana* (or variations thereof) still resonate, through Renaissance art and in Shakespeare[2]. In them, the cosmos and the human microcosm are connected in a universal sonic ecosystem. The energy synthesised into matter and meaning and exchanged within this ecosystem is the raw, disordered and unruly noise banished from the *camera obscura* of Enlightenment empiricism. Earlier classical ontologies, such as Boethius' valued noise not as an antithesis to reason, but as the necessary condition within which meaning manifests, the entropic state from which and to which all returns if left unchecked (as Serres says: 'no life without heat, no matter, neither; no warmth without air, no logos without noise' (1995, 7). It is the grist and the detritus of processes of order, health and sense; haphazard vibration from which all celestial and biological bodies are 'tuned' into being. In such theories, the universe consists, both physically and metaphysically, in the harmonic relationships between nodes of tuning; in an energetic field whose polar extremes are utter chaos and divine simplicity. In this universe, dissonance was a crisis to order (and thus figures of harmony and noise are prevalent in classical drama).

Elsewhere there was the Upanishad mantra *nada brahma*, 'the universe is sound' and the Hindi musical ontology of the *Sangita-Makaranda* conceive of universal noisy energy as the 'unstruck' sound, *anahata*, of which music, dramaturgy and poetry are all technological workings similar to Boethius' third category of music, *musica instrumentalis.* Today one might also think of the sonic tropes of popular science: of a cosmos widely accepted to be energised by the big bang (an acoustic metaphor similar to *nada brahma*), or of *string*, or *n-theory*, theories that very few can understand but many would claim to believe in and which are (apparently) strikingly similar in principle to *anahata*.

If sound is elemental to theatre, as a building and a live event, then acoustemology is fundamental to dramaturgy, which deals with meaning and must therefore understand that audiences *know* sound only as they are culturally equipped to. The categories of aural dramaturgy—voice, speech, music, noise, silence—are not fixed but determined in the cultured ear of

---

[2] See Lindley 2006, 30-50 and *passim*.

the listener. Here, then, we come to aurality, the subjective phenomenology of hearing.

Aurality

Without it there is no sound.

The wave energy that contains the analogue history of kinetic activity within the radius of an earshot is vibration—tactile, and measurable but mute to anything lacking the aural apparatus and psychoacoustic intelligence to conceive of sound as an aural sensation. Bishop Berkeley knew, in positing his famous 'tree falling in the middle of the forest' conundrum, that vibrating air and sound are different things. Sound, is a perceived phenomenon, *nothing but* subjective inference and any meaning made and exchanged through sounding and hearing is contingent, always, on an aural presence at the eventual end of the signal chain. This eventual subject, whose aural presence converts a quivering volume of air or an mp3 data stream into sound, also has potential to mishear, and this potential is also important to the definition of sound. Noise is also in the hearing.

I want, here, to consider three aspects of aurality: i) the practice of listening as an anxious tug-of-war between engagement and distraction; ii) the paradox of sonic objectivity and aural subjectivity; and iii) the notion of *immersivity* (the buzzword of the moment). But first I should explain a little about how we hear.

At some primeval stage of human evolution, hearing began as a whole-body, omnidirectional sensitivity to vibration in the environment. These sensations were conveyed through the skeleton to a primitive receptor, or ear, and thence to the brain, which gradually developed the ability to differentiate between frequencies and amplitudes of vibration and, from these differences, derive information from the environment that served as an early warning mechanism and presented a major evolutionary advantage. Before this, the universe, in all of its noise, was silent. Only with the eventual evolution of far more complex and sensitive external ears, stereophonic hearing and psychoacoustic intelligence, did the proto-human brain become sensitive to, discriminating of and literate in a world not only of sound, but of sounds—individual events/objects of varying degrees of significance: the sound of moving prey, snapping twigs in the forest, babies' cries and eventually, words (another encoded data stream given meaning in their eventual sounding, whether in the ear or in the inner hearing of silent reading). As other faculties developed there was evolutionary advantage in maintaining the dual perceptual modes of listening and hearing in parallel: in being able to concentrate on individual sounds, while also remaining alert to the whole environment.

One may turn one's head towards a sound to bring it into slightly higher definition, but unlike the eye, the ear has no mechanical way of focusing and when one needs to pay attention to, or keep an ear out for, significant sounds (to *listen*) one relies on the psychoacoustic processes of the brain's auditory software. In order to listen, or *intentionally hear*, the brain has learnt a way to apparently filter out insignificance or blur it in such a way that it recedes into the background (becomes *background noise*). Omnidirectional hearing continues unintentionally in the background of listening. This rather quaintly-termed 'cocktail party effect' (as audiologists call it), brings us to the aspect of theatre audience phenomenology I call *engagement and distraction*.

Engagement and distraction

In undertaking the psychoacoustic process known as 'scene analysis' the brain decides which parts of the complex 'plenum' of acoustic activity in the air within the ear canal belong to which causal events in the local acoustic environment (which we might call 'earshot'). It bases these decisions on stereophonic differentials in timing and phase, and on tonal and amplitude variations, but it also draws intelligence from the other senses, particularly vision. It then offers to the consciously perceiving brain a processed map of the acoustic environment that consists of a number of event-objects, or *sounds*. These stand out from a background field of *noise*, which is the remainder of the acoustic energy that the brain has either been unable to lump together into causal event-objects, or has chosen not to, because it has made what we might term a 'cultured' decision that the causal events behind this noise are unimportant to the meaning the brain is looking for or trying to negotiate in a particular moment. When I say in the previous paragraph that the brain 'apparently' filters out such insignificant noise, I mean that it is not made 'apparent' to the attentive brain as significant sound. But it is still heard, semi-consciously, as a background presence, while the processes of the brain, in the peripheries of aural consciousness, continue hearing and inspecting the *plenum* of environmental data for significant sounds. Even when focusing on a sound, the brain continues actively to negotiate meaning within a total surrounding field of noisy acoustic circumstance. Listening is an activity that makes an *event-object* of the focus of its attention, but hearing, in computer terminology, runs in the background, alerting the user to certain programmed categories of event: the breaking of a twig; the rustle in the undergrowth. Listening is thus *subject* to hearing. Actively 'paid' or 'given' attention is continuously tugged and grabbed by events in the heard environment, the listening brain is continuously diverted from and then reinvested in its object. Sound must therefore be understood as ontologically distracting, and theatre must be understood, not as an uninterrupted programme of reception, but as a continual oscillation between engagement and distraction.

Aural paradox

Peripheral awareness of background ambience such as birdsong or waves helps in the recognition of place, while registering spatial reverberation and resonance in the background helps orientate the hearer within the physical environment. We know what we mean when we talk about 'background sound'. But let us unpick the notion of resonance. It is as though the sound has a primary location where it originates, and a secondary location, in the way it resonates (or resounds, the word itself suggesting a secondary event, as though the sound exists twice).

But here we arrive at what I term the aural paradox, because the spatial characteristics of a sound (its reverberation and resonance) are *not* separate to the sound, they *are* the sound, which is indivisibly a space-time phenomenon and may no more exist outside of acoustic space than be frozen in time. If we imagine a sound—say the chime of a bell and the way it echoes around the village—we may think and talk of its point of origin as an object (a discrete event) but the point of origin is not the sound, but the cause of the sound, which is spatial, and these spatial qualities are part of the environment within which the conceptualised event-object of the bell figures. There is only one sound, one event, one thing, and logically a thing may not be both its self and its environment (see O'Shaughnessy 1957).

This seeming paradox is brought about in the perception by the brain's evolved psychoacoustic ability to isolate and thus objectify a programme[3] of significant sounds while blurring the others into an indistinct background. This subject/object paradox is maybe one of the reasons that Cartesian logic tends to be conceived not in auditory, but in visual tropes, where things are far more straightforward.

---

[3] I use the word programme to describe the signal stream / scenography of sound (as a time-space phenomenon it has to be both) that is the object of the listener's attention.

Immersivity

The phrase 'immersed in sound' evokes some kind of ethereal trip or amniotic ambience but my experience of aural immersion consists in the uneasy relationship between listening and hearing. If I am aurally immersed it is in an anxious dialectic between engagement and distraction, or in the paradox between my listening self, which knows languages of sound, and my hearing self, which knows circumstantial vibrations, my place in their environment and certain prescribed categories of event to which it knows to alert me. I suspect my own particular sensitivity is unusual in that has been trained by decades of practice in theatre, which involves almost continual switching between intensely detailed listening to a programme of sound on the one hand and obsessively anxious appraisal of the overall acoustic environment on the other. But I feel some accord between my sense of aural subjectivity and the way in which the trope of immersivity is used to perceptualise theatres of paradoxical multiplicity, rhizomatic web structures, interactive environments such as game-play and so on. I am not sure that theatre companies such as Punchdrunk necessarily mean to invoke aural subjectivity with their use of the word in connection to their brand of theatre, nor that Sky or Sony in trying to sell me ever more immersive HD or 3D televisions do. But following on from the fetishisation of surround sound and of personal stereos, the languages by which the relationship between the consumer and cultural product is described seems to be becoming more characteristically aural.

Whether the current popularity of immersive gaming or 3D cinematography is indeed indicative of such a shift will be for history to decide, but earlier cultural or consumerist 'crazes' that have caught the public imagination (such as the seventeenth century *camera obscura* that I have already mentioned, eighteenth century interest in 'the picturesque' in nature or the nineteenth century *stereoscope*), have convincingly been cited by cultural historians as signs of changing conditions and techniques that constitute a 'modernisation' of perception and thought. Less attended to by the likes of Jonathans Sterne (2003) and Crary (1996), who have written about this in relation to aurality and vision respectively, are the ways in which such modernisation has also often presciently echoed in the theatre. Thus, as Locke and others were considering the *camera obscura* as a model for enlightening empiricism, seventeenth century theatre, in its architecture and the development of a more significant role for the 'scene', was also representing a reorganised model of subjectivity. The noisy resonance of the arena gave way to an increasingly rectilinear 'here and there-ness' and detached observation from one general end-on aspect—a model strikingly similar to Locke's trope of the *camera obscura* as a place of unmitigated conveyance of sensations 'from without to their audience in the brain' (Crary 1996, 42).

One might then consider the popularity of the eighteenth century Eidophusikon, which imbued moving pictures with *mood*, partly though diegetic sonic atmosphere, or the curious fad for the opaque, tinted, portable mirrors known as 'Claude Glasses'[4] used by artists and tourists to view the landscape in a more moodily picturesque rendering. These seem reflective of a growing understanding that what Goethe called *Das Trübe*, (the 'turbid, cloudy or gloomy opacity of experience', Crary 1996, 71) was implicated in any notion of empirical 'truth'. Independently, theatre performance receded from the forestage into the pictorial realm of the scene, auditoria began to darken and thicken with fumes of lamplight, music assumed an ever more important role as an emotional mediator or lens between spectator and dramaturgy that was increasingly structured by pictorial 'situations' and 'effects' (see Meisel 1983, 49-51). Thus, in much the same way as Jacques Attali considers music a prophetic art, whose study reveals early indicators of more far-reaching cultural trends, I would argue that the heated environment of theatre's fast, multidisciplinary, collaborative production processes can constitute, if not a crucible, then a Petri dish where new cultural developments acquire early form.

And thus one might look at theatre's current fashion for interactive immersivity and wonder of what it is redolent. A mode of perspective (which necessarily assumes a detached perceptual position and implies non-participation or involvement) whereby one *watches* television, films or plays, *looks* at art or *listens* to music, seems, in a way that is reminiscent of mid-nineteenth century fashions for exhibitions, stereoscopes and peep shows, to be giving way to modes of wraparound immersivity in which one *wears* 3D glasses, headphones or virtual reality visors, *submits* one's entire field of vision to a huge IMAX screen or *participates* in events. Immersive theatre becomes more the perusal of an environment than show; its audience no longer subjected, from a predetermined viewpoint, to a predetermined story. Rather a multifarious dramaturgy follows and 'subjectifies' them on their personalised promenades of participatory encounter. This is not the 3D of the stereoscope, which was a planar space activated by props and bodies within a framed space, but a surrounding space, perhaps first manifest in the introduction of surround sound to cinemas and theatres (which, barring several experiments in the early twentieth century—see Brown 2010 *passim*—became an increasingly standard practice from the late 1980s onwards).

---

[4] After the landscape artist Claude Lorrain.

The anxiety of theatre silence

Even before surround sound became commonplace in theatre, in the mid-1990s, I remember sound design students were desperate to immerse the audience in noise from loudspeakers all around the auditorium, regardless of my protestations that they should position them carefully and use delay to ensure that the sound image remained properly located within the scene, or else risk distracting the audience (how Lockean of me). I think the point was that they *wanted* to distract the audience from the monolithic unity of the scene. At that time, many directors seemed mystified by the very idea of sound design, hostile to it even, and perhaps as sound designers we tiptoed over-respectfully, during those years of exploding technological possibility, around the venerable tradition of 1950s literary modernism in which directing plays was, as Rebellato describes it (1999, 86-99), all about *noise reduction*. By this he means the minimising of any opaque materiality in production that might mitigate between the writing and its 'audience inside'—in other words, to recreate, as far as possible, the abstract experience of *silent reading*. It was as though the necessity for plays to be staged in the phenomenal world at all was regrettable.

Yes, theatre needs to engage its audience's attention, but the phobia about the audience being distracted by the materiality of production and the extent to which noise became anathema to theatre during the history of its 'modernisation', denies the phenomenology of audience and the ontology of sound as a field both of significant event-objects but also of inevitable distraction. Theatre, after all, situates sentient creatures, evolutionarily predisposed to be distracted as we have seen, not only in a futile construction of noise-abating conventions, but in a *silent crowd*—which Maeterlinck calls "the great active silence [...] the silence of many—silence multiplied, [...] whose inexplicable weight brings dread to the mightiest soul" (Maeterlinck 1897, 8). Since, as Cage demonstrated, silence is noise, this multiplied silence must be one of the most distracting environments imaginable!

When part of a silent crowd, whether in a memorial or a theatrical setting, one's body bristles in omnidirectional attentiveness to the strangeness of the environment. Auditorium silence is now policed by conventional regime, whereas the proto-modern theatres of Elizabethan London, with all their hullaballoo and nut cracking, had to captivate their audience with sonic dramaturgy, with carefully orchestrated counterpoint between wordplay and a sonic metatext (see Smith 1999, 275-283). The three trumpet blasts that heralded the start of proceedings, followed by

frequent prologue pleas for 'gentle hearers' led invariably into some kind
of keynote sound moment (a tempest or a musical exposition) that drew
the audience not only into the narrative, but into a sonic journey from
overture through a succession of flourishes, alarums, musical interludes,
ordnance discharges and aural intrigues, to the finale and the release of
applause. It was a journey programmed with mood changes and
dynamics—like a well-structured mix-tape—not necessarily because the
story demanded them, but because the ear did. Its dramaturgical meta-
function was to keep the ears interested and regularly refreshed; ears that
were, by comparison to today's audiences, differently calibrated by a
different acoustemology and a more panoramic, polyphonically diverse
soundscape.[5] Theatre companies held the degree to which their audiences
kept quiet and listened as a testament to the quality of their work.

The modern demonising of noise (noise, which in the age of
mechanised warfare and industrial oppression certainly had demonic
connotations) seemed, perhaps, to stultify theatre with its nervousness that
any extraneousness—including that of any overt theatricality—might
distract the audience from purer, abstract, intellectual edification. From the
moment Garrick finally dispensed with onstage seating for the chattering
classes, and perhaps in order to set itself above the rowdier music halls,
serious theatre's increasing demands for silence as compliance with a set
of house rules speak of an unhealthy phobia—an irrational fear of
something inevitable and benign. One sits uncomfortably rather than break
the rules by coughing, scratching or stretching. It is as if the breathing,
swallowing and otherwise subjectively-contaminated flesh-bound moment
were an inappropriate aperture through which to appreciate art and that
one should really strain to transcend it; to meet the abstract genius of the
writer half-way in some pristinely abstract space. I now regret telling those
sound students to be so discreet, and think I prefer the Elizabethan notion
of tackling the inevitable tendency to aural distraction through a sonic
dramaturgy that engages with the noise-field and allows the audience the
noisiness of their aural space.

Why theatre noise?

There is a rapidly growing bibliography of philosophical treatises on
sound and auditory phenomenology, theses on sonic arts, theories of
musicology, auditory culture, soundscape studies and acoustic ecology as
well as communications, cultural history and ontology theories, cosmology

---

[5] See Folkerth 2002, 105-121; Brown 2010, 49-65; Smith 1999 *passim*.

and quantum physics that use tropes of music, sound, noise and silence to model new understandings and ways of thinking. Somewhere among them, but not yet ready to be written perhaps, is a theory of noise that cuts across all of these contexts, from the thunder machines of classical drama to the Sex Pistols, and via John Cage, to the big bang, dark material and superstring. My concept of 'theatre noise' merely stakes a claim that in such a theory, theatre should feature prominently as the art form whose self-contained microcosmic scope, whose intermediality and whose governing conventions, whether adhered to or departed from, expose and make play of the interactions between noise, signal, silence and the corporeal subject more than any other.

The multifaceted notion of theatre noise I sketch out here is not by any means an attempt at such a theory; instead it seeks to establish a broader epistemology of sound that allows unruliness and disorder within its eco-system and reconciles dualities within sound that appear paradoxical according to Cartesian reason. In a more polemical way, I object to the pretence that people don't enjoy misfortune, error, malfunction and noise as part of their theatre, or rather I object to the power which is exerted to prevent such noise. Silent listening is socially anxious and anxiety is like noise. The annoyance of phone accidents, rustling sweet papers, coughing and whispering that contaminates the auditorium with intolerance, and the increasing trend for actors to break character and victimise those guilty of leaving their phones on (often to applause), has itself become a new form of auditorium noise (and of public bullying).

Theatre noise, somewhat provocatively, informs tutting, noise-sensitive theatregoers that theatre's meaning is contingent on such noise, or at least the risk of it. It is also suspicious of impossible demands for silence in the body and the environment. It hopes for a more ambitious and confident theatre than that which is so ashamed of its own noise and so insecure in its dramaturgy, that it needs to police the silence of its audiences and criminalise those who offend against its conventions, or which is so precious that it insists that it must only be experienced in the pristine exclusivity of its own sounding or apparition, noiseless, immaterial and sterile. It is bemused by white-walled galleries or black-walled theatres that hope to camouflage their thick, material presence with lighting and by pretending to be quiet and still, but which are all the more noisy for their attempts at stealth.

Theatre noise, or at least my conception of it, does not fetishise and foreground noise in the way that punk rock or Japanese noise music does; rather it valorises the background; the extraneous; the unintentional; the turbid; the noise that is an inevitability of sentience. Meteorological, technological or biological, it is active within the meaning of any moment of perception—including any moment in which art is being perceived. As Serres says,

> There is noise in the subject, there is noise in the object. There is noise in the observed, there is noise in the observer. In the transmitter and in the receiver, in the entire space of the channel. There is noise in being and in appearing. It crosses the most prominent divisions of philosophy and makes a mockery of its criteria. It is in being and in knowing. It is in the real, and in the sign, already (Serres 1995, 61).

I think there is noise, tinnitus, or something mundane like the hum of a fridge or the sound of a tin can rolling in a gutter, even in sensation beyond both the imagination and the calculus of reason, in terrible silence or other profound states of the sublime.

References

Attali, Jacques. 1985. *Noise: The Political Economy of Music*. Trans. Massumi, B. Minneapolis: University of Minnesota Press.

Brown, Ross. 2010. *Sound: A Reader in Theatre Practice*. Houndmills: Palgrave.

Cox, Christopher and Daniel Warner (eds.). 2004. *Audio Culture: Readings in Modern Music*. New York: Continuum.

Crary, Jonathan 1996. *The Techniques of the Observer*. Cambridge (MA) and London: The MIT Press

Erlmann, Velt (ed.). 2004. *Hearing Cultures: Essays on Sound, Listening and Modernity*. Oxford & New York: Berg.

Feld, Stephen. 2005. Places Sensed, Senses Placed. Towards a Sensuous Epistemology of Environments. In *Empire of the Senses: The Sensual Culture Reader*, edited by David Howes, 179-191 Oxford and New York: Berg.

Folkerth, Wes. 2002. *The Sound of Shakespeare*. London: Routledge.

Hegarty, Paul. 2007. *Noise/Music: A History*. New York: Continuum.

Kahn, Douglas. 1999. *Noise Water Meat*. Cambridge (MA) and London: The MIT Press.

LaBelle, Brandon. 2006. *Background Noise, Perspectives on Sound Art*. New York: Continuum.

Lindley, David. 2006. *Shakespeare and Music*. London: Thomson Learning/Arden Shakespeare.

Lingis, Alphonso. 1994. *The Community of Those Who Have Nothing in Common*. Bloomington: Indiana University Press.

Maeterlinck, Maurice. 1897. A *The Treasure of the Humble*. Trans. Sutro, London: George Allen. Digitised facsimile edition available at http://hdl.handle.net/2027/mdp.39015013333235 (accessed February 1, 2011).

Meisel, Martin. 1983. *Realizations: Narrative, Pictorial and Theatrical Arts in Nineteenth-Century England*. Princeton, NJ: Princeton University Press

O'Callagahn, Casey. 2007. *Sounds: A Philosophical Theory*. Oxford: Oxford University Press

O'Shaughnessy, Brian. 1957. The Location of Sound. *Mind*, Vol. 66, No. 264. Oct., *471-490*.

Rebellato, Dan. 1999. *1956 and All That: the Making of Modern British Theatre*. London: Routledge.

Serres, Michel. 1995. *Genesis*. Trans. James, G. and Nielson, J., Ann Arbor: University of Michigan Press.

Smith, Bruce. R. 1999. *The Acoustic World of Early Modern England— Attending to the O-Factor*. London: University of Chicago Press.

Sterne, Jonathan. 2003. *The Audible Past*. Durham and London: Duke University Press.

Toop, David. 2010. *Sinister Resonance: The Mediumship of the Listener*. New York: Continuum.

Voegelin, Salomé. 2010. *Listening to Noise and Silence. Towards a Philosophy of Sound Art*. New York: Continuum.

CHAPTER II

SOUND REPRODUCTION
TECHNIQUES IN THEATRE:
A CASE OF MEDIATIC RESISTANCE

JEAN-MARC LARRUE

Given that theatre is the place where spectators watch, it has also always been the place where they hear—and what they hear varies and comes from different sources: the physical space where the performance leaves its sound imprint, the theatre's own sounds and those of the audience. And then there are also the sounds from the stage—the actors' voices, all the noises they make when performing and the sound of the music and sound effects (rain, wind, thuds, singing birds and so on). All these elements make up the performance's sound universe and, until the advent of sound reproduction technology in the late nineteenth-century, they were created live. This juxtaposition of multiple sounds produced in real time in the same space was about to be disturbed by the intrusion of mediatised sound (recorded and played by an apparatus)—and this intrusion triggered a huge debate on the concepts of sound fidelity, authenticity and reproducibility.

In the following thoughts, I will be less interested in that debate and the ideas propounded on either side than in the repercussions on theatrical practice and its status caused by the phenomena and mechanisms that the appearance of mediatised sound provoked. To come to a conclusion, I have adopted the intermedial perspective, since I feel that it is the most suited to focusing on the technologies, materialities and practices at play in the media in order to discern the issues and interactions triggered by that revolution in theatrical sound.

Even today, to state that theatre is a medium elicits a strong reaction and any attempt to include it in the wide-ranging field of intermedial studies must be justified. It was nonetheless the dual conviction that it is a medium and one that falls within the domain of intermediality that prompted this essay. The essay partakes of current reflections on sound reproduction technology's slow, difficult accession to the theatre stage and on the conceptualisation of the phenomenon of mediatic resistance that it exemplifies. But there is no mediatic essentialism. When one medium resists the intrusion of another or of a new technology—as seemed to be the case with electric sound, for example—it does not act like a living organism and mobilise antibodies to chase off or destroy the intruder. The resistance is always generated by the milieu, made up of men and women, in which the medium functions. To the two basic convictions stated above we must therefore add a third: the fate of media and technology is intrinsically dependent upon the milieu in which they emerge or to which they belong. We therefore cannot afford to dismiss the study of sociomediality or media-related social behaviours.

That is why, while intermediality reflects most centrally on the materiality[1] that necessarily underpins any form of mediation, it has made an effort since its inception to take into account the complex relationships that must constantly be redefined between the users and a medium that is itself constantly changing. It must change in response to the ceaseless influx of new technologies, attempts at penetration by other media, and user pressure in terms of their needs and expectations.[2]

Dissociating technique from its user while ignoring the latter would amount to a form of technocentrism and open the way to technological determinism—and this is exactly what intermedial research is determined to counteract. Such an effort is noteworthy because the opposite might be expected from an approach that came to light in the wake of the major technological revolution produced by the advent of the digital age. We should keep in mind that intermedial studies are not even twenty years old.

The milieu plays an essential role in the constitution—or non-constitution—of media. This apparently obvious statement has considerable heuristic implications. The milieu and the media are engaged in an ongoing process of co-transformation, co-destruction and co-construction. To put it another way, media emerge from the milieu they help to shape. It is in fact to underscore the inextricable nature of media and their related social entities that the CRI (Centre for Research on Intermediality[3])

---

[1] Constituent materials (site, body, voice, image, sound, etc.), substrate materials (celluloid, magnetic tape, set, stage, the body again in its role as the 'recipient site' etc.), techniques, and technology.

[2] Despite epistemological work on intermediality, we have not yet arrived at a fixed definition. The definition I have adopted derives from the work of the University of Montreal's Centre for Research on Intermediality.

[3] At the University of Montreal.

researchers have developed the concept of sociomediality just invoked, which is the central issue to be addressed in this chapter.

From an intermedial standpoint, theatricality is nothing other than the mediality of theatre, or what makes it a medium. To quote the striking formula introduced by Jay David Bolter and Richard Grusin, which could be taken as an intermediality watchword, "[a] medium is that which remediates" (2000, 65). Peter Boenisch presents mediality as remediation (2006, 107). Equating them calls for some nuance: If mediality creates mediation, is it also the result? How can that come about? Echoing Marshall McLuhan's idea that every medium contains traces of previous media (1964, 23-24), Bolter and Grusin open up other avenues, always linked to processes and not to states or objects, which are not without interest for the theatre:

> [A medium] appropriates the techniques, forms and social significance of other media and attempts to rival or refashion them in the name of the real. A medium in our culture can never operate in isolation, because it must enter into relationships of respect and rivalry with other media. (Bolter and Grusin, 2000, 65)

The constant borrowing of techniques, forms and social significance, justified by the proclaimed need to more effectively represent reality, serves to explain the nature and dynamics of media that, like theatre, are "networks or hybrids"(ibid, 19).

Even if the term itself is not always used, the principle of remediation has given rise to a wide range of research that, while it does not always address theatre directly, changes our perception of it. Exactly what is remediated and what remediates? And how? There are obviously major ontological issues associated with remediation and it is no accident that one of the most hotly debated works in the theatre research community in recent years, Philip Auslander's *Liveness: Performance in a Mediatized Culture* deals specifically with the notion of presence. The classical definition of theatre has withered away and nothing is left as ultimate necessity or last bastion but co-presence (of the actor and spectator). Even this last link, which is shared with other 'live' performing arts, is threatening to disappear due to the onset of the new media.

Work on the genealogy of the media (in particular that of André Gaudreault, Philippe Marion, Jürgen Müller and Rick Altman) has given us a better understanding of the process of remediation by showing how under certain conditions the emergence of a new medium can result from a convergence of existing cultural series with media and technological innovation. In the cases these authors have observed, the triggering factor is the advent of a new technology that enters and establishes itself in existing media practices, showing what Altman describes as "a new freckle on a familiar face" (2004, 16). The most dramatic and convincing research has to do with the birth of cinema and illustrates, so to speak, a successful remediation.

Walter Moser's works on "interartiality" open up new perspectives on the remediating process by showing how two media—in this case two artistic practices—react when one tries to remediate the other. According to Moser's dualistic view, there is no fixed process: the remediating practice can impose its opacity while the remediated becomes transparent, but the opposite is also possible. All the occurrences examined by Moser, about the encounter of theatre and cinema, cinema and painting, music and cinema confirm his hypothesis. Ralf Remshardt comes to the same conclusion when he analyses Sarah Bernhardt and The Duse starring in their first movie (Sarah Bernhardt imposing her theatre style and The Duse adopting a new acting more adapted to the screen). But the case of the mediatised sound on the theatre stage shows a completely different type of dynamic.

By sound I mean anything heard by the spectator or the actor during a performance. Some of these sounds are live—produced for the first time—others are mediatised. A mediatised sound is any sound reproduced by a technological device in order to be archived, communicated or "reactualized," as Barbier and Lavenir define it (Barbier and Lavenir 1996, 15). In his book, *The Audible Past*, Jonathan Sterne uses the expression 'reproduced sound'—in preference to 'mediatised sound'—to insist on the performative aspect of the emission of a sound that had already been produced.

Amazingly, the two major technologies for sound reproduction were developed during the same period in the late 1870's and early 1880's. The acoustic technology based on the use of a horn as an amplifier (and a wax cylinder for recording), and electric technology using a microphone. We know that both technologies coexisted until the 1920's when the electrical technologies of sound reproduction became the norm.

The examination of the introduction of sound technologies on stage is very interesting from an intermedial standpoint since it provides a clear example of what happens when the remediation process does not work or is not fully achieved. But it might also exemplify another modality of interaction between two media, between a medium and a new technology that could be cryptomediatic to use Roger Odin's terminology (Gaudreault and Marion 2000, 33-34). Another advantage for examining the dynamic of the introduction of sound reproduction technologies in theatre is that it can be compared to other new technologies that occurred at the same time on stage.

While Western theatre rapidly adopted the innovations that electricity could bring to its lighting systems, it waited almost three-quarters of a century—into the 1950's—before allowing electric sound to enter its stages, auditoriums or creative process. It took barely ten years for Edison's incandescent bulb, invented in 1879, to sweep gaslight from the great majority of Western theatre's stages and halls. But seventy-five years after Bell invented the telephone (1876), after Berliner (1877) and Edward Hughes (1878) introduced the microphone and Edison the phonograph (1877), reproduced sound[4] remained a rarity in these venues. During this period, thanks to the new technology, the cabaret, with its singing and comedy (1936), radio (1920), and talking films (1927)[5] experienced their phenomenal growth! Mediatised sound therefore spawned three major media in less than a half-century—the record-phonogram-phonograph system, radio and talkies, all of which weakened the position of theatre in the growing entertainment field, which it had dominated until then.

While issues of safety undeniably eased and speeded the passage from gas to electric lighting, can they justify a delay of sixty years? Surely not. Mediatised sound's inability to reach the theatre stage from 1877 to the mid-1950s, when stages began to be 'wired' for sound and soundtracks came into use,[6] is attributable to a phenomenon that can occur in any step during the remediating process. I suggest we call it 'mediatic resistance' whose effect is to exclude, avoid, prevent and/or delay the introduction into a given medium of a new technology, a new media object or a cryptomedium. The resistance negates any possibility of remediating the intruder in question at a particular moment. But what is the cause?

Obviously, in the case in hand, a reflex reaction would be to attribute it to the technology's shortcomings. But how can we explain why these 'shortcomings' would have kept mediatised sound on the theatre's threshold while they ensured its phenomenal success elsewhere, for recordings, radio and film screenings? The issue of shortcomings is complicated, involving as it does an underlying auditory expectation—

---

[4] "Mediated sound" is taken to mean all sound that has been technologically preserved, communicated or updated. This includes mediated acoustic sound produced by an acoustical horn on wax rolls, plates or discs, as well as the electric sound produced by a microphone and reproduced on loudspeakers, which developed in tandem, with the second definitely supplanting the first from 1925 on.

[5] These dates indicate their first introductions.

[6] One of the first users of a theatre soundtrack was film director Luchino Visconti. It could be said that in this respect, at least, theatre remediated cinema.

horizon d'attente—that is difficult to reconstruct, with all it entails of ideological determinism, aesthetic suppositions and physical conditioning. As Jonathan Sterne insists:

> We can listen to recorded traces of past history, but we cannot presume to know exactly what it was like to hear at a particular time or place in the past. In the age of technological reproduction, we can sometimes experience an audible past, but we can do no more than presume the existence of an auditory past. (2003, 19)

We cannot dismiss the 'shortcomings' hypothesis. In his study on sound in cinema Gomery enumerates a long series of technological failures that delayed the birth of the talkies, but in the case of theatre this cannot entirely explain away seventy five years of progressive technological advances in the field.

An important cause of any mediatic resistance is certainly sociomedial and comes out of the milieu. It is the milieu's resistance to any change that will—excessively—affect its use of the medium and taint its perception. If the concept of mediatic resistance can be said to apply to all types of media, it is especially active in artistic media.

Without taking an essentialist approach, it can be suggested that mediatised sound could not enter the theatre, in terms of both place—the theatre building—and process, until it had ceased to be perceived as a threat to theatre's fundamental nature—in other words, to its theatricality. Paradoxically, shutting out mediatised sound was perhaps even more harmful to theatre—the measure encouraged the spread of highly successful sound media that then competed with theatre in the entertainment field and brought an end to its status as the leading practice. What's worse, the new media corrupted theatre's audiences and agents. They sometimes even appropriated its institutional organisation and modes, such as frontal presentation and a communal experience, and its spaces, as in the case of the cinema, and pillaged the cultural series of 'theatre' without hindrance, as Jürgen Müller suggests.

Theatre's resistance to mediatised sound remains conditional, of course, in terms of time, since it would in the end be accepted and completely 'naturalised' by the stage, but also in terms of space. In fact, theatre did not hesitate to make use of electric sound production outside its premises for the purposes of outreach, thanks to the Theatrophone, radio plays and recordings made by theatre artists that disseminated the products generated by the stage. In other words, the mediatised sound that was completely acceptable off-stage for theatre artists, and obviously for their audiences, was deemed unacceptable on stage, other than as a curiosity.

And it is not insignificant that the new technology was progressively introduced in the most recent, least structured and least prestigious theatrical forms, such as the revue, variety shows, American vaudeville, Grand-Guignol and burlesque. Mediatic resistance is clearly connected to the traditional stage, its operations and its status.

Regarding its operation, an aspect to be analysed certainly is the potential impact of microphones or even more horns on acting and space. It is clear that, due to their technical limits, early microphones had an effect on the configuration of the dramatic space. There was a conflict between technological constraints—where the microphones had to be positioned—and the space of the action, which also affected the actor's gestures and movements. But to a certain extent we could compare these constraints to the space limitations imposed by previous lighting systems such as gas. Why were these kinds of constraints due to gas lighting acceptable and why weren't the new constraints due to microphones? This raises again the question of theatre *socialités*.

As a consecrating space, performance site, and the historical site for an acting body and its voice, theatre felt threatened by the new medium. We should remember that until the advent of mediatised sound, the stage had been, in the audience's and actors' experience, the only place for artists to be recognised—to be, as Giusy Pisano puts it, "consecrated" (2005).

The sound studio, as the competition in transmitting the voice through recordings and radio, was undermining theatre's unique status, called "sacred" by Pisano owing to precisely that power of consecration the theatre stage was believed to possess. The stage was the site of the constantly renewed performance by the sound body that inhabited it and endowed it with its aural quality. In the days before mediatised sound, a "beautiful voice" was necessarily a "strong voice", and the stage was the site of a "strong" and directly shared vocal performance. But what does that performance become when a machine intervenes between the actor and the spectator, and what does that make the stage?

As Jonathan Sterne recalls, the sound industry's insistence on touting the "fidelity" and then the "high fidelity" (to what?) of its products had as its single objective to counter a feeling of "betrayal" that was widespread among artists and spectators (2003, 215). In addition to the questions of reproductive quality and authenticity raised by mediatised sound, its intrusion onto the stage could be seen as a dual assault. First, what Carolyn Marvin calls the culture of "proto-mass media of the twentieth century" (1988, 3) versus the "other" culture, with its freight of nostalgia at the disappearance of the aura; and then the assault on the actor's "presence", which is so deeply connected to the theatre's episteme. By causing the first historic split between the voice and the body, according to Mladen Dolar (2006, 9-12) mediatised sound destroyed the unity of this age-old presence and launched the practice of "blind listening" to a disembodied voice.

It is hard to conceive that the artists and the audience would have accepted without resistance that their stage be stripped of its historic consecrating power and deprived of the aural quality that constituted its prestige and attraction, so as to become the site of inauthentic performance and fragmented presence.

Why then, several decades later, should mediatised sound take the stage and become part of the theatre's creation process without causing a reaction or sparking a debate? That study remains to be done. But certainly the configuration of media had changed: "blind listening" had become an everyday event and had developed new audience's expectations and behaviours that made mediatised sound more natural or, as Lise Gitelman says, mediatised sound became naturalised.

References

Altman, Rick. 2004. *Silent Film Sound.* New York: Columbia University Press.

Auslander, Philip. 1999. *Liveness: Performance in a Mediatized Culture.* New York: Routledge.

Barbier Frédéric, and Catherine Lavenir. 1996. *Histoire des médias.* Paris: Armand Colin.

Boenisch, Peter. 2006. Aesthetic art to aisthetic act: theatre, media, intermediality. In *Intermediality in Theatre and Performance,* edited by Freda Chapple and Chiel Kattenbelt, 103-115. Amsterdam and New York: Rodopi.

Bolter, Jay David, and Richard Grusin. 2000. *Remediation—Understanding New Media.* Cambridge (MA) and London: The MIT Press.

Dolar, Mladen. 2006. *A Voice and Nothing More.* Cambridge (MA) and London: The MIT Press.

Gaudreault, André, and Philippe Marion. 2000. Un média naît toujours deux fois. In *La croisée des médias—Sociétés et représentations—CREDHESS* 9: 21-36.

Marvin, Carolyn. 1988. *When Old Technologies Were New. Thinking About Electric Communication in the Late Nineteenth Century.* Oxford: Oxford University Press.

Moser, Walter. 2007. L'interartialité: pour une archéologie de l'intermédialité. In *Intermédialité et socialite—Histoire et géographie d'un concept,* edited by Marion Froger and Jürgen Müller, 69-92. Münster: Nodus Publikationen.

Müller, Jürgen. 2007. Séries culturelles audiovisuelles ou Des premiers pas intermédiatiques dans les nuages de l'archéologie des médias. In *Intermédialité et socialité—Histoire et géographie d'un concept,* edited by Marion Froger and Jürgen Müller, 93-110. Münster: Nodus Publikationen.

Pisano, Giusy. 2005. *Questions d'histoire et esthétique du cinéma: images et son du présent, images et sons du passé.* Habilitation à diriger des recherches, Université de Lille 3.

Remshardt, Ralf. 2006. The Actor as Intermedialist: Remediation, Appropriation, Adaptation. In *Intermediality in Theatre and Performance,* edited by Freda Chapple and Chiel Kattenbelt, 41-54. Amsterdam and New York: Rodopi.

Sterne, Jonathan. 2003. *The Audible Past—Cultural Origins of Sound Production.* Durham & London: Duke University Press.

CHAPTER III

PERFORMING SOUND/SOUNDING SPACE

JOHN COLLINS

Target Margin Theater—*Titus Andronicus*

In 1991, just out of college, I took a sound design job with director David Herskovits, who had just founded Target Margin Theater. David had been working as stage manager for Richard Foreman, who insisted on developing the design elements of his shows, especially sound, during rehearsal on the set, with the actors. David shared this unorthodox approach to sound and asked that I be present at every rehearsal. Using only a cassette deck, a cheap microphone and a portable CD player I created *in situ* a sound score for *Titus Andronicus* (1991). I would later understand how rare it was for any designer to spend this much time in rehearsal with actors. It nevertheless suited me—I enjoyed working with the actors—and it suited the project. In all its over-the-top gory violence and revenge drama, *Titus Andronicus*, as David approached it, provided countless opportunities for cartoonish sound effects. I had plenty to do creating sounds to enhance acts of violence that were being played as much for comedy as for shock. Even when the actors weren't acting out barbaric amputations with a circular saw (for which I provided sound), they were literally bouncing off the walls of the tiny theatre and perfecting slapstick routines that I could exaggerate with loud impact sounds lifted from Warner Brothers' cartoons.

Executing my design for *Titus Andronicus* required me to participate more as an actor than as a designer. I saw an opportunity in this assignment to perform—albeit from just off-stage. For instance, in one scene an actor, Thomas Jay Ryan, walked onto the stage and collided with a metal pole (an unavoidable architectural feature of the tiny theatre). On a cassette tape I had a recording of an anvil dropping onto a cartoon villain's head. I had found that I could make my relatively crude playback devices work in perfect sync with their performances. As Tom approached the pole, I punched the play button. Eventually, I calculated the timing of my action in the booth so that Tom's head would snap back just as the horrible 'clang' of the anvil burst through the speakers. This took repeated trial-and-error. The unsophisticated technology I was using *required* that I pay close attention and rigorously develop an intimate familiarity with their actions. Only this way could I create a convincing illusion that it was Tom's head striking the pole that had somehow caused the sound, and not my finger on a tape deck's button. My obsessive drive to sell these comic cause-and-effect relationships suited the director's zeal for a densely packed score and sound became a foundation of *Titus Andronicus*.

The Wooster Group—*Brace-up!*, *The Hairy Ape* and *To You, The Birdie!*

This unusual approach to sound design, full of re-purposed sounds and creatively re-imagined causes-and-effects—where the sound designer is sort of real-time Foley artist—first caught my eye in a Wooster Group production I'd attended about a year before. A minor sight-gag in *Brace Up!* (1990), their rendering of *The Three Sisters*, was a revelation for me. In it, the actor Kate Valk performed a short dance, alone upstage, while several other actors drank vodka and sang a Russian song. In her hand she held an empty shot glass. At the end of each verse of the song, in time with the music, she threw her hand out as if to toss the glass, but instead kept it tight in her hand. At that precise moment her hand snapped out, the sound system produced the sound of a glass smashing on the floor.

This simple action and the perfectly timed sound made immediate sense. Even though the relationship was transparently theatrical and obviously mediated by some outside player (the audience could see she had not let go of the glass), the sound perfectly tracked the imaginary trajectory of the glass. The first time that it happens, Kate glances up toward the sound booth, seeming a little sceptical about the disconnection between the sound and the unbroken glass in her hand. At the end of the next verse, she finishes her dance sequence with the same feigned gesture and again it's accompanied by a loud smash. Now she gets it. With a knowing look to J.J. (the man in the booth with his finger on the 'glass break' key), she finishes the third verse by throwing her hand three times, in three directions, drawing a smash each time and gleefully littering the stage with virtual broken glass. What was played first as a sort of unexpected mistake was transformed into a kind of predictable logic, a truth within the artificial reality of the production.

What happened in this bit of slapstick synthesis was more meaningful than a mere design choice. Kate, with her gesture and her knowing look, assumed agency. She was *performing* the sound and it was clear to the audience that she was causing it to happen. The subtlety of her performance and the suggestion that she had discovered a kind of power gave this performer-and-sound relationship a quality that separated it from theatrical design convention. Here was a sound that the actor seemed to summon. And yet, she did not completely control it. Her performance made clear that there was another person involved and her looks up to the booth suggested a conspiracy. She and J.J. were collaborating on a minor magic trick and deliberately showing their hand in the execution. In that performance there were two players: the actor on stage and the man pressing the key that triggered the sound.

In that moment of watching Kate in *Brace-Up!*, I got an inkling of how sound design at The Wooster Group was unique. Wooster Group sound designers (in 1993 I became one) were called on to perform their work, not design it. There were decisions made about types of sounds and choices made about music; but these decisions were made in the process of executing experiments with sound in rehearsal and there was little time spent working outside of them. As a Wooster Group sound designer I participated in every rehearsal and my ideas evolved through back-and-forth play with the actors. The always changing and technologically adaptable environment of those Wooster Group rehearsals demanded that I participate not as a designer, but as another actor, working with the on-stage actors, in real time.

For *The Hairy Ape* (1994), like many shows created by The Wooster Group during the 1980s and 90s, the physical starting point for the piece was a new configuration of their moving steel set. It had been originally created for a 1984 piece, but was modified to serve almost every subsequent show until 2001. The set completely filled the stage at the group's home, The Performing Garage, and it moved on hydraulic rams that created an intimidating—and noisy—spectacle. This was in place and functioning in early rehearsals and the whole room—from the wooden floor to the metal joints of the set itself—groaned and creaked. This noisy behemoth created an unavoidable aural reality, whether it was moving on its own or being rattled and climbed on by the ensemble. The sound design began as an attempt to gain control of that noise. I began crawling around the set with a microphone and sampling sounds as the big steel wall rose and descended. I took these samples and pitched them down, combined them and ran them through a fairly unsophisticated and limited array of digital processors stacked under the mixing desk. As director Elizabeth LeCompte created action on the set, J.J. and I chased it with these sounds (and an original score by John Lurie). We timed our samples and musical phrases to sync with the slamming doors, the lowering of the set's long steel legs and the steel wall as it rose on the hydraulic rams. We followed the actors' performances as well, adding exaggerated metallic bangs every time Willem Dafoe, in the lead role, raged through the long monologues and these were all opportunities for us to re-associate the sounds we'd collected and perform in lock-step with Willem, the other performers and the set itself.

In 2001, *To You, The Birdie!* provided a design-as-performance opportunity unmatched in any previous Wooster Group project. Joining two other designers, I focused my effort on the sampler keyboard. In past shows, I'd had to divide my attention between sound effects, microphone mixing and music playback. For this new piece, with three of us to run the show, I chose to concentrate entirely on re-purposing and re-assigning sound effects. In *Birdie!*, I created a palette of sounds that filled the keyboard. Over the course of the development of the show, we devised an aural logic whose rules mapped sounds to almost every move the actors made. This set of rules connected the actors to their actions and also to the set, redefining hidden corners of the playing space with the sounds the actors appeared to produce when they moved through them.

Running sound for *Birdie!* was more like playing a video game than following a script with cues. Game play, in fact, had been among the director's first inspirations. An early idea Liz had for the show (a new staging of Paul Schmidt's translation of *Phèdre*) was to build the action around the actors playing court sports, especially badminton (see figure 3-1). In the initial physical development of the piece she designed interludes of net-less and extremely athletic badminton matches between actors Scott Shepherd and Ari Fliakos. This modified badminton was physical, dynamic and highly unpredictable. Attaching sounds to the players and their rackets required quickness and a performer's mindset. Using recordings made from the actors' rackets as they struck shuttlecocks ('birdies'), impact sounds from FX CDs and samples from David Linton's electronic score, I created sounds to associate with Ari and Scott furiously slapping the birdie back and forth on the stage. There was one sound I played in tandem with Ari's racket, another for Scott's and a third that I could use at random. I triggered a sound for the birdie missing the racket and hitting the floor—the sound of a glass bottle breaking. If the birdie sailed upstage and landed in a little trough between the platform and a table, I hit a key with a watery splash on it. I invented a complicated set of rules for myself for the badminton games and they began to redefine the physical world of the set. I didn't have cues, just rules. If someone took a step wearing a particular shoe, I triggered a particular sound. If someone dropped anything (including himself) into the trough behind the stage, I triggered a splash. Most of the sixty-one keys on this keyboard remained active throughout the show. The task of obeying the complex set of rules I'd established for actions and their attendant sounds meant my eyes could never leave the stage.

Figure 3-1: *To You, The Birdie!* Left to right: Dominique Bousquet, Ari Fliakos, Suzzy Roche. Photograph by Paula Court

I had to hit my keyboard a few milliseconds ahead of the very fast-moving performers, consequently I had to be able to predict the contact with the birdie before the actors actually made it. In the half-second before, I might intuit a miss. Timing my sound to land exactly with my expectation of the birdie hitting the floor I would trigger the bottle-break sound and quickly follow it with the buzzer to end the point. Of course, it was not a perfect system and sometimes I misjudged. Ari would sometimes achieve the shot my instinct told me he'd miss. In that case, Ari would perform a wrathful protest. In a less charitable tongue-in-cheek acknowledgement than Kate's of J.J., he would shoot an incredulous look at me in the booth, throw his racket down—to which I would add an explosive sound—and storm off the stage. Even when my logic fell apart, when my performance failed to seamlessly mesh with theirs, a new connection could form between sound and action, actor and designer. That design/performance, with its layers of aurally modulated reality, its real-time execution and its deceptive transparency was the full realisation, the fully evolved state, of an idea that struck me watching Kate's dance with the shot glass.

The work of The Wooster Group and Target Margin suggested that sound was a highly effective creator of a sensation of physical (as opposed to psychological) truth in theatre. Much of my work with those companies employed a tactic of creatively re-associating sounds and live actions. These designs had been heavy on percussive effects and, especially in shows like *To You, The Birdie!*, created unlikely but convincing realities on stage through illusions of precise timing and a sound operator performing in sync with the actors.

Marcus Stern—*Hamletmachine*

In 1990, Marcus Stern, then an MFA directing student at Yale Drama School, mounted an ambitious production of Heiner Müller's *Hamletmachine* in which he staged two daring turns. Firstly, Rob Campbell, playing Hamlet (or 'The Actor Playing Hamlet'), after launching his angry tirade "I am not Hamlet. . . my drama is cancelled," (Müller 2001, 5) leaps off the front of the stage and strides up the centre aisle mumbling to himself as he exits into the lobby and slams the door behind him. In the lobby we hear him explode with rage. He throws a garbage can, repeatedly, against the walls, breaks windows and creates mayhem just beyond the audience's view, but well within earshot. As we crane our necks towards the closed lobby doors and the chaos just beyond them, the trick is suddenly revealed. With loud bangs and screams still coming from behind us, Campbell, with a devilish grin on his face, calmly strolls onto the stage. The violent climax of his monologue has come not from him, but from a loudspeaker strategically placed in the lobby. Yet until he coolly re-enters, there is no question of the reality of the destruction taking place in the lobby.

The second of Stern's daring turns was later in Act IV, wherein Müller's stage directions culminate with a call for an environmental disaster of epic proportions. By this point the sound score has reached a deafening crescendo and the lighting is alternately blinding and pitch-dark. Campbell's 'Hamlet-Actor' is consumed with emotional intensity that reverberates over a body-microphone and he screams as he pushes a large box offstage whose inner walls seem to have talking heads growing from them. The stage directions indicate "...*splits the heads of Marx Lenin Mao*" (Müller 2001, 7). The stage is illuminated briefly by a powerful strobe light—"*Snowfall*" (Müller 2001, 7). Then, with the suddenness of a hard-cut film edit, a completely empty (and silent) stage is revealed, doors open to the empty scene dock, ladders resting idly against the bare brick walls. The elaborate production has vanished and only a long fluorescent light fixture slowly lowered on a fly-bar illuminates the eerily empty stage. The chaotic and deafening scene has been snapped out and the new silence and stark bright light feel larger, more powerful and more ominous than the violent scene that has inexplicably disappeared. *"Ice Age"* (Müller 2001, 7).

In both these events in Stern's *Hamletmachine*—the illusion of the wrecked lobby and the terrifying silence of the empty stage—sound (or the sudden lack of it) created a powerful reality. Sound tells an audience what they cannot see. What is invisible to the audience, but near enough to be heard, becomes the domain of the sound designer. Where sets, lights and even performance can demand suspension of disbelief, sound is a listener's only source of information about an unseen action or actor. One can notice that a three-walled set ends at the edge of the stage; one can look up and see a theatrical lighting unit and know that it, not a streetlamp, is casting light; a closer look will reveal that an actor's chest still rises and falls even though s/he has just played a death scene. But in *Hamletmachine*, no one had any reason to believe that Campbell had not just thrown a trashcan through a window in the lobby. The sound we heard lied to us but still managed to create its own perfectly plausible reality.

Elevator Repair Service – *Cab Legs, Room Tone*

I began directing and devising theatre with Elevator Repair Service in the early 90s with these two powerful images rooted in my subconscious. With ERS I experimented with a new application of sound design while continuing to hone and refine ideas I'd first tested with The Wooster Group and Target Margin Theater—ideas that suggested that sound could play more of an active and integrated role in live performance. Early ERS productions took place on mostly bare stages. Spare to non-existent set design began as an imperative of ERS' economic situation but quickly became a part of the group's shared aesthetic. We worked only with what we had or could find and that translated to treating the architecture of the performance space as a found object. Since ERS did not build sets then, the theatres' stages had to be made to *feel* like imaginative spaces to the audiences. Productions were staged around the existing doors and walls of the theatre and the actors often played scenes in the hallways, stairwells and even outdoor sidewalks that lay just beyond the visible playing area. It was in these invisible places that I found sound's greatest potential to shape the audiences' sense of what was and wasn't real. Here was an opportunity, especially in the oddly configured and somewhat improvised performance spaces of downtown New York, to suggest a different reality to an audience by manipulating what they heard coming from unseen spaces. From ERS' first production, ambient sound played the role of set designer, defining the location and suggesting what lay just beyond its walls. In one of these early productions, that highly charged silence I'd first experienced in Stern's production became the foundation for a new piece. Unexpectedly and entirely by accident in the process of experimenting with silence onstage, I re-discovered the power of off-stage sound that Campbell's apparent Act IV outburst had exploited so convincingly a few years before.

An early production of *Cab Legs* (1998) began with a prolonged period of silence and stillness. Four actors sat almost motionless (but not frozen) on stage and looked around nervously for several minutes. This scene was designed to sensitise the audience to the smallest sounds—even to the sound of their own bodies as they shifted in their seats—and to mine the lower limits of the audience's aural perception. Rather than create suddenly the super-charged silence, this tactic was designed to bring it on gradually. Tragically one night this delicate state was shattered. One of the actors who did not appear in the first few scenes arrived late and, during this silent opening scene, stomped around loudly upstairs in the dressing room just above the stage. Having just settled in to a long, awkward silence onstage, the audience was now treated to the comparatively noisy cacophony of frantic footsteps above their heads. The delicately silent scene was ruined. Afterwards, however, I found that this minor disaster had given rise to a new idea. As the audience filed out, someone sought me out to compliment my use of 'ambient sound' in this scene. The unplanned (and unwelcome) noises had registered with at least one viewer as design. Though I'd kept the memory of that scene in *Hamletmachine* close, I hadn't fully appreciated its potential until that moment when someone misinterpreted the disruption of my perfectly quiet scene. This then became a set piece of *Cab Legs*. We placed speakers in rooms just beyond the theatre, staged shouted arguments on an adjacent stairwell and used sounds of ringing telephones, explosions and distant music to create a delicate frame around a silent and sometimes empty stage.

Five years later, we developed the use of exterior sound when ERS created a play that unfolded in darkness as well as silence. *Room Tone* (2002) began as an experiment with extremely low light and eventually took shape around a re-interpretation of Henry James' *The Turn of the Screw*. This show took place in the same small room where *Cab Legs* was staged in 1997. This small, 75-seat performance space is located on the ground floor of Performance Space 122, which sits at the corner of 9th Street and 1st Avenue in lower Manhattan. Apart from being a busy neighbourhood, this intersection is also on a bus route. When buses stop at 9th and 1st, they idle loudly right outside the windows of the theatre. Covering the windows keeps light from intruding, but there's no good protection from the sounds of these loud city buses and the drunken conversations that spill out of nearby bars. Anticipating this, ERS' then sound designer, Michael Kraskin, hid a microphone in a cinder block next to the sidewalk on 9th Street. With the sound from outside now wired directly into the theatre sound system, he was able to assume significant control over the various noises—especially the M9 bus. He couldn't make the bus sound disappear, but he had the option of making it significantly louder by raising the volume of the outdoor microphone. He had the freedom to do this as frequently, or as infrequently, as he chose and once he had done so, he owned that sound. Successive noises from outside, even those he chose to ignore, were now implicitly a part of his design. He'd found a way to claim the real aural environment around the performance and now any sound that drifted in through walls and blacked-out windows belonged to the show. With this strategy, he'd worked from the outside in, grabbing the real sound and pulling it into the imaginative space of *Room Tone*; in *Cab Legs*, the design had pushed its ideas into the architectural fringes of the performance space, working from the inside outward. In both these cases, the designs harnessed the audiences' instinct to trust their ears, to accept as true what the sound was telling them about what they could not see. *Cab Legs*, both through its silent sensitizing of the visible space and through its careful placement of sounds outside of the stage, forced its audiences to consider everything they heard, both within and beyond the boundaries of the performance space, as part of the reality of the performance. *Room Tone,* by deliberately drawing real-world sounds into the room, processing them and claiming them, achieved a similar end. By preventing its audiences from ignoring even the most seemingly obtrusive aural input, the playing space was effectively boundless. In both cases, the facts of the extended physical environment of the performance were drawn into a charged ambiguity neither provable as real-world fact nor dismissible as mere design and undeniably a part of the reality of the performance.

As a practitioner of experimental theatre, 'realism' has never been a concern of mine. Nevertheless, the question of what is *real* in the theatre has inspired some of my more fruitful experiments. In several of these, sound became my most valuable tool in manipulating a theatre audience's sense of what is and is not true about the immediate physical space of the performance. An invisible medium, sound travels through walls to suggest a reality just beyond the architectural boundaries of the theatre. Inside these confines as well, sound has a remarkable power to create logic. When performed in sync with live actors, sound can imply an alternative physics for the people, objects and architecture that populate the visible world of the stage. Theatre is an imperfect medium and its visible world is awkward compared to the perfect visual illusion of film. For most theatrical design to achieve a sense of 'realism,' suspension of disbelief and a willingness to disregard physical facts is required. Yet sound, even in the lowest of low-budget productions, carves out compelling exceptions to theatre's prohibitive physical limitations. Sound in the theatre is the best liar. The interaction of actors with sounds and sounds with architecture can both exploit and by-pass the artificiality and physically awkward universe of live theatre and create powerful illusions of unassailable physical truth.

References

Müller, Heiner. 2001 (1979). *The Hamletmachine.*, trans. Dennis Redmond. http://www.efn.org/~dredmond/Hamletmachine.pdf (accessed November 20, 2010).

CHAPTER IV

FROM MUSICALISATION OF THEATRE TO MUSICALITY OF FILM: BECKETT'S *PLAY* ON STAGE AND ON SCREEN

DANIJELA KULEZIC-WILSON

Music as model and metaphor

Postdramatic theatre is a "meeting point of the arts," says Hans-Thies Lehmann (2006, 31), a product of a new era in which a yearning for the sensual experience provided by the diverse resources of multimedia has overtaken the conventions of linear narrative and staged drama with its illusory reality. Music, dance, visual arts, film and electronic media are nowadays the legitimate constituents of contemporary theatre in the same way music, dance, ritual and spoken word were essential to the theatre of ancient Greece. A plurality of expressive means is not only inherent to theatre, it is its very *raison d'être*, a purpose enacted from its primary genetic code. It is interesting, though, that in the turbulent and exciting history of postdramatic theatre each of its components has proven to be dispensable or interchangeable at one time or another, except music. Contemporary theatre has been able to thrive without costumes, props and scenography, without drama, narrative and spoken word, even without performers, as shown in Heiner Goebbels's *Stifters Dinge* (2007), but music still seems to be the one element directors are reluctant to abandon. More than that, the concept of theatre *as* music has become prominent in recent decades (Lehmann 2006; Roesner 2008; Chepurova 2009), joining the long list of human creative endeavours influenced by music, which includes not only all other arts but even the origins of modern science.[1]

---

[1] The first scientific explanations of the universe originally proposed by Pythagoras suggest that its laws and proportions are mirrored in the mathematical principles of musical harmony. The resonances of his concept of the "harmony of

The idea of music as an inspiration and model for other arts is so old and pervasive that it would be difficult to pinpoint its exact origins in theatre, but its endorsement by postdramatic theatre has certainly been partly inspired by the work of Samuel Beckett. With his first published essay *Proust* (1931), Beckett declared himself a follower of the Schopenhauerian view of music as the only art which reveals "the true nature of all things" (Schopenhauer 1969, 262). According to Schopenhauer, the perceptual immediacy of music is not only superior to that of other arts but also the key to attaining knowledge through perception, "the means of grasping [...] that we can otherwise know only indirectly by comprehension in concepts" (1969, 265). The influence of this idea can be followed in different manifestations throughout Beckett's oeuvre, from the actual appearance of music in his novels, works for stage and radio, the employment of traditional prosodic and musical devices in language, to the utilisation of music as a metaphor for the processes of consciousness and a facilitator for transforming language from denotative to what Eric Prieto calls exemplificational in Beckett's late novels.

By describing Beckett's function of language as exemplificational, Prieto himself relies on Nelson Goodman's distinction between the three modes of symbolisation in art—denotative, expressive and exemplificational —noting that denotative symbolisation plays the most prominent role in literature, while exemplificational symbolisation has a crucial role in music because "the meaning of a musical work is to be sought in that set of qualities of which it acts as an example" (2002, 33), as opposed to representative or extra-musical ones. Prieto's terminology is useful in this context because it allows one to grasp the audacity and extent of the leap that Beckett made in his refusal to adhere exclusively to the semiotic or purely expressive functions of language. Beckett's vision, however, was not exhausted in changing modes of verbal discourse in literature. His search for a perceptual experience that could compare to that of listening to music guided him to theatre, a medium that turned out to be perfect for exploring the sensual and inherently musical aspects of language, a medium where language not only obtains an actual voice but can also be transformed into a *musical* voice. No other Beckett work confirms this better than *Play* (1963/64), since his experiments with language and form led to its musicalisation on a number of levels, subverting the primarily semiotic function of language in theatre and inviting alternative modes of perception.

---

the spheres" have been felt right up to the present day in the arts, philosophy and esoteric science.

In 2000 *Play* was adapted for the screen and directed by Anthony Minghella for the project *Beckett on Film*. Deeply influenced and inspired by music himself, Minghella responded to Beckett's text by using film technology to foreground *Play*'s inherent musicality both through visual devices and by prompting virtuosic performances from Kristin Scott Thomas, Juliet Stevenson and Alan Rickman (see figure 4-1).[2] Unhindered by the limitations of live theatrical performance, he brought Beckett's vision of performative audio-visual counterpoint to its fully-controlled, perfected stage, transforming the metaphor of music as a model for language into actuality and extending the process of musicalisation to screen.

The musicality of *Play* on page and on stage

Play is a short piece about a man, his wife and his mistress stuck in an emotional triangle. It is structured as a musical piece for three solo parts with choruses and includes stage directions for rhythm, tempo, volume and expression. The actors are buried up to their necks in identical grey urns (see figure 4-1), their speech provoked by a spotlight projected into their faces, as if coming from an invisible conductor. *Play* lasts around eight minutes and then, according to Beckett's instructions, it is repeated from beginning to end, as in the musical convention of *Da Capo*.

Kenneth Gaburo, an advocate of "compositional linguistics" (1987, 83), argues in his analysis of *Play* that the work generates its own language-sensibility because it is composed. However, unlike in some other Beckett works such as *Watt*, where the musicalisation of language is attempted by describing a character reduced to experiencing the world through sensory impacts rather than conceptual comprehension, *Play* strives towards the perceptual immediacy of music in a more straightforward way, by creating a tight rhythmic structure based on repetitions and punctuated by verbal, vocal and visual accents.

Already set in a symmetrical structure through the use of *Da Capo*, *Play* is additionally rhythmitised by internal micro-repetitions: the Man's lines often start by repeating the last few phrases of his previous monologue and a number of words and phrases reappear in the text as refrains, either as characters' "catchphrases" ("poor thing" /Woman 2/;

---

[2] Minghella's first film, *Truly, Madly, Deeply* (1990) is about musicians and was inspired by listening to Glenn Gould's recordings of Bach. While working on *The English Patient* (1996) Minghella repeatedly listened to the Hungarian folk song *Szerelem, Szerelem*, which became "the voice of the film" for him, as did P.J. Harvey's music while writing *Breaking and Entering* (2006) (see: Bricknell 2005).

"get off me" /Woman 1/), or circulated among the characters ("give her up", "poor creature") (Beckett 1969). These repetitions are interwoven through the text together with reappearances of non-verbal motifs such as the hiccups interrupting the Man's speech or the sighs and mad laughter of Woman 2. As the play unfolds, a sense of acceleration is achieved by decreasing the speaking time of each of the characters and shortening their sentences. Their lines become increasingly similar to poetic verses and also more rhythmic, punctuated by full stops, as in the monologue of Woman 2: "She came again. Just strolled in. All honey. Licking her lips. Poor thing." (Beckett 1969, 12) or in the staccato monologue of Woman 1: "pudding face, puffy, spots, blubber mouth, jowls, no neck, dugs you could—" (Beckett 1969, 13). The most illustrative example of a purely musical approach to language, though, is the treatment of the choruses which appear at the beginning, at the end and once in the middle of the play. The characters are instructed to speak different lines simultaneously, as if singing contrapuntally. Their muttering in fast tempo is practically unintelligible, semantic and prosodic concerns both abandoned, and what is left is the Cageian espousal of noise as music, recurring within the play as a refrain. Repetitions often feature in Beckett plays as symptoms of hopelessness, defeat and desperation and in *Play* the recurring phrases and choruses and the instruction for *Da Capo* reinforce the idea of the cyclical nature of the relationships described. Even the added coda does not provide any closure since it ends with the Man's first line starting for the third time, only to be interrupted and swallowed by darkness. However, the repetitions on the micro- and macro-levels are here also undoubtedly employed as musical gestures. They create a highly rhythmic structure which pulsates in a fast tempo with rhythmic accents provided linguistically, visually through spotlights, and vocally through sighs, hiccups, laughter and muttering.

Actors and directors have often remarked that a performer in a Beckett play is not so much an interpreter of his text as an actual instrument. This is particularly obvious in *Play* in which Beckett's obsession with the voice and the need to direct viewers' attention towards it is so strong that he practically annihilates the bodies of his actors, burying them in urns and leaving only their protruding heads. The type of performance he demands in *Play* will be discussed more in the next section, but generally in his work the parameters of "pitch, tone, duration, rhythm, and audibility were not optional extras, or embellishments available to the vocal event," as Mary Bryden says (1998, 43). "Rather they *were* that meaning, that vocal event. They were [...] both 'form and matter, in their union or identity'" (Bryden 1998, 43). A number of anecdotes illustrate this, including those about Beckett using a metronome to control the tempo of his actors' speech[3] and a piano to fix the pitch (Prieto 2002, 165). As Beckett's biographer James Knowlson noted, "for him, pace, tone, and, above all, rhythm were more important than sharpness of character delineation or emotional depth" (1996, 448). Thus, it is not surprising that composers have often responded to the musicality of Beckett's language after hearing particular productions of his pieces, as was for instance the case with Heinz Holliger who composed *What Where* (1988) after hearing that play directed by Alan Schneider, or with Ian Wilson who, inspired by Minghella's screen version of *Play,* created *re:play* (2007) for improvising saxophone, piano, string quartet and double bass.

Silences in *Play* are less noticeable than in some of Beckett's other stage works such as *Come and Go,* but the reason for this is purely musical. As is the case with repetitions, silences have both a musical and a strong dramatic purpose in Beckett's plays. They are often heavy with anticipation, a sense of desperation, or they simply allow us to feel the passing of time. Simultaneously, they are interwoven with the words of his plays in the same way silences render rhythmic figures, melodies and whole musical pieces perceptible by providing them with formal frames. Beckett was intensely aware of the musical function of silences and according to Robert Craft, during his meeting with Stravinsky in 1962 he revealed his interest in the possibility of notating the tempo of performance in his plays, and even more interestingly, of timing the pauses in *Waiting for Godot* (Bryden 1998, 44). That was the same year as *Play* was written and in it both the tempo and the duration of the pauses and blackouts on stage are precisely marked. However, the reason that silences are less noticeable in this work is that its type of musicality is motoric, based on rhythmically conceived sentences and perpetual movement. The tempo of *Play* is among the fastest in all of Beckett's stage works—marked as *rapid* throughout. The duration of the silences varies between three and five seconds, which is approximately the duration of a handful of musical bars in a very fast tempo. So the function of silences in this play is more structural than expressive. They are employed as caesuras within a motorically charged verbal *moto perpetuo,* the cyclical nature of which is underlined by repetitions within the text and the repetition of the whole play.

---

[3] Rehearsals of *Happy Days* with Brenda Bruce, London production 1962 (Knowlson 1996, 447).

The musicality of *Play* on screen

According to some Beckett scholars, the very act of putting his plays on film is heresy because the nature of the film medium, with its use of close-ups and montage, is interpretative and goes against Beckett's wish to have his plays performed, not interpreted. It is also well known that Beckett continuously refused offers to adapt *Waiting for Godot* for the screen,[4] although the reason was not his aversion towards television and film *per se*, but his strong feeling that an inherent part of that particular play was the image of "small men locked in a big space" (Knowlson 1996, 436), which would be lost in a screen adaptation.

Defending the idea of putting *Play* on screen, one of its performers, Alan Rickman, said in a documentary about making the film that some of the qualities Beckett wanted from his actors, like the "ashen and abstract quality of words" (Rickman in: Lehane 2001) for instance, could not have been achieved so well on stage. To that Minghella added that the method of constructing a film through repetitive takes corresponds perfectly to the structure of *Play* and its core ideas of circularity and repetitiveness (Minghella in: Lehane 2001). He thus *visually* suggests the process of going over one's experiences again and again by breaking some of the monologues into several takes shot from different angles. The film version also reinforces the sense of repetitiveness during the opening and closing choruses by revealing in a wide shot not three, but numerous urns with protruding talking heads.

Minghella said on more than one occasion that his experience as a musician informed every aspect of the way in which he made films, but his flair for the musicality of the moving image is nowhere more apparent than in *Play*. Unfettered by the limitations of classical film narrative Minghella here focuses on fluency and rhythm as the principal parameters of communication and uses the challenge of transferring a theatre play to screen as the opportunity to underscore *Play*'s musical character. Consequently, he substitutes a spotlight which is supposed to provoke the speech of the characters onstage by a camera close-up. The monologues sometimes succeed each other in montage cuts and sometimes the camera

---

[4] The fact is, Beckett was very interested in the art of film and with Alan Schneider as director he created *Film* with Buster Keaton in the leading role, which was shown at the New York and Venice Film festivals in 1965. During the process of filming and editing *Film* Beckett grew to appreciate the possibilities of the close-up and editing in particular, which inspired the creation of his television play *Eh Joe* in which a single male figure in a room is gradually approached by the camera, reducing the focus from a whole figure to the detail of the mouth.

takes the position of the viewer and pans swiftly from one face to another. Close-ups and panning of the camera are accompanied by a swishing sound, exchanging theatre noise for a cinematic one—an alternative 'musical' source which underlines the sense of repetition and adds yet another non-verbal refrain to the hiccups, laughter and sighs. Varied framing and rapid changes of camera angle are employed to establish a sense of continuous audio-visual flow, which is consistently punctuated with various sonic and visual accents.

As a consequence of a typical modernist crisis with language, Beckett is known to have discarded not only the expressive attributes of words but even their denotative function in favour of the sensual, musical quality of their sound, the silence that surrounds them and their rhythmic delivery. Although in *Play* this attitude seems to be exemplified most notably in its choruses, indications of expression and tempo are the key to releasing the musical potential of this work: "Voices toneless except where an expression is indicated. Rapid tempo throughout"[5] (Beckett 1969, 9). Knowlson notes that in the first few productions the actors were astonished at the speed at which they were being urged to deliver their lines because it was contrary to everything they understood as the essence of their art.[6] However, as George Devine, the director of the first London production explained to the actors, "the words did not convey thoughts or ideas but were simply 'dramatic ammunition' to be uttered."[7] Consciously responding to Beckett's ambivalent relationship with words Minghella followed his indications about tempo religiously and prompted such virtuosic performances from his actors that it is practically impossible to watch this version of *Play* and concentrate on the denotative meaning of each monologue all the way to the end unless simultaneously looking at the written text, because the *music* of the spoken words always takes over.

---

[5] At the rehearsals of the French production of *Play* (*Comédie*) Beckett described the tone as a "recto-tono," a chanting on a single note which monks adopt as they read from sacred texts at mealtimes (Knowlson 1996, 458).

[6] This also applies to his play *Not I*, which Jessica Tandy performed in New York in 1972 by reading from a teleprompter because Beckett asked her to deliver them without thinking. "It just had to come out" (Knowlson 1996, 523-4). One of his favourite actresses, Billie Whitelaw, said that she hardly had time to breathe when delivering *Not I* in the maddening tempo he requested. "No one can possibly follow the text at that speed but Beckett insists that I speak it precisely. It's like music, a piece of Schoenberg in his head," she said to *The Sunday Times* before the London performance in 1973 (Knowlson 1996, 529).

[7] According to Knowlson, "dramatic ammunition" was Beckett's own phrase presumably used in discussion with Devine (1996, 459).

While completely respectful regarding the presentation of the spoken lines, Minghella is less obedient to the text when it comes to the instructions about the use of silences and blackouts, which can be explained by the nature of the film medium itself. Silence in theatre, if demanded by the text, is exactly that–no sound uttered by anyone on stage. In film absolute silence is almost unimaginable because it is like 'dead air' on the radio. What we usually *perceive* as silence within a film's diegetic world is artificially produced *cinematic silence*, which still has to be designed like any other film soundscape. You cannot simply turn the volume off. In Minghella's film silences and blackouts are replaced by the image of an old film tape going through a projector making a crackling sound and, in one instance, by a sigh from Woman 2. The important thing is that they are employed as caesuras between the speaking sections, which means that they maintain the same structural function as silences within the play while simultaneously inserting another layer of rhythmic punctuation into the musical flow of images and speech.

Figure 4-1: Kristin Scott Thomas, Alan Rickman and Juliet Stevenson in Anthony Minghella's film adaptation of Beckett's *Play,* Blue Angel Films 2001. Still courtesy of Parallel Films.

Beckett's vision of theatre as music

From one point of view, making one's words unintelligible or hard to follow could be understood as a self-defeating result for a writer, but for Beckett that was the aim. He distrusted language and was famous for describing it as "a veil that must be torn apart in order to get at the things (or the Nothingness) behind it" (1983, 171). Prieto thus suggests that the transformation of language in Beckett's work from denotative and descriptive to exemplificational resulted from the writer's realisation that "all the words in the world will not suffice to adequately name the simplest of subjective experiences" (2002, 267), but the way one uses words in relation to each other and how one says them might "exemplify the laws that govern those experiences" (268). In Beckett's case this led to a painstaking filtration and purification of language to the point where whole librettos were reduced to sixteen lines (the opera *Neither*) and grunts, utterances, gestures and silences were equally, or sometimes even more, important than words themselves. As a result of striving to achieve through words the perceptual immediacy of music, his language is sometimes so whimsical that according to Harry White its status in his later work is "downgraded from that of sole intelligencer to compositional technique" (1998, 164-165), although one suspects that in this context Beckett would happily replace the expression 'downgraded' with 'upgraded'.

Unlike in some of his later works, though, the written word in *Play* keeps well within the limits of the discursive and denotative, despite the unintelligible choruses. The banal, exhausting, humiliating and yet so familiar and painful experiences of being caught in an emotional triangle are vividly captured through different structural and prosodic devices, but their perceptual effect is completely dependent on the precision and virtuosity of the performers. In that sense Beckett's inherently musical text is like a score which needs a performer to be recognised and perceived as music and this very fact emphasises the musical origins of Beckett's ideas more than *Play*'s repetitions, staccato lines, rhythmic accents or polyphonic choruses. This is why theatre was so essential to the articulation of Beckett's revolutionary ideas and why he was compelled to continue directing his plays even at a very old age: his imagination was haunted by the sounds, rhythms and music which had to be awakened from the written word and the silence of the page. At the same time, Minghella's screen version of *Play* confirms that in Beckett's theatre works such as this, where the physicality of the actors' bodies and gestures are removed, the visual dimension—bar the lighting—is static and the focus directed towards aural content, it is possible to transfer the perceptual immediacy

of performance to screen without betraying any of the writer's initial
intentions and ideas. Moreover, one could argue that Minghella's direction
of *Play* and the way he conceived its visual representation only added to
the work's musicality.

Finally, it is important to remember that *Play*'s overt musicality
attained through structural, linguistic and performative devices was just
one manifestation of Beckett's reinvention of theatre inspired by music.
The way he employed and re-prioritised linguistic, gestural, visual,
musical and structural elements in his other plays led White to conclude
that the "tensely ironic relationship between exactitude of structure and a
disintegration of verbal meaning" (1998, 168), particularly in his late
work, was a symptom of an essentially serial control of structure. Whether
we agree with White in interpreting the permutations of a single exchange
in *Come and Go*, the patterns of pacing in *Quad*, the repetitions in
Rockaby, the precise instructions for lighting, movement, tempo and types
of expression in most of Beckett's plays as examples of "the serial
paradigm" (White 1998, 168) applied to theatre, or whether we view them
simply as a set of idiosyncratic techniques carefully developed through a
lifetime of searching, there is no doubt that the main inspiration and
driving force behind the ideas that led Beckett to transform the landscape
of modern theatre was music.

References

Beckett, Samuel. 1969. *Play*. London: Faber and Faber.
—. 1983. *Disjecta*. London: Calder.
Bricknell, Timothy, ed. 2005. *Minghella on Minghella*. London: Faber and
    Faber.
Bryden, Mary. 1998. Beckett and the sound of silence. In *Samuel Beckett
    and Music,* ed. Mary Bryden, 21-46. Oxford: Clarendon Press.
Chepurova, Olga. 2009. Concepts in Music Theatre: looking glass.
    http://musictheatre.synthasite.com/looking-glass.php/ (accessed May 9,
    2010).
Gaburo, Kenneth. 1987. The Music in Samuel Beckett's *Play*. *The Review
    of Contemporary Fiction*, Samuel Beckett Number, Vol. 7, No. 2: 76-
    84.
Knowlson , James. 1996. *Damned to Fame: The Life of Samuel Beckett*.
    New York: Simon and Schuster.
Lehane, Pearse. 2001. *Putting Beckett on Film*. [DVD]. Blue Angel
    Films/Tyrone Productions.

Lehmann, Hans-Thies. 2006. *Postdramatic Theatre*. Trans. Karen Jürs-Munby. London & New York: Routledge.
Prieto, Eric. 2002. *Listening In: Music, Mind, and the Modernist Narrative*. Lincoln and London: University of Nebraska Press.
Roesner, David. 2008. The politics of the polyphony of performance. Musicalization in contemporary German theatre. *Contemporary Theatre Review,* Vol. 18, No. 1: 44-55.
Schopenhauer, Arthur. 1969. *The World as Will and Representation*, Vol.1. Trans. E.F.J. Payne. New York: Dover.
White, Harry. 1998. "Something is taking its course": Dramatic exactitude and the paradigm of serialism in Samuel Beckett. In *Samuel Beckett and Music,* ed. Mary Bryden, 159-171. Oxford: Clarendon Press.

CHAPTER V

INTRUSIVE NOISES:
THE PERFORMATIVE POWER
OF THEATRE SOUNDS

KATHARINA ROST

Introduction

Deriving from an interest in how auditory perception takes place within theatre performances and what processes control the spectators' attention I started thinking about theatre noises[1]. In my recent visits to the theatre, I have noticed that some types of contemporary theatre performance use noises in very specific and powerful ways. In an attempt to grasp this energetic force upon the spectator, I have called this quality of the noises 'intrusive'. In this chapter, I will explain this term and argue for its use in performance research.

---

[1] With the term 'noise' I refer to those sounds that are usually found in our everyday environment and physically defined as sounds with an irregular vibration pattern. Noises are sounds that are traditionally viewed as different from musical tones or vocal utterances, though music or voices might contain noisy aspects. In fact, during the last century, noises have been integrated into and composed as music and therefore, cannot be determined as 'non-musical' per se. The English word 'noise' does also implicate that the sound is unwanted or disturbing (compare to the *Shorter Oxford English Dictionary*, 1937). Etymologically, the word 'noise' has derived from the Latin word *nausea*, meaning seasickness (1937). In media and communication theory, noise is considered a disturbing factor that interfered with the transmitted information. All these aspects demonstrate the intrusiveness of noises, but they should not be perpetuated with this paper. The intrusiveness of noises should not be judged as solely destructive and unwanted; rather it can derive from an enticing and wanted character of the sound as well, i.e. when we are taken by the beauty or particularity of a certain noise.

Basic questions that influence this research interest are: Why are noises used in a certain way within specific performances? How do they affect the audience? And, how is it even possible to describe the effect of the noises?

In performances created by directors such as Christoph Marthaler, Luk Perceval, René Pollesch, Michael Thalheimer, Robert Wilson, Einar Schleef and many others audible elements are of great significance. Theatre theory has addressed these aspects in recent years, focusing on the significance of the voice or musical dimensions of these performances. But what remarkably remained a 'blind spot' of these theoretical approaches is an adequate consideration of the significant role of theatre noises. This is even more surprising because acoustic elements have always been fundamental and constitutive parts of theatre.

As the sound designer John Leonard has suggested in his book *Theatre Sound* from 2001, sound effects are generally used in order to give the audience information about the situation of the dramatic action, to reinforce this action, to specify a textual reference, or—and this might be interesting for the questions I would like to raise in this chapter—to create a certain mood and emotional stimulus (Leonard 2001, 142).[2] This list is meant to be a comprehensive identification of the different functions of noises within theatrical practice. However, from my point of view, it needs to be extended in order to grasp the more recent modes of sound application and effects.

In the performances that I would like to focus on in this chapter, noises are not only used in order to illustrate or amplify the onstage action, but far more than that, to create an atmosphere, rhythms, and highly complex arrangements that have a powerful impact on the audience. The intrusive sonic effect does not just add certain information or give some emotional background stimulus; instead it has or obtains the power to touch the listener in a direct physical way and to capture the audience's attention, with or against their will. Furthermore, instead of being a momentary effect it affects the way in which the whole performance is experienced and how meaning is constituted within that performance. I would suggest that this kind of 'auditory captivation' is a central strategy in many contemporary theatre performances and manifests itself in a variety of different ways.

---

[2] Similar assumptions on the function and impact of theatre noises are made in other sound design books. For further reading see the abbreviated original texts in Brown 2010, 16-48.

Intrusive noises

For the following analysis, it is necessary to explain what I mean by the 'intrusiveness' of noises. But due to the complexities involved, it is not possible to give a straightforward definition of the intrusive character of noises. In fact, it should not be conceptualised as a binary opposition of intrusive and not-intrusive sounds, but rather as a whole wide-ranging and manifold spectrum of degrees of intrusiveness.

Noises are not intrusive per se and even though some noises might be more likely to be perceived as intrusive, they still need to be heard and to be perceived in order to have intrusive effects. The intrusiveness of sounds derives from the physical and emotional state as well as from the mode of the perceptual activity (i.e., hearing, listening to, being distracted etc.)[3] of the listener. Therefore, intrusiveness results from specific listening situations and cannot be generally assigned to groups of noises. It appears to depend on the specific configuration of the context, the sound qualities of the noises and the modes of perception, attention and emotion of the listener.

According to several etymological dictionaries the verb 'to intrude' originates from the Latin verb *intrudere*, meaning "to thrust oneself into an estate or benefice". 'Intrusion' in this sense means an "uninvited entrance or appearance".[4] The term generally refers to a movement of someone or something into a geographically or socially defined space without having been invited or legitimised to do so.

Similar to this, the sonic effect of intrusion is determined as "the inopportune presence of a sound or group of sounds inside a protected territory [that] creates a feeling of violation of that space" by the sound researchers Jean-François Augoyard and Henry Torgue. Furthermore, the authors define intrusive sonic effects as "illegitimate intrusions in the body" (Augoyard & Torgue 2005, 65)[5]. It is important to notice that Augoyard and Torgue consider the intrusive power of noises not only as violating spatial boundaries, but also as transcending bodily limits in a

---

[3] Barry Truax, for example, emphasises that there are multiple levels of listening attention and distinguishes between the perceptual activities of 'listening-in-search', 'listening-in-readiness' and 'background listening'. See Truax 2001, 21-25.

[4] *The Oxford Dictionary of English Etymology* (1966, 483). Similar definitions can be found in other dictionaries; compare the *Longman Dictionary of the English Language* (1991 [1984], 828) or the *Shorter Oxford English Dictionary* (2007 [1933], 1421).

[5] Jean-François Augoyard and Henry Torgue have pioneered the task of describing a broad range of sonic effects.

possibly unexpected or even illegitimate manner. Violation in this sense does not only refer to real harm—as very loud noise might do to the hearer's ears or nerves—but more subtly, it also means the intrusion of sounds into the bodily sphere of the exposed human being. The phenomenologist Hermann Schmitz has described the sensation of the individual's body as a dilatation into the surrounding space. The sphere of the body is invasively penetrated by so-called 'half objects', to which he counts all audible phenomena (Schmitz 2008, 81). Thus, the intrusive character of noises does not only depend on their loudness, but can be caused by a certain sound feature like an unusual timbre, pitch, rhythm, timing, loudness, continuation or melodic pattern.[6] Duration can have an influence on the intrusiveness of sounds. Very often noises with a high pitch have intrusive powers, i.e. the squealing sounds of train brakes, whistles or pieces of chalk run over a blackboard. In my opinion, in theatre the bodily sphere is intentionally intruded upon by acoustic means, as they have the power to invade and penetrate each spectator's 'safety zone' in a radical way.

Furthermore, the quality and intensity of intrusive noises depend on the specific spatial, temporal and cultural configuration of the context. In certain conditions, a sound can be much more intrusive than in others. For example, a noise in a quiet library will seem much louder than that same noise in a busy airport. The context has an influence on how sounds will be emotionally perceived, i.e. as interesting, boring, annoying, etc. In theatre, otherwise annoying noises can take on rather fascinating dimensions and provoke a more musical listening mode. Therefore, within theatre performances, the intrusion into the body sphere can result in an oscillating attitude between repulsion and attraction by the noises. Paradoxically, in the extreme case, the two dimensions might even be perceived simultaneously, as will be shown in the following performance analysis.

---

[6] This thought is being supported by tendencies in recent noise pollution research, which considers qualitative dimensions of noise as well as measurement of loudness levels. "Environmental noise affects a large number of Europeans. The public perceives it as one of the major environmental problems. [...] Even though these impacts on human health have long been known, recent research shows that they arise at lower noise levels than was previously thought." See the website of the European Environment Agency http://www.eea.europa.eu/themes/noise (accessed July 7, 2010).

Hearing 'sharpness'

Intrusive noises play a central role in the performances directed by Luk Perceval, especially in *Andromache*, which premiered on December 3, 2003 at the Schaubühne am Lehniner Platz in Berlin. In the following paragraph, I will briefly describe the beginning and first scenes of the performance.

The performance begins with a specific challenge to the audience's perception in that they cannot see anything, but can only hear. A black wall obscures the view of the stage. Erratic sounds are heard that could be described as hollow rumblings. After a short while, the black wall moves to the side of the stage, during which high-pitched sounds are heard, like those of splintered glass moving on a stone floor. On the stage, three actors and two actresses are positioned next to each other on a tall and narrow plinth. The block is surrounded by a vast amount of empty and partly broken glass bottles. The actors do not move, but stand or sit still in different positions. One of the women, the actress Yvon Jansen as Hermione, is leaning down from the pedestal, holding a bottle in one of her hands, which, from time to time, she slides across the rough surface of the pedestal, thereby producing the previously heard rumbling sounds. After pausing for a few seconds, she violently hits the bottle against the hard pedestal and the glass bottle shatters with a loud smashing sound. She pauses, before she grabs another bottle and shatters it against the pedestal. She then quickly repeats this action twenty times. After that, she sits on the pedestal, starring at Pyrrhus, performed by Mark Waschke, for a long half minute. Through the silence, her heavy breathing can be heard; the sounds amplified by loudspeakers in a way that makes them seem very close. All of a sudden she throws herself on Pyrrhus and they start to wrestle on the narrow pedestal. During this fight, the audience hears the sounds of skin moving on other skin, heavy breathing and moaning as well as the rustling of their stiff costumes. Finally, Pyrrhus wins control over her and holds her down as he stares at Andromache, performed by Jutta Lampe. The following stillness lasts another seemingly long half minute, before he starts to speak the first words of the performance, asking Andromache "What are you thinking?" What follows is an even longer silence, after which she answers by repeating his words in a neutral, seemingly nonchalant tone of voice. This is immediately followed by different dialogues taking place—simultaneously and intertwined in such a manner that the utterances never overlap. Instead, there are always gaps of silence in between the spoken words and longer passages.

The overall sonic arrangement of *Andromache* is delicately balanced. It appears that, in addition to the voices of the actors, the noises of smashed glass, which were presented with emphasis in the beginning scenes, are the central audible element of the performance. Obscuring the stage from the audience in the beginning of the performance enhances hearing as the central perception mode, with curiosity and the desire to see what is happening on the stage being aroused. Combined with the minimalist movements of the actors the emphasis on sound provokes a dominance of auditory perception throughout the whole performance, even though the scenery is visible later during the performance. Furthermore, there is no specifically created sound design or musical accompaniment, except for the wireless microphones on the actors' bodies through which not only their voices are amplified, but also vocal sounds are made audible, i.e. like their breathing, groaning and so on. But beyond the use of digital media to technically amplify the heard sounds, the intensity of the sounds mostly derives from the silent background, against which they stand out. The silence is used as an acoustic backdrop and an amplifier through which the sounds and noises appear to be much louder and closer than they actually are. Through this acoustic strategy, the performance plays with a tension between the conflicting impressions of intimacy and distance. Intimacy is created by using the technique of an 'acoustic close-up',[7] through which the bodily noises are made audible to the audience. Thus, the created impressions of passionate emotions and physical overpowering are contrasted by the ascetic and strict aesthetic formality with which the performance is arranged. The formal aspects evoke effects of artificiality, discipline, control and aloofness. Whereas I think that the noises of splintering glass bottles can generally be categorised as intrusive sounds, it is necessary to emphasise that all of the mentioned staging strategies lead to an augmentation of the intrusive character of the sounds.

How can these specific sounds and their intrusive effect be described? In relation to the noises in *Andromache*, I assume that two sound dimensions are fundamental to their intrusive impact. On the one hand the overall temporal structure that includes aspects of rhythm and duration, on the other hand the sound materiality that consists of timbre patterns might play significant roles in this process. I consider timbre and rhythm to be relevant factors for the intrusive character of noises, because they let the physical objects and processes involved in generating the noises, e.g. bodies, energies and movements, become directly perceivable.

---

[7] For further reading on the creation of the effect of 'acoustic close-up' see Pinto (2008, 169-193).

Timbre is most difficult to grasp in words, especially the timbre of noises, as they do not have constant, but permanently changing sound features. Stephen Handel defines timbre generally as the "characteristic quality or 'color' of a sound produced by an instrument or voice" (1989, 169), thereby implying that noises do not possess equivalent characteristic qualities. Traditionally, timbre has been used to differentiate between different musical instruments or voices of the same pitch and intensity levels. Therefore it was analysed predominantly in music theory and psychoacoustics, which did not consider everyday noises (see Risset & Wessel 1982, 26). Ecological acoustics begin to explore the vast variety of different timbres in everyday sounds; however, the timbre of noises has not yet been analysed in detail (see Gaver 1993).

The temporal and rhythmic sound features of noises, e.g. of shattering glass, are very complex. William Warren and Robert Verbrugge have described the sound structure and rhythmic pattern of breaking glass as "an initial rupture burst dissolving into overlapping multiple damped quasi-periodic pulse trains [...]" (1984, 706). Thus, the noise consists of a complex crossover of various interfering sounds of different pitch, duration and intensity. However, even though the perceived sounds consist of several changes and multiple single elements; they will be identified as the sound of 'breaking glass'. As Albert Bregman has pointed out, listening is organised by the identification of auditory streams, which is achieved by acts of grouping and excluding of auditory sensations (1994 [1990], 47 ff.). In complex acoustic environments like theatre performances however, the questions of which grouping mechanisms will be activated or will dominate others cannot yet be answered completely.

Thus, both features are not sufficiently analysed to date and are difficult to put into words as they both escape a simple definition or measure. There remains a significant desideratum in this area warranting further research on the timbre and rhythmic structures of noises.

What can be assumed is that the sound features of characteristic timbre and temporal structure are put to the foreground of auditory perception and attention by the way in which they are employed within *Andromache*. It might be possible to interpret the act of breaking glass as Hermione's expression of rage and despair, but the dramatic action does not refer to this action at all. Even if the breaking of glass bottles would simply be considered a part of the fictional storyline, it would serve the purpose to let Hermione break one or maybe even two or three, but not as many as twenty bottles. The way the noises are created within the performance highlights the performative[8] dimensions of materiality (how they actually

---

[8] For further reading on 'performativity' see Fischer-Lichte (2008 [2004]).

sound) and mediality (how they are experienced by the audience) as well as influences their semiotic potential and function as theatre signs. As Erika Fischer-Lichte describes, the order of representation might be "disrupted and another, if temporary, order would be established: the order of presence", which leads to "an ensuing chain of associative meanings not necessarily related to what is perceived" (2008 [2004], 149 f.). Following Fischer-Lichte, in the order of presence meaning is generated through processes of association, which are unpredictable and not completely controllable by either the staging artists or the perceiving subjects. They are grounded on past meanings that each individual spectator has compiled in his life thus far, which trigger associated ideas and emotions to the spectator's consciousness. Thus, in the case of *Andromache*, the noises of shattering glass might arouse feelings of potential danger and harm, having direct effects on the physical condition of the audience. This effect is augmented by the fact that the sounds are created live on stage and that there are real glass bottles used to produce them. As they could actually get hurt, the actors face real danger during each performance.[9]

Having to watch the actors in such a dangerous stage situation might evoke feelings of excitement and sympathy in the audience. Even though *watching* the actions of this scene actually happening on the stage will certainly amplify the general idea of potential danger, I think that the feeling is primarily and intensely aroused by *listening* to the specific sounds and that vigilance results from the audience being affected by their intrusive power. It is the specific sound patterns of the noises, which convey the impression of danger and harm. While visual perception still allows for a certain degree of distance between the spectators and the observed actions, processes of auditory perception might directly get under the spectators' skin. The impact of the noises does not derive from their potential to represent an absent and culturally coded signified like vocal speech sounds, but rather from their potential to present 'something' insofar as this 'something' emerges and manifests itself to the listeners

---

[9] In an interview conducted at the Edinburgh International Festival, the director Luk Perceval explains: "Everyone is in a situation between life and death," he says. "To realise a space on stage where this death threat is tangible, we've put the actors on an altar with only 50cm depth so they can hardly pass each other. There are 300 real broken bottles below, so if an actor falls down he really hurts himself. We have trained very well so they don't fall down. The glass, the height and the restricted movement creates [sic] a very high tension. I wanted people to be involved not only with the play but also in the fear and danger." See the article "Short, sharp shock as actors walk a tightrope over real danger" by Mark Fisher at http://living.scotsman.com/features/Short-sharp-shock-as-actors.2554887.jp (accessed June 25, 2010).

through the perceived sounds. I consider this 'something' to be the objects in their shape and materials, the movements with their specific power, tempo and duration as well as the energetic forces as for example in- and decreases, frictions or collisions, which altogether are generating the perceived noises and physical as well as emotional effects. Bregman has stated that through listening the subject will gain "information about the nature of events, defining the 'energetics' of a situation" (1994 [1990], 37).

Crucial in this regard is the statement of William W. Gaver who assumed that "a given sound provides information about an *interaction* of *materials* at a *location* in an *environment*" (1993, 4). In this sense, what the audience can hear, when the actress Yvon Jansen smashes the bottles against the pedestal, is a sound event, which in its specific sound features of timbre and rhythm conveys information about the materials and energetic processes involved in causing the sound. As Handel points out listening processes evolve on multiple simultaneous levels, as the listener perceives the physical features of a sound, but also "features of a sound that are not directly translatable into physical measures (warmth, roughness, hollowness, brightness)" as well as "objects" (1989, 181). I would suggest that both of the latter levels of listening are relevant to the experience of intrusive noises in *Andromache*, as, beyond the pitch and intensity patterns, the audience can perceive the hollowness of the empty glass bottle, the hardness of the concrete surface, the energetic and explosive power of the multitude of bursts, the quickness of the shattering, the smallness and sharpness of the thousands of glass shivers scattering on the floor, the spatial dispersion of the many pieces. What is heard is the fabric and matter of the material as well as the confrontations, movements and coactions of different materials.

Hearing these attributes—or *affordances* as James J. Gibson (1979) has termed the perceived combination of certain attributes in regard to visual perception—gives insight on properties of the perceived sound event, which is not to be confused with the sound source identification. In fact, it is important to differentiate between the processes of perceiving these properties and assigning a known source to these sensations, though both are fundamentally intertwined. The perception of these properties that cannot be physically measured on specific intensity or pitch scales is not a semantic process, which means that the identification of the sound event and its signification proceeds on a different level.

In my opinion, perceiving these attributes is crucially connected to the intrusiveness of certain noises. Their intrusive character derives from the audibility of the dynamics of clashes, bursts and dispersion. Hearing sharpness corresponds to the intrusiveness of the noises of smashed glass.

Auditory perception of the involved energies, dynamics and temporal structures thus can have a direct impact on the physical and affective condition of the spectators. In fact, while this applies for almost all sounds in general, for example voices or musical tones also carry sound information about their production processes;[10] it is much more extreme with intrusive noises. I think that in the case of the noises in *Andromache*, their intrusive power originates in the violence and vehemence of the sound dynamics, which are directly linked with the sensations of potential danger, harm, damage or violation.

Due to the fact that the noises are part of a theatre performance, they will presumably not provoke real fear and anxiety in the audience. I assume, however, that they possess the power to provoke vigilance and alertness in the spectators, their auditory attention being intensely activated and focused on the sounds. The listeners cannot really guard against being affected by the sounds, as they are 'attacked' on a physical level. Even so, it is highly probable that the theatrical context will bring forth an oscillating dynamics in the listening mode insofar as the sounds will also be perceived as sound art events. Thus, their intrusive character obtains rather fascinating and interesting qualities as the listeners might be absorbed by the specific sound structure of the noises. At the beginning of the chapter, I have referred to this as the ambivalence of the spectators as simultaneously they are being intrusively affected and intrigued by the sounds. I assume that theatre noises predominantly evoke such paradox conditions since in the theatre the intrusive impact of the noises is employed for aesthetic purposes in that it can arouse feelings like curiosity and fascination as well as bewilderment and overpowering at the same time.

Future prospects

What I have undertaken in this chapter is a first step towards analysing the phenomenal properties and effects of noises used within theatre performances. I think that it would be most fruitful for theatre theory to furthermore address the question of intrusive noises as it appears to give insight into processes of auditory perception that take place beyond sound localisation or source identification. The ear conveys the dynamics, energies, objects and materials involved in the sound production process and is affected by their intensity, power or tempo.

---

[10] Roland Barthes has pointed out the 'grain in the voice', the *grain de la voix*, as marks of the body within the speaking voice (Barthes 1982, 236-245).

Intrusiveness appears to derive from specific sound 'layouts' insofar as it seems to be linked to certain sound dynamics, for example frictions, collisions, scraping among many others. This does not mean that there is only one kind of intrusiveness; on the contrary, there are many different ways in which noises are or can become intrusive. But in the case of the noises of shattering glass in *Andromache*, I assume that it is the process of hearing 'sharpness', among other related attributes, which predominantly causes the intrusive impact of the noises. Certainly, it cannot be seen as completely independent from the specific context and situation as well as from the perceptual mode of the spectators. Sound source identification as well as the interaction with the other senses leads to further associations of potential physical harm, caused by scattered glass splinters, and adds to an overall sense of the performance. In this sense, the noises are not employed to solely articulate Hermione's emotional state. As was pointed out by Fischer-Lichte, the sound materiality of the noise evokes a number of connoted ideas and associations. I suppose that in *Andromache* the shattering glass provokes vague ideas of danger, rage and despair in the audience. Thus, they create an overall sense of the performance, which is expressed in the tension between audience and stage and derives from the possibility of real harm and the aroused physical and emotional state of ambivalence. In this sense, the semantic potential of the shattering glass is utilised to generate an overall meaning and idea of this performance, which is made directly perceptible to the audience in their own bodily experience through the intrusive noises.

In future, it would be important to develop a descriptive and classificatory vocabulary to further analyse certain noises in their particular qualities and effects. This vocabulary would be helpful for establishing a 'Phenomenology of (Theatre) Noises', which would reflect on the increasing use of specific noises in theatre practice. In my opinion, analysing various theatre performances, which provide complex or particular acoustic arrangements, can provide fruitful insights for theatre theory and aesthetics, reflecting on the recent tendencies in theatrical practice. Furthermore, it is revealing to continue research on the intrusive character of noises, because on the one hand, for noise and sound studies, it might further our understanding of the way in which noises function and affect the hearer in general and on the other hand, for theatre studies, it seems to open up ways to conceptualise the relationship between stage and auditorium with regard to its auditory dimension.

References

Augoyard, Jean-François and Henry Torgue. 2005. *Sonic Experience. A Guide to Everyday Sounds*. Montreal: McGill-Queen's University Press.

Barthes, Roland. 1982. *L'Obvie et L'Obtus. Essais Critiques III*. Paris: Éditions du Seuil.

Bregman, Albert. 1994 [1990]. *Auditory Scene Analysis. The Perceptual Organization of Sound*. Cambridge (MA) and London: The MIT Press.

Brown, Ross. 2010. *Sound. A Reader in Theatre Practice*. Basingstoke/ Hampshire: Palgrave Macmillan.

Fischer-Lichte, Erika. 2008. *The Transformative Power of Performance. A New Aesthetics*. Transl. by Saskya Iris Jain. Oxford/New York: Routledge [Original: *Ästhetik des Performativen* (2004)].

Fisher, Mark. Interview with Luk Perceval conducted on August 15, 2004. "Short, sharp shock as actors walk a tightrope over real danger" at http://living.scotsman.com/features/Short-sharp-shock-as-actors. 2554887.jp (accessed June 25, 2010).

Gaver, William W. 1993. What in the World Do We Hear? An Ecological Approach to Auditory Event Perception. *Ecological Psychology* 5 (1): 1-29.

Gibson, James J. 1979. *The Ecological Approach to Visual Perception*. Boston: Houghton Mifflin Company.

Handel, Stephen. 1989. *Listening. An Introduction to the Perception of Auditory Events*. Cambridge (MA) and London: The MIT Press.

Leonard, John A. 2001. *Theatre Sound*. New York: Routledge.

McAdams, Stephen. 1993. Recognition of Sound Sources and Events. In *Thinking in Sound. The Cognitive Psychology of Human Audition*, ed. Stephen McAdams and Emmanuel Bigand, 146-198. Oxford: Clarendon Press.

Pinto, Vito. 2008. (Zeige-)Spuren der Stimme. Zur technischen Realisierung von Stimmen im zeitgenössischen Theater. In *Deixis und Evidenz*, ed. Horst Wenzel and Ludwig Jäger, 169-193. Freiburg: Rombach.

Risset, Jean-Claude, and David L. Wessel. 1982. Exploration of Timbre by Analysis and Synthesis. In *The Psychology of Music*, ed. Diana Deutsch, 25-58. New York/London: Academic Press.

Schmicking, Daniel. 2003. *Hören und Klang. Empirisch-phänomenologische Untersuchungen*. Würzburg: Königshausen & Neumann.

Schmitz, Hermann. 2008. Leibliche Kommunikation im Medium des
    Schalls. In *Acoustic Turn*, ed. Petra Maria Meyer, 75-88. München:
    Fink Verlag.
Truax, Barry. 2001. *Acoustic Communication.* 2nd edition, Westport, CT:
    Ablex Publishing.
Warren, William W., and Robert R. Verbrugge. 1984. Auditory Perception
    of Breaking and Bouncing Events: A Case Study in Ecological
    Acoustics. *Journal of Experimental Psychology: Human Perception
    and Performance* 10 (5): 704-712.

Dictionaries

The Oxford Dictionary of English Etymology. 1966. Ed. by C. T. Onions.
    Oxford/New York: Oxford University Press.
The Longman Dictionary of the English Language. 2nd Edition. 1991
    [1984], Essex: Longman Group.
The Shorter Oxford English Dictionary. Vol. 2, 6th Edition. 2007 [1933],
    Oxford/New York: Oxford University Press.

content of what a speaking person is saying. In this sense, the human voice may be revealed as having the potential to *show* what cannot be *said*. And it is also in this sense that the voice as a topic of interest for a multitude of disciplines may be considered as a gauge or marker of the 'performative turn' in the humanities.[3]

Performativity is at its core a philosophical term, coined as it was by J. L. Austin to underline the way in which language is not just used to identify pre-existent things in the world but that it also, and essentially, has the power to brings those things about, and thus to constitute, shape and change reality. Yet strangely enough, despite being a philosopher no one could accuse of lacking voice (there is an effusive theatrical vocal presence in Austin's texts), and despite his recognition of the ritual dimension of performative language which implies a shift of focus from semantics proper to the role of embodied citation, i.e. vocality, Austin appears to have paid little heed to the actual role of voice in performative utterances. Yet surely, it is not just the words that a priest must utter in order for a baby to be baptised or for a couple to be wed that define the success of a performative ritual. The quality, tone and sheer presence of the voice that speaks the quasi magical words contributes equally essentially to the uncanny power of the (always intricately theatrical) performative event.[4] The words, one could argue, are in a sense but empty placeholders for the voice in such ritualised, ceremonious practices. So it was with Austin and the question of performative language in mind that I originally came to ask: what of the place of voice in philosophy?

The voice in philosophy: three pathways

Tracing the place of voice in philosophy is a complex and confusing endeavour in which one is led to confront a host of seemingly contradictory perspectives and conclusions. There are several intertwining routes one can take.

---

[3] For a detailed description of this performative turn, see e.g. Lagaay 2001, Carlson 2004.

[4] In May 2010 the news was announced in Japan of the first couple to be married by a robot—apparently 'female'—known as the iFairy. The fact that this news hit the headlines around the world confirms the initial assumption that performative acts can generally only be carried out by *human* voices. But it also raises and complexifies the question of what actually constitutes the performativity of a voice. For a recording of the iFairy in action, go to: http://www.youtube.com/watch?v=uguH2dN2uvE&feature=fvw (accessed January 1, 2011).

The tone in philosophy

One route is to look for the place of tonality in philosophy, to consider the often tense relationship between *what* is said or written, i.e. what a particular philosophy explicitly stands for, and *how* it is said, i.e. what tone can be detected in the speaking/writing of a particular philosopher. Does a philosophy reflect its own tonality and is there a sense in which the voice—as meaningful sound—can be distinguished and even perhaps perceived to be saying something else, something slightly or totally different, than the main propositional content of the utterance it carries? Deconstruction and the reading/listening methods developed by Jacques Derrida have clearly sharpened our ears and made philosophers aware of the crucial difference between voice and language and the tendency of the voice to defy conscious rational control.[5]

Philosophers' words on voice

Another pathway is to consider the place of voice in a particular philosophical system. Here it is a question of attending to what philosophers have explicitly had to say about voice. Given the metaphysical tradition of Western philosophy and its quest to establish abstract, rational ideals over concrete phenomena and emotion, one might initially be inclined to assume that philosophers throughout the ages have tended to overlook—no, failed to *hear!*—the significance of the human voice beyond its mere function as a vehicle for language. Yet this is blatantly untrue. A host of philosophers have shown keen interest, indeed at times an uncanny obsession, with the human voice and tonality of language. Quite contrarily to what one might expect, the physical and musical aspects of human vocality have in fact been very well perceived not only by Plato and Aristotle, but by philosophers throughout the ages e.g. Lucretius, Saint Augustine, Rousseau, Herder, Humboldt, Nietzsche, Heidegger, Levinas, Derrida and Agamben, to name just a few.

At least two general movements of thought can be identified that many philosophers have shared when it comes to reflecting upon voice.

---

[5] Almost any text by Jacques Derrida can be taken to demonstrate this, e.g. Derrida 1973.

1) Ambivalent feelings in response to vocality

Firstly, perception and analysis of the musicality of language, which naturally goes hand in hand with a perception of the conceptual difference between words and their embodied sounds, has often tended to attract ambivalent feelings. Thus the sounding nature of spoken language or in particular the sounding nature of singing has often been described by philosophers as something ecstatically beautiful. Yet the very same phenomenon has just as often, and often at the same time, been perceived as potentially dangerous: dangerous in the sense that it is depicted as tempting the senses away from the sober path of reason. In the eyes of many a philosopher it is almost as if there were something about the medium of voice (as distinct from the word) that were potentially mad, or at least maddening.

Consider for instance this passage taken from Saint Augustine's *Confessions*:

> In earlier days the pleasures of the ear enthralled me more persistently and held me under their spell, but you broke my bonds and set me free. Nowadays I do admittedly find some peaceful contentment in sounds to which your words impart life and meaning, provided the words are sung sensitively by a tuneful voice; but the pleasure is not such as to hold me fast, for when I wish I can get up and go. [...] Yet sensuous gratification, to which I must not yield my mind for fear it grow languid, often deceives me [...]. [W]hen in my own case it happens that the singing has a more powerful effect on me than the sense of what is sung, I confess my sin and my need of repentance, and then I would rather not hear any singer (Augustine 1998, Book 10, 229-230).

Augustine makes a clear distinction here between the aesthetically pleasing sound of the words and their meaning. And it is the meaning side he associates with divine reason whereas the sounding aspect, mere noise, is perceived as something to be wary of for fear that one may get carried away by the pleasure of hearing.

Jean-Jacques Rousseau's references to the sounding nature of language would be another, quite different example here. For him, as is well known, it is the sounding, musical, affective dimension of spoken language, or its dramatic intonation that is the very holy source of the origin of language and thereby stands in a privileged relation to truth. The more structural, monotonous, grammatical, side of language is associated with reason rather than with passion, and is thus, quite contrary to Augustine's sense, where the corruption lies (Rousseau 1974).

2) Outer vs. inner voice

The second striking feature that many philosophies of voice seem to share is that in almost every case in which the outer, acoustic resonance of the speaking or singing voice occurs, it seems to be accompanied by a reference or an attempt to describe a very different experience of voice: the experience of an *inner* voice enters the scene which, whilst lacking the external nature or acoustic resonance of the embodied, musical voice (i.e. no sound waves), is nevertheless clearly audible. Moreover, this voice is almost always distinguishable from the constant murmur of the author's or thinker's own thought-process, flow of consciousness or interior monologue. The *inner* voice enters the scene as the voice of an *other*. And what characterises this voice is that it tends to have an undeniable *authority* which is impossible to ignore and is associated with clear moral guidance.

An example of this thematisation of an inner voice is to be found in the famous passage in Plato's *Apology* in which Socrates describes and invokes a personal 'daemon', which, he says, manifests itself in his mind in the form of a strange voice-like noise:

> Perhaps it may seem strange that I go about and interfere in other people's affairs to give this advice in private, but do not venture to come before your assembly and advise the state. But the reason for this, [...] is that *something divine and spiritual comes to me*, [...] I have had this from my childhood; *it is a sort of voice that comes to me, and when it comes it always holds me back from what I am thinking of doing, but never urges me forward*. This is what opposes my engaging in politics. (Plato, *Apology* 31 cd, here Plato 1966, 115 my emphasis)

Interestingly, what appears to define the authority of this inner voice is not *what* it says (indeed whatever the voice were to say, Socrates, it seems, would be driven to obey), but the very *fact* that it is perceived. Which brings me to question the nature of this kind of auditory experience, since what characterises the perception of this voice is not what it says but its sound. Yet curiously it is a *sound that lacks acoustic resonance*.

How to relate this silent yet nevertheless audible *inner* voice to the outer, acoustically resonant voice? What is the nature of the sound of the inner voice and how does it compare with the physical resonance or musicality of spoken language? Is there a connection at all? And if so, how or where is one to place the ethicality or moral call associated with this voice? Could the seeming morality of the call of the inner voice actually have something to do with its silent resonance, or indeed, with the very different sounding nature of the outer voice? In other words, could it be that there is something sensual and rhythmical about human consciousness or indeed conscience itself? And if so, could this sensuality of conscience (which here takes the form of an inner voice) be connected to the idea that *there is a silent dimension that is in fact intrinsic to the nature of the audible, acoustic, physically resonant, noise-like, sounding human voice?*

In a nutshell, it would seem that the quest for a philosophy of voice leads to the need to investigate the sounding nature of the inner voice on the one hand and a dimension of silence intrinsic to the outer, resonant voice, on the other. Could the two dimensions be intertwined in a kind of chiasmic structure? I will return to this question of the place of silence in voice in further detail a little later on, but first I would like to point to another route from which to explore the enigma of voice and its place in philosophy.

3) A phenomenology of voice

Filtering out all one's habitual assumptions, theoretical prejudices and acquired knowledge pertaining to voice(s) and simply attempting to concentrate on the sound—and colour—of a voice can be a fruitful philosophical method leading to some quite surprising discoveries. For a start, the difficulty involved in separating voice from language is striking: the moment I begin to listen to what a voice is saying I tend to lose focus of the sounding materiality of the medium, and inversely, when I focus on the fleshy, melodious noise of the words as they are formed in a speaker's mouth and resonate through his or her body, I tend to lose track of their meaning. A phenomenological approach also quickly brings into relief the dramatic quality of a voice as *address* or *appeal*: as soon as an acoustic sound is recognised as a voice it immediately leaves the realm of mere sonorous noise and becomes 'more' than just a bodily vibration. I instantly become aware that someone is (possibly) trying to say something, possibly to me and possibly requesting my response.[6] Indeed it would seem to be in the very sounding nature of voice that in speaking or even just emitting noise, it *evokes*, perhaps even *invokes*, i.e. implies, appeals to and *brings about* an audience (even if the audience is the speaker him or herself or someone not physically present). In this sense an ethical quality is inscribed within the very phenomenality of voice to the extent that it is

---

[6] Consider for instance Kurt Schwitters' Dadaist sound poem the *Ursonate* (1922-32). There are hardly any decipherable words in it but the rhythm, intonation and above all voice make it sound like an almost familiar language.

always already affective, perceived as a call appealing for a response. Moreover, as the mind and senses focus yet more attentively on the sounding resonance of the voices that surround us, a host of paradoxes gradually emerge which seem to have to do with the peculiar threshold character of this mysterious and ephemeral phenomenon:

a) A voice is both individual *and* communal: On the one hand, every human voice is unique; no two voices are ever quite the same. In this sense every voice is the signature of an individual. Yet on the other hand, no voice ever resonates alone but emerges as a singular current brought about within a sea of other mimetically interwoven voices. Thus, every voice, each particular grain, is not only constituted through interaction with other voices, but as a result of this process, it also contains uncanny traces of a company of others. In a voice, that which is most personal cannot therefore be quite separated from that which is shared. Again, though now from a slightly different perspective, an ethical contour appears to define the phenomenon.

b) Linguistic *and* non-linguistic: As a medium the human voice is distinct from language; it has its origin in a time *before* language (i.e. in the noise of prelinguistic babble), and functions as an index for that which goes *beyond* or cannot be expressed in language (e.g. in the display of inconceptualisable emotion). In another sense, however, it is dependent on language (as this is distinct from noise), coloured by language (e.g. the particular 'grain' of a French or Spanish voice), and points to the taking place of language (as in its calling nature it signifies a 'wanting-to-say').

c) Temporal *and* transcendent: On the one hand, the human voice is a physical production of the concrete human body, and as such is bound to a concrete, immanent materiality, existing in a particular space and time. As such it is a deictic marker.[7] Yet, on the other hand, insofar as it (and the body from which it emanates) is not only perceived by the other's physical ear but also by his or her acoustic imagination, and thereby connected to a logic of desire (attraction or aversion), the voice resonates beyond its physical transience; as 'phantasmagoric' voice it transcends the body, becoming in a certain sense atemporal.

d) Sounding resonance *and* silent potential: On the surface of perception voice is of course sounding resonance, a physical vibration perceivable

---

 a detailed analysis of the relationship between voice and *deixis* in the work of io Agamben, see Lagaay and Schiffers 2008b.

by a biological ear. But voice is not just the random disturbance of sound waves or the consequence of spontaneous or involuntary, arbitrary friction; not simply parasitical to communication, not just noise. To formulate a thesis: what distinguishes voice from noise is its intrinsic relation to the possibility of silence. For, inasmuch as silence can be considered as a mode of vocal expression, voice cannot be defined in clear opposition to silence (nor vice-versa).[8] It follows from this that the philosophy of voice is not exhausted in a philosophy of human performance qua activity but must also take into account and articulate itself as a philosophy of human *potentiality*.

I have named and outlined three different pathways towards uncovering the place of voice in philosophy. Of course in a given philosophy, all three paths may often intertwine or fold into each other in the complex manner of a labyrinth: what a particular philosopher has said or written about voice may or may not reveal something about the phenomenology of voice and may or may not reflect upon its own tonality. I would now like to explore the latter, the relationship between voice as sound and voice as silence, in the move towards a 'negative' philosophy of voice. Articulating this negative philosophy involves dwelling for a moment on the passage from noise to voice; with noise conceived here as perhaps always already 'more' than just random friction, insofar as it is perceived, and as such it relates as disturbance to a realm of potentially intentional meaning, and voice as never quite reducible to linguistic signalling.

Towards a 'negative' philosophy of voice

Most recent theories of voice tend to focus on the acoustic, embodied, actualised, speaking/uttering sound of voice (e.g. Meyer-Kalkus 2001; Cavarero 2005; Dolar 2006). But do we not experience on a daily basis the reality and power of voices that are withheld, voices that refrain from actually speaking, silent voices? I expect that a voice that were only ever in an active mode of actual speaking performance, a voice that knew no silence, could not be a real voice nor even identified as an hallucination. My quest is thus for a theory of voice that does not reduce voice to mere sound. Or stated differently: I'm looking for a concept of sound that allows it to be stretched beyond the actual moment of its resonance; a philosophy of voice, if you like, that resonates or echoes into and beyond silence.

In attempting to grasp this negative philosophy of voice, Giorgio

---

[8] For a detailed account of the potential meanings of silence, see Lagaay 2008c.

Agamben has much to offer. In *Language and Death* (1991) he describes a philosophy of voice that is not built upon the idea that the human voice in question speaks continuously and from the start. The fact that humans are born *without* being able to speak is essential here. It means that our first experience of voice—including hearing our mother's voice and the voices of people around—is an experience of voice that says nothing. Yet neither is it meaningless noise. This voice is negative in the sense that unlike the voice of animals who are always already in harmony with their own language—they don't generally have to learn to speak—it is *no longer* mere noise but *not yet* meaning. This experience of voice at the threshold to meaning is of fundamental importance for Agamben's concept of potentiality, the source of which he considers to reside in human infancy. This experience of potentiality is not only to be interpreted as an experience of the possibility of speaking. More profoundly at stake here is the experience of a fundamentally human *in*ability. Indeed, for Agamben, even when voice becomes articulated language there remains on a deep level a trace of this pure vocality which cannot speak.

Agamben pursues this idea of pure vocality throughout the history of Western philosophy—and poetry—and discovers a link between it and the idea of nothingness and the relationship of humans to death. Both Hegel and Heidegger recognise a close connection between the relationship of humans to language and their consciousness of mortality. For Hegel, human articulation begins in the suspension or transcendence of animal 'voice': man begins to speak at the point when the animal cries out at the moment of death—a vocal utterance on the brink of articulation. The animal's death is thus conceived by Hegel as a threshold of sorts to human language.[9] For Heidegger, on the other hand, Dasein is always already thrown into being *without* a voice. However, this negativity—Dasein's thrownness—leads to an opening, which, conceived as an "acoustic of the soul brings about the 'Stimmung' in which the call of consciousness as a *silent* voice is heard—thus enabling Dasein to articulate its relationship to nothingness" (Heidegger 2001, § 54-62).

At this point, the inner and outer voice appear to intertwine. The sound of the inner voice conditions, as it were, the possibility of the outer voice which in the face of death remains silent. And whoever knows this silence will recognise more than mere noise in the sounding nature of the other's voice, one's counterpart. In this experience of a call without content lies an

---

[9] "Every animal finds a voice in its violent death; it expresses itself as a removed-self (*als aufgehobnes Selbst*). [...]. In the voice, meaning turns back into itself; it is negative self, desire. It is lack, absence of substance in itself" (Hegel from *Jenear Schriften* quoted in Agamben, op. cit., 45).

ethical potential which is rooted in the phenomenal voice, understood here as the interdependence of inner and outer vocality. A consequence of this recognition is that our attention must not be directed solely to the outer, sounding voice. For the voice that is withheld is in many ways just as telling. And only when voice remains silent, can silence begin to speak.[10]

But where does this philosophy of voice leave us, or rather take us, when we turn to the realm of theatre and performance? One perhaps most obvious thing to note is that in its implicit theatricality, the phenomenon of voice shares much with that which constitutes theatre/performance. This is apparent in its ephemeral temporality, implicit indexicality and eventness (the (a) live here-and-now both of voice and of that which makes a theatrical event), as well as in its always already beingness-for-another, beingness-for-an-audience and the implicit request of a response. But what a meditation upon the sounding nature of vocality also—and perhaps essentially—reveals is that, quite curiously, its experience is not exhausted in its sounding materiality. Together, the complex relationship between inner and outer levels of voice on the one hand and the various dimensions of silence within voice on the other, when transferred to or confronted with the realm of theatre and performance, gesture towards the dimensions in which a theatrical event is never quite reducible to the simple materiality of what occurs in the theatrical/performative space. Intriguingly, indeed almost ironically, the very 'performative turn' that has led critics and philosophers to concern themselves more intensely with the specific materiality, embodiment and temporal liveness of what is carried out within and thereby constitutes theatre also points, in a certain sense, to the transcendence of these elements. Thus it would seem, and this is what the prism of voice certainly appears to reveal, that an intense preoccupation with that which is present/presence necessarily leads to an increased attentiveness towards that which is not yet fully there—but might be, could be on the brink. Stated bluntly: a conscious focus on sound sharpens the listener's ears to the surrounding pregnant silence. Yet the 'transcendence' of performance gestured towards here must not be misunderstood as transcendence in an absolute sense, not something that necessarily takes us beyond the material or out of the body, for it clearly takes place *within* immanence: it is a transcendence, if you like, that relies centrally on the human senses to the extent that these are capable, essentially, of sensing beyond themselves and the moment—towards the silent yet resonant potential *within*.

Thus, what the voice in relation to theatre reveals is not simply on a

---

[10] Considered from another perspective: "Silence is not the absence of sound but the beginning of listening" (Voegelin 2010, 83).

banal level that theatre/performance is never just visual but always also
sonorous and synaesthetic, but that what happens on stage is constituted as
much by that which occurs on the immanent level of concrete phenomenality
(creaking floorboards, dense, airless space, moving, calling bodies all
combining to underline an urgency of the present moment) as by what
does *not* occur, what could have, what might have, but doesn't quite.
Theatre is made, one could say, for the ears as much as for the eyes; and
by action and occurrence as much as by inaction and non-occurrence. The
philosophy of voice reveals this much but also more: that it is never just
eyes on the one hand and ears on the other, not action on the one hand and
refrainment or potentiality on the other. Although these different dimensions
can be separated and distinguished on a theoretical/theatrical level, what
the enigma of voice in fact suggests is that a real challenge of
theory/theatre is precisely to understand, grasp and bring to expression the
intrinsic, chiasmic interrelation of these various dimensions: eyes *as* ears,
ears *as* eyes and action *in/as* inaction on the level of the phenomenon.

References

Agamben, Giorgio. 1991. *Language and Death: The Place of Negativity*.
    Trans. Karen E. Pinkus with Michael Hardt. Minneapolis/London:
    University of Minnesota Press.
Augustine. 1998. *The Confessions*. Trans. Maria Boulding. New York:
    Vintage Books.
Barthes, Roland. 1977. The Grain of the Voice. In *Image-Music-Text*.
    Trans. Stephen Heath. 179-189. New York: Hill and Wang.
Blödorn, Andreas, Daniela Langer, and Michael Scheffel, eds. 2006.
    Stimme(n) im Text. Narratologische Positionsbestimmungen. Berlin: de
    Gruyter.
Carlson, Marvin A. 2004. *Performance: A Critical Introduction*. 2nd ed.
    New York, London: Routledge.
Cavarero, Adriana. 2005. *For More than One Voice: Toward a Philosophy
    of Vocal Expression*. Trans. Paul Kottman. Stanford, Calif.: Stanford
    University Press.
Derrida, Jacques. 1973. *Speech and Phenomena*. Trans. David B. Allison.
    Evanston: Northwestern University Press.
Dolar, Mladen. 2006. *A Voice And Nothing More*. Ed. Slavoj Žižek, *Short
    Circuits*. Cambridge (MA) and London: The MIT Press.
Heidegger, Martin. 2001. *Sein und Zeit*. 18th ed. Tübingen: Max
    Niemeyer. Original edition, 1926.

Jaynes, Julian. 1976. *The Origin of Consciousness in the Breakdown of the Bicameral Mind*. London: Penguin Books.

Lagaay, Alice. 2001. *Metaphysics of Performance. Performance, Performativity and the Relation between Theatre and Philosophy*. Berlin: Logos.

—. 2008a. Between Sound and Silence: Voice in the History of Psychoanalysis. *Episteme* Volume 1 (1): 53-62.

Lagaay, Alice and Juliane Schiffers. 2008b. Das Stattfinden der Sprache in der negativen deiktischen Struktur des Pronomens. Zur Figur der Stimme bei Giorgio Agamben. In *Deixis und Evidenz*. Eds Horst Wenzel and Ludwig Jäger, 217-239. Freiburg: Rombach.

Lagaay, Alice. 2008c. How to Do and Not to Do Things with Words. Zur Frage nach der Performativität des Schweigens, in: *Performanzen des Nichttuns*. Edited by Barbara Gronau and Alice Lagaay, 22-32.Vienna: Passagen.

Meyer-Kalkus, Reinhart. 2001. *Stimme und Sprechkünste im 20. Jahrhundert*. Berlin: Akademie Verlag.

Plato. 1966. *Euthyphro, Apology, Crito, Phaedo, Phaedrus*. Trans. Harold North Fowler. Cambridge (MA): Harvard University Press.

Rousseau, Jean-Jacques. 1974. *Essai sur l'origine des langues*. Paris: Aubier.

Voegelin, Salomé. 2010. *Listening to Noise and Silence. Towards a Philosophy of Sound Art*. New York, London: Continuum.

Waldenfels, Bernhard. 1993. Hearing Oneself Speak, Derrida's Recording of the Phenomenological Voice. In: *Southern Journal of Philosophy*, vol. 32, 65-77.

CHAPTER VII

VOCAL LANDSCAPING:
THE THEATRE OF SOUND IN AUDIOWALKS

MISHA MYERS

Introduction

As an innovative form of site or context-specific performance, audiowalks create a theatrical auditory space through the sound of voices speaking in the ear. Such works involve the listener-walker-participant as an active performer in the work through a multi-sensory involvement within specific places and landscapes. Their attention is conducted through particular techniques and technologies of and for voicing and listening. In this "theatre of sound" places are perceived from multiple sensorial vantage points, through "earpoints" as much as "viewpoints" (Edmund Carpenter in Feld 1996, 95). This mode of performance challenges prevalent conceptions of meaning production, forms of discourse and sense making involved in the experience of theatre. Furthermore, it contests notions of landscape and of spectatorship of theatre as predominantly visually orientated experiences or constructs. It could be argued that the central criteria of the medium of theatre are no longer present: co-presence of performance and audience in shared time-space. However, previous theatrical hierarchies, relationships between performer and audience and the phenomenological reality of the stage have been challenged and subverted by the use of innovative technologies in contemporary performance (Carver and Beardon 2004, 181). Indeed, as these authors have argued, the use of technology could be understood to reaffirm the centrality of immediacy in the theatrical experience, where ephemerality and contingency are augmented or enhanced. In this chapter it will be argued that the combination of practices of walking with those of listening presents a particular way of knowing landscape that situates or contextualises an audience in the visual and imaginary space that is already involved in the experience of theatre. In particular, it considers how the use of technology in the audiowalk expands the phenomenological space in which theatre happens and the sensory modes of audience engagement within that space.

For example, particular attention is given here to the practices of listening involved with movement through auditory spaces in audiowalks through the mediation of audio technology in works such as: Mike Pearson's *Carrlands* (Pearson 2007), which he describes as a series of original sound compositions that combine spoken word, music and effects inspired by and set at three locations in North Lincolnshire (Pearson 2007); Duncan Speakman's *sounds from above the ground* (Speakman 2008, 2006), a site-responsive guided walk that combines text, performance and live sound with a group following a lone walker with his internal monologue transmitted to headphones; and Platform's "operatic audio walk" *And While London Burns* (Platform 2006), in which recorded voices guide the ambulant listener through London's Square Mile. While it is not possible within the scope of this chapter to analyse each of these works in great detail, this discussion moves alongside or accompanies these works to focus on the general techniques and technologies of and for listening employed in audiowalks. Consideration will be given to how such works affect and produce particular theatrical experiences of landscapes through kinaesthetic, mobile and multi-sensory experiences of sound within everyday environments.

With *Carrlands* a series of audio works can be downloaded[1] from the Internet to either listen to at home or to take on a walk in one of the three rarely visited locations in which the work was set. When experienced in these landscapes, the work becomes what Pearson describes as an innovative form of site-specific performance "from which performers are *absent* but within which the audience member plays an active and generative role in meaning creation, as a participant" (Pearson 2007, 2). This is a complicated sense of absence, as it is not simply that there is no performer there. This is addressed further in a discussion of issues of embodiment and speech that will follow. However, I have previously referred to the participant engaged in this active role within such modes of performance as a *percipient*. Where the locus of meaning creation or content is shifted away from conventional performers, I have employed this term to refer to a participant as a locus of place and knowledge production who alters and determines a process and its outcomes through their skilful, embodied and sensorial engagement (Myers 2006, 2008,

---

[1] *Carrlands* can be downloaded at http://www.carrlands.org.uk/project.asp (accessed November 20, 2010).

2010). In *Carrlands* the percipient is guided through the integration of spoken texts for solo voice with musical composition and suggestive instructions of particular actions for the user to take. Pearson describes the instrumental and vocal components, sound effects and electronically generated material of the musical composition as providing "a matrix within which the text is embedded" (Pearson 2007, 6).

In *sounds from above the ground*, a group of percipients are given stereo wireless receivers and follow behind the work's creator and guide Speakman as he leads them through the streets of a city. He asks the percipients to walk behind him at such a distance that if they were to raise their voice, he couldn't hear them. Speakman's internal monologue is transmitted to the audience's headphones and is instantaneously remixed with sounds of the city via a laptop, which he carries in a backpack. Speakman instructs the percipient suggestively in the way that Pearson does in *Carrlands*: "Listen through my ears. Things that happened before will happen again" (Speakman 2008). The percipient listens to the manipulated ambient sounds Speakman encounters and "collects" as he walks just ahead. Meanwhile, the soundscape of the percipient's immediate surroundings is drowned out by the sounds that precede them. Although a performer is present in this work in the conventional sense, he is also absent or displaced in a related, but different way to that of Pearson's absent performer. Speakman's voice is not recorded, but transmitted live and he is seen by the percipient walking up ahead and then he vanishes around corners. However, he is displaced sonically within the body of the percipient as his voice is heard through headphones. There is also a shift of the locus of meaning production in this work as the percipient is engaged both in meaning creation and in a role as a performer. A percipient of the work commented:

> The artist is murmuring in my ear like a friend, telling me where to go. My inner monologue rises to tangle with him [...]. I've followed instructions. I've had space to look around, to be puzzled, to disagree, to feel stubborn" (Osunwunmi 2006).

And While London Burns is an operatic audio walk produced by the arts organisation Platform with composer Isa Suarez, that takes the listener, equipped with an MP3 player, on a walk "through the web of institutions that extract oil and gas from the ground [...] the 'carbon web' that is London's Square Mile" (Platform 2006). The MP3 files of the walk can be downloaded[2] from a website along with a map. The recorded voice of a narrator, or guide, gives directions for walking, relays factual information about the buildings and landscapes passed through, and sets a pace with the sound of her footsteps. This landscape is also seen through the eyes and experience of the operatic audio walk's fictional protagonist, a financial worker implicated in the "carbon web". These voices speak directly to the percipient and, similar to *Carrlands*, invite them to perform particular actions along the way, such as looking into a luxurious window display in the Royal Exchange, walking around and around the Swiss Re Tower, leaning up against a tree, climbing to the top of the monument to the Fire of London and then looking out over the city imagining a new future. While directing the attention of the percipient to their reflection in Swiss Re's mirrored windows, the protagonist whispers: "You in there, I'm here, in here between your ears, inside you. Look inside the windows [...] Do you see me [...] or is it you?" (Platform 2006). In this moment of the audiowalk, the performer of *And While London Burns* also directly addresses a distinct experience of entanglement of internal and external space offered by this mode of performance.

Listening that speaks, voices that sound: intimacy, touch and proximity

Each of these three works utilises the mediation and transmission of recorded or live voice and ambient sound through headphones to direct percipients' direct and active engagement and sensual attention within a specific environment. In each audiowalk solo voices speak monologues, which could be understood as the sound of inner speech. In Frances Dyson's critique of vocal production of mainstream radio, she finds that the,

> characteristics of inner speech—that it is silent, atopic, self-directed and timeless—enable it to establish a philosophical system where the mind can be conscious of itself without reference to the world, and without interruption or interference from the uncertainty of life (1994, 169).

This inner speech can assume the sensuous characteristics of voiced speech, which leads to the association of personal presence, sincerity, depth of character and truth with the sonorous quality of the voice. Dyson

---

[2] *And While London Burns* can be downloaded at http://www.andwhilelondon burns.com (accessed November 20, 2010).

argues that a simulation of interiority is produced by the media through the transmitted and amplified voice cleansed of any noise of the body. With the addition of reverberation projected onto the amplified voice by reverb, this atopic voice can be "placed" in an idealised space. It acquires spatial solidity and dimension suggestive of that of a natural voice reverberating in a somewhere, although this somewhere is nowhere as it is absent of noise. However, the percipient in the audiowalk, and in some cases the performer, such as in the example of Speakman, will almost inevitably be amidst the "noisy" uncertainties of life where contingent and ephemeral ambient sounds of wind, passers-by, traffic, footsteps contribute significantly to the work. This contrasts with the conventional theatre space, which has been designed over time, like the radio studio, to be sound-proof and impermeable to the outside with its thick walls, cushioned seats and carpets. This section will primarily focus on a discussion of the transmitted voice rather than address the permeability of external noise as a central part of this mode of performance. While the latter will be considered in the next section, it is nevertheless worth noting that this aspect of the audiowalk increases the sense of immediacy that is central to the theatrical experience, as discussed in the Introduction.

The notion of the solipsistic, atopic and authoritative voice is inherited from the early Christian theological notion of *logos* and Plato's institution of this metaphysics into an ideal: the revelation or truth of *logos* is only possible through the medium of speech and the technology of language, expressing ideas already in the mind. With this conceptualisation of speech, there is a consequential separation of the voice of the body and the voice of the mind, a dematerialised voice. Sound is eliminated from the voice to be replaced with the inner voice, the metaphor for reflection and intellection.

With the traditional conventions of Western theatre and acting inherited from the Greek theatre and this idealisation of a dematerialised voice, the actor, like language, is the transparent medium of truth and language, and is viewed as the primary sign system transmitting meaning. But what of the percipient in *sounds from above ground*, whose inner monologue tangled with Speakman's or the protagonist of *And While London Burns* who gets inside the listener? This mode of a soundless and placeless inner speech does not adequately describe the mode of speech or indeed the spatial dimensions of theatrical speech involved in *And While London Burns, Carrlands* or *sounds from above ground*. Indeed, it was suggested earlier that the locus of meaning in these audiowalks is shifted to the percipient or listener. What alternative forms of listening and voicing, of meaning production, of sensing meaning and making sense are offered, then, by the mode of performance they employ?

The interrelationship or implication of interiority and exteriority is significant to audiowalks where there is a certain intimacy constituted in the particular mode of listening mediated through the technologies and techniques they employ. Proposing a joining of a history and phenomenology of interiority with a history and a phenomenology of listening, Roland Barthes describes a kind of listening that followed from the internalisation of religion in Judeo-Christian civilisation as *"taking soundings"*, where an intimacy is "plumbed by listening" (1991, 250; emphasis in original). In Barthes' account of forms of listening, the development of interiority leads gradually from the exterior voices of demons or angels to the object of listening becoming the conscience itself. He suggests that the shift from public confession to private listening within the confessional advanced a limited and clandestine listening that "brings two subjects into relation" (1991, 251). With the development of the instrument of the telephone and psychoanalytic listening Barthes suggests a new mode of aural attention has progressed that is active, dialogical and intersubjective: *"listening speaks"* (1991, 259; emphasis in original). A transference or a kind of touch between two subjects is constituted through "the quasi-physical contact of these subjects (by voice and ear)", where *'listen to me'* means *touch me, know that I exist"* (1991, 251; emphasis in original). With telephonic listening, Barthes suggests a return to the tactility or embodiment of hearing: the speaker is invited to collect the body into the voice and the listener to collect themselves into their ear (1991, 252).

Steven Connor suggests that amplified voices close up space through what he calls an aggressive-sadistic use of voice. He writes, "For when we shout, we tear. We tear apart distance" (Connor 2000, 34). The voice is brought closer in proximity to the receiver in an imposing closeness and intimacy. A range of organic vocal sounds such as that of the lips, tongue, and breath can be heard where in ordinary hearing they would not:

> Microphones permit the use of a range of dynamics and the projection of nuances; even very small and inward elements of dialogue and expression can carry a lot of force (Salzman and Desi 2008, 28).

The voice has an embodying power to produce bodies, to manipulate itself into an object and to occupy space. This is the case with the voice that has an identifiable source, but exceeds that source, such as the singing voice, as well as the voice that seems to be separated from its natural source. As Connor suggests:

This voice then conjures for itself a different kind of body; an imaginary body which may contradict, compete with, replace, or even reshape the actual, visible body of the speaker (2000, 36).

Or indeed, in the audio walk this visible body of the speaker is conjured within the imagination of the listener. As the protagonist intimates in *And While London Burns*, the listener staring at their own reflection in Swiss Re Tower's windows might envision the voice they hear as their own. The audiowalk then reshapes the dimensions of theatrical space and the relationship between audience and performer. It is not enough to say that the performer is not present in this theatre of sound.

Vocal acts of landscaping: spatialisation of voice and sound

With the technology of the headphone and personal stereo, audiowalks suggest an additional space and instrument of intersubjective listening that not only extends or transfers this touch between two subjects within an interior bodily space, or "body-as-site" associated with discourse (Barthes 1991, 255), but also externally with and within a specific landscape with its spectrum of ambient sound. As Barthes suggests "listening is the very sense of time and space" (1991, 246). In *And While London Burns, sounds from above the ground* and *Carrlands* the voice is placed somewhere where a range of ambient sounds of a material place, including the soft and nuanced, are amplified, imposed and transformed as elements of musical composition.

In recent thinking on landscape in cultural geography, as seen in John Wylie's work on the specific practice of coastal walking, narrative and writing, the dimensions of bodily space and landscape become enmeshed. As Barthes finds a metaphor in the "folds and detours" of the ear for the folding of the body into the voice and the self into the ear, Wylie suggests, "The circulation and upsurge of affects and percepts is precisely that from which these two horizons, inside and outside, self and landscape, precipitate and fold" (Wylie 2007, 215). The audiowalk might be understood as what Hayden Lorimer refers to as "embodied acts of landscaping" (Lorimer in Wylie 2007, 166), that is "the ongoing shaping of self, body and landscape via practice and performance" (Wylie 2007, 166).

Charles Stankievech notes that the "*technique* of listening" that was initiated with the stereo stethoscope, the techniques of isolation and amplification, have persisted with the "*technology* of headphones", but they have been enhanced to produce imaginary voices and spaces:

But while the stereo stethoscope allows for a transportation of a real space into an imaginary space (from heart chamber to headspace), headphones allow for the creative manipulation of any kind of sound—from natural to technical to musical—to create imaginary spaces within *another* imaginary space (Stankievech 2006, 94).

Furthermore, current headphone technology permits the transmission of binaural recordings, M-S stereo recordings, or ambisonic recordings, which create a 3D impression "that accurately replicates an exterior perception of the world" (Stankievech 2006, 94). Stankievech suggests that audiowalks utilising binaural recording create a realistic immersive environment, such as those of Janet Cardiff and George Miller, where in their case a fictional element is combined through the use of *film noir* elements. The listener enters into "a hybrid reality where they are given a dramatic role to play" (2006, 94). Stankievech suggests that the success of their work is in the contrasting quality of Cardiff's voice, recorded in mono and proximity to the microphone, with the binaural recording of the soundscape; as the guide's voice feels like it speaks "not just from within the soundscape, but from within the listener's own body" (2006, 95).

Different senses, spaces and sounds become fore-grounded as the audiowalk directs the listener's attention to various levels of detail and sensorial experience, which is not unlike everyday experience:

Lived experience involves constant shifts in sensory figures and grounds, constant potentials for multi- or cross-sensory interactions or correspondences. Figure-ground interplays, in which one sense surfaces in the midst of another that recedes, in which positions of dominance and subordination switch or commingle, blur into synaesthesia (Feld 1996, 93).

With audiowalks the artists carefully compose such shifts of figures and grounds to direct percipients' attention to details and narratives of particular landscapes. The voices of the guides involved in each of the works discussed above invites actions that activate other senses and/or sensations are amplified by musical elements. As Barthes suggests:

It is against the auditive background that *listening* occurs [...] if the auditive background invades the whole of phonic space (if the ambient noise is too loud), then selection or intelligence of space is no longer possible (1991, 247).

This relationship between figure and ground might be considered similar to that between signal and noise. The ambient sound and the noise of the body in motion may not always be composed, but may be accepted as a condition of this theatrical mode. Where it may be most effective in terms of an intelligence of space, is where the audiowalk allows for and anticipates the contingency and uncertainty of ambient sounds encountered in the landscape, and the particular gait of the walker into its composition. In such case, noise is no longer a distraction of unwanted sonic debris, but rather an element of the composition that enhances and augments the theatrical experience and space.

Listening through the feet. Mobility, multi-sensoriality, interanimation

It is significant that with the audiowalk, the self that is collected in the ear is mobile and moved by the body. Indeed, Tim Ingold suggests that sometimes auditory perception is also "heard" through the feet in the form of vibration (2004, 330-331). But the motion of walking itself enables a different mode of sensory perception, as do other forms of mobility that move at a human pace. The tactile, sonic and visual senses are drawn upon and coordinated with the motion of the body, "the kinaesthesia and sonesthesia of shaped place, [is] encountered and learned by the moving, sensing, experiencing body" (Feld 1996, 105). This kinaesthetic, synaesthetic and sonaesthetic mode of perception (Casey 1996, 22), "the whole body sensing and moving", is an "actively passive" mode, both absorptive and constitutive at the same time (Casey 1996, 18). Places are vivified through what Keith Basso refers to as a process of "interanimation": "As places animate the ideas and feelings of persons who attend to them, these same ideas and feelings animate the places on which attention has been bestowed" (1996, 55). This idea is perhaps related to how Pearson suggests *Carrlands* enhances appreciation of "a seemingly featureless terrain" by "animating that which is observable through story" (2007, 3).

Filipa Matos Wunderlich argues that the Walkman or iPod affects bodily disengagement in modes of walking, which she refers to as "purposive", that is walking as a task of everyday necessity, a rapid paced and "anxious mode, in which we long for arrival at a destination" (2008, 131). The ambient sound of the actual environment and the sounds of the body, of breathing, of footsteps, of clothing are sometimes dampened, become background or are amplified or displaced. This is not dissimilar to the lived experience of shifting sensory grounds and figures described by Feld above. Ian Chambers contends: "[The Walkman] does not subtract from sense but adds to and complicates it" (1994, 51). There is a destabilisation of the senses that does arise in all of the works discussed, as what is heard is not always what is seen. With *sounds from above ground* the delayed sound or intimate proximity with a sound source that can be seen at a distance is disconcerting. The conversation of a couple of passers-by walking up ahead is audible. By the time they reach me I no longer hear them. We are in a disjunctive time, as if we were in different worlds. However, there are also instances where what is heard and what is seen are conjoined in the synaesthetic and sonaesthetic perception of place.

While auditory perception may be conceived as the primary mediating sense in audiowalks, that you are being called to collect all of yourself into your ear (Barthes 1991, 252), the involvement of the other senses is significant to the experiences and opportunities for understanding they invite. "The more apparently distanced, disembodied, or deboned a sound might seem to be, the more substantial, the more bodily our relations find a way of becoming" (Connor 2004, 171). This multi-sensorial engagement potentially intensifies the emotional, imagistic and metaphoric associations, attachments and connections made with places (Wunderlich 2008, 130).

Conclusion

Michael Bull has described personal stereos as "technologies of accompanied solitude" (2004, 177). He suggests this technology "shrinks space into something manageable and habitable" through the combination of noise, proximity and privacy (2004, 177). Bull focuses on the privatising and colonising aspect of this technology through which users can reconfigure, aestheticise and familiarise the spaces of the everyday and faraway with their own private experience. With this technology users can,

> create a seamless web of mediated and privatized experience in their everyday movement through the city and [...] enhance virtually any chosen experience in any geographical location (Bull 2004, 182).

The audiowalk does aestheticise particular spaces of the everyday. However, this mode of performance interanimates and shapes landscapes through a theatre of sound that is not simply or primarily a visually orientated or directed experience. In this mode of performance, voices conjure bodies and landscapes in the imagination, voices are touched and touching and voices are placed somewhere amidst the amplification, imposition, transposition and transformation of ambient sound of material place. In addition, it is not necessarily a solitary experience in a shrunken and isolated space. The audiowalk is a theatre of intersubjective listening that both closes the distance and extends touch between two subjects within an interior bodily space, as well as within a landscape. Indeed, there is a particular way of touching the world and of being touched with the particular landscaping practice of walking while listening to voices and sounds through headphones: "Landscape becomes the close-at-hand, that which is both touching and touched, an affective handling through which self and world emerge and entwine" (Lorimer in Wylie 2007, 167). In this theatre of sound, self, body and landscape are shaped and enmeshed through voicing and listening bodies in motion.

Ongoing innovations in locative media technology and the increasing use and access to basic mobile recording devices, GPS-enabled technology, and other hyper-media offer a range of applications that can further expand the dimensions of the theatrical space of the audiowalk. As well as making possible alternative modes of co-presence of performers and audiences in new dimensions of shared time-space, they also present modes of theatrical experience that are customised by and responsive to percipients and their presence within specific locations. Acting as multi-sensory receptors, transmitters, recorders and amplifiers, these technologies offer new modes of theatrical landscaping, as well as new opportunities to experience, create and express changing cultural, social and political landscapes.

References

Barthes, Roland. 1991. *The Responsibility of forms: critical essays on music, art and representation.* Berkeley, CA: University of California Press.

Basso, Keith. 1996. "Wisdom Sits in Places: Notes on a Western Apache Landscape," in *Senses of Place,* edited by Keith Basso and Steven Feld, 53-90. Santa Fe, New Mexico: School of American Research.

Bull, Michael. 2004. "Thinking about Sound, Proximity, and Distance in Modern Experience: The Case of Odysseus's Walkman," in *Hearing Cultures: Essays on Sound, Listening and Modernity*, edited by Veit Erlmann, 173-191. Oxford: Berg.

Carver, Gavin and Colin Beardon. 2004. *New Visions in Performance: The Impact of Digital Technologies.* London: Taylor and Francis.

Casey, Edward. 1996. "How to Get from Space to Place in a Fairly Short Stretch of Time: Phenomenological Prolegomena," in *Senses of Place,* edited by Keith Basso and Steven Feld, 13-52. Santa Fe, New Mexico: School of American Research.

Chambers, Ian. 1994. *Migrancy, Culture, Identity*. London: Routledge.

Connor, Steven. 2000. *Dumbstruck: A Cultural History of Ventriloquism.* Oxford: Oxford University Press.

—. 2004. "Edison's Teeth: Touching Hearing" in *Hearing Cultures: Essays on Sound, Listening and Modernity*, edited by Veit Erlmann, 153-172. Oxford: Berg.

Dyson, Frances. 1994. "The Genealogy of the Radio Voice", in *Radio Rethink: Art, Sound and Transmission,* edited by Daina Augaitis and Dan Lander, 167-186. Banff: Walter Phillips Gallery.

Feld, Steven. 1996. "Waterfalls of Song: An Acoustemology of Place Resounding in Bosavi, Papua New Guinea" in *Senses of Place,* edited by Keith Basso and Steven Feld, 91-136. Santa Fe, New Mexico: School of American Research.

Ingold, Tim. 2004. "Culture on the ground: The world perceived through the feet." *Journal of Material Culture* 9 (3): 315-340.

Osunwunmi. 2006. "Duncan Speakman: Echo Location." *Real Time*, no. 72 (April-May), http://www.realtimearts.net/feature/Inbetween_Time /8397 (July 1, 2010).

Pearson, Michael. 2007. *Carrlands.* http://www.carrlands.org.uk/project.asp (July 1, 2010).

Platform. 2006. *And While London Burns*, operatic audio walk, dir. John Jordon and James Marriott, comp. Isa Suarez. London: Platform Production, http://www.andwhilelondonburns.com (July 1, 2008).

Salzman, Eric and Thomas Desi. 2008. *The New Music Theater: Seeing the Voice, Hearing the Body*. Oxford: Oxford University Press.

Speakman, Duncan. 2008. *sounds from above ground, Roam: A Weekend of Walking* (15-17 March). Loughborough: Loughborough University.

—. 2006. *sounds from above ground.* http://duncanspeakman.net/?p=162 (July 1, 2010).

Stankievech, Charles. 2006. "Get Out of the Room, Get into the Head: Headphones and Acoustic Phenomenology". In *Responsive Architectures,* edited by Philip Beesley et al., 93-95. Cambridge, Ontario: Riverside Architectural Press.

Thibaud, Jean-Paul. 2006. "Les mobilisations de l'auditeur-baladeur: une sociabilité publicative." http://en.scientificcommons.org/23510915 (September 5, 2008).

Wunderlich, Filipa Matos. 2008. "Walking and Rhythmicity: Sensing Urban Space." *Journal of Urban Design* 13 (1): 125-139.

Wylie, John. 2007. *Landscape*. London: Routledge.

CHAPTER VIII

RADICAL VOCALITY, AUDITORY DISTRESS AND DISEMBODIED VOICE: THE RESOLUTION OF THE VOICE-BODY IN THE WOOSTER GROUP'S *LA DIDONE*

PIETER VERSTRAETE

In recent years, vocal performance has generally established itself through and in relation to the experimental concert scene and new forms of music theatre by escaping established definitions and resisting against certain historical traditions of opera and musical drama. This resistance is accompanied with many boisterous vocal experiments and a legacy of performance art as well as popular culture. Nonetheless, it has also produced a certain level of *continuity* with the past in vocal research on the stage.

One way of going against the grain of historical conventions and categories was, what I would call, a 'radical vocality', which was recharged by the espousal of performance art with new audio technologies, a development that ran parallel to the new forms of postdramatic theatre. Vocality is understood to indicate a broader spectrum of utterance, including the purely sonorous, bodily aspects of the vocal utterance. I would like to claim that a significant manifestation of this radical vocality on the postmodern stage is the disembodied voice, also referred to as the acousmatic (Chion 1994) or ventriloquist voice (Connor 2000). I thereby do not want to disregard the different theoretical contexts in which these terms have their proper meaning and function. Instead, I would like to discuss the conceptual ramifications of these terms in relation to each other, as far as they help me to explain how disembodiment, as one particular expression or trait of radical vocality in performance, has particular implications in the meaning making processes of the auditor-spectator.

After briefly exploring the historical significance of radical vocality in relation to the development of music theatre, I turn to the basis of my conceptual framework: 'auditory distress'. I would like to coin this new term as a concept that materialises itself foremost as an *excess* of intensities in the listener which, according to my hypothesis, is inherent to every auditory perception. This rather rigorous thesis helps me to explain the necessity in the listener to act in response to sound. As such, auditory distress is an austere metaphor that corresponds to the act of response in the spectator, in order to relate to the impulse of auditory intensities by means of meaning making. Although auditory distress may be perceptually materialised as noise in the sense of an unwanted or (deliberately) irritating sound, however minute that may be, it is rather a wider-ranging concept that has value in understanding the necessary process of meaning making and of channelling all manifestations of sound, including voice. As a metaphor that weds psycho-acoustics to semiosis, it corresponds to Michel Serres' (1995) sense of noise as inherently part of and always present in, indeed as the very basis to our perception of all phenomena.

Starting from this concept as a premise of our listening experiences, I will demonstrate the aesthetic implications of responding to disembodied voices on stage through a case study, The Wooster Group's production of *La Didone* (2007).[1] Through this performance, I will demonstrate how the conceptual implications of auditory distress can help us understand our urge—and our limitations—to find meaning through our responses in listening to disembodied voices. But first, I return to my departure point and contextual framework: how radicalism in vocal experiment on the postdramatic stage, with its concomitant explorations of noise and ensuing auditory distress, has contributed to relations of resistance and continuity to traditional models and opinions of voice in performance. For this, we need to explore the precise meaning and relation between noise and auditory distress.

Noise as impetus

The notion of noise in recent theories of sound and philosophy has shown much productive ambiguity and polysemy. In its most commonsensical definition, noise is a manifestation of sound that interferes. Soundscape Studies regards noise as contaminating what we desire to

---

[1] I saw the production on 30 May 2007 in the Stadsschouwburg Rotterdam during the opera festival 'Operadagen Rotterdam'. It premiered in Brussels on 19 May 2007 as part of the KunstenFESTIVALdesArts in Brussels for which The Wooster Group originally created the production.

hear. It should, therefore, be filtered or blocked out. In (Acoustic) Communication Studies, noise is also seen as undesirable: it creates interference to the production and distribution of meaning. However, as Serres has pointed out in his lyrical work of philosophy, *Genesis (1995)*, with regard to meaning-making noise is unavoidably part of any system to which it operates in a parasitic relation. Noise is the very matter of communication or 'logos':

> Background noise is the ground of our perception, absolutely uninterrupted, it is our perennial sustenance, the element of the software of all our logic. It is the residue and the cesspool of our messages. No life without heat, no matter, neither; no warmth without air, no logos without noise, either. Noise is the basic element of the software of all our logic, or it is to the logos what matter used to be to form. Noise is the background of information, the material of that form (Serres 1995, 7).

As Serres suggests, noise can be the background level of (sonic) energy in our daily environments and technologies. It is the "ground of our being" (1995, 13) which never ceases. R. Murray Schafer (1977) has coined the term 'keynote sound' for such defining background noise as it makes up the tenor of someone's habitat as a specific 'acoustic horizon' which is always there. As such, all our relations and consequent meanings that we attribute to sounds are pitched to this defining ground, this background noise.

Aden Evens (2005) supports this claim through his phenomenological approach that includes a psycho-acoustic understanding of sound as contraction, a fluctuation of air pressure that can only be heard as it changes over time:

> Sound is a modulation of difference, a difference of difference. This eternal return of difference, noise, is what gives to be contracted but it is not in itself contracted. The contractions of frequency into pitch, of pitch into timbre and harmony, and the further contractions of melody, duration, rhythm, meter, are unproblematic, analytic; none of them can yet give sense to sound. Noise is the uncontracted, the depth from which these contractions of perception are drawn, and, though sense-less and insensible, it makes sense or gives sense to sound by providing sound with its direction and by focusing it to a point of clarity. Noise is the reservoir of sense, the depth in which sounds connect to each other, the difference whose modulation is signal (Evens 2005, 15).

In acoustic terms, noise seems to be separate from any air pressure contraction that surpasses the acoustic horizon in order to reach our ears, and from any ensuing semiosis in our perception of this contraction, this 'difference'. However, Evens seems to agree with Serres on the idea that, although uncontracted and senseless, noise is the condition and the catalyst for our perception and meaning making. Serres qualifies noise further as "a silhouette on a backdrop, like a beacon against the fog, as every message, every cry, every call, every signal must be separated from the hubbub that occupies silence, in order to be, to be perceived, to be known, to be exchanged" (1995, 13). Equally, Evens argues that noise gives sound its direction and clarity. It is the 'depth' to which all sounds and their specific qualities (frequency, timbre, harmony, etc.) are pitched and receive their meaning.

A concrete example of how noise lends sound its direction and sense is predicated by the distinction in psycho-acoustics between 'attack' and 'decay' in the impact of sound. Attack is the moment of intervention, disturbance, or difference when the sound surpasses the threshold of the acoustic horizon and calls for attention in the ear. Decay is the temporary resonance and the quality of the sound before it disappears or it is superseded by another sound. The intervention determines how the listener will hear and interpret the sound, or rather the timbre. For instance, if one takes away the sound of the hammer hitting the string of a piano, it would be very difficult to identify the decaying resonance as piano sound. What is commonly heard as incidental and often subliminal noise unfolds as the tonic of our experience, which does not only determine the appeal to the listener, but also the direction for its meaning. Without it, the sound loses its clarity.

As the example of the missing attack in the piano sound suggests, a significant aspect in the meaning of sound is its mark of a source. This is an important realisation for the way we listen to a very peculiar and dominant sound system, the human voice, particularly when we are confronted with a voice without an immediately identifiable source: a disembodied voice. Without its material attack, or what Roland Barthes (1977) termed the 'grain', a voice loses its phenomenal substance, its body or immediate embodiment. I would like to argue later in this chapter that because of this lack of access to an immediate source body, the disembodied voice conversely contributes to a re-enchantment of the body in the voice, as an attempt to re-inscribe, re-imagine its place in relation to other sounds and their acoustic horizon. As such, for all its resistance to embodiment, disembodied voice reminds us that every sound is always embodied because of its *need* for a body.

Radical vocality

Because of its potential to resist hegemonic ways of perceiving and understanding, the sourceless or disembodied voice has contributed to a radicalisation of vocality in performance parallel to the development of poststructuralist theories of voice such as those by Julia Kristeva and Barthes. The radical vocality on the stage is to be understood as a pervasive multiplicity of vocal art forms, orality, chorus and voice modalities, predominantly as a project to regain the voice's distinct sounding and corporeal qualities over its signifying properties, or in Kristevian/Barthian terms, its 'genotext' (genosong) rupturing the 'phenotext' (phenosong; the verbal or cultural content of the voice). Such drastic rupture is aimed at undoing the voice of a single, unified subject, an *authoritative voice* determined by its verbal content.

Concomitant to these vociferous breaks with traditional models of voice and vocality, the development of the disembodied voice has significantly contributed to the resistance of music theatre and experimental performance against traditional compositional and performance practices. However, as Carolyn Abbate has argued through her reading of Mozart's *The Magic Flute* in her influential book *In Search of Opera*, the disembodied voice is already inherently part of many historical opera works. Opera, Abbate argues, confuses disembodied voices and invisible music, granting omniscient authority to the latter.

That is why, as a significant aesthetic strategy, the disembodied voice shares as much *continuity* with its musical past as it performs *resistance* to it. This radical vocality, marked with as much vocal disembodiment, is in line with the postdramatic shift in theatre. As discussed by Hans-Thies Lehmann, this is a shift from a logocentric hierarchy in favour of the delivery of text and linguistic content as the ultimate target, to new spaces *beyond telos*, auditory landscapes that call upon new ways of reading and meaning making by the spectator-auditor (Lehmann 1997, 57).[2]

---

[2] Especially with the general acceptance of audio technology in the theatre, the possibilities to create soundscapes have become almost unlimited. "In electronic music it has become possible to manipulate the parameters of sound as desired and thus open up whole new areas for the musicalisation of voices and sounds in theatre" (Lehmann 2006, 92). Lehmann thereby stresses the instrumentalisation and control of sound to create desired auditory landscapes. However, I want to pose against this idea that musicalisation brings a great deal of uncontrollability by means of the interventions of sound and the auditory distress it creates. This uncontrollability would mean that the fragmentation and the 'space beyond telos' as a result of musicalisation is less intentional than Lehmann would assume.

Through its call for expressions of radical vocality, music theatre takes position against both theatre and operatic practices on equal terms of resistance and continuity. It does not only participate in the postdramatic stage and its ongoing musicalisation in order to break free from certain confinements of the text, as an authoritative voice in the theatrical construct. Music theatre's renewed interest in the voice is also informed by a desire to reinstall the body and with it, the ritualistic, since opera had become, according to Michelle Duncan, "an ('enlightened') art form with metaphysical properties that transcend the body" (2004, 299). Especially in the Wagnerian tradition, by concealing the modes of labour in musical performance and by means of highly trained, immaculate singing, opera had widened the gap between the *voice as body* (a surface phenomenon), and the *voice as language* (a linguistic category). No need to over emphasise here how this gap reproduces the split between spirit and matter as the origin of a quite dominant epistemological structure in Western philosophy; nor how music theatre's appeal towards a radical vocality in the postdramatic paradigm would call for the antithesis of that structure.

By no means do I want to suggest a preference for either side of the binary, but I do intend to debunk the so-called 'enigma' of voice, as Duncan suggested, "it is always potentially and profoundly multiplicitious" (2004, 296). My main concern is how the enigmatic experience of the disembodied voice challenges the regimes of perception to the extent that they shift the attention between the signifying and corporeal aspects of the voice. The radicalisation of 'voice as body', however, does call for a radicalisation of metaphor that is informed by the ostensible opposite in 'vocal disembodiment' or, to borrow the terms from Michel Chion, a process of *acousmatization* that always almost immediately implies *de-acousmatization*. In what follows, I propose a conceptual framework for discussing how voices lay bare their bodies in a flux of veiling and revealing, of absence and presence, of noise and meaning, according to how the disembodied voice plays upon the spectator's modes of perception and interpretation.

The enigma of the disembodied voice: auditory distress

The radical vocality in contemporary performance calls for a more radicalised understanding of the effects of disembodied voices on the spectator-auditor than that the polysemy surrounding noise in philosophical terms can provide us for analysis. Hence, I suggest the notion of 'auditory distress' as a departure point of such an understanding. Auditory distress materialises foremost as an *excess* of intensities in the listener, which, according to my hypothesis, is inherent to every auditory perception. This excess is a result of the intervening power of sound and as such forms a parallel to the notion of noise as both an impetus and a ground for meaning-making.

I find confirmation of this thesis in, among others, Schafer's Soundscape analysis, as formulated around the same time when Barthes put forward his notion of *psychoanalytical listening* as a 'panic listening' in 1977. Schafer demonstrated through his notion of the soundscape that sound is always spatially transgressing a certain acoustic horizon as well as some personal perceptual thresholds in the listener, in order to be heard. Similarly, Barthes had said earlier that "listening is that preliminary attention which permits intercepting whatever might disturb the territorial system; it is a mode of defence against surprise; its object (what it is oriented toward) is menace" (Barthes 1991, 247). Based on the rather evident observation that our ears have no earlids that could be closed at will and therefore are susceptible to any sound vibrations at all times, it is suggested that sound always necessarily intervenes before it becomes audible and calls for our listening attention. In this sense, for a sound to be heard and, therefore, attract the attention, it actually needs to act as a noise disturbing the ear's territorial system before it can become meaningful.

As a consequence, any auditory perception is marked by a constant threat of disturbance and a desire to control the so-called 'menace', which does not have to include high decibels for it to be intervening at all. It is not hard to imagine this menace as a constant threat of noise in the primary sense of an unwanted, unexpected sound. But the point is here that sound is always necessarily intervention when it is perceived. It burgeons on an excess of intensities that needs to be controlled. It is territorial when it calls for our attention, and it is therefore in need for de/re-territorialisation through our perceptual systems.

As Soundscape analysis suggests, we have developed psychological (read: cognitive) mechanisms over time to position ourselves in relation to this excess of intensities in our ears: a wide range of listening modalities that function as silent responses to the auditory distress. With these responses the listener relates to sound in order to make that relation meaningful. Through this relation, the listener gains back a level of control over the territorial intervention of sound. I therefore propose a model to discuss the spectator's responses in terms of *modes of relation*. What is important is that these modes include certain virtual positions of the listener-spectator towards the performance with which she or he attempts to regain control over the auditory distress.

and listening, in order to gain control over the acoustic excess, and thereby, the auditory distress.

As such, *La Didone* demonstrates how the vocal disembodiment takes a central place in how our responses to auditory distress are channelled by the mechanisms of the performance. Depending on the perspectives given in the performance, the disembodied voice invites the listener to conjure an imaginary body, as Connor suggests, that "may contradict, compete with, replace, or even reshape the actual, visible body" (Connor 2000, 36). This imaginary body is based on the excess that it poses in proportion to its visually identifiable source body. Connor seems then to advocate a connection between this excess and the listener's imaginary production—an 'invocation', so to speak—of the voice-body, which includes certain postures, gestures, movements, ways of expression:

> The leading characteristic of the voice-body is to be a body-in-invention, an impossible, imaginary body in the course of being found and formed. But it is possible to isolate some of the contours, functions, and postures by means of which vocalic bodies come into being (Connor 2000, 36).

I argue that it is through this voice-body that the listener synthesises what she or he hears, sees and imagines. In this respect, I contend that the excess of the voice, being the reason for the creation of the voice-body, is a vital part of the response to auditory distress.

The production of a voice-body is, however, challenged at another instance in the performance, the moment at which a male actor lip-syncs a female voice with angelic qualities (as he is meant to represent Cupid or Amor), whilst playing a toy guitar. Suddenly we are confronted with an impossible body in our perception of two contradictory bodies. The guitar sound 'sticks' as it coheres with the kid's guitar—or is it a ukulele played off-stage? Similarly, the disembodied female voice sticks to the male body of the mimicking player on stage, whilst we are aware of the off-stage source body. In both cases, we constitute imaginary bodies in our pursuit to give the sounds a temporary habitat. Not only does the auditory distress cause us to restore bodies to the acousmatized sounds in a causal mode of listening; the ensuing vocal bodies also get sticky in our constitution of a narrative, constituting a whole, as a reaction against the fragmentation on stage. These imaginary bodies help us then to relate to the sounds as discursive responses to the excess of meanings and intensities, which would otherwise be discharged as noise. In this way, as a response to dissociation and disembodiment, new fictional characters and meandering narratives come to life as a consequence of the way we position ourselves through our modes of perception in meaningful ways.

However, Connor's concept of the voice-body does not only give an answer to the way we give temporary bodies to disembodied sounds in order to regain 'control' over the theatre noise and its consequent auditory distress at the level of perception and interpretation. By isolating contours, functions, postures we should also acknowledge the potent directions that theatrical mechanisms provide in terms of virtual positions of the intended auditor-spectator to relate to the disembodied voices in particular ways. The voice-bodies are, therefore, not ad-hoc fictions of the mind but do correspond to the particular modes of perception that are triggered by those mechanisms.

Once more in the example of the full-bodied, masculine actor lip-syncing to a very feminine voice, one cannot help but observe the striking dissociation in gender, and yet, a vocalic body easily supersedes in our imaginations. This oddity demonstrates the multiplicity not only in the propensity of the disembodied voice to present us with excess over and above meaning, but also in the voice-body itself as a semiotic slippage between performance and the spectator's imagination: a slippage that unfolds a body that is 'more than' or 'other than' the difference between sound and image seems to promise. Hence, the disembodied voice posits a limit to its framing in looking and listening. Its disembodied nature highlights that voice always retains a level of nonsensicality, of noise and fundamental alterity, "always itself and potentially something else" (Duncan 2004, 296).

Epilogue: a limit to imagining the voice's body double

Disembodied voices call for a different attention to the 'drama', the performance, the promise of discursive content and the sound of words. As a particular type of noise due to their intervening and seemingly sourceless occurrence, they equally reveal that auditory distress constitutes the impetus of every sound perception, which calls for a necessary response in the listener, a meaningful relation that compensates for the noise. In their excess of intensities, they remind us that listening to a voice is always an embodied experience, and that meaning making is necessarily an embodied effect of how the listener relates and responds to this excess. At the same time, this urge for meaning may result in a revelation of an imaginary body that exceeds the body that we see, complementary to the voice. It is in this slippage between perception and imagination bringing to life amalgamated bodies, that the voice finds its temporary refuge.

Through the disembodied voice, as part of a radical vocality on stage, the voice-body discloses its constitutive body politics to the attentive listener: it poses a challenge to place the voice back to its otherness, its unknown origin; yet, it will always remain an enigma to us. The distance that stands between our resonant bodies and the disembodied voice is the noise that lends it its message. The voice's body double as virtual voice-body speaks to us, to the way we both embody and read voices in response to the excess and unframeability that they exert on their source bodies and, ultimately, on our own.[5]

References

Abbate, Carolyn. 2001. *In Search of Opera*. Princeton, NJ and Woodstock, Oxfordshire: Princeton University Press.

Barthes, Roland and Roland Havas. 1991 [1977]. Listening. In *The Responsibility of Forms: Critical Essays on Music, Art, and Representation*, trans. Richard Howard, 2nd edn., 245–60. Berkeley and Los Angeles: University of California Press.

—. 1995 [1977]. Ecoute. In Éric Marty, ed., *Oeuvres complètes, Tome III: 1974–1980*, 727–36. Paris: Seuil.

—. 1977. The Grain of the Voice. In *Image, Music, Text*, ed. and trans. Stephen Heath, 179–89. New York: Hill and Wang.

Chion, Michel. 1994. *Audio-Vision: Sound on Screen*, ed. and trans. Walter Murch and Claudia Gorbman. New York: Columbia University Press.

Connor, Steven. 2000. *Dumbstruck: A Cultural History of Ventriloquism* Oxford: Oxford University Press.

—. (2004) The Strains of the Voice. In *Phonorama: Eine Kulturgeschichte der STIMME als Medium*. Catalogue, Zentrum für Kunst und Medientechnologie Karlsruhe, Museum für Neue Kunst, 18 Sept. 2004–30 Jan. 2005, ed. Brigitte Felderer, 158–172. Berlin: MSB Matthes & Seitz.

—. 2005. Ears Have Walls: On Hearing Art. Lecture presented at the series Bodily Knowledges: Challenging Ocularcentricity, Tate Modern, 21 February 2003. *FO(A)RM* 4, Topography: 48–57.

---

[5] This chapter is based on a keynote lecture on invitation by Prof Dr Morten Michelsen, entitled "Radical Vocality in Performance: On Voices that Lay Bare their Bodies", as part of *The Voice Seminar* at the University of Copenhagen (5 November 2009). I am grateful for all the comments by the participants at this seminar series as well as at the International Conference *Song, Stage, Screen V, Interdisciplinary Approaches to 'Voice' in Music, Theatre and Film* at the University of Winchester (3-5 September 2010), where I presented a shortened version of this text.

Doane, Mary Ann. 1980. The Voice in the Cinema: The Articulation of Body and Space. *Yale French Studies* 60, Cinema/Sound: 33-50.

Dolar, Mladen. 2006. *A Voice and Nothing More*. Cambridge (MA) and London: The MIT Press.

Duncan, Michelle. 2004. The Operatic Scandal of the Singing Body: Voice, Presence, Performativity. *Cambridge Opera Journal* 16.3: 283–306. Cambridge: Cambridge University Press.

Evens, Aden. 2005. *Sound Ideas: Music, Machines, and Experience*. Minneapolis, MN: University of Minnesota Press.

Lehmann, Hans-Thies. 1997. From Logos to Landscape: Text in Contemporary Dramaturgy. *Performance Research* 2.1: 55–60.

—. 2006. *Postdramatic Theatre*, trans. & with an introduction by Karen Jürs-Munby. London and New York: Routledge.

Poizat, Michel. 1992. *The Angel's Cry*, trans. Arthur Denner. Ithaca, New York and London: Cornell University Press.

Restivo, Angelo. 1999. Recent approaches to psychoanalytical sound theory. *Iris* 27, Spring: 135-41.

Schaeffer, Pierre. 1966. *Traité des objets musicaux: Essai interdisciplines*. Paris: Éditions du Seuil.

Schafer, R. Murray. 1969. *The New Soundscape*. Vienna: Universal Edition.

—. 1977. *The Tuning of the World*. Toronto: McClelland and Stewart.

Serres, Michel. 1995. *Genesis*, trans. G. James and J. Nielson. Ann Arbor: University of Michigan Press.

CHAPTER IX

AURAL ACTS:
THEATRE AND THE PHENOMENOLOGY
OF LISTENING

GEORGE HOME-COOK

Listening is, in all senses, an *act*. Not only does the act of listening require us to *do* something but listening itself is inherently theatrical; in listening we set both sound and ourselves 'at play.' Conceiving listening as a form of research into phenomenology this chapter provides an account of aurality in contemporary theatre that considers the embodied and particular position of the listening-spectator. Developing Alva Noë's assertion that perception "is something we do" (2006, 1), the claim is made that listening-in-the-theatre is a specialist mode of attention that involves an embodied, enactive, and exertive engagement with our environment and its "affordances" (Gibson 1977, 67).[1] In offering a rereading of Merleau-Ponty's "true theory of attention" (2002, 36) and drawing from the work of Aron Gurwitsch (1964;1966), this chapter counters the familiar, ocularphobic conception of attention as a one-dimensional, objectifying spotlight and instead urges us to reconsider attention as a dynamic and essentially embodied activity.

The phenomenological investigation of listening-in-the-theatre is an area of enquiry that remains comparatively unexplored and under-thematised within Theatre and Performance Studies. Recently, however, in coalescence with the emergence of Sound Studies and the so-called "sonic turn" (Drobnick 2004, 10), a growing number of theatre scholars have

---

[1] As Gibson has clarified, "an affordance is not what we call a 'subjective' quality of a thing but neither is it what we call an 'objective' property of a thing if by that we mean that a physical object has no reference to any animal. An affordance cuts across the dichotomy of subjective-objective and helps us to understand its inadequacy" (1977, 69-70).

begun to take note of the aural dimensions of the theatrical phenomenon.[2] Ross Brown has even gone so far as to suggest that theatre might be entering a "new age of aurality" (2005, 105). Yet, what is at stake in such a pronouncement?

In his ground-breaking essay, "The Theatre Soundscape and the End of Noise" (2005), Brown provides us with a masterful and perspicacious summary of the history of sound in theatre and has done much to pioneer the ear in theatre. That said, I would like to argue that his enterprise is in coalescence with a more general and near-pervasive trend within scholarship that, in its vehement attempt to challenge the hegemony of the spectatorial eye and its gaze, serves only to perpetuate this sensory and critical hierarchy by focussing on or essentialising difference.

My contention, primarily, concerns methodology. In my view, Brown's treatise is weakened by his *a priori* reliance on Joachim-Ernst Berendt's far-fetched model of ontology. Whilst Brown has boldly attempted, for the first time, to sketch out the profound relationship between the theatre soundscape and Being (a relationship described by director Peter Sellars as sound speaking to theatre "as ontology" (2009, vii)) he operates, largely, by way of analogy and in so doing overlooks the aural-as-encountered. In other words, generally speaking, Brown reasons by resemblance, from an abstracted, theoretical position that is to some extent totalising and where the contingencies of the particular are disavowed.

Michel Serres exhorts that "background noise is the ground of our perception [...] No life without heat; no warmth without air, no logos without noise" (1995, 7). Here 'noise' is both the sonic context in which speech, language and thought take place and, hence, metaphorically is that which, as Brown describes, is "*extra* to meaning" (2005, 118). However, whilst Brown has rightly declared that the theatre soundscape prompts us to widen our attentional and significative frame to phenomena that would otherwise be considered marginal or irrelevant, this does not mean that we have to lose sight of the dialectic that exists between background and figure, theme and margin: background noise is not the 'world' but the *ground of perception*. Gleaned from my experience as a listening-spectator and from my reading on attention, I would like to offer an alternative approach that neither excludes the particular nor the whole but accounts for the ever-changing, chiasmic and inherently theatrical attentional relationship that exists between background and theme; noise and signal.

---

[2] Notable pioneers of the ear in theatre include: Andrew Gurr, Bruce R. Smith, Ross Brown and Wes Folkerth.

Thus, in order to investigate and begin to account for theatre's "aural phenomenology" (Brown 2010, 138ff) we must engage in the rigours and particularities of phenomenological description: phenomenology must be *practiced*. Indeed, as Don Ihde has made clear, "*without doing phenomenology, it may be practically impossible to understand phenomenology*" (1977, 14); or, as Merleau-Ponty once put it, "phenomenology is only accessible through a phenomenological method" (2002, viii). Offering an alternative approach that investigates the essential "interchangeability" (Ingold 2000, 285) of the senses and that attempts to account for the phenomenal dynamics of the attentional "sphere" (Arvidson 2006, 7), this chapter suggests that the soundscape of contemporary theatre not only demands that we engage in increasingly complex attentional manoeuvres but that, by *staging* perception, theatre invites us to attend to ourselves attending.

The act of attention is inherently linked to Alva Noë's concept of enaction. Perception, as Noë has suggested, is enactive; it "is determined by what we are *ready* to do [...] we *enact* our perception, we act it out" (2004, 1). In other words, there is no such thing as an "inert" or "inactive" perceiver (Noë 2004, 17): our sensorimotor skills are always, to some degree, implicated in perception. As its etymological root attests,[3] to perceive is 'to grasp'; to move out, touch and make contact with the world. Thus, as Merleau-Ponty declares, "to experience a structure is not to receive it into oneself passively: it is to live it, take it up, assume it and discover its immanent significance" (2002, 301). In attending a given phenomenon, phenomenal event or environment we are called to *stretch ourselves*. The word 'attention' derives from the Latin compound *adtendere*, meaning, 'to stretch.' Hence, at the very core of the notion of attention is the idea of a kind of embodiment that entails a dynamic movement through space. This movement is not only sensed but actual. Moreover, in *stretching* we become aware of ourselves as a body. Stretching also implies a sense of exertion, work and elasticity; in stretching ourselves we experience a sense of being pulled in different directions, a dynamic of 'push-pull' that manifestly generates onto-phenomenological variation and adventure. Thus, attention is, fundamentally, a dynamic act of embodiment.

One of the most insightful, though somewhat overlooked philosophical discussions of the phenomenology of attention is that of Merleau-Ponty.[4]

---

[3] The word 'perceive' is of Anglo-French origin and stems from a combination of the Latin *per* (thoroughly) and *capere* (meaning to grasp or take).

[4] That said, Merleau-Ponty conspicuously overlooks listening as a mode of attention.

It has often been assumed that he was against attention altogether.[5] Such an assumption would appear to have some justification: early on in *Phenomenology of Perception* (2002) Merleau-Ponty states, quite categorically, that "the notion of attention is supported by no evidence provided by consciousness" and is "no more than an auxiliary hypothesis, evolved to save the prejudice in favour of an objective world" (2002, 7). Yet, he is not taking issue with the phenomenon of attention *per se* but with how attention has been conceived either by empiricism on the one hand or intellectualism on the other. From the perspective of empiricism, as he makes clear, attention "is a kind of searchlight that shows up objects pre-existing in darkness" (2002, 30). Thus, as conceptualised by empiricism, attention is rendered passive and impotent since "the objects of perception are already there and just need to be lit up" (2002, 30). Conversely, from the perspective of intellectualism, attention is overwhelmingly virile: as he asserts, "since in attention I experience an elucidation *of* the object, the perceived object must already contain the intelligible structure which it reveals" (2002, 31).

Moreover, as Merleau-Ponty discloses, neither empiricism nor intellectualism "can grasp consciousness *in the act of learning*, and that neither attaches due importance to that circumscribed ignorance, that still 'empty' but already determinate intention which is attention itself" (2002, 33). In other words, he is opposed to a concept of attention that is either all-ignorant (empiricism) or all-knowing (intellectualism) and instead suggests that attention inscribes a kind of paradox, which, in itself, is the paradox of perception: the dialectical relationship between body and world:

> [...] attention is neither an association of images, nor the return to itself of thought already in control of its objects, but the active constitution of a new object which makes explicit and articulate what was until then presented as no more than an indeterminate horizon. At the same time as it sets attention in motion, the object is at every moment recaptured and placed once more in a state of dependence on it (Merleau-Ponty 2002, 35).

Merleau-Ponty concludes "the result of the act of attention is not to be found in its beginning" (2002, 36). Rather, as he goes on to exhort, "consciousness must be faced with its own unreflective life in things and awakened to its own history which it was forgetting: such is the part that philosophical reflection has to play, and thus do we arrive at a true theory

---

[5] Jonathan Crary, for example, has asserted that Merleau-Ponty "rejected the philosophical relevancy of attention" (1999, 56).

of attention" (Merleau-Ponty 2002, 36). Merleau-Ponty's discussion of attention suggests that it is an embodied act that entails a sense of movement and that the relationship between attention and the affordances of our environment is essentially dialectical: the perceptual object motivates attention but is not the *cause* of this "knowledge bringing event" (2002, 35). Further still, by depicting attention as an inherently dynamic phenomenon Merleau-Ponty's account disrupts, if not dismantles, the attention/distraction binary. Indeed, as Natalie Depraz has pointed out, "attention contains quite essentially in itself inattention" (2004, 18).

Rather than segmenting attention from distraction we must focus on the essential interpenetration, indeterminacy and co-presence of these phenomena. Indeed, as Aron Gurwitsch rightly proclaims, "the 'searchlight theory' of attention has to be abandoned altogether" (1966, 218). Experience, he explains, "always presents us with objects, things, events, etc., within certain contexts and contextures, and never with isolated facts and scattered data and facts" (1964, 1). Hence, as "absorbed though our attention may be with our problem, we never lose sight of our actual surroundings nor of ourselves as situated in those surroundings" (Gurwitsch 1964, 1). Thus, Gurwitsch attempts to describe not only a given attentional theme but "the totality of co-present data:" namely, the "field of consciousness" (Gurwitsch 1964, 1). Recently, his notion of the attentional 'sphere' has been exposited and substantially developed by P. Sven Arvidson who provides the following summary:

> When something captures our attention, or when we concentrate or pay attention to something, it is presented within a context...Working from the centre of the sphere of attention to its outer shell, there are three dimensions...: *thematic attention* (attention in the dimension of theme or focus), the *context of attention* (consciousness in the dimension of the thematic context), and the *margin of attention* (consciousness in the dimension of margin as halo and horizon). (2006, 1)

As a fecund means of exploring this model of attention and as an initial 'way in' to a phenomenology of theatrical listening, I will now reflect upon my experience of attending two performances, Robert Lepage's *Lipsynch* and Complicite's *Shun-Kin*. This provisional investigation responds to the following questions regarding the phenomenal relationship between sound, listening and theatricality: what *happens* when we listen?; how is our body implicated in the act of listening and what role does movement play in perception?; what is the phenomenal relationship between listening and looking and how is hearing 'activated' by the "co-option" of looking? (Ingold 2000, 278) and in what sense is sound spatial and what kinds of attentional structures and spatialities does the *act* of listening make manifest? In short, what happens when we begin to attend to the phenomenal dynamics of theatrical attention? An example of where the enactive, exertive, and existential qualities of listening-as-attending are clearly brought to the fore is in the theatre of Robert Lepage.

Lipsynch received its world premiere at London's Barbican Theatre in September 2008 and required the audience to sit through a nine-act epic lasting nine hours. Whilst there were fairly regular intervals, being asked to pay attention to this kind of theatre takes some work and, boy, do we have to stretch! Attending *Lipsynch* was 'hard work' but not simply on account of its scale, pace and our consequent struggle to piece it together to form a coherent narrative, as suggested by James Reynolds (2008). *Lipsynch* exhorted us to stretch our attentional, sensorimotor skills as well as our imaginative, narrative-creating, macroperceptual faculties.[6] By performatively staging the complex phenomenal relationship between voice, speech, and language, *Lipsynch* required the audience to engage in complex and inherently playful attentional manoeuvres. A memorable example to recount was at the beginning of Act 5, subtitled 'Maria'.

The Act opens with Maria, centre stage, sitting at a table with a laptop. She has just had brain surgery and has lost her ability to speak. Her doctor tells us, the operation will mean that she loses her speech but not her voice. Behind her is a huge projection of what she sees on her laptop; a voice-graph. In the minutes that follow the audience experiences the creation of a composition (four part harmony in Gregorian style) composed in real-time. Maria begins by producing a series of vocal ejaculations somewhere between singing and speaking. As she makes these sounds we see them in their visual/scientific form as frequencies on the voice-graph. Once she has recorded this initial base-line, she stops the recording and starts again using this soundscape as the basis for producing a descant which is overlaid on it. This happens twice more so that by the fourth time she improvises (or appears to improvise) over this vocal score a kind of four-part harmony is produced.

This section of *Lipsynch*, like so many other moments in the production, invites or prompts the listening-spectator to pay attention not

---

[6] The distinction between micro- and macro-perception was originally conceived by Don Ihde (1991). Vivian Sobchack provides the following summary: "first through the specific material conditions by which they latently engage and extend our senses at the transparent and lived bodily level […] our 'microperception,' and then again their manifest representational function by which they engage our senses consciously and textually at the hermeneutic level of what [Ihde] calls our 'macroperception'" (Sobchack 1992, 138).

only to *what* is being heard but to start to think about *how* we hear. The verb 'to listen' derives from the word *hlysnan*, an Old English term of Germanic origin meaning 'to pay attention to.' Thus, etymologically and phenomenologically speaking, listening is an act of *attention*: to listen is to attend to sound(s); to hone in, foreground and attempt to capture the particular shape, character or essence of the sound-object in question. The experience of attending this segment of the performance revealed that there is a lot more to paying attention than mere forward facing, one-dimensional attentiveness. For instance, listening can operate on more than one level at the same time. In listening to, or rather attending, this sequence of *Lipsynch*, and having more than one sound in play at the same time, I had to engage in a kind of sonic/aural juggling. In addition, unlike listening to a piece of choral music on the radio, the existence of the visual embodiment of the sounds played a crucial role in the experience of listening. These traces, these marks, enabled me to cling on to the sounds within the soundscape more tangibly, thus assisting the process of aural juggling. In other words, and as Tim Ingold has asserted, looking is not the enemy of listening but its facilitator: "*it is the very incorporation of vision into the process of auditory perception that transforms passive hearing into active hearing*" (2000, 277); looking and listening, "co-opt" one another (Ingold 2000, 278). Furthermore, this scene exemplifies the ways in which the body has to stretch itself in order to perceive. Throughout this scene I was aware of movement not just at the level of temporality (the music/sound passing through time) but I was also aware of the physical and ontological movement that I, the theatregoer, necessarily enacted *in* listening. Thus, listening not only entails an ongoing engagement with the affordances of a given environment but creates space: listening *spaces*.

In order to further explore this idea and to suggest ways in which our experience of sound in contemporary theatre may problematise established notions of auditory experience, in particular the phenomenal relationship between sound, source and space, I will now reflect upon my experience of attending Complicite's production of *Shun-kin*. Staged at the Barbican Theatre in February 2009 and inspired by one of Japan's most important twentieth century writers, Jun'ichiro Tanizaki, *Shun-kin* charts the life of an aristocratic, sadomasochistic, blind shamisen player (Shun-kin) and her devoted, much-abused, servant-cum-lover, and student, Sasuke, who spends his life slavishly practicing the shamisen and pandering to her every whim, eventually blinding himself as a symbol of ultimate union.

Our location in the theatre has an important part to play in our perception of the theatrical event not only in terms of 'sight-lines' or in terms of 'ear-lines' but, more precisely in terms of attention: different

positions require different modes of attention. This is particularly the case
for productions like *Shun-kin* that use supertitles. My seat was on the far
right hand side of the Barbican's enormous auditorium and about half way
up the stalls. On the stage there appeared to be four speakers, two of
different sizes, on each side, one on top of the other. Importantly, being at
the tail end of the row, my seat was sharply angled. Consequently, whilst
the supertitles, mounted on the wall, were directly adjacent to me, four or
so metres above my line of sight, the stage itself felt slightly peripheral.
Being closer to the stage and positioned where I was, meant that it was
almost impossible, or least so it felt, to scan the supertitles whilst
maintaining some kind of peripheral awareness of where and what these
words were coming from. Yet, ironically, it was the existence of playback
sound that made this task more difficult. In the case of *Shun-kin* the stage
was heavily amplified with numerous microphones, so much so that my
perception of the relationship between sound and source was brought into
question. This was particularly true in the case of speech.

Rick Altman has proposed that in theatre "we never have any doubt
whatsoever about who is speaking [...] our ears tell us" (1992, 22). Yet,
Altman's assertion is based on the assumption that the actors on stage are
voicing naturally without the aid of either microphones or amplifiers of
some kind. Thus, in cases such as *Shun-kin*, and to a lesser extent
Lipsynch, where actor's voices are increasingly amplified through
complex speaker-arrangements and configurations, our ears often get it
wrong. When sound seems to be dislodged in some way from its source
our ability to 'zoom in' on its originating location is adversely affected and
thematic attention often becomes fragmented and dispersed.

For instance, at the beginning of *Shun-kin*, Sasuke, as an old man,
slowly walks forward to address the audience. At this moment, I heard the
voice of an old man originating somewhere far up to my right. For a
second, I didn't even realise that this voice originated from Yoshi Oida,
the actor playing Sasuke. There was a strange and uncanny poly-
dimensionality to the sounds of speech that I perceived. Not only was my
sphere of attention stretched but, more radically, noise and signal were set
in flux. It was not so much that I was distracted by this uncanny
disembodiment but that the sudden uncertainty concerning the originating
source of this disembodied voice manifestly registered at the very centre
of my attentional theme: marginal and thematic content momentarily
seemed to co-exist in a state of extreme and innately theatrical equivocality.
Far from being fixed and homogeneous, this example revealed the
dialectical and dynamic nature of attention. Such occurrences pique our
attentional faculties and, in doing so, motivate us to attend not only to the

indeterminacies of the attentional sphere but to the dynamics of the attentional act itself. It is in and by means of attending that the background noise of the seemingly irrelevant is brought into relief and heard amidst the structured order of diegetic and artistic intention. Indeed this example indicates that we should move away from the natural tendency to segment attention from distraction and instead aim to discuss and describe the phenomenal emergence of a given attentional theme within and in relation to its corresponding attentional context.

Interestingly, a similar phenomenon occurred during the opening sequence of *Lipsynch*, The piece begins with Ada the opera singer, played by Rebecca Blankenship, standing alone, apparently 'immersed' within the mournful and ubiquitous soundscape of Górecki's mournful Third Symphony. At first I was mesmerised, indeed overcome, by what I encountered—the image of a prepossessing woman against a rich red background, with the soundtrack enveloping this scene with a certain texture and weight. Then, after a few seconds, I realised that this woman-in-the-scene was the *source*, or rather the co-source, of this astonishingly beautiful sound: Ada the opera singer was seemingly 'immersed'[7] in the sound(s) of her own making. Such displacement of sound from source results in other curious effects, most notably, the momentary creation of the theatrical equivalent of Michel Chion's "acousmetre" (1999, 21).[8]

For example, at one point in *Shun-kin* I heard the voice of an old man speaking in Japanese but could not, for the life of me, locate the body from which it originated. Glancing around in search of clues, feverishly looking at the supertitles and the speech-less actors on stage, I found none. Importantly, this voice was not straightforwardly *acousmatic*, a voice heard but whose source cannot be seen or located. Rather, since the voice was experienced as being located at the very centre of the diegetic and scenographic context, it manifested as an uncanny absent presence, setting listening—and looking—in flux. However, this experience was very short lived; by scanning the environment for information and with a slight

---

[7] The notion of 'immersion' has become a popular trope within contemporary critical discourse. Yet, as I have argued elsewhere (see unpublished PhD thesis by the author), immersion-as-lived is never simplistically spherical but is always polymorphous and dynamic: 'total immersion' is a myth that resonates closely with another popular belief, the idea that 'sound is round.'

[8] Chion's neologism is a portmanteau derived from the French 'être acousmatique' or acousmatic being (1999, 21); Chion explains that "[w]hen the acousmatic presence is a voice, and especially when this voice has not yet been visualized – that is, when we cannot yet connect it to a face – we get a special being, a kind of walking and acting shadow to which we attach the name acousmetre" (Chion 1999, 21).

stretch to my right this quasi-acousmetre was "de-acousmatized" (Chion 1994, 131). Stretching around and within the tapestry of bodies before me I came across the body to which this acousmetric being had so convincingly detached itself: namely, Sasuke. This phenomenon arose as a direct result of the displacing effects of powerfully amplified sound *combined* with the fact that my visual access to this part of the stage was momentarily occluded. Usually, as Altman observes, we are able to identify the precise location of an actor, even if the lights are low and he or she has their backs to us, on account of the spatialising and honing characteristics of auditory perception. Yet, in this example, what might normally be described as an unimportant moment of visual eclipse became an intensely equivocal and hence, inherently theatrical, moment of perceptual ambiguity where my enactive abilities were considerably, if momentarily, stretched. As this example demonstrates, with the rise of the theatre soundscape comes the manifestation of interesting, challenging and unusual spatio-sonic experiences. However, the theatre soundscape does not herald a new age of aurality where sound, or rather, 'noise' resounds. Nor, moreover, do the experiences of equivocation and ambiguity, as described above, pertain exclusively to the province of distractedness. Such quasi-acousmetric phenomena are not only the motivator of our attentional faculties but are, to some extent, generated by the enactments of dynamic embodied attention. Furthermore, although many have suggested that sound is nonspatial,[9] this conception not only relies on a Euclidian/geometrical notion of space that forecloses a discussion of how space is felt but implies and presupposes a linear, mono-directional, static notion of perception that is untenable. The phenomenal experience of felt space and spatiality is evident in my final example.

In the last few minutes of *Shun-Kin* was a phenomenon of exquisite beauty and captivating charm: on two or three occasions, a flock of large white birds rose up diagonally from the back of the stage and subsequently disappeared as they flew off into the 'wings'. The experience of these birds was extremely life-like. They were, of course, mere projections on a large screen. But this empirical fact was perceptually cloaked by the co-use of sound; each instantiation of projected footage was synchronised with the sounds of a flock of birds flapping their wings. Nothing unusual about that one might say; the phenomenal effects of synchronising vision and sound being so common-place as to be habitual. Yet, *as perceived* this phenomenon was anything but banal. First and foremost this example troubles the notion that the senses are discrete; my visual and aural

---

[9] Notable proponents of this view include: Peter Strawson, Stephen Handel, Jonathan Rée and more recently Matthew Nudds.

experience of the birds was one and the same thing: *"hearing [was] seeing"* (Ingold 2000, 279). Like Ingold's example of the thunder bird (2000, 279)[10] these birds *were* the sound they made as they traversed the space; scenography sounded and the soundscape was seen. Secondly, this experience complicates the source/sound debate. Zuckerkandl, following a classical conception of sound, states that unlike vision, which he conceives of as being 'out there', sound is experienced as a "from-out-there-toward-me-and-through-me" (1956, 277). In this conception, audition is passive and sounds are thought to be located, perceptually, not at their source but at the ear. However, my experience of the birds of *Shun-kin* seems to suggest quite the opposite. In paying attention to these flying-sounding beings, I felt an overwhelming sense of outward movement; my body not only followed and traced the route of these beings through space but moved with them. In short, I was 'moved': emotionally, physically and ontologically. Recently Casey O'Callaghan has proposed that sounds are located at their source (2007, 31). But, in this case, we experience sound to be located neither at a fixed source nor at our ears; neither out there nor in here, but rather, we experience both ourselves and the sound we perceive within a heterotopic zone, a no-space which is constantly *on the move*. In stretching out through and in space to grasp these strikingly ephemeral percepts it became clear that, as Ingold exhorts, "looking, listening, and touching are not separate activities, they are just facets of the same activity: that of the whole organism in its environment" (2000, 261).

In this chapter I have claimed that it is not only problematic to uphold that attention is diametrically and simplistically opposed to distraction but also that it is untenable to associate 'attention' with vision and 'distraction' with audition. Furthermore, it has been suggested that the seemingly intractable binaries of looking/listening, attention/distraction, signal/noise and spectator/audience can be effectively navigated and set at play by reconsidering the puzzle of 'theatre perception' from the perspective of attention. Rather than understanding theatre 'noise' as unwanted or unintended sound, a broader usage of the term has been offered that sets 'noise' in dialectical relationship with "dynamic embodied attending in the

---

[10] Ingold explains that "the thunderbird [unlike the cuckoo] is not a thing of any kind. Like the sound of thunder, it is a phenomenon of experience. Though it is by thunder that the bird makes its presence heard, this sound is not *produced* by the thunderbird as the cuckoo produces its call. For the thunder *is* the bird, in its sonic incarnation. Therefore to see it is not to resolve the cosmic mystery of the sound, [...] One is rather drawn further in [...] *hearing is seeing* [...] As a specific form of the experience of light, the thunderbird is not set over against the perceiver as an object of vision, but invades the perceiver's consciousness" (2000, 279).

world" (Arvidson 2006, 7). Far from being diametrically opposed to the phenomenon of attention, we must reconsider noise as both a product and motivator of attention. In sum, contemporary performance increasingly invites, and even requires us, to find new ways of playing with the sounds, states of being and 'noise' made manifest *in* the practice of attending theatre.

Being a spectator implies a passive, motionless attendance. Yet, the practice of listening in theatre actually entails shifts of movement, yawns, stretchings, that may appear insignificant—the mere noise of a restless body—but are in fact a vital and implacable aspect of theatre perception itself. Not only does the phenomenal multiplicity of contemporary theatre allow and demand the spectator to make ever greater and more complex attentional manoeuvres but it increasingly makes us aware of our own embodied position and experience within this phenomenal matrix. In close correspondence with Brown's suggestion that the theatre soundscape affords a new degree of flirtation with what would traditionally have been considered as mere background noise (2005, 117), I have suggested that contemporary theatre invariably invites or urges us to pay attention to our 'sphere of attention'. This inference, however, does not signal the "end of noise," nor does it suggest the triumphant return of "ear-thinking" (Brown 2005, 106). Rather, and perhaps more than ever, theatre is *staging* perception: we are being called to reflect upon the intricate connections between the senses and the role of the body in the perceptual event. Sound in theatre first and foremost is *felt*; but this phenomenon is not at odds with the semiotic; signs are sensed and the senses signify. Indeed, it is this indeterminate and dynamic intertwining that affords a variety of creative attentional acts. Thus, being-in-sound is only disclosed by and in our active engagement with the world of sound: or, in the words of Heidegger, "only as phenomenology is ontology possible" (1962, 50).

References

Altman, Rick, ed. 1992. *Sound Theory/Sound Practice*. London and New York: Routledge.

Arvidson, P. Sven. 2006. *The Sphere of Attention: Context and Margin*. Dordrecht: Springer Press.

Brown, Ross. 2005. "The Theatre Soundscape and the End of Noise," *Performance Research* 10 (4): 105-119.

—. 2010. *Sound: A Reader in Theatre Practice*. Basingstoke: Palgrave MacMillan.

Chion, Michel. 1994. *Audio-Vision: Sound on Screen*, translated by Claudia Gorbman. New York: Columbia University Press.
—. 1999. *The Voice in Cinema*, translated by Claudia Gorbman. New York: Columbia University Press.
Crary, Jonathan. 1999. *Suspensions of Perception: Attention, Spectacle and Modern Culture*. Cambridge (MA) and London: The MIT Press.
Depraz, Natalie. 2004. "Where is the Phenomenology of Attention that Husserl intended to perform? A Transcendental pragmatic-oriented description of Attention," *Continental Philosophy Review* 37 (1): 5-20.
Drobnick, Jim, ed. 2004. *Aural Cultures*. Toronto: YYZBooks.
Folkerth, Wes. 2002. *The Sound of Shakespeare*. London and New York: Routledge.
Gibson, James J. 1977. "The Theory of Affordances," in *Perceiving, Acting and Knowing: Toward an Ecological Psychology*, edited by Robert Shaw and John Bransford, 67-82. Hillsdale; New Jersey: Lawrence Erlbaum Associates.
Gurwitsch, Aron. 1964. *The Field of Consciousness*. Pittsburgh: Duquesne University Press.
—. 1966. *Studies in Phenomenology and Psychology*. Evanston: Northwestern University Press.
Handel, Stephen. 1989. *Listening: An Introduction to the Perception of Auditory Events*. Cambridge (MA) and London: The MIT Press.
Heidegger, Martin. 1962. *Being and Time*, translated by John Macquarrie and Edward Robinson London: SCM Press.
Ihde, Don. 1977. *Experimental Phenomenology: An Introduction*. New York: Capricorn Books.
—. 1990 *Technology and the Lifeworld: From Garden to Earth*. Bloomington: University of Indiana Press.
Ingold, Tim. 2000. *The Perception of the Environment: Essays in Livelihood, Dwelling & Skill*. London and New York: Routledge.
Merleau-Ponty, Maurice. 2002. *Phenomenology of Perception*. translated by Colin Smith. London and New York: Routledge.
Nanay, Bence. 2006. "Perception, Action, and Identification in the Theater," in *Staging Philosophy: Intersections of Theater, Performance, Philosophy*, edited by David Krasner and David Z. Saltz, 244-254. Michigan: University of Michigan Press.
Noë, Alva. 2004. *Action in Perception*. Cambridge (MA) and London: The MIT Press.
Nudds, Matthew. 2007. "Sounds and Space," *Edinburgh Research Archive*, http://www.era.lib.ed.ac.uk/bitstream/1842/1774/3/sas.pdf (accessed August 20, 2010).

O'Callaghan, Casey. 2007. *Sounds: A Philosophical Theory*. Oxford: Oxford University Press.

Reynolds, James. 2008. "Hard Work: Robert Lepage's *Lipsynch* and the Pleasures of Responsibility," *Platform* 3 (2): 130-135. http://www.rhul.ac.uk/Drama/platform/issues/Vol.3No.2/13.%20Perfor mance%20Response.pdf (accessed August 24, 2010).

Serres, Michel. 1995. *Genesis*. translated by Genèvieve James and James Nielson. Ann Arbor: University of Michigan Press.

Sobchack, Vivian. 1992. *The Address of the Eye: A Phenomenology of Film Experience*. Princeton: Princeton University Press.

Zuckerkandl, Viktor 1956. *Sound and Symbol: Music and the External World*, translated by Willard R. Trask. London: Routledge & Kegan Paul.

CHAPTER X

THE BEWITCHED:
HARRY PARTCH AND THE LIBERATION
OF ENSLAVED MUSICIANS

TIM WHITE

Writing of the necessity of noise to the mutation of one sonic code into another, Jacques Attali notes "[…] the transition from the Greek and medieval scales to the tempered and modern scales can be interpreted as aggression against the dominant code by noise destined to become a new dominant code" (1985, 34) hearing further ruptures in Monteverdi and Bach (noise amidst polyphony), Webern (tonal order) and La Monte Young (serial order): "What is noise to the old order is harmony to the new" (Attali 1985, 35). Yet American composer Harry Partch, though he proposes a radical mutation, though his strange-sounding works invite invocation of the term 'noise' as a pejorative, he listens with an ear attuned not to the future but to the past, to the very same Greek and medieval scales from which Attali commences his chronology. In so doing, Partch stands apart from the prophetic, evolutionary nature of music, ahead of the rest of society because it "explores much faster than material reality can, the entire range of possibilities in a given code" (Attali 1985, 11) and posits a notion of the musician before capital: "Shaman, doctor, musician. He is one of society's first gazes upon itself; he is one of the first catalysers of violence and myth" (Attali 1985, 12).

Such an efficacious and distinctive role for the musician runs counter to that prescribed by the performance spaces of the late twentieth century, which, through dress, placement and deportment separate and marginalise musicians from dancers and performers. Partch's works for the theatre propel him to challenge these assumptions that are bound up in the consensus of the well-tempered scale, which, once unpicked, calls into question the circumstances of performance.

Two productions of Harry Partch's dance satire *The Bewitched* grapple with the challenges of rethinking the relationship between music and performance, striving toward what the composer termed "corporeality" (Partch 1974, 8). Defined at the outset of Partch's treatise, *Genesis of a Music*, Corporeal Music is posited as "emotionally 'tactile'" and the antithesis of Abstract Music. Whereas Abstract Music is concerned with form, the Corporeal is "a music that is vital to a time and place, a here and now" (Partch 1974, 8). Thus, all instrumental music (excepting that intended for narrative dance) and vocal music with words that convey mood rather than meaning, "musicalized" in Partch's parlance, are characterised as Abstract, whilst music that is "physically allied with poetry or the dance" (Partch 1974, 8) is considered Corporeal. The 1957 premiere of *The Bewitched*, overseen by Partch in collaboration with choreographer Alwin Nikolais,[1] and a 1980 staging directed by composer Kenneth Gaburo[2] offer distinct means of approaching the corporeal while simultaneously acknowledging and exploring the tensions between the constituent elements of such a production, not only between the presupposed specialists of music and dance but also between composer and choreographer and, in the latter production, between the work and its director. The following remarks consider the extent to which the corporeal can both evade the turn toward abstraction (becoming 'musicalised') and resist being subsumed within a theatrical frame that would render it supplemental.

The distinctiveness of Partch might equally apply to his existence as to the legacy that remains in the form of his writings, recordings and films. The impact of Partch's contemporary, John Cage, continues to reverberate across the arts; indeed, is a foundation stone for the American avant-garde, while Partch, one of the last century's great iconoclasts, still remains in comparative obscurity. Though there are a number of initiatives that now seek to promote Partch's work,[3] the composer resisted cultivating a legacy. Ben Johnston, who served what might loosely be termed an apprenticeship with the composer, recalls "He told me that if I or anyone else ever claimed to have been a student of his, he'd cheerfully strangle us" (Johnston 1975, 93) and the non-conventional aspects of his works exacerbate the issue of preserving what he accomplished; Johnston concludes his tribute following the death of Partch in 1974 by noting that

---

[1] Champaign-Urbana campus, University of Illinois Festival of Contemporary Arts, 26 March 1957.

[2] Akademie der Künste, Berlin, Festival 20-23 January 1980.

[3] These include The Harry Partch Institute at Montclair State University, New Jersey and the Enclosure series of books, films and audio material concerning Partch.

the problem of maintaining his legacy "staggers conception" (Johnston 1975, 97).

The difficulty of continuing to perform and to further study the work is a consequence of the problem Partch himself identified in Western music, founded on what he regarded as the lie of equal temperament, the division of the octave into twelve equal intervals that aids transposition and modulation rather than employing pure intervals derived from the ratio between tones, termed "just intonation."[4] Dispensing with the arbitrary assignment of tones, Partch composed music that required new instruments, new forms of notation and the acquisition of new skills in order to perform his works, employing as many as fifty-five tones in the octave.[5] Had his dissatisfaction been quelled by such endeavours, Partch might have been more readily embraced by the musical establishment as an experimental composer though his exasperation extended beyond this to encompass the formal expectations of musical performance, rejecting both the orchestra pit and "the inhibitory incubus of tight coats and tight shoes" that constricted the classical musician on the concert platform (Blackburn 2008, 13).

Emboldened by the experience of working with director Arch Lauterer on the first staging of his *King Oedipus*,[6] Partch tested the water for the development of his notion of corporeality. Being specifically designed and constructed for the performance and being of such a size that they could not but lend an architectural frame to the movements they circumscribed as much as the sounds they produced provided momentum for the narrative, Partch's instruments act as sounding markers of the here and now.

Later, Partch was to assume responsibility for all the relationships between text, music, instruments and performers and though the positive collaboration with Lauterer could be seen as the catalyst for this move, its theoretical basis can be traced back to earlier writings. Partch scholar Philip Blackburn, writing on the 2007 production of Partch's most expansive stage work, *Delusion of the Fury*, sees the composer's concept of corporeality arising from his earlier notion of Monophony (Blackburn

---

[4] For a visual and aural demonstration of the distinction between the two see Kyle Gann. "Just Intonation Explained" http://www.kylegann.com/tuning.html (accessed June 20, 2010).

[5] Partch, to his annoyance, was often summarised as the composer who worked with the 43-tone scale, even though he explored many different divisions according to requirements.

[6] Mills College, Oakland, 14-16 California March 1952. For an account of the collaboration see Gilmore 1999, 199-205.

2008, 5). Partch, in his theoretical treatise, *Genesis of a Music*, begins his definition of Monophony thus:

> A tone, in music, is not a hermit, divorced from the society of its fellows. It is always a relation to another tone, heard or implied. In other words it is a musical interval, the relation between two tones. This relation is continually mutable, to be sure, but it never ceases to exist. (1974, 86).

This denial of isolation is extended beyond the musical to encompass all activities that might occur in performance; in place of isolation or, as he expresses it, abstraction (Partch 1974, 8-9), one has corporeality that enters into each and every aspect of performance and, specifically, the relation between each and every element. To rephrase his comment on Monophony, these relations are continually mutable, but they never cease to exist. This sense of relatedness finds expression in his abhorrence of discrete activities and those who would practice them. He berated what he termed "the age of specialisation" (Partch 1974, 5), which would curtail the expressiveness of the musician, denying her the possibility of broaching the limits of her training as well as consign "music to the specialisation of the symphony, drama to the specialisation of the Broadway success" (Partch 2000b, 241).

Partch's railings against specialisation in the arts are the basis of a number of essays he wrote in the late 1940s and early 1950s including "No Barriers" in which he declares:

> Experience does not exclude, because the eye, the ear, the body and the mind register, react, store away and therefore evolve, consciously or otherwise. The mind does not put its reactions into little locked rooms to be opened labouriously, one at a time (Partch 2000a, 181).

The sentiment is in accord with Cage's definition of theatre as something that engages both the eye and the ear (1965, 50). Yet whereas Cage moves off into the realm of non-intention, Partch works toward a considered notion of the artwork that can be constructed with reference both to the incidental writings of this period and the text of *Genesis of a Music*. Corporeal music is contrasted with abstract music, which from the examples given suggests that it is a conflict between the breadth of expression available to the musician and the limited subset of this range that the musical establishment deem to be acceptable. Partch frustrates recourse to external referents, abstract notions of how music should sound and how instruments should look and be played, forcing the spectator to attend to the here and now of the corporeal.

This division between corporeal and abstract might already be detected in the move from the arbitrary twelve-tone scale toward a plethora of harmonic ratios and from the circumscribed palette of pre-existing instruments to the smorgasbord of sound-making tools that Partch created to realise the compositions.[7] In regard to the musicians themselves, Partch is frustrated that the correlation of action to sound is either denied, as when the musicians are sequestered in the orchestra pit or else attenuated through distance and the synchronicity of serried ranks of musicians on the concert platform. He states:

> I use the word ritual and I also use the word corporeal, to describe music that is neither on the concert stage nor relegated to a pit. In ritual the musicians are seen; their meaningful movements are part of the act and collaboration is automatic with everything else that goes on (Partch 1970).

Implicit within this remark is the sense that the ritual is inseparable from the instruments, irrespective of whether the work calls upon individuals who might dance or act.

The first production of *The Bewitched* is perhaps indicative of the inherent tensions awaiting to surface between a composer finding limitation and precedent circumscribing his every initiative and any collaborator not as attuned to this new way of working. The work is conceived as "A Dance Satire", divided into ten scenes plus a prologue and epilogue. The Bewitched of the title are those from all walks of life who are enslaved by pre-existing conditions—prejudice, self-imposed limitation, circumstances of appearance, gender, age and so on, in fact any limit that serves to enslave an individual. The central character of the drama, the Witch, is the means of release, as Partch comments in his introduction to the work: "The Witch belongs to the ancient pre-Christian school. She is an omniscient soul, all-perceptive, with that wonderful power to make other people see also when she feels so inclined" (2000d, 307).

Completing the cast are two groups: the Lost Musicians, whom Partch refers to as the Chorus, and the dancers. The chorus is described as the instrument of The Witch, implying that her power to dispel limitations is channelled through its members, not simply as musicians but as performers, as this critical comment makes clear:

---

[7] An extensive selection of these can be viewed and 'played' online at "American Mavericks—Harry Partch's Instruments" http://musicmavericks.publicradio.org/features/feature_partch.html (accessed June 20, 2010).

The Chorus is a corporeal part of the drama—more directly than it would be as mere instrumentalists. It both sings and plays; it stamps its feet, it whistles, it says Woof! and Bah! In low and aspirate exclamations. More it is a child of magic (Partch 1957a, 242).

A synopsis of one of the scenes will serve to illustrate the extent to which the work could almost be construed as another medium by which Partch's unfailing belief in the tyranny of Western music can be espoused. Scene 4 has none of momentum of a dramatic situation and its title is unashamedly didactic; "A Soul Tormented by contemporary music finds a humanising alchemy". The notes regarding this scene not only amplify Partch's dissatisfaction with Western music but provide insight into the corresponding humour and playfulness that accompanied even his most passionate and vigorous dismissals of the status quo, indicative of his perpetual awareness of his audience, whether in his writings or his works:

Of all the sad tales sung by the poets of old, some are sadder than this, some more poignant, many more tragic, but none more pathetic, for this is a scene of inner conflict—a conflict arising out of an absorbing regret over the passage of time.

The story of this soul began with the injustice of having been born at such a miserable time in history as the present. But as the years passed, the regret became equivocal, because—except for such modern trivia as the current price of baby-sitters—it became so immersed in the bewitchment of some preceding century as in fact to function only in that century (Partch 2000d, 314).

After the revelatory experience of *King Oedipus*, Partch seems empowered to venture into the realm of staging itself. Here, his directions unite all participants within the stage space:

The instruments dominate the set. They are on risers of different heights, the risers being connected by a stairway, or a nexus of stairways, which mature into an ascent without evident end, at one of the far corners of the rear. Some of the instruments may be only partially visible. […]

Generally the Witch is on a throne near the front of the stage, facing the opposite entrance, draped in robes which assume different colours with the changing lights […]. She sits immobile, she stands, she moves rhythmically on the throne and occasionally assumes command of her Chorus as ostensible conductor (Partch 2000d, 308).

Perhaps further emboldened, Partch's introduction ventures into advice to the dancers and it is at this point that two disparate readings of the intent need to be considered, the first that acknowledges the necessity of broaching the divide between areas of expertise, such as the composer having the ability to contribute to the movement language of those on stage, whether they be formally identified as musicians, actors or dancers—how else might the specialisation in the arts that Partch so abhorred be countered other than in practice? The second consideration, running counter to the first is a recurring suspicion that an amalgam of disciplines undermines the spirit of collaboration; why work with someone else if the synthesis of the different disciplines is effected within one individual? Whilst there is value in bringing together those with disparate skills, uniting two like-minded souls who reject the idea of specialisation seems less beneficial. Given that Partch had a pronounced dislike of his work being used as background music,[8] one wonders whether he would have entered into a working relationship in which a collaborator, empathising with Partch's belief in non-specialisation, had strong ideas about the role of music within the work and made suggestions that would place in it a position any less dominant, both visually and narratively, than is the case in Partch's scores, librettos and scripts.

The tendency toward domination can be found in Partch's comments about dancing. Partch makes three points; first a personal preference for avoiding arms and eyes being raised heavenward at the same time as he felt that this was the dance equivalent of a melodramatic declaration of 'Woe is Me!'; second, that the dancers on occasion employ statuesque immobility, noting that there should be "no innate compulsion to move constantly, simply because one is on a stage" (Partch 2000c, 309) and, lastly, that the dancers refrain from touching another dancer:

> In a serious love duet or a fight duet, a dancer never touches another dancer, in a gesture of endearment or anger. I noted, long before I ever saw oriental dancing, how tension was likely to drop the moment two such characters became physically embroiled (Partch 2000c, 309).

Leaving aside the first of these, the other two observations seem to constrict the dancers in ways that the musicians are not; the latter are encouraged to display a greater sense of visibility on stage as the dancers are simultaneously invited to become less evident. Partch issues the following instruction regarding the musicians:

> At no time are the players of my instruments to be unaware that they are on stage, in the act. There can be no humdrum playing of notes, in the bored

---

[8] Bob Gilmore notes that *The Bewitched* owed its genesis in part to background music, which Partch found "fascinatingly repulsive" (Partch in Gilmore 1995, 228).

belief that because they are 'good' musicians their performance is ipso
facto 'masterly'. When a player fails to take full advantage of his role in a
visual or acting sense, he is muffing his part—in my terms—as thoroughly
as if he bungled every note in the score. (Partch in Blackburn 2008, 11)

As for the second point, forbidding touching in moments of emotional
intensity is at odds with the tactility not simply necessitated but provoked
by his strangely alluring instruments. Partch's period on the road
embraced not only his time as a hobo[9] but the majority of his adult life as
he moved from place to place, not so much for his own personal well-
being but rather to find suitable homes and players for his ever growing
family of instruments. Talking to Kenneth Gaburo, who would later direct
a production of *The Bewitched* after Partch's death, the composer's
priorities become apparent: "My instruments need a home while I'm here,
I can sleep on the ground" (Partch in Gaburo 1985, 164). Gaburo recounts
this comment in the context of his own programme notes for *The
Bewitched* alongside a poetic invocation of what might constitute
corporeality—interaction between entities (humans and objects)—that has
no small echo of Michael Fried's "Art and Objecthood", though more
sensuous than censorious:

> I am in this room; Partch's Marimba Eroica is in this room. I am not alone.
> I am staring at it; wondering about it. Even though I can't call what it's
> doing: 'staring or wondering' at-about me, its presence is made clear
> because it, too, is present. (We) are each sitting in the presence of the
> other. It 'tells' me it is here.
>   Somehow, (we) each got here and now are facing each other. I slowly
> walk to it, and touch it. It feels cold. I feel its coldness, not mine (I am not
> cold). Its coldness is evident to me, because it is cold. Even though it
> doesn't say 'I am cold' (in my language) it does say it; (in my language).
> Now its coldness resides in me. It didn't before I touched it. Its coldness is
> now in both of (us). (Gaburo 1985, 164)

In settling on Alwin Nikolais, an emerging choreographer whose work
displayed its own challenges to orthodoxy (including a number of
productions that sought to obscure and or constrict the dancer (see
Gitelman 2007), surely the antithesis of Partch's revealing of the individual),
the first production of *The Bewitched* was set for a tempestuous gestation.
No clearer indication of the divergence between the two collaborators can
be found than in comparing Partch's remarks on the style of each scene

---

[9] See Partch's journal *Bitter Music* that recounts eight months of his travels on the
road. Partch, Harry 'Bitter Music' unpublished, 1940 in Partch 2000c.

along with his titles and those of Nikolais. It would require a meeting of minds to have a common understanding of what is meant by Scene 2's style "Eighteenth-century formality, with satiric twentieth-century expressionism, in part" and, after all the Western and Eastern stylistic diversity, Partch's magnanimous relinquishing of the reins in the final scene, "I leave this open", is small consolation for any collaborator wishing to bring their own contributions to the work. Partch's descriptive, evocative and elusive titles such as "Two detectives on the tail of a Tricky culprit turn in their badges" or "The Romancing of a Pathological Liar comes to an Inspired end" are dripping with possibility and awaiting further elucidation yet are reduced, in Nikolais' version to the distinctly prosaic 'Melodrama' and 'Dance Hall' respectively (see Gilmore 1998, 249).

Where one might find allegorical references to an artist's aesthetics in their work, Partch, it could be argued, inverts this such that one discovers compositions lurking within his aesthetics; each of the ten "unwitchings" in the piece could be taken on a surface level to indicate a general reference to enlightenment but it is not difficult to regard each instance as a further expression of the plight of the contemporary musician. It is tempting to consider Partch's continual return to the emancipation of the musician as obsessive, but to grasp corporeality a less harsh appraisal is required. If music is accorded status as something vital and an inevitable function of human existence (a quality Partch observes in Ancient Greek society and lacking in the present) then it is possible to follow Kenneth Gaburo's understanding of the term. Gaburo's sensual encounter with the Marimba Eroica, cited above, is preceded by the following distinction to permit discussion of the interactions that occur:

> Observing an entity;
> Describing that entity;
> Making sense of that entity;
> (An entity can be one's self; another human; another life-form; another so-called "thing". In what follows, I shall occasionally refer to life-forms by the symbol: 'I'; non-life forms by the symbol: 'it'; and the interaction between them as follows: I $\longleftrightarrow$ I; I $\longleftrightarrow$ it) (Gaburo 1985, 149).

One could argue that the terms are so encompassing that their usefulness is questionable but Partch's assault upon the very terminology and associations by which the work is described—dance, dancers, instruments, musicians—invites just such recourse to the ontological so as not to be ensnared by the assumptions and preconceptions against which Partch rails.

Interestingly, Gaburo elaborates an understanding of the expression 'physicality' as a means to creep up on the term that really demands explication, corporeality. He constructs a series of notations that express the extent of what physicality might entail. Whether one is convinced by this graphical presentation of his argument or not, it fulfils an important secondary function of allowing Gaburo to make the work coherent for himself. At every turn Partch is evident in his work but in order to engage with *The Bewitched* or indeed any of Partch's provocations as anything other than self-contained works they need to be the pretext for an encounter. Gaburo provides an instance of this with the Marimba Eroica (an I←→it encounter in his formulation) though many other encounters are to be found in the performance of the work: to list them would be to slip back into prioritising certain specialists (who fall into the I group) and certain things (the it group) rather than holding on to the understanding of all these relations—simply human-human, human-object—taking place. Additionally this taking-placeness makes a connection between the scripted action and the observed action. Now, the coincidence of those playing instruments—the musicians—and their simultaneous appearance in the drama—'the lost musicians'—can be understood as both presenting and re-presenting change. Musician and performer are coterminous, an instance of Lyotard's figural as proposed by Bill Readings,

> in which two incommensurable elements (such as the visible and the textual) are held together, impossibly, in the 'same' space; a kind of superimposition without privilege. (1991, xxx)

This 'blocking together' frustrates assimilation of the figure on stage as musician or performer, denying a reading that assigns the abstraction of recognisable form. Instead, the audience are required to attend to the actions of the figure as the evolving instance of what a musician might be, just as the sound invites consideration not in terms of its distinctiveness from previously heard arrangements of sonic material but instead as relating to the specific circumstances in which it is produced.

Partch starts from the position that the musician is a given and, if one considers that his theoretical work and his compositions begin with the voice, capable of dividing the octave in ways beyond conventional twelve tone notation, then this is not a title bestowed after years in the conservatoire but inherent in the inhalation and exhalation of air; as much a given as the instruments that frame every action that he conceives in his stage works. And if the instruments together with the individuals needed to play them are the point of origin from which all other stage relationships flow (rather than commencing with either the text or the performer) then one can begin to accept the often 'incidental' quality of the dancing or action (a quality one would normally assign to stage music) and indeed the seemingly cavalier treatment of setting and mood as found in the sad/comic Japanese/Ethiopian hybridity of the two act stage work *Delusion of the Fury* (1969), and the perplexing titles and often contradictory instructions that accompany *The Bewitched*.

The musicians, freed from what Partch regarded as the shackles of the concert platform or the orchestra pit, are encouraged to perform rather than simply play their instruments and so the distinction between what were formerly discrete activities—musician, performer, dancer—is less clear. However, is it the case that, emerging from a position of invisibility and inferiority, the newly-enfranchised Partch musician now dominates the work? Certainly there is a discrepancy between the call to challenge specialisation and the reality that the new instruments not only require new playing techniques but often the ability to read a new form of notation, variously written in extended staves or with additional accents to denote the more numerous intervals or, perhaps even more alarmingly, set out as a series of ratios rather than notes. The musicians may well contribute gestural elements to the stage work but the opportunities for a dancer or actor to dabble with such specialised instruments and esoteric notation seems remote. This is the continuing challenge of Partch's stage works; leaving to one side the not insignificant matter of building and mastering the instruments, the metaphorical, and at times literal, elevation of the musicians threatens to effect a simple inversion of the existing order as the musician overshadows the performer. Instead, rather than regarding this as replacing one specialist at the heart of the work with another, it allows one to think anew about the relations that obtain on stage, now not an empty space but one already delineated by instruments and defined by those who surround them, caress them or perhaps are dominated by them that elsewhere we might variously have called dancers, musicians, performers.

References

Attali, Jacques. 1985. *Noise: The Political Economy of Music* translated by Brian Massumi. Minneapolis: University of Minnesota Press.

Blackburn, Philip. 2008. Delusion 2.0; Harry Partch and the Philosopher's Tone. *Hyperion* Vol. 2 No. 1: 1-20.

Cage, John, Michael Kirby and Richard Schechner. 1965. An Interview with John Cage. *The Tulane Drama Review* Vol. 10, No. 2: 50-72.

Fried, Michael. 1967. Art and Objecthood. *Artforum* Vol. 5 No.10: 12-23.

Gaburo, Kenneth. 2000. In Search of Partch's Bewitched, Part One: Concerning Physicality. In *Harry Partch: An anthology of critical perspectives* edited by David Dunn, 147-77. Amsterdam: Harwood Academic Publishers. Originally published in *Percussive Notes Research Edition* 1985: 54-84.

Gilmore, Bob. 1995. "A Soul Tormented": Alwin Nikolais and Harry Partch's "The Bewitched". *The Musical Quarterly* Vol. 79, No. 1: 80-107.

—. 1998. *Harry Partch: a biography.* New Haven and London: Yale University Press.

Gitelman, Claudia. 2007. Sense Your Mass Increasing with Your Velocity: Alwin Nikolais' Pedagogy of Unified Decentralisation. In *The Returns of Alwin Nikolais: Bodies, Boundaries and the Dance Canon* edited by Claudia Gitelman and Randy Martin, 26-45. Middletown CT: Wesleyan University Press.

Johnston, Ben. 1975. The Corporealism of Harry Partch. *Perspectives of New Music* Vol. 13, No. 2: 85-97.

Partch, Harry 1970. Harry Partch Lectures. Edited transcript of lectures given by Harry Partch 1950-1970 transcribed by Danlee Mitchell and Jonathan Glasier. Http://www.singingeye.com/eng/text/partch.htm (accessed June 20, 2010).

—. 1974. *Genesis of a Music: An Account of a Creative Work, its Roots and its Fulfillments* Second Edition. New York: Da Capo Press

—. 2000a. No Barriers. In Harry Partch *Bitter Music: Collected Journals, Essays, Introductions and Librettos*, edited by Thomas McGeary 181-3 Urbana and Chicago: University of Illinois Press. Originally published in *Impulse* 1952: 9-10.

—. 2000b A Soul Tormented by Contemporary Music Looks for a Human-izing Alchemy. In Harry Partch *Bitter Music: Collected Journals, Essays, Introductions and Librettos*, edited by Thomas McGeary, 239-243. Urbana and Chicago: University of Illinois Press. Originally given as a lecture-demonstration, 24 Mar. 1957, University of Illinois at Urbana-Champaign.

—. 2000c [1940]. Bitter Music, In Harry Partch *Bitter Music: Collected Journals, Essays, Introductions and Librettos*, edited by Thomas McGeary, 3-132. Urbana and Chicago: University of Illinois Press.

—. 2000d [1957] The Bewitched:—A Dance Satire. In Harry Partch *Bitter Music: Collected Journals, Essays, Introductions and Librettos*, edited by Thomas McGeary, 305-318. Urbana and Chicago: University of Illinois Press.

Readings, Bill. 1991. *Introducing Lyotard: Art and Politics* London and New York: Routledge.

CHAPTER XI

NOISES *ON*:
SIGHTS AND SITES OF SOUND
IN APOLLINAIRE'S *THE BREASTS OF TIRESIAS*

ADRIAN CURTIN

Staging sound

Guillaume Apollinaire's *Les Mamelles de Tirésias* (*The Breasts of Tiresias*) is an acknowledged classic of the modernist theatrical avant-garde and a prototypical surrealist work. Written in 1903, but revised and expanded in 1916 and 1917, the play received a one-off performance at the Théâtre Renée-Maubel in Montmartre on June 24, 1917, presented under the auspices of the artistic review *SIC* (*Sons, Idées, Couleurs*), whose founder and editor, Pierre Albert-Birot, directed the production with Apollinaire's assistance. Performed one month after the infamous *première* of the ballet *Parade*, for which Apollinaire coined the term *sur-réalisme* on account of its dissonant artistic registers, *The Breasts of Tiresias* was intended to continue the same spirit of artistic innovation in which the ostensibly natural bonds between media and the presumed logicality of commonplace ideas and everyday relations were disregarded in favour of their contrary disunion and fracture. Hence the unusual, madcap story, in which the eponymous character ditches her husband, lets her breasts fly off like toy balloons, becomes a man, and then an army general (among other careers and guises), while her beleaguered husband single-handedly 'gives birth' to 40,049 children in a single day. Concurrently, an apparently unrelated duo of characters, Presto and Lacouf, continually argue about their whereabouts (Paris or Zanzibar?) and kill each other in pistol duels, only to revive repeatedly. All in all, the play celebrates life liberated from structure and convention, although it is not wilfully devoid of meaning (à la dada); rather, it is conducted in the spirit of farce and music hall, albeit on a serious theme (that of repopulating France after the war). The production, which was hastily put together on a shoestring budget, used amateur actors, a makeshift stage design of patchwork paper arranged in a 'cubist' style designed by Serge Férat (who also made cubist-inspired costumes), and music composed by Germaine Albert-Birot (née de Surville, a.k.a. the director's wife), intended to be played by an orchestra but played instead by a pianist (Niny Guyard) reportedly on account of the rarity of musicians during the war (Melzer 1980, 128).

Typically noted as just another quirk of the play and an example of its whimsy is the "collective speechless person" referred to as the 'People of Zanzibar', who functions as a type of one-man chorus, commenting on the action not with words but with sound effects that he makes live on the stage (Apollinaire).[1] Here is Apollinaire's description of the People of Zanzibar, as provided in the stage directions for Act I:

> In the background, the collective speechless person who represents the people of Zanzibar is present from the rise of the curtain. He is sitting on a bench. A table is at his right, and he has ready to hand the instruments he will use to make the right noise at the right moment: revolver, musette [a musical instrument], bass drum, accordion, snare drum, thunder, sleigh bells, castanets, toy trumpet, broken dishes. All the sounds marked to be produced by an instrument are made by the people of Zanzibar, and everything marked to be spoken through the megaphone is to be shouted at the audience (1964, 67-8).

Apollinaire's innovation of dramatising an 'effects man' and including this person (meant to represent a multitude) in his cast of characters has been overlooked in the criticism of this play, with the result that the People of Zanzibar has faded into the textual background. However, when the play is considered in terms of performance, it is evident that this figure, positioned upstage at the Théâtre Renée-Maubel, was a key part of the novelty and jocularity of the production; multiple mentions are made of him in the reviews.[2] Apollinaire's play is replete with instructions for sound effects, the collective impact of which the reader may overlook when presented in the form of stage directions (at least when one is not reading for sound), but not, arguably, in the context of performance, where the People of Zanzibar was both seen and heard throughout. The proposal

---

[1] For the sake of simplicity I use the term 'sound effects', although this term did not enter into usage until 1927 (the term 'stage effects' was used instead) (Brown 2005, 106).

[2] Alas, although the reviews mention the People of Zanzibar they do not describe his contribution in detail or comment on how he performed his role.

that this figure was to be interpreted as a de facto member of the dramatis
personae is evident not only from the fact of his naming (which appeared
in the programme) and his visibility on the stage, but from the fact that the
actor/technician playing him (known only as 'Howard') was costumed and
wore a half-mask (other members of the cast wore full-masks). A
photograph of some of the actors shows 'Howard' as the People of
Zanzibar, dressed as a 'Red Indian' with a feather sticking out of the top of
his head (Albright 2000, 251).[3] The black-and-white image does not show
the redface makeup that 'Howard' reportedly used (presumably, redface
was a visual gag or else a signifier for 'Red Indian') (Melzer 1980, 128).
The costuming may also indicate a usage (or possibly a satirizing) of the
primitivist idea that the principal mode of communication of Native
Americans is not speech but a specialised array of non-linguistic sounds or
noises (the racist trope of the 'primitive' being closer to nature), so that the
perfect person to represent a chorus of people from the 'distant' land of
Zanzibar ('distant' from the 'centre' of Paris) is imagined as another non-
speaking but noise-making primitive.

The People of Zanzibar was not just a glorified stagehand but part of
the artistic and intellectual programme of the surrealist performance
jointly developed by Apollinaire and Albert-Birot. It bears emphasizing
that the act of locating (not to mention dramatizing) the production of
sound effects onstage in this manner was (to my knowledge) a theatrical
innovation for the time, and one that predates related practices in
postmodern/contemporary theatre.[4] By staging the creation of sound
effects in *The Breasts of Tiresias*, Apollinaire supplanted the long-standing
tradition of 'noises off', which relegated the *technê* of sound to the wings
where it functioned as a notional offstage presence, and instead
instantiated a practice of 'noises *on*' in which sound effects were made
visible (as it were) or at least *made visibly* so that their operational
procedure was made apparent. Apollinaire offered his audience the
spectacle—or rather the actuality—of how illustrative sound effects were

---

[3] The 'Red Indian' attribution was presumably a production choice because no
mention of it is made in Apollinaire's text (although Tiresias is noted as having a
blue face). Victor Basch, in his review for *Le Pays*, referred to the People of
Zanzibar as a 'Red Indian' ("une sorte de peau-rouge") ("Extraits De La Presse"
1917). Jeffrey Weiss appears to misidentify 'Howard' in his discussion of this
photograph; the captioning on the image is confusing (Weiss 1994, 249).

[4] For example, Richard Foreman mixed sound live in his productions in the front
row of a theatre in his 1975 production of *Rhoda in Potatoland* (Whitmore 1994,
177). U.K.-based company *Sound & Fury* also experiment with combining the
roles of performer and operator, as in their work-in-progress *Going Dark* at the
Roundhouse in London in 2010 (Lauke 2010).

achieved, lifting the curtain on a long established but hitherto 'invisible' stage tradition. In so doing, Apollinaire revealed the craft of sound making: the practical means by which a human operator uses an instrument (manipulating it in some fashion or breathing into it) as well as the artifice of sonic conventions (e.g. shaking a sheet of metal to simulate thunder). In stipulating that illustrative (diegetic and non-diegetic) sound effects be used transparently in the production (i.e. not in an illusionistic manner) and in subverting the supposed normality and logicality of sound making, Apollinaire staged a surrealist action. The audience was encouraged to hear one thing (for example, 'thunder') but see another (a man shaking a sheet of metal), thus calling attention to the conventionality of sonic mimesis.[5] Sound may appear to be 'natural' or 'authentic', but it has a singular capacity to deceive, especially when generated for theatrical performance.[6]

The *bruiteur*

Apollinaire's innovation is important, not just as a point of interest in the history of theatre scenography, but because of the potential significance of the People of Zanzibar both as a player on the stage and as a generic intermediary: in other words, as a figure that calls to mind a separate but related performance tradition. The tradition in question is that of the cinema sound effects man, known in France as the *bruiteur* (noise man), whose job it was to provide sonic accompaniment for screenings of silent films.[7] Typically paired with a pianist, the *bruiteur* (and the equivalent designation elsewhere) functioned in the manner of a theatre 'effects man' (and often came from the theatre, in fact), 'punctuating' and ornamenting the events on the screen in order to enhance the enjoyment of an audience by providing a sense of sonic actuality and verisimilitude.[8] The location of the *bruiteur* varied according to the specifics of the venue, but

---

[5] A similar effect is achieved in the beginning of *Monty Python and the Holy Grail* when the sound of approaching horse hooves is revealed to be the work of a man (King Arthur's servant) banging a pair of coconut halves together. Ironically, a Foley artist likely dubbed the sound of these coconut halves (Gilliam *et al.* 2001).

[6] As sound designer John Collins has remarked, "sound in theatre is the best liar" (see chapter III).

[7] To the best of my knowledge there were no female *bruiteurs*; hence my use of sex-specific language.

[8] The *bruiteur* was known as an "effects worker" or "effects boy" in Britain, a "drummer" or "trap drummer" in the United States, and a "Schlagwerker" in Germany (Bottomore 1999, 490).

he typically operated behind the screen, in an orchestra pit, or from the wings (provided that the angle of visibility allowed him to see the projection) (Meusy 1995, 251). The *bruiteur* was never prominently displayed but was cordoned off from view so as to focus attention on the screen and to enable (or at least to suggest) the illusion of the sound originating from the projected image and being synchronous with it. The tradition of providing live sound effects in cinema began in the early years of the twentieth century (circa 1906/1907 in France) with the rise in popularity of narrative films, and was well established by 1917 (the year of the performance of Apollinaire's play) (Bottomore 1999, 487). The following is an account of *bruitage* (sound making) at the Théâtre du Cinématographie Pathé in Montmartre (the district in which the Théâtre Renée-Maubel was situated) in 1906:

> In the pit, one finds a skilful *bruiteur* by the name of Barat, an artist of his kind, a former music-hall singer. With a very simple set-up, he is able to recreate every imaginable sound without fail: the waves of the ocean with a metallic sphere containing a lead shot, all kinds of wind from a gentle breeze to a storm with strings stretched over a metal mesh, not to mention bells, gunfire, sounds of chains, and many other things. He has beside him a young assistant, a 14-year-old kid who learns the trade. "You know, boy", says Barat, talking about the spectators, "they have full eyesight, but we need to give them an earful!" [...] "You must understand that I need a conscientious boy. It's not a sudden get-out [*'le coup parte'*] when the guy is dead! We need someone who can anticipate the next effect! I'll tell you, little one: it is a work of art!" (Meusy 1995, 144, my translation)

The professed conscientiousness and dedication of this particular *bruiteur* seems not to have been typical, or at least it was not universally shared. There was much consternation about the role, efficacy, and competence of *bruiteurs* and their ilk at this time, with audiences complaining about effects being inaccurate, superfluous, too loud, or exaggerated (Bottomore 2001). It would appear that some *bruiteurs* were overenthusiastic in their efforts, or else chose to perform for laughs, 'punning' or 'kidding' the film in the manner of a vaudeville drummer who would call attention to himself and to the whole apparatus of sonic accompaniment as part of the show, as another potential attraction (or distraction).[9] While the *bruiteur* may not have been visible to the audience,

---

[9] "As narrator, the [vaudeville] drummer regularly destroys the illusion for the sake of a laugh. According to a schedule dictated by onstage action—but always punctual and periodic—the drummer reminds spectators that they are watching an attraction designed expressly for their pleasure. Whereas audiences for realistic

Figure 11-1: "Entr'acte" by Germaine Albert-Birot

Albert-Birot's pieces are a patchwork of short (two-bar, four-bar) phrases of contrasting character, a collage of musical ideas in miniature, like the strips of contrasting coloured paper that Serge Férat used to cover the wings of the stage. It is music that aims to attract the ear by virtue of its discrete effects and charms.

The music in this production did not just provide a simple background accompaniment (hardly possible given the visual prominence of the pianist); it was not merely 'incidental' to the production but intervened upon it, like the sound effects, and complicated the onstage action. Moreover, it jockeyed for position and pre-eminence, competing with the other elements of the stage spectacle.[19] At the beginning of Act II, the curtain is directed to go up during the entr'acte (as indicated in the score) while the People of Zanzibar provides sound effects for crying children; the husband subsequently makes a passing remark that "modern music is amazing", a possible meta-theatrical reference to Albert-Birot's work or else a sardonic remark on the abrasiveness and discordance of modernist music in general (equating it to the cries of infants) (Apollinaire 1964, 80). In 1.4, Albert-Birot's funeral march for Presto and Lacouf—a morose series of chromatically-led chord progressions—precedes the event of their duel and in actuality accompanies the comic bit of stage business that sees Tiresias overpower her husband, strip him of his clothing, and don it herself: a pronounced mismatch of sound and spectacle.[20] Another tension in the aural and visual registers is presented at the end of the play when Tiresias is reunited with her husband and releases her toy balloons (breasts) at the audience, at which point the company sings an ostensibly jolly and celebratory ditty (the People of Zanzibar accompanies with jingling bells):

And then sing night and day
Scratch if you itch and choose
The white or the black either way
Luck is a game win or lose
Just keep your eye on the play (Apollinaire 1964, 91)

---

[19] As with 'Howard', the historical record does not provide information about how Guyard executed her duties as pianist. It is possible (and perhaps even probable) that she interacted with 'Howard' and/or with the onstage actors in some manner, thus adding to the semantic noise of the performance.

[20] The music for the funeral march, which finishes as Presto and Lacouf "die" onstage, also (unexpectedly) resolves with a major chord: another possible audio-visual disjunction.

Albert-Birot's music for this section consists of an unresolved, four-note, chromatically descending ostinato figure in octaves: an established musical trope, which in this instance appears to function as an indicator of menace rather than celebration, perhaps recalling the seriousness of the play's central thesis (the French need to have more children) (see Figure 11-2).

Figure 11-2: Untitled incidental music by Germaine Albert-Birot

It is also possible that Albert-Birot's chromatic ostinato was meant to 'sour' or subvert the supposedly happy reunion of Tiresias and her husband, along with the restitution of patriarchal order and gender norms. Once again, the acoustic field complicates the visual field so that the performance as a whole is made deliberately ambiguous, if not downright contradictory.

Sights and sites

Apollinaire's play aimed to have competing and overlapping planes of attention as part of the aesthetic experience. As the director explains in the prologue, the aim of the production was to bring a new 'spirit' into the theatre, one in which the audience was fully immersed in the experiential noise of life. The director imagines the theatre that might suit the purpose of this intent:

A circular theatre with two stages
One in the middle the other like a ring
Around the spectators permitting
The full unfolding of our modern art
Often connecting in unseen ways as in life
Sounds gestures colors cries tumults
Music dancing acrobatics poetry painting
Choruses actions and multiple sets (Apollinaire 1964, 66).

This is understood to be a version of Pierre Albert-Birot's proposed *théâtre nunique*, a theatre of 'nunism' ('nun' from the Greek for 'now'), which prioritised simultaneous, multiple actions conducted on a grand scale and promised a fully immersive and dynamic theatrical experience.[21] The one-off performance of *The Breasts of Tiresias* only attempted this in miniature, yet it successfully expanded upon the perceptual "frames" of the theatre to engage multiple sites of performance and modes of address (Aronson 2006). As well as presenting the sights of sound onstage by way of the People of Zanzibar (and the pianist), sound also came from the wings (voices of men and women shouting exultations to Tiresias in 1.7, in addition to an offstage chorus instructed to sing at three different points in the theatre as part of the entr'acte), and also from the audience, who reportedly offered their own verbal contributions to the proceedings.[22] Likewise, the actors' speech was sometimes delivered through a megaphone, delivering another form of sonic barrage made visually apparent. The total effect of all this was to interrelate "the thing seen" and "the thing heard" so that the sights and sites of sound became activating principles in theatrical reception, contributing to a noisy surplus of meaning. Apollinaire used the multiplicity and variability of sound to enable a surrealist experience in which what one sees and what one hears may or may not correlate. This potential lack of correlation was presented to the audience of watching listeners as a productive, enjoyable, and

---

[21] The musical aesthetic of Alberto Savinio was also a likely inspiration. Apollinaire collaborated with Savinio in 1914 on an un-staged pantomime entitled *A quelle heure un train partira-t-il pour Paris? (What Time Does a Train Leave for Paris?)* (Bohn 1991).

[22] As Paul Souday remarked in the *Paris-Midi*, "The show was also in the room. It was two hours of relaxing madness" ("Extraits De La Presse" 1917). This performance is also notorious because of Jacques Vaché (a friend of André Breton), who threatened to shoot his revolver at the audience (Breton 1996, 9). The audience of this production perhaps behaved in a manner similar to that of early ('silent') cinema (i.e. noisily) (Châteauvert 2001).

deliberately mischievous irresolution, inviting them to perform audiovisual double takes.

References

Albert-Birot, Pierre. 1918. "Le 24 Juin 1917." *SIC* 27.

Albright, Daniel. 2000. *Untwisting the Serpent: Modernism in Music, Literature, and Other Arts.* Chicago: University of Chicago Press.

Altman, Rick. 2004. *Silent Film Sound.* New York: Columbia University Press.

Apollinaire, Guillaume. 1918. *Les Mamelles De Tiresias; Drame Surréaliste. Avec La Musique De Germaine Albert-Birot Et 7 Dessins Hors Texte De Serge Féret.* Paris: Sic.

—. 1964. The Breasts of Tiresias. In *Modern French Theatre: The Avant-Garde, Dada, and Surrealism.* Ed. Michael Benedikt. New York: Dutton.

Aronson, Arnold. 2006. Avant-Garde Scenography and the Frames of the Theatre. In *Against Theatre: Creative Destructions on the Modernist Stage.* Eds Alan Ackerman and Martin Puchner, 21-38. London: Macmillan.

Bohn, Willard. 1991. *Apollinaire and the Faceless Man: The Creation and Evolution of a Modern Motif.* Rutherford, N.J.: Fairleigh Dickinson University Press

Bottomore, Stephen. 1999. "An International Survey of Sound Effects in Early Cinema." *Film History* 11, no. 4: 485-98.

—. 2001. The Story of Percy Peashaker: Debates About Sound Effects in the Early Cinema. In *The Sounds of Early Cinema.* Eds Richard Abel and Rick Altman, 129-42. Indiana: Indiana University Press.

Breton, André. 1996. *The Lost Steps = Les Pas Perdus.* Lincoln, Neb.: University of Nebraska Press.

Brown, Ross. 2005. "The Theatre Soundscape and the End of Noise." *Performance Research* 19, no. 4: 105-19.

Châteauvert, Jean and André Gaudreault. 2001. The Noises of Spectators, or the Spectators as Additive to the Spectacle. In *The Sounds of Early Cinema*, eds Richard Abel and Rick Altman, 183-91. Indiana: Indiana University Press.

Collins, John. 2009. Theatrical Sound Design: A Binary Paradigm. Keynote Address, Theatre Noise: The Sound of Performance, 22 April, 2009, Central School of Speech and Drama, London.

"Extraits De La Presse Concernant La Représentation Des Mamelles De Tirésias. Le 24 Juin 1917." 1917. *SIC* 19-20.

Monty Python and the Holy Grail. Directed by Gilliam, Terry, Terry
    Jones, Graham Chapman, John Cleese, Eric Idle, Michael Palin, Monty
    Python (Comedy Troupe), Python (Monty) Pictures. and Columbia
    Tristar Home Entertainment (Firm). Burbank, CA, 2008.
Lauke, Karen. 2010. "The Placement of Sound in Artistic Contexts."
    Body, Space & Technology 9.1,
    http://people.brunel.ac.uk/bst/vol0901/karenlauke/home.html (accessed
    June 9, 2010).
"Le 24 Juin 1917." 1917. *SIC* 18.
Melzer, Annabelle. 1980. *Latest Rage the Big Drum: Dada and Surrealist
    Performance.* Ann Arbor, Mich.: UMI Research Press.
Meusy, Jean Jacques. 1995. *Paris-Palaces, Ou, Le Temps Des Cinémas
    (1894-1918).* Paris: CNRS Editions.
Stein, Gertrude. 1935. *Lectures in America.* New York: Random House.
Weiss, Jeffrey S. 1994. *The Popular Culture of Modern Art: Picasso,
    Duchamp, and Avant-Gardism.* New Haven: Yale University Press.
Whitmore, Jon. 1994. *Directing Postmodern Theater: Shaping Signification
    in Performance.* Ann Arbor: University of Michigan Press.

CHAPTER XII

HEAR AND NOW:
HOW TECHNOLOGIES HAVE CHANGED
SOUND PRACTICES

ERIC VAUTRIN

The first track of *Desperate Attempts at Beauty*, by the American artist Joe Colley (2003), seems to be nothing more than a 'buzz' in a loudspeaker, in other words the sizzling sound typical of the imperfection of sound broadcasting—or perhaps what is called *white noise*, all sound frequencies produced at once in a continuous and monotonous way chiefly used to characterise or set the standards for amplifier and loudspeaker devices. Yet something *within* the sound turns this noise, at first perceived as technical and trite, into something surprising and even attractive, provided it is broadcast through an appropriate device enabling us to hear the subtle and almost sensual work on frequencies. The subsequent tracks combine various field recordings with electronic manipulations of exceptional sensitivity composing a sound space as a field of acoustic forces varied in nature in which all qualities of sound—tonality, tone, pitch, graininess, source, frequency—seem to have an influence on one another to create a peculiar hearing experience. Listening to those sounds is not like hearing music, but sitting in on a multimodal phenomenon composed by music, sound, flows, accidents, sensuality, vibrations, attractions.

Joe Colley is the kind of artist whose activity is hard to define. A composer without a system, a genius sound engineer, a craftsman experimenting with everything, a musician, a 'sound artist'—he eventually seems to be all these through his recordings, installations and performances in which he mingles frames and sources of sound, mixes recordings and

manipulates these via microphones, piezzos,[1] loudspeakers and any
electric phenomenon. In this chapter I will develop an analysis inspired by
Colley's composition which is best summarised by this question: what do I
hear when I hear a *buzz* in a loud speaker? *Desperate Attempts at Beauty*,
says Joe Colley.

Today creative composition calls upon the whole 'sound chain' (in
reference to the graphic chain from conception to print). A composer or a
musician, especially if working for the theatre, cannot imagine a given
sound without considering its means of production. This is not just a
matter of interpretation, as Cage or Ravel had done so, but also, after rock
and since digital technology, involves technical mixing, acoustic context
and speaker systems. My proposal is the following: technical possibilities
have recently opened a new arena for sound creation in theatre—I will
refer to this space as *sound matter*. I will explore the main developments
of this and examine three implications: the evolutions in creative practices,
the new conception of sound as experience and the theory and practical
perspectives—particularly those concerning the return of the musician/
engineer/composer as improviser and the consequences of this for
theatrical projects.

A brief and imaginary history of sound in theatre through the evolution of technical possibilities

In order to understand specific contemporary composition, it is no
doubt necessary to broadly outline a history of sound in theatre. This
history is not conceived here as a linear and progressive evolution, but
rather as a classification of functions as Riegl suggested for the visual arts
(see Riegl 1992). The emergence of a technology at a given moment is
often linked to prevalent practices and theories; but it does not rule out the
possibility of the coexistence of different approaches. Thus, for instance,
digital technologies are suited almost 'naturally' for empirical and
experimental composition techniques without, of course, preventing
anyone from working with these through classical means. In the same
way, while contemporary sound practices have been encouraged by recent
technical evolutions, nevertheless they have not been strictly determined
by them.

---

[1] An electro-mechanical or electronic device that allows electric current to pass
when pressed or distorted. It can be used as a very basic microphone also called a
contact microphone.

There is a prehistory to sound in theatre, then we were able to notate sound, inscribing it to recollect it because we did not have the means of recording, but also because compositions were the framework for musicians in which they could play, as Lionel Salter, a baroque specialist recalls (cit. in Bailey 1982: 40). The sounds or the music were produced on stage or in the wings; words and voices, footsteps, various sound effects or accompanying melodies made up the most part of the sound of the stage. This sound was directly linked to the performance in its construction and/or its conventions. In the second half of the nineteenth century, as soon as we were able to record and diffuse sound, this enabled the creation of fictional spaces outside of the stage's boundaries. Sound became a complement to the fiction, an accompaniment and an amplifier, and established a strictly acoustic dramaturgy.[2] Then, when recording sound became simpler, after World War II, sound truly acquired a new sort of efficiency. Being reproducible and easy to manipulate as desired, sound seems to have become an autonomous matter with its own dramaturgy: any change in sound, as rhythm, intensity, localisation, cause or trigger participates in the whole dramaturgy of the performance *in a sound manner* (which means: not only as an extension or a prolongation of any other element).

This brief history is no doubt less chronological than practical, or shall we say less marked by breaking points than by virtual possibilities, which present themselves or not (in this case, through technical evolutions). It joins another history inherent to theatre: this one is marked by a similar evolution, between two spectator practices: *hearing* and *seeing*. Indeed, theatre has for a long time been marked by the conjunction of hearing with seeing—hearing is therefore seeing, in the same way as speaking or producing a sound on stage makes visible something which is not there. Then, at the turn of the twentieth century, particularly developed by the Symbolists, hearing is seeing but seeing is hearing too: there is no longer any distinction between the two, a sound is a presence, and a presence reveals its complex nature by sound, within the sound, in its matter (in light, in a body, in a space). Sound—a voice or otherwise—is no longer the sign of that which is absent, but rather reveals the metaphysical strength of that which is present. Seeing *through* sound, and not only *by* sound.

After 1945, and especially during the eighties, hearing and seeing became separated; one no longer structures, no longer complements, no longer mixes with the other. We witness here a radical disjunction of

---

[2] This element can also be linked to the upheaval caused by Wagner at the same time, who indeed substituted music for words as the key element of drama.

sound and scenic presences or actions, of which the work will redefine and reconstruct for itself the possible links, of all sorts, between one and the other.

Contemporary practice

Today, the ordinary technical equipment of a large number of theatres and the technologies present in most personal computers of the members of theatre companies enable us to do pretty much everything that the twentieth century had dreamed of: incredibly realistic sound amplification; musical accompaniment as close as ever to the performers and the narration; surprising off-stage effects; elaborate compositions; multiple and simultaneous broadcasting; editing from various sources ... and all with such wonderful ease. And yet, even if interesting virtual acoustic experiments exist, and the research on sensors and translations of various signals into sonic events has never stopped since the *9 evenings* in New York (1966), it is remarkable to note that these 'dreams [which] become reality' are not what motivates the majority of the contemporary theatre we can see today. Contemporary practices aim to reformulate the links between seeing and hearing in yet another way.

However, this reformulation isn't surprising and gives us a first idea, an intuitive sense that something in the creation process imprints itself on sound beyond its sole acoustic qualities. Composers such as Tristan Murail or Iannis Xenakis are amongst those who have precisely linked their music to new technological possibilities. However, they have both remarked that once a procedure is made simple by technology (for example compositions based on complex mathematical calculations), the result was no longer pertinent. Murail explains this by the fact that the time spent on this kind of practice, and the thought process which nourishes the work and himself, are necessary. Xenakis endlessly transformed his compositional procedures to test the limits of technological possibilities.

But what are we working on today? On sound itself, on its diffusion, that's to say both its production on stage—by the manipulation of objects or by working on the technical set-up, tables, loud-speakers, cables—and on the site, the space and its acoustic characteristics. In other words, we are working on that which makes the sound present, the non-neutrality of that which makes it appear, the 'medium of listening', we could say, its 'basis'. This means we are giving attention to the site, the place and space, its resonances, its volumes (of the space and of the sound), and the movements of the sound (stereo, Dolby 5.1 surround sound, or the physical movements of the speakers). It is this work on the sound system itself manipulating objects or an electric signal to produce a sound on stage, which means that we are working on noise, the materiality of sound, the medium, on continuity and accidents.

1. The sonic place

If the conceptual idea of an 'in situ' sound creation is relatively recent, working on the importance of space and the given acoustics of a performance space reveals the convergence of two major trends of the twentieth century. On the one hand there is the increasing significance of performance space in contemporary music (with the Group of Musical Research, Boulez and Stockhausen, to name just a few of those most involved in this kind of research). This kind of research however, works with the idea of sound in a 'neutral' concert space. On the other hand, there is the experience of popular or experimental music and particularly rock, the culture from which most sound technicians come: popular music is very often performed in spaces that are not at all neutral if not say acoustically awful, therefore the performance space must be taken into consideration. Today contemporary theatre practices, linking the two heritages, take into account the space, its resonances, its volume, its specific texture—inspiring for instance the likes of Scott Gibbons (with Castellucci), composing for electronic and pop music, or Alain Mahé (with choreographer Josef Nadj).

2. The sound signal

Sound creation which starts from the sound device itself, also comes from popular music—it is a little bit like an electric guitar without the guitar. The electric guitar was the first instrument to integrate an amplifier, whose sound came from the alteration of an electric signal. Working on this signal brings about a particular sort of composition, made up of cycles (electrical sine waves) and of loops (the sound within the sound, made possible by the dissociation of the instrument and its source of diffusion, allowing all sorts of feedback to occur). A radical form of this kind of sound work is that of Peter Rehberg in his composition for the choreographer Gisèle Vienne where a mixing table is looped to itself (in short, plugging the *input* into the *output*): the sound produced is therefore the amplification and the variations of different forms of electrical resistance—the 'buzz' of the machine. Another example would be the work of Gibbons,[3] who for a long time re-recorded the sounds emanating from all kinds of speakers (even old and broken ones) until the original sound was no longer recognisable and became just a sort of 'memory' of the electric signal.

In any case, 'conception' of the sound is no longer distinct from its 'diffusion'—sound is therefore matter and gesture, or in other words an experience. This principle of working with sound analogically brings us back to Murail and Xenakis's impression that their practice 'marks' sound creation—it is not about making sound, it is about marking it with traces, imprinting on it, charging it with a memory which will enrich listening; as though listening was not just getting pleasure from a sound, but rather an exploration of something like the thickness of sound; as though listening was hearing without hearing, hearing something which cannot be heard and cannot be expressed.

The issues of these new practices are no doubt multiple, but I would argue that here is an attempt to render sound *diegetic*—meaning that it represents itself. It is neither illustration, nor illusion, nor the expression of an idea, or innerness nor even a singular matter. Taking into account the space and working on the sound system set-up as the principal source results in the consideration of sound as something not pure, not ideal or ideational, and turns away from all conceptualisation or representation of a sound happening. A diegetic sound event enables sound to no longer be an image of itself, or an idea but rather it becomes something which could link gesture, matter, concept, space, movement and memories indistinctly. This approach to *sound event* is about imagining how different materials can be interlinked, how any sound source can interact with any other stage matter—body, voice, text, light, space—beyond any predefined hierarchy. It is also a dramatic or dramaturgical structuring of certain political and social questions of today: how to create a common experience out of heterogeneity, collectiveness out of differences, vitality out of that which is ordinary, banal or anonymous? These are the questions Castellucci, Rodrigo Garcia, Christoph Marthaler and others are asking in their theatre forms. We must therefore try to imagine to what degree dramaturgy may be shaken in its foundations and pushed into a new era by this *diegetic* presence of sound, or whether this is insignificant and confronting us with little else than its own presence, being about nothing apart from being, concretely, physically, materially.

---

[3] An American musician and sound creator, Gibbons has frequently worked with the Italian director Romeo Castellucci for about ten years. See his website for example: http://www.red-noise.com

New practices, new team, new experience of sound

In this type of sound work, which I believe to be of our time, the musician is no longer 'just' a performer, an engineer, or even a composer, but all three at once. He or she must have full knowledge of how the set-up works, complete mastery of his/her movements, and the ability to organise and conceptualise series of sound events. The musician therefore resembles an improviser, similar to the free-jazz and rock musician and the experimenters from all different horizons, including the descendants of the Italian Futurists, of Walter Ruttmann or John Cage, the illegitimate children of David Tudor or the *Gruppo di Improvvisazione*. Tudor is perhaps a significant case as the first to have grasped what motivates the practices I am describing here: that sound is not an image, stocked away in a memory somewhere, but rather it is a matter, a fluid, a field, a production in the process of happening, taking place.

Derek Bailey defines, as do others, the practice of improvisation as having three basic aims: the freedom of work, the misappropriation of the object, and the collective work—which we could say is 'listening' between musicians and the audience, but I prefer the expression 'collective negotiation of space and time'. This partly explains the fact that certain creators today still prefer analogue processes, which offer a matter and a form which resist, from which the musical gesture can take place, outside of all preconceived ideas or images. These improvisations are those which Bailey refers to as "non-idiomatic" (1982, 4) meaning they are not based on any prior existing forms. Indeed, the resulting music/composition is not about editing or 'collage', in which it is the distance between sounds which structures the composition and invites listening, but rather a form of mixing in the sense of a weaving of various fields (electric, phonic, libidinal or others), within which each sound/tonality/texture/resonance retains its autonomy in a space constantly redefining itself.

The engineer-musician defines him/herself as a sound creator working on a selection of sources, on a mix of electric or sound flow as much as on the specific possibilities of its amplification and diffusion system and on the acoustic reactions of his/her workspace—that is to say, eventually, on every type of alteration of the sound flow at any stage of its creation. This sound creation is not only enabled by digital technologies, but also clearly about a way to play with sound matter only encouraged by digital developments. This sound creator, who in part improvises compositions and to whom the available equipment is particularly significant holds a new position in the creative team. The stage director, the performer or the scenographer cannot know what the available sound disposal enables them to do, and what its potential is in a given space. Then it is necessary to figure out another model to understand theatrical ways of creation and hierarchies in the team,[4] less determined by the interpretation of a text or a preconceived idea than organised by a flat and empirical network of propositions, an ongoing negotiation.

A sound experience

The notable consequence of these described developments is without doubt a new conception of sound matter: a sound is not pure, an image of sound does not exist, a sound does not exist outside of that which creates it, be it the performer or speakers. Sound matter can essentially be defined as a series of *resistances*—between the instrument and sounds; between the performer and the gestures they know only too well; between the flow of sound and the space it meets, speakers and resonances in space, resistances which modulate the electric flow etc.—a *resistance* to reducing sound to a representation, paradoxically.

How can we speak about a way of listening which is not purely the pleasure derived from harmony or orchestration, nor losing ourselves in a melody, nor the appreciation of a logical arrangement? A way of listening which would be enriched by all that which is not heard—from different types of silence, to that which is not in the sound itself, the 'memory' of its conception and the manifestation of its 'means' (electric signal, loudspeakers and space). Working on sound matter more than on sound involves taking listening into account, here conceived as a kind of widened dimension of perception. If, for instance, a rhythm cannot be heard without space around, or a melody without a gesture, listening is no longer or not only about finding analogies or deciphering sounds, but it becomes an aptitude to perceiving complex harmonies between heterogeneous elements or matters. A non-identifying listening or a listening which would be enriched by everything it does not hear, such as different qualities of silence, occurrences of its vehicles, the technical device (electric signal, loudspeakers and space) and the memory of its own creation? What is the equivalent of the sound creator's empiric and critical listening for the audience?

Therefore it is necessary to turn to a more anthropological approach to sound matter. It is well known that sound draws attention, foreshadows *something:* listening is at the same time being alert, and trying to immerse,

---

[4] This rethinking of hierarchies is not necessarily new: Meyerhold and Brecht, to name the most famous examples, already experimented with alternative forms of collaboration.

to lose ones identity and to merge with the non-personal, the non-private—trying to enter right into the 'natural' world, like a hunter alert to noises in the forest—or at least, trying to be out of ourselves. Listening is thus defined as a hesitation between succumbing to exteriority and taking part in archaic communion with others. Dealing with 'listening' in those terms broadens the perspective of studies on sound creation in theatre: work on sound comes down to building a certain relationship with the stage and its propositions based on attention or immersion. It is easy to understand when assessing dramaturgical or narrative sound choices: one can perceive how some sounds trouble the audience or arouse their concentration whereas others let their attention slip into a slower, or on the contrary, a livelier mood. But this type of *listening* in the broadest sense is worth even more than fictional and narrative constructions since it involves the sound properties of the building, the technical disposal, the movements or the objects, and eventually of the very body of the spectator.

Conclusion: working on the sound matter

Thinking about sound matter allows another dimension to the theoretical approaches to contemporary creation in the theatre. The practices discussed here suggest a way to turn sound matter into a renewed perception of the world, alert and uncertain. Working on sound matter as 'only' sound, as a sound quality peculiar to the project, the space and the concrete conditions of a performance, would counteract music as an unconscious elation and, in the same way, as the expression of oneself. And by giving priority to sound as a flow and a process, by working on sound production conditions, more than on a conventional memory of tones, sound creators would propose a type of listening to the world. In the same time, they would invent a unique and renewed relationship between sound matter and the various elements of the performance. This experience of listening which we are suggested to try, as listeners, for the duration of the performance, is at the edge of what we can hear—because it isn't possible to disconnect the acoustics from the broadcasted sound, nor to undo logically the produced complex networks, but it is possible to perceive and to investigate this intricacy. In any case, this listening is an attention to sound flows, on unsettled schemes of various elements, and not on the imaging evoked or summoned by sound—even if it means accepting, for a time, the enigma of the "hide-and-seek between the visible and the audible" (Quignard 1997: 149).

It is an approach to sound matter, to sound creation and also to listening as a *"type of deafness"* (Guionnet 2009). *Deafness* means here a

way of listening which starts when a spectator doesn't recognise a sound
as a sound, but as anything (or nothing) else—an event, a presence, a
movement: if, for a few moments, you don't try to understand the world
around you *through* its sounds, then, temporarily *deaf*, you perceive your
surroundings in an unfamiliar way, as a perpetual noisy variation, a
continuous mix of different events and presences. This is the kind of
experience that is possible to exercise, today, on stage—theatre as a *way of
listening* more than a place for hearing.

Joe Colley defines his work as the search for "the mystery of the
obvious" (2004), for how composition may not produce an image, of itself,
of the composer, of a project, of music, of the world or oneself, but rather
give itself as a sound experience. He has called one of his albums *Stop
Listening* (Colley 2000).

Translated from French by Deborah Lennie-Bisson
and Marie Lamardelle.

References

Bailey, Derek. 1992. *Musical Improvisation: Its Nature and Practice in
Music.* Upper Saddle River: Prentice-Hall.
Colley Joe. 2004. Projet pour un LP, ou comment se passer au mieux du
compositeur. In *Revue & Corrigée*, 61: 16-19. Nota Bene: Sievoz.
—. 2000. *Desperate Attempts at Beauty*, Auscultare Research.
Crawl Unit (aka Joe Colley). 2000. *Stop Listening*, Ground Fault
Recordings.
Quignard Pascal. 1997. *La Haine de la Musique*, Paris: Gallimard.
Guionnet Jean-Luc. 2009. Le bruit de fond. Text for an "Atelier de
Création Radiophonique" (France Culture, 1998) realised with Eric La
Casa. http://www.jeanlucguionnet.eu/Le-bruit-de-fond (accessed
December 12, 2010).
Riegl Aloïs. 1992. *Questions de style*. Trans. Henri-Alexis Baatsch and
Françoise Rolland, preface by Hubert Damisch. Paris: Hazan.

CHAPTER XIII

THE MECHANICS OF NOISE: THEATRICALITY AND THE AUTOMATED INSTRUMENT IN HEINER GOEBBELS' THEATRE AND PAT METHENY'S JAZZ

DAVID ROESNER

Introduction: noise and the mechanical

In this chapter, I will investigate different performative approaches towards the automated instrument on stage, their relation to liveness and to noise. The understanding of noise that I want to accentuate here (fully aware that this addresses only one of many aspects of noise in performance) is its relation to its cultural encoding as mechanical or automated sound. I will look at how two examples of live performance negotiate this cultural encoding and reinterpret the mechanics of noise in different ways.

Noise is a cultural phenomenon: it requires a listener, who interprets certain sounds as 'noise'. It occurs, as musicologist Paul Hegarty states, "in relation to perception—both direct (sensory) and according to presumptions made by an individual" (2007, 3).[1] One of these presumptions, which has grown out of Western civilisation and industrialisation, is that noise is something often considered mechanical or at least associated with machines. We do not mind the sound of waves crashing on a beach or of the wind in the trees, but the sound of an air conditioning system or a nearby motorway robs us of our sleep—it is not, however, necessarily the quality or volume of the sound itself but the cultural encoding as 'pleasant and natural' or 'annoying and artificial' respectively, which guides our (mis)appreciation of sounds as noise.

---

[1] See also Ross Brown's chapter in this book (chapter I).

Luigi Russolo, the Futurist ambassador of excessive noise, proclaimed that "in the 19th century, with the invention of machines, noise was born" (Russolo in Hegarty 2007, 5). It was also not by accident that in his quest for *l'arte dei rumori* (the 'art of noises'—the title of his 1913 manifesto), he turned to finding, inventing and building *machines*, so called *intonarumori,* to realise his vision of a noise orchestra. Humans, by contrast, were less suited for the job: they harbour too many cultivated inhibitions towards creating excessive noise and also pale in comparison where sheer volume is concerned.

But even when we consider *human* noises, it seems that an important factor for distinguishing between speech, utterance or song on the one hand, and noises, such as laughing, coughing, sneezing, rustling, burping, or farting on the other, is that the latter are mostly considered 'mechanical' by which I also mean: unintentional and involuntary. In suggesting this, I am following Henri Bergson's theory on comedy in *Laughter* (*Le Rire*) (1956 [1900]) in which he investigates society's dismissal of the mechanistic in human behaviour, for which laughter is suggested to be a powerful sanction and corrective.

Bergson discusses the "mechanical inelasticity" (1956, 65) or "automatism" (1956, 71) of certain acts of an involuntary, habitualised, or absent-minded nature. These stand, says Bergson, in stark contrast to "what life and society require of us", namely, "a constant alert attention that discerns the outlines of the present situation, together with a certain elasticity of mind and body to enable us to adapt ourselves in consequence" (1956, 72). By definition and design, machines lack intention, are automated, habitual and characterised by the absence of a mind. In social interaction, Bergson claims, we resort to laughter to appeal to or even punish those who fail to meet the social requirements of adaptability and presence of mind. And with regard to noise, particularly when it is of a mechanical, automated nature, we equally respond with strategies to avoid, suppress or stop the source of noise.

I am interested now in investigating how two different live performances, both of which I would characterise as 'theatrical'[2] even though one of them would conventionally be called a 'concert', negotiate

---

[2] Heiner Goebbels' piece, while having been called a "no-man show" (Bell 2010, 151), and playing with characteristics of an installation, is still clearly indebted and shaped by a theatrical dramaturgy and a theatrical stage-audience relationship. Pat Metheny's *Orchestrion* concerts display theatrical elements in that they include narrative elements within their presentation: there is for example a segment in which he explains and explores the possibilities of the "orchestrion" he uses almost in the style of a lecture-performance.

the dominant presence of mechanical instruments on stage: Heiner Goebbels'
"performative installation / music theatre" *Stifters Dinge [Stifter's Things]*
from 2007 and jazz-guitarist Pat Metheny's *Orchestrion* Tour 2009.[3] One
unifying factor between these distinct performances is that they both
elevate noise to the level of music, and do so by creatively engaging with
the *theatricality* of the mechanical instrument in a variety of ways that
invite the audience to reconsider the status of the emanated sounds through
a performative suggestion of naturalisation, humanisation and intentionality
after all.

The automated instrument in performance

The two performances I will interrogate differ significantly in their
style, genre, and target audience, but they share an interest in bringing
automated instruments on stage and engaging with them performatively.[4]
Composer and director Heiner Goebbels presents an entire stage in his
production *Stifter's Dinge [Stifter's Things]* that functions as an instrument.
It is a hybrid performance, which combines elements of theatre, installation,
radio-play and exhibition—with a hint of a physics lab—which results in a
contemplation on nature, culture, technology and voices and is characterised
by an almost complete absence of human performers.[5] The continuous
sound-track of the piece is produced by five automated pianos, stacked on
top of each other (see figure 13-1) as well as a number of cymbals, tubes,
wires and other mechanical constructions that produce ticking, grinding,
crashing, thumping, cracking and humming sounds. The stripped-open
pianos have been rigged with different complex robotic mechanisms,
which extend the pianos' expressive range from 'normal' playing to
different techniques of scratching and plucking their strings directly. All
this is programmed and operated from a bank of computers via MAX/MSP

---

[3] See the list of online references at the end of this chapter for more detailed
information on both performances.

[4] In this, they differ for example from the recent production of *Kleiner Mann—was
nun?* (Dir. Luk Perceval, Munich Kammerspiele, April 25, 2009) where a purpose-
built orchestrion was the sole feature of the stage design and provided most of the
incidental music, but was otherwise hardly involved *performatively*. See
http://www.muenchner-kammerspiele.de/programm/stuecke-a-z/kleiner-mann-
was-nun/ (January 15, 2010) for more details.

[5] In one instance, two technicians enter the stage to modify the water basins, but
they are clearly meant to be seen as stagehands, not performers. See more detailed
descriptions of the piece in Bell 2010 and Eiermann 2009 as well as the
documentary material on Goebbels' webpage www.heinergoebbels.com (January
12, 2011).

software—low tech sound production[6] (e.g. a stone being drawn over a rough surface) meets high-end steering technology.[7]

Figure 13-1: The stage as instrument in Heiner Goebbels' *Stifter's Things* (2007)[8]. Photograph by Mario Del Curto.

---

[6] Gelsey Bell describes this further: "The pianos reinforce the decidedly steam punk aura of the whole thing—proud Victorian-era instruments shown in Frankensteinian derangement. Mechanical technology that—compared to the sleek digital sterility of today—seems somehow more organic, replete with dirt, rust, mold, even bacteria, as if the gilded-era Armory exists as a greenhouse for forests of wild pianos and steam-powered drums" (2010, 152).

[7] An article in the *Bühnentechnische Rundschau* from 2008 (Anon. 2008) describes the technical setup in more detail. The article is also available via Goebbels' website www.heinergoebbels.com (January 12, 2011).

The renowned jazz-guitarist Pat Metheny equally mixes the possibilities of latest technology and the old idea of the 'orchestrion' in his project of the same name. About ninety years ago, orchestrions were the next step up from the so-called player piano: instruments that could be mechanically operated and programmed, initially by feeding punched paper rolls through a mechanism that translated this information into playing keys. Metheny employs a wide range of instruments in his orchestrion: guitars, basses, pianos, organs, tuned bottles, mallets, and plenty of percussion (see figure 13-2). Modern technology allows him not only to operate each instrument from his guitar, but also to loop and program them, so that even in a live situation the actual instruments playback highly complex musical pieces, but also remain open to improvised interaction.

Figure 13-2: Pat Metheny surrounded by some of the instruments of his orchestrion in the live setup. Photograph by Ralf Dombrowski.

Particularly for those familiar with Metheny's work with the Pat Metheny Group, one cannot help but note an absence as well in this setting: the musical idiom is very close to that of the group, but Lyle Mays, Steve Rodby, Antonio Sanchez and other group members are absent from the stage. At the same time, the technological setting also means a

---

[8] The sculpture of automated pianos is mirrored in two of the three shallow basins that form an integral part of the set.

multiplication of Metheny, the splitting of *one* inventive musical mind into a wide range of instrumental disciplines and mechanics all controlled by the one guitar(ist).

Both Goebbels and Metheny transform the kind of interaction historically associated with automated instruments in significant ways, which also, I will argue, change our notion of the relationship between noise and the mechanical in performance. Historically, it was a key transition in the development of automated instruments, when the player pianos that had populated homes and bars for some time transformed into 'reproducing pianos' from around 1911 onwards. The transition from arranged rolls to hand-played rolls meant that live performances of an actual pianist could now be reproduced by the instrument, including the individual timing and dynamics of the human performance. The somewhat mechanical and 'noisy' clunking of the player piano gave way to a technology that not only captured a tune but an individual rendition of that tune or even "the performance of a master" (Armstrong 2007, 3). Following my earlier argument, this audibly brings back the element of intentionality into the mix: the instrument now echoes the presence of an interpretive musical mind, renders 'noise' into music by 'emancipating' it as Walter Benjamin might have described it (Benjamin in Armstrong 2007, 16).

It is particularly the theatrical aspect of this transition I am interested in. Both Goebbels' and Metheny's settings, however different in their musical idiom, are built not to store *music*, but to recreate the *performance of music*. They could both have used playbacks of the same kinds of sounds, captured by samplers as digital files, but have gone to great lengths to ensure that the audience (and in Metheny's case the performer) do not engage with recorded sounds, but recorded performances, recreated by machines and actual instruments. The key difference to the reproducing piano is that the performance is no longer integral, but is assembled from layers and layers of acts of performing, programming and editing. It is for the most part not performed on the actual instruments, but consists of a translation from a controlling device (a keyboard for Goebbels, a guitar for Metheny) to a plethora of instruments and playing techniques. The machine, one could argue, is built in such a way that it does not remember and reproduce a sound, but remembers the *gesture* that produces a sound.

In addition, both Goebbels and Metheny exploit the sheer space needed and the spectacle produced by the both intricate and enormous apparatuses by using them as theatrical set design, as well as instilling them with aspects of theatrical dramaturgy, for example by creating a sense of expectation, entrance and revelation. At some point in *Stifter's Things* the wall of pianos glides to the front of the stage like an actor stepping forward to deliver a soliloquy; in *Orchestrion*, Metheny raises the expectations by playing a number of solo pieces on acoustic guitars in front of the still-hidden machinery before unveiling it to great visual and acoustic effect. Both artists use elements of rhythmically synchronised lighting to highlight and pinpoint which parts of the apparatus are currently 'acting' and playing.

Figure 13-3: Advertisement for an Orchestrion built for the Chicago World's Fair, in 1893.[9]

The old nickel-operated orchestrions of the 1920s actually mostly *concealed* the mechanics of music production behind elaborate wardrobe like front pieces (see figure 13-3). They performatively played with the contrast of the simple nickel that went in and the abundance and complexity of sound that came out. In contrast, Goebbels and Metheny have an interest in revealing the sound source and the technology used on

---

[9] The use of this image is courtesy of the Tim Trager Archives (www.timtrager. com).

them: most of their mechanical devices replace actual musicians and point at their ostentatious absence. At the same time, they draw attention to the 'noise' of musicking[10]—here, the *effort* and the *materiality* of sound production.

All of this emphasises the continued performative "difference" (in Deleuze's sense, 2001) between the sounds produced, the way they are produced, and our expectations. In both cases there is a friction between sound source and sound event, like an interfering noise between signal and receiver. But rather than being a disturbance, both performances exploit the challenge this posits on the audience and make it a central part of the attraction. The audience is put in a very active mode of investigation about 'how is this done?' or 'where does this come from?' and need to employ a dual consciousness[11] which engages both with what is being said or played and how it is conveyed.[12] Other modes of performance, such as Hollywood films, realist dramas or blockbuster musicals, seek to *reduce* the 'signal-to-noise ratio' and allow for a more uninterrupted immersion, but here there is a conscious engagement with noise in the sense of what Douglas Kahn calls "that constant grating sound generated by the movement between the abstract and the empirical" (Kahn 1999, 25). Metheny and Goebbels both make use of this friction, but do so—at least generally speaking—in almost opposite ways: in the *Orchestrion* project, musical sounds are organised mechanically; in *Stifter's Things*, mechanical sounds are organised musically.

Goebbels and Metheny share a strategy that negotiates the potential "inelasticity" (Bergson 1956, 65) of the mechanical instrument in their respective aims to create, on the one hand, a thought provoking,

---

[10] Musicking, as Christopher Small defines his neologism, emphasises that music is not a thing, but an activity: "To music is to take part, in any capacity, in a musical performance, whether by performing, by listening, by rehearsing or practicing, by providing material for performance (what is called composing), or by dancing" (Small 1998, 9).

[11] I suggest we adapt the concept of a dual (or double) consciousness for the audience member, which has originally been established for the *actor* (most prominently by Coquelin in *The Art of the Actor,* 1894) as a necessary split between the emotionally charged presentation of a character and a careful attention to the technical necessities of the performance (hitting lighting marks, handling props, sticking to certain agreements with your acting partners on stage etc.). See also Merlin (2010, 27).

[12] Gelsey Bell's description is interesting here: "I literally cannot tell how the sounds were being made. Directionally, it is clear that most of them are created live on the stage, but it is not easy to identify the individual parts that make the sonic whole" (Bell 2010, 151).

contemplative performance on the immediacy and the uncanny of nature and, on the other hand, a vibrant and lively jazz concert. As I will now explore in more detail, they reinstate a sense of the organic, human(oid) and intentional in the way they prepare, present and interact with their respective apparatuses.

In the specific way in which they programme their machines, Goebbels and Metheny make use of their intuitive and personal relationship with their primary musical instrument, the keyboard and the guitar respectively, so that the process of inputting data, programming tracks, but even, in Goebbels' case, of controlling elements of stage technology, are connected to their body memory and expressive vocabularies as *musicians* rather than mediated and defamiliarised by today's equivalence of the mechanically produced piano roll; i.e. the creation of MIDI impulses on a computer screen via mouse clicks and entered numerical parameters.[13] So if in the early days of barrel organs and orchestrions a *machine* controlled the musical instrument, Goebbels and Metheny now make use of the possibility that they can again use a *musical instrument* to control the machine that operates another musical instrument. But other than the reproducing piano, which repeats the identical performance of a human being made on the very same instrument, Goebbels and Metheny use the element of translation between instrumental idioms in search for the sound yet unheard, the image yet unseen. They create a world of sounds that could not be reproduced by human performers, but at the same time give it a 'human touch' in the process of programming it.

On stage then, there are also strategies of anthropomorphism which allow the audience to see the automated instrument both as man and machine.[14] Metheny amplifies this notion by walking in between sections of his enormous orchestrion, which looked to me as if he was seeking contact with particular musicians in a dialogic exchange while playing, as jazz musicians often do. For particular moments of improvisation they seek the acoustic but also the physical presence of and sometimes eye contact with different performers, and the continuation of this practice in a fully automated setting instilled a sense of personality and intentionality within the orchestrion.

In a different, but related sense, Goebbels also animates the objects and instruments of his stage in the way he arranges their sounds and movements

---

[13] See Heiner Goebbels' chapter "'It's all part of one concern'. A 'keynote' to composition as staging" in Rebstock/Roesner 2011.

[14] Bell also describes the stage in *Stifter's Things* as animated but likens it to an animal rather than a human: "The set groans and hums like a waiting beast" (Bell 2010, 151).

rhythmically and spatially. There is a section where three gauze curtains appear to 'dance' to the water reflections of light on their surfaces (which also look like waveforms of sounds), a spotlight, whose shutter mechanism is amplified to produce a percussive sound, seems to wilfully interject into a recording of aboriginal incantations. In a curious way, I would even argue, that the animation and emancipation of the instruments as stage and of the stage as instrument[15] in Goebbels' work is supported and enabled by his understanding of theatre as a machine; a machine, however, whose blueprint we have to re-design and re-read with each production, rather than relying on the well-tried, 'well-oiled' mechanism to kick in, which would inevitably reproduce more of the same, but nothing new. Goebbels elaborates:

> The students at Gießen[16] have called the form of presenting their work "theatre machine"; this machine includes everything, not just the hardware of the fly tower, but all people, materials and means involved. Only by extending the term in this way, 'machine' is to be understood. If you like, the whole staging concept of my pieces *Black on White, Max Black* and *Eislermaterial* is that each is a machine, which sets its own, new rules. From these all the artistic consequences emerge and the aesthetics and impact of the performance. These rules have to be worked on; all those involved in the production have to learn to read their blueprint (Goebbels 2003, 23, my translation).

Seeing the theatre as a whole as a machine brings into focus how *all* elements contribute to a final production and necessitates Goebbels and his team to actively reflect on and artistically shape their interplay, rather than relying on established relationships, hierarchies and artistic effects. This in turn affords the audience an "evenly hovering attention" (Freud 1912, 111), which acknowledges both the novelty and virtuosity made possible by the process of automation and the familiarity of the personal theatrical and musical vocabularies of Goebbels and Metheny, whose signatures remain clearly present.

What is interesting to me here, is that all this amounts to an exchange of two concepts of noise; a 'castling'[17] of noises, if you wish: on the one hand, both artists use the movement towards mechanisation, which bears

---

[15] See also Roesner 2010 on the question of the stage as (musical) instrument.

[16] He refers to the Justus-Liebig-Universität Gießen, where he has been Head of Department of Applied Drama ("Angewandte Theaterwissenschaft") since 1999.

[17] Castling is the only movement in chess where a player moves two figures at the same time, moving one (the king) towards the other (the rook), which takes the place of the king.

the 'danger' of being noisy in the sense described earlier by being associated with that which is inflexible, soulless, and predictable. However, in Goebbels' theatre the automation also serves as a productive defamiliarisation from a well-known instrument like the piano into a material object, a visual sight, an automated performer, a sculpture. The musical sounds of the piano become mechanical, industrial, foreign, 'dinghaft' ('thing-like') and the music of things becomes the prevalent soundtrack of the performance. It thus follows the aesthetical strategies of Adalbert Stifter, whose descriptions of nature—a forest in winter, for example—manage to defamiliarise it to the reader, make it new, unknown, unpredictable and uncanny.

Metheny, however, captures in his *Orchestrion* the wonder and childlike curiosity he experienced on encountering the player piano in his grandfather's basement, unashamedly uniting nostalgia with an almost 'nerdy' interest in pushing the boundaries of music technology. Again, there is a productive musical and performative tension between re-encountering the musical idiom that Metheny has developed over the 30 years of his career (and I would argue that nearly everyone who went to see his orchestrion tour was familiar with this idiom) and the subtle acoustic differences and visual irritations created by this 'forest' of instruments playing 'on their own'.

On the other hand they both use strategies of 'humanisation', which bring back the 'elasticity' and intentionality of human musicking. This enables Goebbels to make his stage sound not like a factory, but like an organism (a 'beast') and render it a performer. It enables Metheny to use the intimacy of a solo tour, while being in a complex dialogue with multiple versions of himself.

They both replace—or at least place side by side—the mechanics of noise, (evoked by its insistent perfection, but also the cold physical materiality of its moving parts, the performativity of its inner or outer workings) with the 'organic' imperfections of human communication, which is abundant with its own set of noises. In musical terms, there are the imperfections of agogic rhythms, which intentionally deviate from a chronologically-absolute time, of intonation, of timbre and phrasing. These are manifest in Metheny's performance as the involuntary sounds guitar-strings make when changing frets, the unintentional aspects of his "guitar-face" (Auslander 2006, 112),[18] when being lost in the act of

---

[18] "This phrase refers to the distorted expressions that appear on the faces of rock guitarists, particularly when playing a solo. These expressions are nonessential to the actual production of musical sound but serve as coded displays that provide the

improvisation. Similarly, in Goebbels' use of voice recordings for *Stifter's Things* there are many examples of rich, layered, imperfect voices and an intentional embrace of the "grain" (Barthes 1997), the unmistakable, the unique in these voices and/or their methods and materials of preservation, as in the example of the Papua New Guinean incantations, recorded on wax cylinders by an Edison phonograph.[19]

The mechanics of noise make room for the organics of noise, where the 'empirical' of language—the 'grain' of "parole" (Saussure 1983, xiv)—is grating against the systemic purity of "langue" (Saussure 1983, xi).[20]

Conclusion

Metheny and Goebbels—with very different aesthetic outcomes, in very different genres and to very different audiences—seek to embrace and utilise noise, both in a physical and a conceptual sense as a *productive* friction between signal and receiver[21] where the idea of an immediacy of artistic expression and aesthetic perception is rendered problematic and becomes therefore, as a process in itself, noteworthy and invites reflection on "the thing seen / the thing heard".[22]

They play with noise as a concept of counter-rotating movements: Metheny and his technical support team advance music technology and instrument making in visionary ways by putting an actual orchestra (not virtual instruments) at the fingertips of one musician but at the same time

audience with external evidence of the musician's ostensible internal state while playing" (Auslander 2006, 112).

[19] "Incantations for the south-westerly winds so vital to sailors ("Karuabu") in Papua New Guinea, recorded on 26th December 1905 by the Austrian ethnographer Rudolf Pöch, renowned pioneer of documentary films and sound recordings. Using his so-called "Archivephonograph" he was able to make unique recordings of indigenous songs and stories performed in the Papuan language by the native inhabitants." from the press kit for *Stifter's Things* at www.heinergoebbels.com (January 15, 2010).

[20] On Saussure's distinction between *langue* and *parole* see also Normand (2004, 89).

[21] This applies both to the signal the artist sends and the receiving and reproducing machine and the kinds of distortions, losses and gains achieved in this process as well as to the signal then emitted by the automated instrument and the interferences experienced by the audience due to the sonic and visual sense of 'difference' achieved.

[22] Heiner Goebbels used this quotation from Gertrude Stein's *Lectures in America* for the title of his keynote at the 'Theatre Noise' conference at the Central School of Speech and Drama 2009.

revert the continuing current of digitisation, which has brought the music industry the often cold perfection and virtuosity of drum computers and synthesizers with a perfect signal to noise ratio. He brings back some of the charm of the slightly battered jazz club ensemble into this mix of sleek melodies and advanced steering technology. But it is particularly in *performance* that the 'noise' of music making, the mechanical effort and slightly gritty feel of nineteenth century industrialisation takes hold. There is 'noise' in the discrepancy between the almost grotesque machinery it needs to produce the elegant flowing idiom of Metheny's music, between the solo performer and the plethora of sounds. There is also a sense of noise as excess and residue (cf. Hegarty 2003, 2004); noticing the 'too much' of an effort with music-technological wizardry results in a kind of music that a small ensemble of musicians could have played equally well.

Goebbels, on the other hand, uses this excess more critically: he very consciously does not attempt to emulate the experience captured in Stifter's account of a forest in winter time by imitating nature in its simplicity, immediacy and reduction, but affords the audience a complex and self-conscious version of this experience mediated through a plethora of sonic and visual impressions, for which it is, however, vital that despite the high-end stage technology employed there is again a sense of liveness, of the mechanical vs. the digital. It makes a difference that almost all of the sounds are produced live (even if produced by robotic construction), that visual effects such as the beautiful dancing water reflection, bouncing off alternating gauze curtains, are not pre-recorded projections, and that the chemical reactions that make the water basin bubble with tiny volcanoes of steam happen there and then, in real time.

In different ways then, Goebbels and Metheny use the noisy machinery, the mechanical instruments, the 'intonarumori' they have built with their teams as a vehicle for a contemplation of beauty.[23] They subvert and question some of the common cultural encodings of noise as the mechanical, unintentional and unnatural. In contrast, it is characteristic of both performances that, other than many of the more common attempts at beauty, which accentuate the flawless, the impeccable, the crystal-clear, the untouched, etc., they both do not 'suppress' or 'filter' the noise of the excess, the imperfection. They thus facilitate for the audience a confrontation with something that by being both alluring and repelling at the same time touches on the sublime.

---

[23] I am using a notion of beauty here, which follows John Danvers' thought, that beauty is not a "quality inherent in particular objects" (nor, I should add merely in the proverbial eye of the beholder), but a "mode of engagement, a function of a particular kind of relationship between subject and object" (Danvers 2005, 1).

References

Anon. 2008. Technisches Wunderwerk belebt "Stifters Dinge". Eine Theateraufführung ohne Akteure von Heiner Goebbels. In *Bühnentechnische Rundschau*, 1/2008. At http://www.heinergoebbels.com/en/archive/ texts (April 4, 2011).

Armstrong, Tim. 2007. Player Piano. Poetry and Sonic Modernity. In *Modernism / Modernity*, 14, 1, 1-19.

Auslander, Philip. 2006. Musical Personae, *TDR: The Drama Review*, 50, (1, 2006), 100-119.

Barthes, Roland. 1977. The Grain of the Voice. In *Image-Music-Text*, by Roland Barthes, New York: Hill and Wang.

Bell, Gelsey. 2010. Driving Deeper into That Thing: The Humanity of Heiner Goebbels's Stifter's Dinge. *TDR: The Drama Review* 54 (3, 2010), 150-158.

Benjamin, Walter. 1963 [1936]. *Das Kunstwerk im Zeitalter seiner technischen Reproduzierbarkeit*. Frankfurt am Main: Suhrkamp.

Bergson, Henri. 1956 [1900] Laughter. In *Comedy*, edited by Wylie Sypher, 61-190. New York: Doubleday Anchor Books.

Bowers, Q. David. 1966. *Put Another Nickel in: a History of Coin-operated Pianos and Orchestrions*. New York: Vestal.

Danvers, John. 2005. In Beauty I Walk. Beauty, Nature and the Visual Arts. In *The Future of Beauty in Theatre, Literature and the Arts* edited by Daniel Meyer-Dinkgräfe, 1-11. Newcastle: Cambridge Scholars Publishing.

Deleuze, Gilles. 2001. *Difference and Repetition* London/New York: Continuum.

Eiermann, André. 2009. Wenn die Dinge stiften gehen. Theater der Objekte / Stifters Dinge von Heiner Goebbels. In *Postspektakuläres Theater - Die Alterität der Aufführung und die Entgrenzung der Künste*, edited by André Eiermann, 238-268. Bielefeld: Transcript.

Freud, Sigmund. 1912. Recommendations to Physicians Practicing Psycho-analysis. In *The Standard Edition of the Complete Psychological Works of Sigmund Freud, Vol. 12*, edited by J. Strachey. London: Hogarth Press.

Goebbels, Heiner. 2003. 'Den immer andern Bauplan der Maschine lesen'. Widerstände zwischen Theorie und Praxis. In *TheorieTheaterPraxis*, edited by Kurzenberger, Hajo / Matzke, Annemarie, 17-26. Berlin: Theater der Zeit.

Hegarty, Paul. 2003. Residue—Margin—Other: Noise as Ethics of Excess. At http://www.dotdotdotmusic.com/hegarty1.html (January 20, 2011).

—. 2004. Noise as Weakness. At http://www.dotdotdot music.com/hegarty
   2.html (January 20, 2011).
—. 2007. *Noise/Music: A History.* London: Continuum International
   Publishing Group.
Kahn, Douglas. 1999. *Noise, Water, Meat. A History of Sound in the Arts.*
   Cambridge (MA) and London: The MIT Press.
Merlin, Bella. 2010. *Acting: The Basics.* London and New York:
   Routledge.
Normand, Claudine. 2004. System, Arbitrariness, Value. In *The Cambridge
   Companion to Saussure,* edited by Sanders, Carol, 88-106. Cambridge:
   Cambridge University Press.
Rebstock, Matthias; Roesner, David. 2011. *Composed Theatre. Aesthetics,
   Practices, Processes.* Bristol: Intellect.
Roesner, David. 2010. Musicking as *Mise En Scéne. Studies in Musical
   Theatre. Special Issue: Music on Stage* 4 (1, 2010), 89-102.
Saussure, Ferdinand de. 1983. *Course in General Linguistics; edited by
   Charles Bally and Albert Sechehaye with the collaboration of Albert
   Riedlinger; translated and annotated by Roy Harris.* London:
   Duckworth.
Small, Christopher. 1998. *Musicking: the Meanings of Performing and
   Listening* Hanover: University Press of New England.

Online Resources

http://www.heinergoebbels.com/ (accessed January 7, 2011).
http://www.patmetheny.com/orchestrioninfo/ (accessed January 7, 2011).
Pat Metheny—The Orchestrion EPK at: http://www.youtube.com/watch?v
   =9VymAn8QJNQ (accessed January 7, 2011).

CHAPTER XIV

MELODIC INTENTIONS:
SPEAKING TEXT IN POSTDRAMATIC
DANCE THEATRE

ZACHARY DUNBAR

Introduction

Presentant l'action d'une voix passive.[1] (Igor Stravinsky, 1948)

In this chapter, I will reflect on historical and critical aspects of narration, voice, and musicality. These issues were prompted by a postdramatic multimedia dance theatre piece entitled *The Cows Come Home* (2008) in which I had to speak lines from a text. Postdramatic environments self-consciously disavow programmatic or teleological intentions. Consequently, spectators and performers alike experience a dislocation between auditory and visual connections. When sounds manifestly avoid their associations with objects or become asynchronous with movement in space, the utterance of text acquires greater significance. Under these conditions, as the performer of the text I was forced to consider how the intonation of speaking might veer between intentionality and objectivity, naturalism and melodrama, phonetic utterance and semantic conceptualisation. As a way to overcome these vexations, I decided to treat the text like a piece of music; that is, to interpret the words on the page as groupings of rhythms, pitches, or phrases, rather than as mnemonics or prompts to access inner memories as an actor might do; in short, to think in terms of *melodic* intentions.

Within the larger discussion of the phenomenon of 'theatre noise', my probing into the materiality and the organisation of vocal sound correlates

---

[1] In the preface (*décor*) to his opera-oratorio *Oedipus Rex* (1927), Stravinsky comments that the narrator should "Present the action in a passive voice".

with clusters in this book that interrogate the interpretive or metaphoric status of musicality. The uses of musicality as part of praxis is discussed in recent scholarly accounts of contemporary German *Musiktheater* productions. David Roesner's rigorous and wide-ranging study of musicality in this field raises the notion of musicalisation to a hermeneutical level.[2] Whereas postdramatic theory has replaced logo-centric accounts of text, musicalisation, according to Roesner, re-introduces a "full range of textual potential: as rhythmical, gesticulatory, melodic, spatial and sounding phenomenon *as well as* a carrier of meaning" (Roesner 2008, 3).

Further afield, musicality is a concept that helps us to understanding the new rules of audience reception and of directing drama. In America, the intertextual and interdisciplinary formations in for instance the music theatre of Meredith Monk, Eric Salzman, Laurie Anderson and Robert Wilson have subverted the phenomenology of listening to music or text to that of 'seeing' the music and text. In contemporary French drama, the emphasis in the current trend for *Theatre de la parole* is to break with drama's epic-lyrical diegesis and the actor-ly traditions of enunciation, and thus to explore the act of speaking itself. Contemporary French practitioners working within the premise of unstable objectives and plot-less drama no longer ask, when analysing the spoken text, about what one "thinks" or "feels", but something like "what is its rhythm" (see Ryngaert 2007a and 2007b). In this chapter, I locate the notion of musicalisation to the experience of the performer and foreground this within historical and current theoretical discussions. These discussions will focus on the word-tone relationship in history, postmodern drama theory and narrative voice, and uttering text in postdramatic theatre. There are reasons for this.

From a historical perspective, the word-tone relationship has been an abiding dialectic in Anglo-European theatre. Since the Renaissance, the interplay of poetry and music has represented a vexing point around which discourses on privileging either text or song have formed. In the early modernist movement of twentieth century Paris, the mimetic realism of language and of music, and the Aristotelian principles on which they were mainly based, were dispensed with in favour of eclectic or synaesthetic forms of theatre. The self-conscious deconstruction of text as the primary source of semiotic encounters in a performance space set the early groundwork for the forms of postdramatic performance practices observed today. As a practitioner operating within the postmodern zeitgeist, I am

---

[2] See David Roesner on 'musicalisation' (Roesner 2008). The discussion of musicality also adds to a growing field of inquiry in postdramatic music theatre, which touches on the shared meanings, processes and terminologies in theatre-making and music-making.

interested in the diachronic development of the word-tone dialectic alongside how notions of musicality are inlaid within current theories on the narrative voice in theatre. Postmodern theory on drama is also concerned about the formation of the narrative voice and its musical nuances. Hans-Thies Lehmann's account of postdramatic theory includes the notion of musicality in relation to speaking text. Through these issues of the word-tone dialectic, narration, voice and musicality I contextualise a critical framework for performing text in a postdramatic setting.

Performance context

In 2008, alongside a choreographer, I devised a multimedia postdramatic dance theatre piece entitled *The Cows Come Home*.[3] The work re-imagined a mute chorus in the after-hour of a tragedy. Through a kind of glass darkly, the work evoked the Bible-believing world of a farmer who comes to terms with his plague-ridden cattle. Simultaneously, this was also the theatre of Greek myth, particularly the story of Oedipus and the dysfunctional relationship between humans and gods. Under thunder-heavy Texan skies, five dancers gestured and signified individual and collective sites of illness; little cellular gestures evoked gently remembered days and these visions fast forwarded and rewound to the hyper-realistic nightmare of the pitch and fall of life's great going down.

A postdramatic symptom of the work was manifested in the treatment of text. Within a dense sensorium of throbbing multi-shaped light bulbs, rambling voice-overs, radio white noise, live electro-acoustic guitar, and morphing clouds, a narrator-protagonist (played by me) sat under a dim light bulb away from the dancer's performance space. The text was culled from Samuel Beckett's death-obsessed novel *Malone Dies* and Sophocles' *Oedipus*. Lines of text were chosen with an ear more for their expressive soundings on the theme of death rather than for specific explanations or signifiers of happenings in the space. My intention would be to resist the natural propensity toward story-like narrations.

On the face of it, my role seemed easy enough. There would be no grappling with subtexts, defining actor-ly intentions, accessing emotions or sorting out gestures. Yet being immersed in a multi-layered sensorial

---

[3] *The Cows Come Home* was performed in Camden People's Theatre (London), the Underbelly (Brighton Festival), and at the Junge Hunde Festival (Denmark); for images see www.youtube.com/watch?gl=GB&hl=en-GB&v=YoSt8oT1rKg; for critical reception www.musicomh.com/theatre/cows_0508.htm; www.london theatreblog.co.uk/the-cows-come-home; http://magazine.brighton.co.uk (all accessed October 20, 2010).

performance brought with it an unforeseen set of challenges for the speaker of text: one's voice had to be tangibly present and yet characterless. Moreover, the complexity of sensations in the performance space made the timing and execution (i.e., the entrances and exits) of the text all-important. Added to this tension was how the dramatic actions of the dancers and the images, in contrast to my stillness, exerted strong inertial forces on my breathing, posture, and concentration.

As a musician, it made sense for me to imagine the performance of the text in melodic terms—in other words, thinking about musical timbre, rhythm, pitch, cadence and tempo. But musical readings and emotional tabula rasa are not necessarily coterminous. For example, a simple musicalised line of text like "let me say before I go any further that I forgive nobody" (Beckett's *Malone Dies*), when immediately following an intense sequence of images and movements, could have several kinds of melodic intentions and achieve different affects:

MELODIC INTENT	DRAMATIC AFFECT
Pitch: "**Let me say** before I go any further, that I forgive nobody".	Starting in the upper range of the speaking voice overly anticipated the intensity of the moment and added unwelcome melodrama.
Timbre: mixing reverb on the microphone	Ghostly and disembodied.
Cadence: "Let me say before I go any further that **I forgive nobody**".	A kind of diminuendo in the phrase sounded resigned.
Periodic phrasing: "Let me say / before I go any further / that I forgive nobody".	Unnatural measures of phrases gave the text a sense of being 'read' rather than 'said'.
Rhythmic/syllabic: "*Let-me-say-be-fore-I-go-an-y-fur-ther-that-I-for-give-no-bo-dy*".	Overtly denotative account evoked an automaton rather than a live being.

A similar set of performance parameters may have concerned Stravinsky. In his *Oedipus Rex* (1927), the composer anticipated the balance of the narrator being present in, and also distant from, the action. Like a *conférencier*, the narrator must speak his text in a manner that suits the static *décor* of a macabre opera-oratorio which included a chorus in bas-relief singing in Latin, and statue-like protagonists singing in styles that ranged from Monteverdi to Verdi. This eclectic gamesmanship of visual and musical styles was wedded to the aesthetics of French interwar neoclassicism. The anti-semantic treatment of language and experiments corresponded to the disembodiment of meaning and voice, and this process anticipated the postdramatic theatre in the retextured and restructured place of text and speech. The ontological uncertainty of the theatrical and the musical, in the dialectics of the word (as text) versus tone (as melody) relationship, takes us first to a historical overview.

Melody and text in ancient and modern drama

Our modern concern in the theatre about the songfulness of text is rooted in ancient Greek drama. In this highly innovative form of theatre our ancient forebears experienced the mutual interdependence of modes of music and rhythm, as well as the synaesthetic effect of song, dance and text. The theoretical implications of poetic language and music were systematically (and retrospectively) disseminated in Aristotle's *Poetics*. Although he omits any formal analysis of music that he gives tragic poetry, Aristotle speculates about *Melopoiia* (composition of songs). This, and *opsis,* which is concerned with visual appearance, form the two out of six elements that obtain to tragic mimesis. The term *melos* itself constituted poetic order as well as songfulness. *Melos* served the purpose of heightening emotion in the lyric parts of drama. For the classicist, Gregory Sifakis, the mutuality of melody and ethical mode established a uniform musico-poetic language through which (according to Aristotle) melodic intonation combined properly with the language to move the listener's soul (Sifakis 2001, 30-1).[4] In the *theatron* of Attic Greece, the democratic principle of spectatorship in a ritual space synchronised seeing as well as hearing as a way of knowing.

With the rise of the professional actor in ancient Rome, who performed the dramas to musical and choral accompaniment, the synth-aesthetic practices of the fifth century BCE *polis* dissolved into more formal roles. In the public sphere, the political efficacy of speech, enshrined in the writings of Cicero and Horace, would influence the cultural sphere of drama and position rhetoric above music. Throughout the Renaissance and the modern Classical period, the educative and the rhetorical function of speech, as prescribed by ancient writers, eclipsed music as the highest art, though increasingly, the development of the expressive palate of musical instruments, and innovations in song writing (especially in art songs and

---

[4] For a diachronic analysis of the word-tone relationship from antiquity to modernity in Greek tragedy, see Dunbar 2007.

arias) continued to influence the way composers explored melodies as mimetic structures of human temperament and speech.

In the German classical-romantic era, music secured an esteemed position to a degree such that the romantic poet's ear was said to be more receptive to the musical *Ton und Klang* rather than to the rhetorical patterns of language. The fact that poetic images and musical sound were interrelated reflected in Schlegel's aphorism, "many musical compositions are merely translations of poems into the language of music" (Schlegel 1991, 90).[5] It was Nietzsche (influenced by Schopenhauer's sense of music as the dynamism behind the universal will) who envisioned the collapse of logos-driven language. The philosophical import of the melody and of lyrics, as part of the *Gesamtkunstwerk* impulses in art, was developed to the nth degree by Wagner who, in his notion of the *Unendliche Melodie,* expressed through opera the dissolution of poetic language into music.

During the early twentieth century, ideas such as those in Artaud's *Theatre and its Double* (1938) helped resurrect in the theatre the ancient mutuality of *melos* and speech. Artaud was interested in the way text operated as an evocative, pre-literate sound prior to being attached to semantic meanings. The implicit de-naturalised language, as part of the wholesale disavowal of mimetic realism of nineteenth century romantic drama, played into the interwar French neoclassical zeitgeist. Cocteau's and Stravinsky's theatre were both interested in the denotative/phonetic, as opposed to connotative/semantic, impact of words.

In Stravinsky's *Oedipus Rex,* a narrator stands outside the drama yet through his demeanour and dress he is configured between urbanity and antiquity. He speaks both like a compere and also like a tragic messenger. But in the trade-off between appearing and sounding both significant and insignificant, Stravinsky recommended that the narrator introduce each section of the drama in a "passive voice". In the theatre of Cocteau, the naturalistic connection of character and speech is self-consciously dismantled when Cocteau creates de-humanised narrators and choruses who speak a language that is simple and stripped of any representation or melodramatic temperament. An interplay of illusion and reality through

---

[5] Music's simultaneous effect on both seeing and hearing was expressed by one of Germany's leading nineteenth century court poets, Ludwig Tieck: "Und dennoch schwimmen in den Tönen oft so individuell anschauliche Bilder, so dass uns diese Kunst, möchte ich sagen, durch Auge und Ohr zu gleicher Zeit gefangen nimmt" (cit. in Atkinson 1947, 168). [And still in the notes often float individually vivid images, so that this art (form), I would like to say, captivates us via our eyes and ears.]

the juxtaposition of colloquial language and the disembodied voice was pursued as part of Cocteau's self-styled, neo-classical aesthetic of *nouveau simplicité* and *style dépouillé* (Messing 1996, 153). For instance, the life-like figure of the narrator was absented in Cocteau's *The Infernal Machine* (1932-33), and in its place was a disembodied but amplified human voice in a lifeless, Anubis-like figure. In his reworking of *Antigone* (1922), and throughout its re-stagings, the treatment of the chorus evidenced a self-conscious separation of character and voice. This manner of staging problematised what the audience was supposed to hear in the text and also see in the action of the drama.

The synthetic process of hearing, seeing and knowing in an art form of ancient Greek drama evolved into hierarchical formulations in the post-classical world. Speech and text, as the privileged elements of theatre, was problematised in early modernist theatre. In the postmodern non-linear writing, the voice of the narrator goes in search of new functions.

Voice and narration: the postmodern and postdramatic reflections

Musicality and narrative voice are concerns in postmodern drama. Andrew Gibson is unequivocal about the 'musicality' implicit in the materiality of voice: "to deal with the voice *per se* in drama would be to deal with [...] material questions of timbre, cadence, emphasis, and vocal nuance" (Gibson 2001, 711-12). Brian Richardson, critiquing the place of narrative theory in the staging of postmodern writing, suggests that mental states and narrations have been neglected in his survey of the field (Richardson 2001, 691). Richardson suggests three types of narrator in postmodern drama. One type exists in memory plays, such as Tennessee Williams' *Glass Menagerie* (1944), in which a main character in the play also identifies himself as "the narrator" of the drama. Another type of narrator is a "generative" narrator who narrates diegetically; that is, directing events or meanings during the action of the play. The generative narrator grew out of Brecht's epic-style plays, and also from Beckett's later plays in which, as Richardson states, "dramatic narrators and monologists create the world around them as they name it" (Richardson 2001, 683). The third of the narrator-type plays is represented by an off-stage style narrative voice. Its sonic world is that of the disembodied voice that propels the actions forward, or comments on proceedings. The Anubis figure in Cocteau's *The Infernal Machine* suggests the narrative tone of this type of play. According to Richardson, the interlocking monologues in

Pinter's radio play, *Family Voices* (1980) suggests that this is another example of the spatially dislocated narrator.

Reflecting on these three examples, the speaker in *The Cows* would seem to be situated in between the style of narration described as the generative and also the disembodied; that is, between the presented, literal voice of Beckett's narrator, and also the absented, incorporeal voice of Cocteau's commentator. By culling text materials from *Malone Dies*, the narrator in the performance of *The Cows* encounters, additionally, another voice, which is the narrator's voice in Beckett's novel. The literary fictional voice impresses itself upon the performance-based narrator and creates another layer of complexity in the delivery of text. Given that the narrator's voice is embodied in this twinned setting of narrative personalities, and that there is a reduction in the role of the text as a narrative device, it is incumbent upon the speaker that the text is "treated very carefully to manoeuvre it into position" (Barnett 2008, 22).

There is another way to understand the problems encountered in a multi-voiced narrator, which enacts text as a sound rather than as semantics. The intellectual provenance by which "words are treated purely as sounds rather than as sign-vehicles" (Allen 2000, 65), has entered postmodern discourse through Derrida's neologism of *différance*, in which words contain an infinite regression of meanings from their functional source.[6] If we revisit the example of spoken text from *The Cows* (which was analysed earlier)—"let me say before I go any further that I forgive nobody"—there is anarchy implicit in the infinite variety of qualitative (musical) parameters for saying it. Nevertheless, this anarchy, according to Barnett, is necessarily met by a "raft of performance rigours" that coincides with simultaneous modes of representation and of liveness (2008, 22). Understood from Derrida's notion of *différance*, the speaker in *The Cows* necessarily encounters the "difference" among conceptual locations found in the world of Beckett, a Midwestern Farmer, and ancient Oedipus. At the same time, the speaker's utterances exist in a "deferred" state, and reject any of the three worlds. The coexistence of these opposing processes is articulated in postdramatic theory.

Within postdramatic discourse, the notion of musicalisation flags up the problem of meaning and coherence, for performer and spectator alike, in the interstices of aural and visual actions. Lehmann, has commented on the dichotomy of narrative voice and musicality within a sensorium where logical correlations between seeing and hearing are subverted. In such an

---

[6] For further reading on intertextuality and narrative voice in dance theatre see Janet Lansdale. 2004. Ancestral and Authorial Voices in Lloyd Newson and DV8's *Strange Fish. NTQ* 20.2: 117-26.

environment, the spectator and the performer alike experience "condensations and multiplications of possible meanings" (Lehmann 2006, 91-3). Perceiver and perceived are highly sensitised to sources of meanings so that, according to Lehmann, when a "'human' moment flares up, the whole subject is momentarily found when the [spectator's] gaze has located the voice and returns it to the body" (2006, 150). Lehmann suggests that actors who speak text in performance in a postdramatic field are operating within the principle of ontological "polyglossia". This means that the performer's and the spectator's reception of the voice's narrative powers is hyper-realised (Lehmann 2006, 147). The danger inherent in the act of speaking is that, in a dramatically incoherent or indeterminate space, the embedded "ethnic" and "cultural peculiarities" in the actor's voice—its melodies, cadences, and accents—are also magnified (Lehmann 2006, 91). The tension the performer experiences is the pressing need to speak in a decipherable and coherent manner without signifying the voice with character or intention. The principle working in postdramatic space is that the more abstract the visual and aural images, the more indeterminate their ontological sources in the performance event, the greater the onus is felt by the performer to convey meaning.

How does musicalisation, then, represent a process that allows the dialectic of speech and music to collapse in performance? Is musicalisation a process by which an actor can abstract the musical structures and soundings from text? When a de-literate text acquires *melos* (in the Aristotelian sense of finding a proper way to the poetry), does a process of musicalisation help to negotiate the unison of subjective and objective utterance of text? This unfixed counteraction between conventional forms and postmodern fluidity can be found in current re-thinking of music. For instance, the musicologist Philip Bohlman makes the point that music is conventionally defined metaphysically as an "object". Melody can be analysed in terms of its structure and function in relation to rhythm and harmony. On the other hand, melody can also exist due to its adumbration. A melody is predicated upon the analysis of attending formal structures, and can also be conspicuous by its absence (Bohlman 1999, 17 and 19). While performing the text in *The Cows*, my voice became materially identified as part of the performer who 'presents' his sound in the space and of the actor-narrator who conveys a representative sound. In a postdramatic performance space, the sonic act of speaking and of being mutually and dynamically present and absent exclude each other. The difficulty I experienced in generating the sound world of the protagonist-narrator was in shading a character-ful sound into unison with a non-specific sound.

From an ontological perspective of the postdramatic performer, *who* speaks also longs for the musical language of *how* to speak. In a sense, to play it by ear is to re-imagine speech situated in the continuum between a theatre noise and a concert song.

References

Allen, Graham. 2000. *Intertextuality.* London: Routledge.

Aristotle. 1987. *Poetics* (tr. S. Halliwell). London: Duckworth.

Atkinson, Margaret E. 1947, *The Relation of Music and Poetry as Reflected in the Works of Tieck, Wackenroder and Brentano*, MA thesis (University of London).

Barnett, David. 2008. When is a play not a drama? Two Examples of Postdramatic Theatre Texts. *New Theatre Quarterly* 24.1: 14-23.

Bohlman, Philip. 1999. Ontologies of Music, *Rethinking Music,* ed N. Cook and M. Everist, 17-34, Oxford: Oxford University Press.

Dunbar, Zachary. 2006. *Science, Music and Theatre: An Interdisciplinary Approach to the Singing Chorus of Greek Tragedy*, unpublished PhD thesis (University of London).

Gibson, Andrew. 2001. Commentary: Silence of the Voice. *New Literary History* vol. 32: 711-13.

Lehmann, Hans-Thies. 2006. *Postdramatic Theatre* (tr. K. Jürs-Munby). London: Routledge.

Messing, Scott. 1996. *Neoclassicism in Music: From the Genesis of the Concept through the Schoenberg/Stravinsky Polemic.* Rochester, New York: University of Rochester Press.

Richardson, Brian. 2001. Voice and Narration in Postmodern Drama. *New Literary History*, vol. 32, 681-94.

Roesner, David. 2008. The Politics of the Polyphony of Performance: Musicalization in Contemporary German Theatre. *Contemporary Theatre Review* 18.1: 44-55.

Ryngaert, Jean-Pierre. 2007a. Writing *on* the stage / writing *for* the stage, Research Seminar, Scarborough University, (7th Feb).

—. (2007b), Speech in Tatters: The Interplay of Voices in Recent Dramatic Writing. *Yale French Studies* 112: 14-28.

Schlegel, Friedrich. 1991. *Philosophical Fragments* (tr. P. Firchow). Minneapolis: University of Minnesota Press.

Sifakis, Gregory. M. 2001. The Function and Significance of Music in Tragedy. *BICS* 45: 21-35.

Stravinsky, Igor. 1948. *Oedipus Rex.* London: Boosey & Hawkes.

CHAPTER XV

APPLIED AURALITY:
NOISE AND THE AESTHETICS OF ACCESS
IN GRAEAE'S *REASONS TO BE CHEERFUL*

LYNNE KENDRICK

The Deaf and deafness are familiar tropes in sound and noise theories. From Paul Hegarty's example of the silent "noise [...] of deaf people using sign language" (2010, 4), to Don Ihde's more exiled deaf person who, unlike the "ordinary listener [...] hears from *only* the fringe" (2003, 66), the deaf appear as a measure by which to demarcate the accepted fields of sound and hearing for an auditory—or perhaps 'audist'[1]—culture. Though such references are not necessarily ill-meant, the presence of the 'non-hearing' is, more often than not, as an 'other' in theories of sound, signal and reception of sonic material. Jonathan Sterne captures the problem as one which is culturally embedded in the history of sound and reproduction technologies in which, "*deafness* often appears as a metaphor for the refusal of intersubjectivity" (2006, 346). Moreover, as Sterne has effectively argued, the archaeology of sound technologies reveals a troubled history with deafness, for instance a preference for the auricular produced telephonic inventions modelled on the receptivity of the ear—the "tympanic" (Sterne 2006, 22)—and at the extreme, these became instruments for the attempted eradication of deafness:[2]

> Western culture has fetishized and generalised certain aspects of deafness as a condition in its development of sound reproduction technologies, all

---

[1] The term 'audist' is used in the same sense as racist; the term here is cited from Davis (1995) in Bradford (2005, 87).

[2] Alexander Graham Bell, inventor of the telephone denied the existence of the deaf culture and "most often appears as a villain in cultural histories of the deaf since he is (correctly) seen as seeking to eradicate deaf culture altogether" (Sterne 2006, 40).

the while maintaining a strong stigma against deafness itself. Sound-reproduction technologies were connected with an ongoing project to make the deaf like the hearing. They wound up making the hearing more like the deaf (Sterne 2006, 347).

As co-editor of this book, I felt we couldn't produce a volume on 'theatre noise' without attention to the sound of performance by theatre makers who do not conform to normative concepts of hearing: deaf artists who make theatre, as a culturally defined group as well as with/for the 'hearing audience'. Thus, this chapter focuses on a form of applied theatre:[3] disabled performance, and will review—or more aptly, rehear—both the art of creating and the act of audience to this form of theatre. The case study of this chapter is Graeae, the UK's foremost disabled theatre company.[4] My focus is on its creative practice that includes sensory and physically disabled artists and in addition embraces integration with non-disabled performers and audiences. This chapter pays attention to the aural strategies and acts of sounding by the deaf artists involved; in the case of *Reasons to be Cheerful* both director, Jenny Sealey and lead actor, Stephen Collins. This is not an analysis of Theatre for the Deaf, nor an attempt to theorise the culture of the non-hearing, but is a series of reflections on the applied aurality[5] of theatre making by these deaf artists that, in turn, offer a reconsideration of the theories of sound and noise in relation to performance. Rather than a 'refusal of intersubjectivity', I argue that the act of sounding by the Deaf is an act of emerging subjectivity which, when considered in relation to theories of noise, is more than readily available to be heard.

---

[3] Applied Theatre encompasses drama, theatre and performance principally made for, by or with specific participant and community groups. Key forms include Disabled Performance, Theatre for Development, Theatre for Young People (including DIE and TIE) Reminiscence Theatre, Theatre of Witness and Verbatim Theatre and embraces the broader categories of Radical Theatre and Community Performance.

[4] For this reason I consider Graeae's work as situated well within the territories of disabled performance, though this has been contested by those who consider this form of applied theatre as only applicable to work made solely by and for the disabled.

[5] I use the term applied aurality to specify the company's approach, which is to apply models of practice in order to create work with those artists for whom ordinary production processes deny access. For instance, a deaf actor ordinarily learns the lines and actions of all other personae present onstage; Graeae eschew such approaches as hegemonic practices.

Applied theatre and ocularcentric analysis

Applied theatre practice is primarily concerned with effect and aims for transformation, "to effect changes in world outside the theatrical discourse" (Prentki and Preston 2009, 10). A key concern is that applied theatre practice is merely transportative, with communities and participant groups returned to the hegemonies that designate them as such after the brief sojourn of the theatrical experience. One of the reasons for this is that applied theatre theory is ocularcentric, concerned with the visual emergence of identity and representation and, as a consequence, preoccupied with visibility. Despite the fact that applied practices take issue with the form and material relations of theatre (models and ethics of practice, border crossings, participatory and interventionist forms etc.) and, in particular, attends to the aurality and vocality of the marginal and the other (such as 'speaking' on behalf of, or making 'voices heard'), the results of these analyses are, more often than not, measured in terms of their appearance. For instance, Petra Kuppers' (2003) account of the efficacy of disabled performance describes this as a "sliver of difference" (2003, 6) which is but "momentarily visible" (2003, 6), a brief but significant dent in the visual stage. However, in terms of disabled performance an emphasis on the ocular presents a particularly troubled past. The disabled are both invisible, culturally, historically and socially and yet highly visible in their perceived 'difference'. As such a history of disabled performance is marked by the production and consumption of the disabled body for scopophilic pleasure—the spectacle of the freak show, the theatre of the public surgical demonstration—as Colette Conroy (2008) has termed, acts of "enfreakment [...] making the subject perform as an unusual object" (2008, 342).

The problem is that the act of looking, the *spectatorial* analysis, is not that far removed from the objectifying stare.[6] Even the politically expedient Brechtian analyses, phenomenological readings, and the layers of performativity function as 'lenses' and cannot escape the emphasis on the visible: the appearance of the body. Even if that appearance is one that is deemed discursive or disruptive, witnessed or encountered rather than 'seen', this still bears a relation to the dominant ocular discourses that objectify disability as the negative other in the first place. Though

---

[6] Rosemarie Garland Thomson (2005) identifies 'staring' as an act which "starkly registers the perception of strangeness and endows it with meaning" (2005, 31) and as such just as "the male gaze produces female subjects; the normative stare constructs the disabled" (2005, 32).

temporarily disrupted by the act of performance, the binary oppositions arguably remain intact.

But what happens if we shift emphasis from the gazer to the performer? From the spectator to the sounding body? From the receiver to the maker? What about silence as an act of withholding? What about the act of sounding, or the vessel of sound? In the field of applied theatre there is a dearth of analysis from the perspective of the aural, the sonic—particularly noise. This is curious considering the fact that some significant disabled performance innovations are at the forefront of sonic technological development.[7] Though some theorists of disability performance studies have hinted at an interest in noise. Kuppers, for instance, in her discursive deconstruction of the 'signs' of disabled performance declares that:

> My approach focuses on the value [...] of using silence within political representations. But the silence that I want to look for is not the silence of non-representation, the non-visible, but the glaring blank and empty noise of the present invisible. The invisible refuses the pat play of the signifier and signified, and hints at that which is outside speech but not outside culture (Kuppers 2003, 25).

Kuppers uses the term 'noise' to infer not only that which resists but *exists* in distinction (not annihilation) to received meaning and, furthermore, is empirically understood and culturally owned by the 'present invisible' —the disabled performer. Can noise analysis shift emphasis from the disabled performer as silenced to the performer as sounding—or in the case of this chapter, *noise-making*—a form of sonic agency? I will demonstrate how sonic agency is possible by means of the varied theories of noise (Voegelin and Serres) and sonority (Nancy), which might allow us to encounter the 'otherness' of disabled performance as *not* consigned to the cusp of appearance but as *arrived*, as Nancy's embodied sonority and Voegelin's articulated noise suggest, and as *present*, as Serres' noise always is.

Aesthetics of access, aural strategies and noise

Reasons to be Cheerful is a musical—or according to Sealey, "a Graeae musical" to be more precise. It's also a "memorial gig" (Sealey

---

[7] For example see Extant Theatre Company's sonic experiments with soundscape design (by Braunarts) and hand-held haptic devices that trigger scripted soundtracks www.extant.org.uk/projects/the_question (accessed April 4, 2011).

2010),[8] organisationally as well as narratively, as it is the company's tribute to its former patron, Ian Dury.[9] And it is noisy. Literally noisy because the entire live score is composed of the discography of Ian Dury and the Blockheads, including late 1970s punk anthems *Hit Me With Your Rhythm Stick, Clever Trevor, Plaistow Patricia* and *Spasticus Autisticus*. The tribute band, who are onstage throughout the production, include radical disabled artists Mat Fraser (resurrecting his former career as a drummer) and cabaret singer John Kelly. The memorial gig is also a dramatic device, set in 1979 the narrative centres on this event organised in an East End pub by Vinnie (Stephen Lloyd) in order to commemorate his father's (Bobby played by Garry Robson) death. Throughout the gig characters replay the series of events leading towards this, framed by Vinnie, his best mate Colin (Stephen Collins) and (potential) girlfriend Janine's (Nadia Albina) attempts to procure tickets to see a gig by Ian Dury from the malevolent boss of a supermarket where they reluctantly earn a living. This classic musical, play-within-a-play, structure is one means by which Graeae's 'aesthetics of access' are incorporated, through a meticulously directed set of *aural strategies*.

In terms of access, the aural strategies at first appear purposefully aesthetically explicit. For blind audiences the audio-description is threaded into the narrative, delivered entirely as a durational call on the pub's payphone, with the describer also functioning as a character within the frame of the gig. Audio-description is also textually embedded within the movement between the memorial gig and the play-within-the-play. Vinnie as the master of ceremonies articulates the imaginary scenes as they unfold, "Mum's in our sitting room giving Dad a shave. Our sitting room: Brown leather three-piece suite just here. Tele in the corner. Window here. Woodchip wallpaper" (Sirett 2010, 7). Though the audio description is not only functional: at the denouement of the play Bobby, a wheelchair user and blind due to terminal illness, requests the visual world is described not in actual but in fantastical ways:

> Bobby: I love the smell of the sea. Turn me around. Turn me to face the sea. What colour is it? What colour's the sea? Describe it to me.
> Vinnie: Sort of ... brown.
> Bobby: Brown? The sea is blue.
> Janine: No it's not –

---

[8] All quotations by Jenny Sealey are from an interview with the author March 8, 2010 (available from http://cssd.ac.uk/content/dr-lynne-kendrick).
[9] Ian Dury, who died in 2000 was, according to Sealey "a really important role model for disabled people."

Bobby: Yes it is. If I say the sea is blue, the sea is blue. Where's the bloody romance? Now describe it for me. Paint a picture. And make it beautiful. (Sirett 2010, 58).

Consequently, Vinnie and Janine describe a (not very) typical English seaside, one which is visibly present for no-one other than in the theatrical imagination. Thus the act of audio description becomes a dramaturgical device, a means of access but also dramatic expression: narratively and theatrically. Equally, visual-interpretation is incorporated into both layers of the production. Sealey was keen to "give deaf audiences a multitude of platforms to access the play [...] because you cannot watch a signer for hours and hours." These platforms included projected text, films and a performing interpreter. Not in every theatre production can you witness the sign-interpreter beat the audio-describer over the backside with a pool cue—but considering the presence of a pool table and plenty of alcohol consumed, narratively it was that time of the 'evening' when someone usually performs a lewd act with the instruments of the game—and the act performed to *Hit Me With Your Rhythm Stick* encapsulated the company's anarchic punk approach to the whole production. This is most explicit in the company's unashamed, overt performance of disability. It is Janine, who refers to herself as "a raspberry"[10] (Sirett 2010, 69), who introduces the anthem of the production with the declaration "I'm Spasticus!" (Sirett 2010, 69)[11] There's the sense that these aesthetics of access are also a critique of the banality of accessibility usually offered in theatre production (ordinarily, in the case of sign interpretation, adjacent to, and isolated from, the visual frame of theatre) but these are also bold, anarchic gestures about access, and a sort of 'two-fingers-up' to a culture of theatre production which deems access as concessionary and disabled performance a rarity.

The aesthetics of access also disrupt the aesthetic of the musical form, but not because it is performed by a disabled theatre company but because of the sonic presence of a diverse community of disabled performers actively performing their distinctive approaches to generating sound. Such a mix of disabled subjectivities, it is argued in postmodern pluralistic fashion, would be more effective if grouped according to their cultural specificity. The argument against integrative practices is made chiefly for

---

[10] 'Raspberry ripple' is Cockney rhyming slang for 'cripple.'
[11] The radicality of disabled artists performing Dury's anthem to the disabled, *Spasticus Autisticus*, was the significant "keynote" (to borrow R. Murray Schafer's phrase) of the production. Sealey described the rendition by "the four physically impaired performers" as a "seminal moment."

fear of the potential dilution of subjectivity, particularly when integration includes the non-disabled. However, analysed from the alterity of sound theory, such gatherings of difference are far from reductive, as arguably these are acts that bring noise in. In the integrative aesthetic of *Reasons to be Cheerful* the performers are able to enact discourse across divisions, engaging in that which Salomé Voegelin (2010) suggests is a transaction of "noisy voices" (2010, 71).

Figure 15-1: Performing *Spasticus Autisticus,* left to right: Nadia Albina and John Kelly. Photograph by Patrick Baldwin.

Voegelin's philosophy of sound art rejects the dominant ocularity of modernity but she also offers noise as a critique of postmodernity because, while in a postmodern culture "more and different voices have been allowed to speak [...] they have not necessarily always been heard" (2010, 71). Voegelin's noise, in common with noise theory *per se*, has nothing to do with language and received meaning; it is the un-heard voice, one which cannot 'speak' within dominant, hegemonic discourses, but when it does (in radical forms of performance) it emerges as other, as 'noisy' and when asserted it engages with "a sonic particularity" (Voegelin 2010, 52) that arrests the listener and cannot be ignored. This 'particularity', is unique to noise, it is a specific form of sound that doesn't just demand the hearer listens but grabs hold of the receiver in the moment, because "it deafens my ears to anything but itself" (Voegelin 2010, 44). This version of noise becomes particular not because of its deafening quality (i.e. being louder than any other present signal) but because it draws attention to and disrupts the primacy of its sounding context. The result of this is a "contingent subjectivity" (Voegelin 2010 51) between performer and audience, because without recourse to received ideas about the sounding context, the audience is reliant upon the performer's performance in order to engage in the meaning of the production. The audience is amidst listening and thus immersed in what the performance critiques, while simultaneously the performer's subjectivity is asserted by means of being heard. This contingent subjectivity hinges upon the 'noise' of the performance as this not only demands we listen but in doing so throws the meaning of the sounding context into question.[12]

Graeae's production positions the performer in this contingent subjectivity, by ensuring that the performer's self is *cited*.[13] Stephen Collins' character 'Colin' is deaf, a directorial decision that, according to Sealey, gave the performer "the freedom to be deaf." 'Colin's' deafness is Stephen Collins' deafness. Colin, like Collins, is also in a band, and has a zealous love of music which punctuates the narrative with repeated plays of the 'lyrics game'[14]. The 'particularity' is that the audience sees—or hears—the act of sound by a deaf person, theatrically and actually. Stephen Collins' subjectivity is cited and asserted; it is unavoidable, and the act of audience is contingent upon this. Furthermore, this act blatantly critiques the sounding culture that others the Deaf. In this sense, a

---

[12] For instance Voegelin cites Charlemagne Palestine's piano performance—"an assault in sound"—as one which "referenc[es] as well as negat[es] any piano concert ever seen […] it is a theatrical noise that destroys the rationality of the piano and its role in the concert hall" (Voegelin 2010, 50).

[13] As Kuppers asserts, the citing of the self is integral to the dialogic relation between audience and disabled performer. It distinguishes between the act of performance as 'beneficial' to one which is interventionist. "On the one side, disabled performance is seen as therapeutic–the relationship between body and performance is unproblematic, performance is an 'opportunity' for disabled people to discover themselves as 'whole' and 'able' […]. On the other side, disabled performance can be seen *as* performance: challenging dominant notions about 'suitable bodies', challenging ideas about the hierarchy between (led) disabled people and (leading) non-disabled people. Here, disabled performance can be seen as political intervention, aimed at the whole community. A split can be created between the performer and the performance, body and representation: the 'truth' of the bodily expression is manipulated, cited and rewritten by the performer" (Kuppers 2003, 56).

[14] The lyrics game is a test of music knowledge, one player blurts out the line of a song, other players must respond immediately with the subsequent line to win the game.

'contingent subjectivity' is not just about the all-encompassing experience of noise but identifies how the aesthetics of access of the production demand we listen to music theatre made by those ordinarily denied access to it. This noise of the aesthetics of access demonstrates the potential intersubjectivity between audience and performer, reversing the assumption that deafness is a refusal of this, as Sterne demonstrated. We cannot ignore the subjectivities present, not because they are visually explicit but, by means of the 'noisy voice', we are brought into the disabled artists' discourse. However, Voegelin's theory of noise is one which focuses almost entirely on the experience of the listener. In *Reasons to be Cheerful*, noise is not just an effect of such aesthetics of access; noise also exists in the creation of the work.

Noise and the aural placing of sound

Sealey's approach to directing sound in theatre is multifarious. It is essential that she works with musical directors who understand, first and foremost, that her initial encounter with music is ocular—but this is merely the superficial route into the process of directing a musical, utilising the score as a "visual musical map" (Sealey 2010). Sealey works to "isolate the specific sounds" (Sealey 2010) and to read these as integral aspects of the *mise en scène* as it emerges. There is no clear-cut distinction between the musical director and the director's roles—the assumption might be that the musical director is solely responsible for the sonic aspects of the production and Sealey for the visible. Sealey directs the sonic aspects of the musical by treating these as *material*. At first this appears a pragmatic choice, for example situating the band centre stage and ensuring that all cueing is visually initiated. But this material approach is a strategy for ensuring that the music is materially embodied between the actors, the sound source, the space and the receivable adumbrations of sound. As a directorial act, this treatment of sound as simultaneously corporeal, spatial and scenographic is highly complex. For instance, when directing Stephen Collins, Sealey placed an emphasis on rigorous vocal training, the collaborative support between the ensemble, intensive research into the quality or "grain" (Barthes 1977, 185) of vocal sounds (particularly Dury's), and Collins' physical relation in the theatrical space in order to effectively perform his acts of sound. All this Sealey describes as a process that allows the deaf actor to "interpret the sounds that deaf people will have"[15] (Sealey 2010). These meticulous negotiations are all directorial aural strategies. This score of visual, material and embodied sound, becomes a template for what Sealey describes as the "aural placing of sound" (Sealey 2010).

The directorial aural strategies, as outlined above, become part of the fabric, the material of the production, the very means by which the sound is created. Thus these aural strategies are sonically generative and as such render the act of 'aural placing' something of an *event*, a *becoming* of sound. And this is because the deaf actor is also positioned within this aural place, his body is a part of the material, he is *of* that space. Aural, in this sense, can be understood not simply and etymologically in terms of the ear, or "specifically to the middle ear, the inner ear, and the nerves that turn vibrations into what the brain perceives as sound" (Sterne 2006, 11) but as "referring to the phenomenological and discursive field of sound" (Dyson 2009, 6). The aural strategies, including complex aesthetics of access and the sonic particularity of 'different' voices, and the aural placing of sound, including the production of sound by precise material means, produce sound that is more like a discursive event. Because it is *not* solely created from the vantage point of auricular reception but from the point of view of how sound might be created without hearing and what, politically, might be heard. And this is how Graeae are, in essence, 'noisily voiced' in Voegelin's terms, because their aesthetics of access are created from the vantage point of subject specificity, of all disabilities not just the deaf, and as a consequence the sound generated is embedded in the discursive, the meeting of differences that Voegelin suggests is the essence of the 'noisy voice'.

The aural placing of sound also has a specific relation to noise. Sealey refers to that which she does hear as 'noise'. But this is not a meaningless cacophony that diverts her engagement in the aural environment; in fact it is the opposite, as she points out, "that we can hear 'noise' is really important because it does allow you to have a relationship with music" (Sealey 2010). Noise is Sealey's route into music, the point at which the sounds she possesses come into relation with the aural environment. Immersed in the aural placing of sound, noise becomes readable and "interpretive", not in itself but in terms of what its material offers the deaf artist. Such a functionality of noise raises questions as to why it is

---

[15] Sealey's point is that few deaf people hear no sound at all, a form of silence, and that most deaf people receive some frequencies of varying interpretability. It is not insignificant that she describes these sounds as possessed rather than received, this indicates that the act of sound for the deaf actor is a generative act (which I will return to later).

frequently deemed pejorative,[16] firmly and confidently placed as a
negative in binary opposition to sound, and the purity of musical signal,
whatever the cultural, economic and/or ideological reasons therefore.
Sealey's more pragmatic experience of noise aligns with Serres' argument
that this should *not* be considered a negative because of its intrinsic
relation to—or in Sealey's case a channel towards—meaning. This suggests
that noise, in the production of theatre, is far from reductive, excessive,
wasteful or just plain unwanted, and the term 'noise' is something to be
reclaimed: "[...] we will have to retain the word *noise*, the sole positive
word for describing a state we otherwise can only designate in negative
terms" (Serres 1995, 20).

Breath and vocality

In the creation and reception of Graeae's theatre, noise has
productivity, which in turn demonstrates the potential of this performance
practice in reconsidering and repositioning some of the axiologies of
theory. An example of this is the productivity of breath in the production
of voice within the aural placing of sound. In order for the deaf actor to
rehearse sound, Sealey places great emphasis on breath. "With all deaf
actors, and myself included, we forget to breathe. A lot of actors forget to
breathe, but deaf actors in particular because we can't hear our voices"
(Sealey 2010). A rigorous process of vocal training focuses on "that
education of how sounds are made," and "taking that breath right down to
the belly" (Sealey 2010). While there is an emphasis on articulation, the
deaf actor's voice is encultured in the body. For instance the sound Collins
makes begins in his body; it is not received and regurgitated, it is made
within, it is generated. This is not just a procedural necessity but also a
crucial act that demarcates the disabled artist's particular cultural
subjectivity. Douglas Khan (1999) captures this cultural specificity as a
matter of the body playing host to the voice in differing ways, the voice a
sort of signifying guest that "inhabits bodies differently" (1999, 290).

This generative vocality is one example of how disability performance
can challenge theory, in this case the production of the signifying voice.
For instance, Collins' embodied vocality would disappoint Barthes' thesis
of the grain of the voice as its signifying presence, and refute his denigration

---

[16] For instance Hegarty raises the common assumption that, "Noise is negative: it
is unwanted, other, not something ordered. It is negatively defined [...] but it is
also a negativity" (2010, 5) and Dyson explores this existence of negativity in
relation to philosophical discourse in which "it does not make sense to talk of
meaningful noise" (Dyson 2009, 89).

of "the myth respiration" (1977, 183), in particular his dismissal of the lung, "a stupid organ" (1977, 183). For the deaf actor, the grain can be imagined and performed but it carries no significance other than its significances to his other, the hearing audience. The deaf actor's embodied sound is generated in the lung, expressed through breath and shaped into significance by the uttering organs of the larynx and mouth. This is in part because the embodied sound is a *performance*, not a performance *of* (just as Barthes' vocalists are in service to the musical score). But it is also because the deaf actor is amidst noise—the noise of what they do hear, the sounds they possess, the sonic material of the production and the dramaturgical aesthetics of access—breath is key to how their bodies are positioned within the aural placing of sound. Significantly, Sealey describes this aural strategy as an act of teaching "their bodies to be resonators" (Sealey 2010).

Resounding and emergent subjectivity

It may seem churlish at this stage to introduce a theory that relates to the act of hearing, but Jean-Luc Nancy's theory of listening is more a treatise on sonority or *resounding* than one of auricularity. He demarcates between hearing, as an engagement in meaning, and listening as "something other than sense" (Nancy 2007, 32). Moreover, Nancy suggests that a state of active listening is not necessarily predicated on the act of sonic receptivity alone, on the primacy of hearing. Michelle Duffy (2010) offers a pertinent précis of the distinction between hearing as engaging in the exterior and listening as more aligned with interiority, with the self:

> Nancy defines *hearing* in terms of understanding and comprehension, while *listening* (the French term *écouter*) is an experience of sound in which we don't fully interpret the experience. Listening, then, is perhaps more aligned to our emotional and bodily responses than to our sonic environments (Duffy 2010, 43).

The body is at the centre of Nancy's listening process, which he attributes to the act of sounding which "resounds, that is, it re-emits itself while still actually "sounding," which is already "re-sounding" since that's nothing else but referring back to itself. To sound is to vibrate in itself or by itself" (Nancy 2007, 8). This process reconstructs the body as a sonic vessel, and suggests an act of sonic agency. Furthermore Nancy identifies the act of sonority is a matter of subjectivity in itself, without recourse to the sonic environment:

So the sonorous place, space and place—and taking-place—*as* sonority, is
not a place where the subject comes to make himself heard (like the
concert hall or the studio into which the singer or instrumentalist enters);
on the contrary, it is a place that becomes a subject insofar as sound
resounds there (Nancy 2007, 17).

The *resounding body* is a sonic subject and the act of resounding is the
act of encounter with self, a form of "being as resonance" (Nancy 2007,
21) by means of which the self comes into subjectivity. This theory of
subjectivity through resounding, not necessarily hearing, reveals how deaf
actors might perform their own subjective 'non-hearing' identity. Collins'
generative, embodied vocality can be seen as an act of resonance, an
emergence of self. Furthermore, in performing without recourse to
normative modes of auricularity, it is arguable that Graeae's deaf actors
and director are engaged in an act of sounding that is unshackled from the
hegemonic sounding context—they are free to sound without recourse to
received signal and dominant discourses. Thus, they are also free to
resound and to meet (as Nancy would have it) or perform their selves,
their emerging subjectivities. It is an act of other without the constraints of
being othered, a form of sonic agency. And this act is tantamount to noise,
in that while noise is the other of sound, of music, it also exists entirely in
distinction from these culturally defined signals. Furthermore noise is a
form of sound not only not subject to logos; but also forms the basis of it,
as Serres declares there is "no logos without noise [...]. Noise is the basic
element of the software of all our logic, or it is to logos what matter used
to be to form" (Serres 1995, 7). If noise is the basis of meaning, the
permanent form of sound from which the accepted, transient signal is
cleaved, then the deaf actor's resounded subjectivity is arguably as ever
present. I consider Stephen Collins' performance an act of noise. Not only
in its effect—received as an intersubjective 'noisy voice', grasping the
audience in an act of 'contingent subjectivity'—but as resounded as an
assertive act of subjectivity.

Conclusion

Critics at the forefront of disability studies have asserted that disability
has the potential to tackle and alter existing theory. I have suggested some
ways in which the aural strategies of Graeae's endeavours towards an
'aesthetics of access' call into question some of the axiologies of sound
and vocal theories: aurality as pertaining merely to the aural, Barthes'
denigration of the breathing body, and the designation of noise as
negative. Graeae's practice draws attention to an audio-aural litany (to

adapt Sterne's audio-visual version), the ease of the commingling of "mixed seeing and hearing" (Stein 1935, 99), and the assumption that sound in performance is predicated on hearing. Furthermore, the aural strategies critique the privileged assumptions of the ways in which we generate signal over and above noise in theatre practice. Graeae's artists resound, and they also *re-sound*, literally, by adapting technologies that render drums playable, lyrics readable etc. But ideologically they attack the culturally specific promulgation of signal that designates them as 'other', by a process of resounding that is radically severed from the received meanings and ideologies associated with normative receptive modes. Through noise, Graeae's 'aesthetics of access' can be considered a radical act not just of making themselves heard, but as already sonorously present, ready to be listened to.

References

Barthes, Roland. 1977. The Grain of the Voice. In *Image-Music-Text*, translated by Stephen Heath. New York: Hill and Wang.

Bradford, Shannon. 2005. The National Theatre of the Deaf. Artistic Freedom & Cultural Responsibility in the Use of American Sign Language. In *Bodies in Commotion. Disability and Performance,* edited by Carrie Sandahl and Philip Auslander. Michigan: University of Michigan Press, 2005

Conroy, Colette. 2008. Active Differences: Disability and Identity beyond Postmodernism. *Contemporary Theatre Review* Vol. 18 (3): 341-354.

Davis, Lennard J. 1995. *Enforcing Normalcy: Disability, Deafness, and the Body.* New York: Verso.

Duffy, Michelle. 2010. Sound Ecologies. *Cultural Studies Review* Vol. 16 (1): 43-59.

Dyson, Frances. 2009. *Sounding New Media: Immersion and Embodiment in the Arts and Culture.* Berkeley, Los Angeles and London: University of California Press.

Henderson, Bruce and Ostrander, R. Noam. 2010. *Understanding Disability Studies and Performance Studies.* London and New York: Routledge.

Ihde, Don. 2003. Auditory Imagination. In *The Auditory Culture Reader (Sensory Formations),* edited by Michael Bull and Les Back, 61-66. Oxford: Berg Publishers.

Garland Thomson, Rosemarie. 2005. Dares to Stares. Disabled Women Performance Artists & the Dynamics of Seeing. In *Bodies in*

Commotion. Disability and Performance, edited by Carrie Sandahl and Philip Auslander. Michigan: University of Michigan Press.

Hegarty, Paul. 2007. *Noise/Music: A History.* London: Continuum.

Kahn, Douglas. 1999. *Noise, Water, Meat. A History of Sound in the Arts.* Cambridge (MA) and London: The MIT Press.

Kuppers, Petra. 2003. *Disability and Contemporary Performance: Bodies on Edge.* New York and London: Routledge.

Nancy, Jean-Luc. 2007. *Listening,* translated by Charlotte Mandell. New York: Fordham University Press.

Schafer, Raymond Murray. 1977. *The Tuning of the World.* Toronto: McClelland & Stewart.

Sealey, Jenny. 2010. Interview with Lynne Kendrick on 8 March 2010. http://cssd.ac.uk/content/dr-lynne-kendrick.

Serres, Michel. 1995. *Genesis,* translated by Geneviève James and James Nielson. Michigan: University of Michigan Press.

Sirett, Paul. 2010. *Reasons to be Cheerful,* dir. Jenny Sealey. Graeae Theatre Company and Theatre Royal Stratford East.

Stein, Gertrude. 1935. *Lectures in America.* New York: Random House.

Sterne, Jonathan. 2003. *The Audible Past: Cultural Origins of Sound Reproduction.* Durham: Duke University Press.

Prentki, Tim and Preston, Sheila. 2009. *The Applied Theatre Reader.* London and New York: Routledge.

Voegelin, Salomé. 2010. *Listening to Noise and Silence. Towards a Philosophy of Sound Art.* New York, London: Continuum.

Online Resources

www.graeae.org
www.reasonstobecheerfulthemusical.co.uk

CHAPTER XVI

THE SOUND OF HEARING

MARIE-MADELEINE MERVANT-ROUX

The long oblivion of sound

The sense of vision has been dominating French theatre studies since they appeared in the 1970s: the specificity of theatre has been identified by many scholars with 'la *mise en scène*' [stage direction], this itself being perceived as a scenographic, *visual*—or audio-visual (i.e. an enriched form of visual)—phenomenon. According to this point of view, which remains undoubtedly dominant, theatre is a *teatron*, 'un lieu où l'on regarde', literally: a place where one watches. The word generally used in French to speak about theatre goers is 'spectateurs' ('spectators'), a term that privileges visual activity and presents the audience member as a 'viewer' rather than a 'listener'.[1] The clearest sign of this (mostly) implicit theoretical domination of the eye in theatre studies is the near complete oblivion of rich sound archives, which I would definitely distinguish from audiovisual archives. Researchers, theatre historians, specialists of stage production etc., hardly ever use audio recordings of performances, nor even remember that they are available and could be consulted.

Unintentionally, I myself have been driven to consider the theatre venue as a listening place. My first research examined the possible role that the spectator plays in theatre performance. By listening to a recording of a performance of the play I was studying, I discovered that if onlookers remain unseen—apart from exceptions or transgressions—, they are always audible: eyes are heard. The permanent undesigned *noises* of the audience (coughs, laughs, murmurs, movements, breath, and silences)

---

[1] The designation of the audience member as 'spectator' (the one that is watching) became common only in the middle of seventeenth-century. Before, the word 'auditeur' was used much more than 'spectateur'. In Corneille's *Discours*, we find 59 mentions of "auditeurs"/"auditoire" and only 26 "spectateur[s]". See Louvat-Molozay 2008, 26.

cannot always be clearly distinguished from what are usually called the *sounds* of the stage. The reason why they had always been strictly separated is a conception of the theatre place as a visual one, clearly divided into two parts: the zone of the viewed (the stage) and the zone of the viewers (the audience), without taking into account that theatre is also an acoustic place, where the notions of limit and frame do not have the same value.

Sounds/noises. An artificial partition of space

Stage sounds (voices, sound effects, aural scenography, soundtrack, sound design…) have been considered and studied, but as audio elements of a basically visual stage production. Audience noises have sometimes been evoked, but most of the time as anecdotal or 'magical'. In this respect, theoretical elaborations are few. According to semiotic approaches, audience noises are supposed to be 'responses' to the 'discourse' of the stage. But for a long time, semioticians have criticised their unsuitable linguistic model. According to psycho-physiological approaches, audience noises are supposed to express the biological life of the audience's body. This idea does not take into account that in theatre, to quote Peter Brook, the spectator is at the same time "there and not there"[2]. In both cases, audible elements have been located inside of *a clean divided space*.

An original soundscape

Between 1986 and 1994, I conducted a study on multiple performance runs of the same scenic productions. I placed my microphone in the heart of the audience. What emerged from this recording strategy was a very strange theatre space, totally different from the one which is generally described, designed, photographed and filmed: a space which was absolutely unified, which had no limits.

It incited me to resort to musician and researcher R. Murray Schafer's concept of "soundscape" (Schafer 1977), translated as "paysage sonore" in French[3]. I remembered some metaphors used by writers, critics or actors to describe spectators' subtle noisy movements as rumbles, rustles, swells,

---

[2] "It is hard to understand the true notion of spectator, there and not there, ignored and yet needed. The actor's work is never for an audience, yet always is for one. The onlooker is a partner who must be forgotten and still constantly kept in mind" (Brook 1968, 51).

[3] *Le Paysage sonore. Toute l'histoire de notre environnement sonore à travers les âges* (1979) trans. Sylvette Gleize. Paris: Lattès.

waves... as if the audience's reactions were a kind of meteorological dimension, colouring, illuminating and animating the play differently every evening. However, this image, too naturalist, is not satisfactory.

Past metaphors of audience noise

"A living resonator"

At the beginning of the twentieth century, some directors evoked audience activity through the image of a 'resonator'—Meyerhold described the spectator as 'a living resonator' (Meyerhold 1912, cit. in Picon-Vallin, 1990, 123)—referring to the device created in the 1850s by Hermann von Helmholtz: a spherical vessel made of metal or glass with an opening and an earpiece on opposite sides. Placed in the ear, it acts as an acoustic filter, allowing only sounds of a particular pitch to be heard:[4]

> The audience creates, so to speak, a psychological acoustic. It registers what we do and bounces its own living, human feelings back to us (Stanislavski 2008, 238).

> Sensing his own resonator [the spectator], the actor immediately reacts, by improvisation, to all the demands coming from the audience (Meyerhold 1912, quoted by Picon-Vallin, 1990, 123).

The two comparisons of the theatre with acoustic phenomena are rather different: Stanislavski evokes spectators' emotional movements expressed through audible signs; Meyerhold had in mind the most physical effects of actors' biomechanics on the members of audience (later, in 1925, his assistants would precisely note down and calculate different audible audience reactions: silences, noises, whistles, etc.)[5]. But most important here is the fact that the two directors chose the field of acoustics to explain their conception of the theatrical event.

---

[4] Studying the ear, Helmholtz formulated the resonance theory of hearing, in which certain organs of the inner ear were believed to function as tuned resonators. With the publication of *On the Sensation of Tone as a Physiological Basis for the Theory of Music* (1863), he further refuted the vitalists by demonstrating that the aesthetics of music was a function of the ear's mechanical ability to pick up wave motions of musical sounds.

[5] See Picon-Vallin 1990, 233.

"A vibrant instrument"[6]

The resonator metaphor corresponds to a period when the stage-audience relationship was assumed by actors and when theatre-goers were collectively active. Later, other great actors used a similar metaphor, describing the audience as a musical instrument. Less mechanical, this metaphor evokes an ideal audience that gives an artistic and beautifully audible resonance to stage players.

Now, the image of 'vibration' is still valid, but the new 'live resonators' no longer react directly to the actors' work. They react to sequences of scenic action and to anonymous elements of a performance:

> The actor doesn't directly impact the spectator—at least this is what I think. This is why when a strong reaction is manifested by the audience, it is impossible for the actor to directly combat it (Dréville 2008, 30).

An acoustic modulation of scenic production

In order to understand the importance of the audience, I studied a series of performances of the same production: observations of the performances (writing up notes shortly after leaving the theatre), sound recordings made inside the auditorium, a large number of interviews with spectators and an even larger number of questionnaires (hand-written, impromptu questionnaires distributed at the beginning of the show or handed out during the interval to volunteers, who were given two weeks to return them to me). The corpus of productions was deliberately restricted to those performed in 'traditional' theatres, strictly end-stage (such as the large auditorium at the Théâtre des Amandiers at Nanterre) or Italian style proscenium arch (such as the Théâtre de l'Athénée), with a seated, immobile and virtually silent audience. The productions themselves were —equally a deliberate choice— extremely varied in style as can be judged from the following examples: *Elvire-Jouvet 40* (Brigitte Jaques, Théâtre de l'Athénée, 1986), *The Play of Faust* (Théâtre du Radeau, several different venues, 1988-89), *Hamlet* (Patrice Chéreau, Avignon, Nanterre, MKHAT Moscow, the Great Hall at La Villette, 1988-89), *I Shall Never Return* (Tadeusz Kantor, Pompidou Centre, Théâtre de Chaillot, 1988-89), *Iphigenia in Aulis* (Théâtre du Soleil, 1990-91). The analyses I carried out

---

[6] "It [the old Old Vic] is warm, alive, and it has a tattered magnificence about it. […] It is able to transform a collection of human beings *into that curious vibrant instrument for the actor, an audience*" (John Gielgud quoted in Mackintosh 1993, 81, my emphasis).

on audio-recordings of these performances led me to the conclusion that the audience is always producing a permanent acoustical modulation of the scenic action, a true modulation of *acoustics*. What we may call "the sound of hearing" is working directly on the production and constitutes a structural character of theatre, which essentially differentiates it from cinema. As Jorge Semprun noted,

> a theatre piece is retransmitted on television with ambient audience noise included. This never occurs for the retransmission of a film on television, even if it does make a difference for the film spectator whether the movie theatre is packed or empty (1994).

I could distinguish three chief acoustic variations of the audience's audible, mostly nonverbal movements. These are: rhythmic variations; tonal variations (accordant and discordant) and variations of intensity (degrees of silence). The result is a transformation of the performance, which could become more precise, more comical, more intense... or could be impoverished, simplified, sometimes destroyed... Moscow's audiences (1989), for example, were affected very differently and did not underline the same scenes of Chéreau's *Hamlet* as French audiences (1988-89). Reasons were not linguistic, but cultural, historical, socio-political. If Hamlet (played by Gerard Desarthe) remained of central importance, other characters that most affected the audience were not the same. Secondary characters stole attention from the most important roles on the dramatic level (such as King Claudius, Queen Gertrude, Ophelia). The sequences arousing the most reaction, next to the Ghost on horseback, were those of Rosencrantz and Guildenstern and the arrival of the Players and of Osric. In this Elsinore, the Russian audience saw first and foremost a grotesque universe of masks and underlined the connection between Hamlet and the Players (see Mervant-Roux, 1998, 195-217).

This phenomenon remains largely unseen, unobserved; ordinary spectators don't notice it. I myself had to attend several occurrences of the same performance before becoming conscious of its efficiency, and I had to study a great number of recordings before discovering its different aspects: the audience actually modulates the performance. Each evening is absolutely unique. Finally, applause appears to be a kind of auditory self-portrait of the community of spectators, formed itself during the play (Mervant-Roux, 1998).

Present theatre: a listening place

Among the outstanding acoustic phenomena today in French theatre venues, the most noticeable is the importance of *silence*. Just a few years ago, Daniel Deshays deplored the state of theatre, which illustrated a notable lack of reflection on silence (2006, 95).

Theatre historians usually comment on the imposition of silence and immobility in theatre halls at the end of the nineteenth century as depriving the spectator of his freedom and making the theatre "bourgeois", as an effect of the "tyrannies of intimacy" (Sennett 1974). Spectator silence is still often attacked as a sign of passiveness, a kind of sleep. But in our very cacophonic and strident societies, silence has a new value (see the "Acoustic Manifesto", published in Linz a hundred years after the Futurist Manifesto).[7] Theatres transform themselves into places of stillness, into quiet asylums in the middle of cities, into places allowing and inviting people *to listen*.

Hearing stages

Some directors, who also frequently work in the visual and plastic arts, will prioritise listening. This is often done by working with musicians, or sound engineers: contemporary stages listen to the whole theatre space: characters—and actors—are 'soundboxes', their audible perception-attention is apparent. We see them listening with spectators to sonic elements of the performance (music, voices, noises), or listening to the spectators themselves (audience noise, audience silence).

In the theatre of Claude Régy, the whole stage with its scenic figures is attentively, completely, physically listening to what is happening. Régy refers to ancient monastery silence, which was not understood as an absence of noise. It was not a condition to achieve before reading, but a state obtained via the act of reading. Régy evokes a "cavity of subterranean silence found inside every person, for which the imagined immensity of the empty stage could be a representation ["cette cavité de silence souterraine chez les gens, dont l'immensité rêvée de la scène vide serait un figuratif"] (Régy 1991, 145). The large, bare, often slow and quiet stage (figure 16-1) is a kind of reflection of the spectators' mute interiority, inaudible silence.

---

[7] See http://www.hoerstadt.at/ueberuns/das_akustische_manifest/the_acoustic_ manifesto.html (accessed December 12, 2010)

This perfect stillness obtained by Régy works like an audio magnifying glass: it permits sharp and delicate nuances; it makes every word, every movement, strange and new. We can speak of an art of meditation.

Figure 16-1: *Quelqu'un va venir* [*Someone will come*], a play by Jon Fosse, created by Claude Régy. Scenography by Daniel Jeanneteau, Théâtre de Nanterre-Amandiers, 1999. Photograph by Michel Jacquelin.

In a very different way, no one can easily forget the intense collective silences created in Avignon in 2007 by Romeo Castellucci, his actors and his technicians, with the gifted collaboration of Scott Gibbons, a musician who has worked with him for the last ten years: in *Inferno*, inspired by Dante's text, an acrobat climbs with his bare hands the high, nocturnal façade of the Palais des papes; one after another, a child, adolescents, adults come to face the audience, a ball in their arms. Immobile, they tranquilly watch the audience; characters throw themselves backwards into a void; a crowd rolls on the stage like a wave. Each time the public becomes absolutely mute and motionless. But how can such perfect silences be created? Through alternating strong, loud, full acoustic sequences that awaken our sense of alertness with sequences of very soft noises. Or by a specific use of music to suggest an infinite and choral realm, a new cosmic, mythological "soundhouse", to quote Peter Sloterdijk (2002), a space leaving room for the spectators' silent chorus.

Listening eyes

The new use of the ear modifies seeing (as simple perception of scenic images) into watching (a view from afar). Silence contributes to an extension of time and space, to a broadening of the spectator's imagination. These modern pauses are "times to see", according to Frederic Maurin's formula about Robert Wilson's theatre ("a time to see, a space to listen", Maurin 1998). Attending *Inferno,* the spectators watch, during some very long minutes, a real piano on fire. The first image Romeo Castellucci experimented with was a burning microphone. This transformed into a burning, black grand piano. Here, music is simultaneously arising and dying before the audience, so alive and so beautiful—like a musical memory, remembered by both the stage and by the auditorium. About ten characters stay motionless near the piano and listen to the crackling of the fire, then to the same dawning music as the spectators of the performance ('Spiegel im Spiegel', Arvo Pärt). Hearing of hearing constitutes perhaps the true heart of our modern stage.

A "quasi spatial" sonosphere

How can we define contemporary theatrical space, taking into account these last and intense versions of theatre listening?

The most inspiring references are no longer metaphorical, but still theoretical. They appear in the field of sound studies and in recent scientific and philosophical attempts to describe and modelise sounding and listening spaces. The figure of stage as a listening double of audience, or the figure of audience as a listening double of stage, used today by certain actors, evokes Sloterdijk's *Spheres* peopled with acoustic "nobjets"—a word borrowed from Thomas Macho (see Sloterdijk 2002, 320, note 1)—, illustrating that sounds are not objects, that listening is not a face to face activity.

Because of their acuteness, the "thought experiments" elaborated by Roberto Casati and Jérôme Dokic, working in the field of Philosophy of Mind (see 1994), offer rich material for a new theory of theatre performance. Two cognitive postulations must be underlined: the fragility of the "sound image" concept (a sound's reproduction is not an image, but a re-production, i.e. another *true physical* sound event). Secondly, the fact that it is difficult to localise sound (see 1994, 96). This idea is illustrated by the fictional figure of the "Akustiker" (Heymans 1905, cit. by Casati and Dokic, 124-127), whose representation of the world would be based solely on auditory impressions. As they serve to describe acoustic phenomena as events and not as perceptual objects, both can help us find a relevant model for modern theatrical space and the mutual "tuning" of the performances by actors and by spectators.

References

Brook, Peter. 1968. *The Empty Space*. New York: Touchstone.

Bénédicte Louvat-Molozay. 2008. L'émergence de l'instance spectatrice. In *Le Spectateur de théâtre à l'âge classique (XVIIe-XVIIIe siècles)* ed. B. Louvat-Molozay and Franck Salaün, 23-27. Montpellier: L'Entretemps.

Casati, Roberto and Dokic, Jérôme. 1994. *La philosophie du son*. Nîmes: Jacqueline Chambon.

Deshays, Daniel. 2006. *Pour une écriture du son*. Paris: Klincksieck ("50 questions").

Dréville, Valérie. 2008. *Conversation pour le festival d'Avignon 2008*, Avignon : P. O. L / Festival d'Avignon.

Mackintosh, Iain. 1993. *Architecture, Actor and Audience*. London, New York: Routledge.

Maurin, Frédéric. 1998. *Robert Wilson. Le temps pour voir, l'espace pour écouter*, Arles: Actes Sud ("Le temps du théâtre").

Mervant-Roux, Marie-Madeleine. 1998. *L'Assise du théâtre. Pour une étude du spectateur*. Paris: CNRS Éditions.

Picon-Vallin, Béatrice. 1990. *Meyerhold*. Paris: CNRS Éditions.

Régy, Claude. 1991. *Espaces perdus*. Paris: Plon ("Carnets").

Schafer, R. Murray. 1997. *The Tuning of the World*. New York: Knopf.

Semprun, Jorge. "Enfin adulte". *Le Monde,* 9 December 1994.

Sennett, Richard. 1974. *The Fall of Public Man*. New York: W.W. Norton & Co. French translation: *Les tyrannies de l'intimité*. 1979, Seuil.

Sloterdijk, Peter. 2002 [1998]. *Sphères I. Bulles* trans. Olivier Mannoni Fayard, Paris: Hachette Littératures ("Pluriel").

Stanislavsky, Konstantin. 2008. *An Actor's Work: A Student's Diary* (1936) trans. Jean Benedetti. London: Routledge.

CHAPTER XVII

NOISE, CONCEPTUAL NOISE AND THE POTENTIAL OF AUDIENCE PARTICIPATION

GARETH WHITE

Figurative noise and actual noise

This chapter is a discussion of actual noise, and the sounds that are manipulated by theatre makers, but also a concept of noise as described by Jacques Attali, amongst others, as "the term for a signal that interferes with the reception of a message by a receiver, even if the interfering signal itself has a meaning for the receiver" (1985, 27). My strategy is to read audience behaviour, both its explicit participation in a performance and its ambient activity in the theatrical event, through the concept of noise, paying particular attention to the noise making and silences of audiences. My aim is to discuss how this may help to develop ideas of the value and purpose of participatory performance, which involves considering the politics of the differentiated roles in theatre events—that is the differences between the behaviour that is proper to audience members and performers —and what the alteration of these roles can mean.

In London theatre there has recently been a consistent undercurrent of experimentation with audience activity; not a movement, but a definite trend. I will use examples from work by two of the companies that have been leading this trend: Shunt and Punchdrunk, the latter of which characterises itself as "the UK's leading exponent of immersive theatre" (Machon 2009, xv). There are micro-politics to the imbalances in the audience-performer relationship of the conventional model of theatregoing: the performers retain authority over the action, while the spectators retain the right to stay out of the action, to watch and hear it. There are politics too, to the experimental audience formations and actor-audience relationships that are proving popular with performance makers and audiences alike, though it is not evident that the practitioners creating this work are consciously engaged with these politics, or whether they are particularly interested in their implications. To change such relationships is an act of surrender for both parties, where both give up some of the control that belongs to their place in the event. The social structure of the conventional theatre event is coded and exhibited through a domestication of noise-making, chiefly through the silence of the audience, and through their use of approved vocalisations and other bodily noises. The question I will consider is whether and where there are strategies at play in Shunt and Punchdrunk's performances which succeed in escaping or undoing this domestication.

Well-trained audiences

To begin with a picture of this tamed and disciplined audience, I will choose a convenient straw man in W. A. Darlington's comments from 1949, on the trained audience:

> An audience which, in a comedy scene sees the point of a line at once and laughs quickly is a godsend to an harassed actor, who otherwise must wait to see whether the laugh is coming, and contrive his speech before the wait becomes noticeable if no laugh comes at all. If he times this wrongly, and begins to speak again just as the belated laugh comes, his next line is drowned and he has to make up his mind whether to repeat it or let it be lost.
>
> An intelligent audience smoothes out such difficulties in the actor's way and increases enormously the speed and precision of the performance as a whole. But let me here make clear once and for all that by an intelligent audience I do not mean an audience composed of intelligent people; for such an audience can on occasion be very slow witted indeed. I mean an audience trained to the theatre so that it can follow the dramatist's meaning like a pack of hounds on a scent (1949, 29).

Darlington uses laughter as his exemplar of audience training: laughing out of place is unfortunate, and not to laugh at all impertinent. Though we might think of laughter as a spontaneous expression of independent response, he has drawn it for us in this passage as one that is choreographed and cued. The audience as a pack of hounds is an unfortunate image for an analysis of a theatre practice that aims to realise the potential of all involved: in it the spectator is simultaneously dehumanised, domesticated and potentially vicious. Compare this to Alfred Jarry's image of his audience; writing of his need to goad his public, he says: "It is because [they] are an inert and obtuse and passive mass that they need to be shaken up from time to time so that we can tell from their bear-like grunts where they are—and where they stand" (Jarry in Blackadder 2003, 323). These are caricatures of the tamed audiences of their time, both using noise-making as a key indicator of their state of engagement with the work. Which is more flattering, to be an inert and grumpy bear or a well trained hound?

This is historical, of course, and the current appetite for a different kind of audience is historical too. The passive audience is a part of the bourgeois-ification of the theatre in the eighteenth and nineteenth centuries, before which a sudden and spontaneous interruption to the stage events could be seen as complementary rather than inconvenient[1]. Audiences were homogenised by this revolution, as they learned to signify their qualified presence through restraint, and a kind of absence through their silence. The famous response to Jarry's *Ubu Roi* (1896) was a provoked rebellion, ostensibly against the play itself, but also implicitly against this domestication. It was a vestige of the tradition of 'damning' a bad play at its first performance, as were the so-called riots at the first performances of Synge's *Playboy of the Western World* (1907), when the managers of the Abbey theatre covered the floor of the auditorium with felt to muffle the stamping of sections of the audience, and allow the play to be heard. These practices have fallen away: the theatre-going public no longer insists on conformity to its expectations, and no longer protests vocally when they are offended. Why go to a play one doesn't expect to like, as the protesters at Jarry and Synge's openings evidently did? And if one does so by accident, protest is registered through walking out, with its subtle shuffling and muted 'excuse-me's. One can still disrupt the event through ignorance or accident, of course, and the worst such offence is not to switch one's phone to silent. In all of this the role of the audience is to avoid making a noise—we can make sounds, but only those which complement the signal being transmitted from the stage. Unwelcome noise, then, is interference, with the capacity to interrupt the flow of the significant, privileged, material.

Against this background I will sketch the practice of two companies who produce 'immersive' theatre that involves creating ambitious physical and sonic environments for audiences to inhabit. Punchdrunk and Shunt have generated a kind of anti-West End commercial success, and have gained their buzz partly because of the activity they ask of their audiences. In pieces like *The Ballad of Bobby Francois* (2000), *Dance Bear Dance* (2003) and *Money* (2009), Shunt lead us through their dank railway arches, and other curious spaces, and might contextualise us as airline passengers or UN ambassadors. They play spatial tricks and leave

[1] As discussed in detail by Susan Kattwinkel (2005) and Neil Blackadder (2006).

obstacles in our path. In *Faust* (2006), *Sleep No More* (2003), and *Masque of the Red Death* (2007), Punchdrunk ask us to wear masks and wander freely through elaborate environments, and lure us into one-to-one encounters with characters from well-known stories. These formal interventions are meaningful in themselves, but are also strategies that can make us feel special, as if we've taken part in something new and exciting because it is unlike the majority of theatregoing practice, and because the uniqueness of our experience is foregrounded unequivocally. And as ever, part of the meaning of these experiences is the kudos of being there: the cultural capital gained by attendance at something new, exciting, and exclusive.

Noisy audiences and unsettled subjectivity

It is possible to develop an analysis of this by following a thread from Nicolas Bourriaud's *Relational Aesthetics* (2002), in which he asserts a trend for the participatory and interactive in contemporary fine art. The work he considers is "a set of artistic practices which take as their theoretical and practical point of departure the whole of human relations and their social context, rather than an independent and private space" (Bourriaud 2002, 113). It is work that creates conviviality (a favourite Bourriaud word), not for its own sake, but for the outcomes that can be generated when people are led to 'live together' in an unfamiliar, unsettled way for a little time. Bourriaud makes use of Félix Guattari's aesthetics of subjectivity, in which the subject is not a secure point of departure, but a "set of relations that are created between the individual and the vehicles of subjectivity he comes across" (Bourriaud 2002, 91). These vehicles include elements of culture associated with family, religion, art and so on, along with consumerism, and its 'ideological gadgets', and informational machinery itself, in the guise of communication media. This subjectivity is never settled, which Guattari celebrates, finding that it is stasis which is unhealthy; subjectivity is enriched by becoming unsettled. For Bourriaud it is Guattari's recognition of this interdependence, and his anticipation of its rise in contemporary art that makes this a suitable theoretical model. The artists producing Bourriaud's 'relational art' refuse the privileged autonomy that the tradition offers them, creating relational procedures, vehicles of subjectivity that employ their interlocutors as similar vehicles themselves. We don't meet the subjectivity of the artist in a fixed work, but are de-territorialised by our encounter with the work in process. The idea of territorialisation is developed in Guattari and Deleuze's *A*

Thousand Plateaux (1988) as a term for the centrifugal effort to secure subjectivity, and a tool for this is the refrain, (or ritournelle):

> A child in the dark, gripped with fear, comforts himself by singing under his breath. He walks and halts to his song. Lost, he takes shelter, or orients himself with his little song as best he can. The song is like a rough sketch of a calming and stabilizing, calm and stable, centre in the heart of chaos. Perhaps the child skips as he sings, hastens or slows his pace. But the song itself is already a skip: it jumps from chaos to the beginnings of order in chaos and is in danger of breaking apart at any moment (Deleuze and Guattari 1988, 311).

Or less poetically:

> [...] we call a refrain an aggregate of matters of expression that draws a territory and develops into territorial motifs and landscapes (Deleuze and Guattari 1988, 323).

Their musical analogy (partly analogy, and partly direct reference to strategic use of sound and rhythm in nature as well as culture) is that the repeatable patterns and images we use to mark out our home ground, to make it safe and secure from the chaos of the wider world, can also be inverted to become the material with which we improvise with that world. The refrain can both resist and engage with the chaotic outside, and can become both signal and interference. Clearly the theatre is territorialised in part by the domesticated sound making of the audience, and might be de-territorialised by a sudden, unsettling change in that behaviour. The sonic exchanges at the early performances of *Ubu Roi* and *Playboy of the Western World* were invasions of territory; though the physical space of the stage was not disturbed, its claims to distinction—asserted through sonic discipline—could be challenged.

The project of unsettling the culture of art is as old as modernity, of course. Its latest manifestations in the theatre we have taken to calling 'postdramatic', particularly in the special status given to the "irruption of the real" (Lehmann 2006, 99-104) out of representational forms; Nick Ridout has gone so far as to say that "theatre is a machine which sets out to undo itself" (2006, 168), that the act of de-territorialisation is what makes the whole exercise worthwhile. Clearly unsettling spectators can be achieved without asking them to become more active, and without asking them to make noises of their own. This might be achieved through provocative content, but it might also result from a more than usually immersive theatrical environment, one which does not merely surround the audience member, but invades their space, whether through scenographic strategies which deny a defined audience space in the first place, through physical contact from performers, or through some kind of sonic assault and reciprocal opportunities for sound-making by the audience member.

An example of the sensation which can still arise out of such attempts to unsettle can be found in the minor scandal surrounding Badac Theatre's *The Factory*, at the Edinburgh festival in 2008. A reviewer (Wilkinson 2008) reported that the work initiated a confrontation with the audience in which spectators were harangued by actors playing concentration camp guards and surrounded by makeshift metal gongs played at loud volume, but that unscripted feedback from spectators was not welcome, and apparently unsettled the performers themselves: to the degree that they confronted uncooperative participants (including the reviewer himself) after the show, blaming them for deliberately vandalising the work. The way this story unfolded in online media at the time, and stimulated an extensive discussion of the obligations of interactive theatre performers as well as reviewers and audience members, could be a bookend to periodic reports of performers' onstage admonitions of audience members whose phones ring during a show, or who eat noisily, or otherwise do not keep performance discipline[2]. Between these two tropes of unhappy performers: the earnest experimentalist who invites but cannot handle participation and the offended traditionalist, we might find a range of expectations for audience behaviour, and in particular for audience noise-making. The willingness to reciprocate unsettling gestures, and to join in the noise, may be read as a sign of the times, either in today's immersive performance or in a different way in what might be considered a golden age of participatory culture. Guattari was associated, in 1968, with Julian Beck of The Living Theatre, who made use of literal and figurative noise in participatory performances like *Paradise Now* (for an account see Kostelanetz 1994), unsettling audiences by showing what should not be shown—naked bodies, chiefly—and inviting chaos in the show and around it, using both literal and figurative noise through semi-coherent vocal elements in the performance. Living Theatre's invitation to be de-

---

[2] See for example reports of Richard Griffiths scolding audience members in both London and New York, in productions of *The History Boys* and *Heroes*, BBC online, 2/11/2005, http://news.bbc.co.uk/1/hi/england/london/4458810.stm; The Independent, 2/6/2006 http://www.independent.co.uk/arts-entertainment/theatre-dance/news/now-broadway-gets-a-mobile-broadside-from-richard-griffiths-480728.html; along with Daniel Craig and Hugh Jackman in *A Steady Rain*: The Telegraph, 29/9/2009, http://www.telegraph.co.uk/culture/theatre/6241626/Daniel-Craig-and-Hugh-Jackman-stage-mobile-phone-protest.html (all accessed October 4, 2010).

territorialised might amount to an invited disobedience, quickly appropriated
by the mainstream and recycled in the musical *Hair* (1967), but it stands as
an emblem of theatrical excess—for those who value that as well as those
who don't.

In both *Paradise Now*, and *The Factory* the environment was sonically
challenging as well as socially and aesthetically demanding. Unfamiliar
and high-volume sounds were used in both productions to make audience
members feel uncomfortable. For The Living Theatre this had the result,
initially, of making the performance more noisy in the figurative sense, as
audiences joined the performance in ways that seemed genuinely
surprising and disruptive; their eventual abandonment of this show and its
strategies was partly due to the appearance of predictability in these
responses. When large-scale participation became an expected element of
their work, it ceased to be interesting to the company, or to many in their
audience: it was no longer unpredictable, evidently no longer uncomfortable
for those who took part, and because it had come so much under their
control, no longer noise in the sense I have been using the word here. For
Badac it seems that the figurative noise produced by some audience
members in response to their provocations—including the use of actual
noise—was not what they desired, they wanted to maintain a greater
control of the signal.

Some cautious sonic innovations

With Shunt and Punchdrunk, however, different kinds of restraint are
the norm, which allow an unsettling of theatrical conventions, without
stimulating their audiences to action which would lead them to encounter
the work in a way that might be called 'relational' in Bourriaud's sense.
Punchdrunk's most significant innovation is to mask audience members, a
move which facilitates exploration of their huge, rambling performance
environments and intimate interactions with performers[3]. As well as
facilitating, however, the mask inhibits. In the majority of Punchdrunk's
work (for example *Sleep No More, Faust* and *The Masque of the Red
Death*), the audience's masks have been 'full face', in some cases with
attached hoods, and sometimes with the large beak-like projection over the
mouth seen in some Venetian Carnival masks. They cover facial
expression, make eye-contact less communicative, and muffle speech, so
that their audience members speak to each other much less than those at

---

[3] For a longer discussion of their use of mask see my chapter in Oddey and White,
2009.

other promenade performances. The masks isolate people, and make the experience of watching and exploring much less communal than it might otherwise be. Though there are verbal elements to their pieces, often in one-to-one encounters or set-piece performances, the intimate interactions between performer and spectator are likely to be more physical, or to happen in seclusion. The mask focuses attention on the gaze in a way that can feel akin to being disembodied, and strangely un-present. Clearly this has the potential to be very unsettling, but it does not fit the description of mutual, convivial de-territorialisation that Bourriaud suggests as the potential for relational performance. The pervasive, looping sound design also serves to inhibit speech between audience members: this is a functional, as well as atmospheric, device that allows scene changes to be cued to performers in different parts of the environment, as the same sounds are played throughout, at a volume that is also loud enough to cover much conversation. It is ironic that the atmospheres usually produced by these soundscapes are eerie, unnerving and apparently chaotic but their effect is to maintain control over the event. The audience member's experience can be radically unstructured, in that they can wander as they like through the environment, but the potential for it to become rewarding, to produce impressions of encounters with actual events, is made possible through the structuring mechanism of the sound design.

Shunt's performances tend to have a more structured route for audiences to navigate their environments, they provide some spaces in which to speak out, and expect an answer, both between spectator and spectator, and spectator and performer. In *Money* this includes interactions framed as if the audience were in a waiting room with characters from the story, in a shareholders meeting, at a seminar for investors and at a champagne reception. In each of these the configuration of the space, with performers sitting next to audience members and talking to each other across the room, for example, implies that interaction is invited, and when it is offered it is accepted and incorporated skilfully, though not in a way that alters the progress of the scene. Shunt also use sound design in an instrumental way, to unsettle their audience in a way that puts them on edge or sensitises them: a favourite trick used early in a performance (in *Money* and several years earlier in *The Ballad of Bobby Francois*), is to bring the whole audience into a small space, plunge them into total darkness, and play very loud noises before bringing back the lights to reveal a radically changed physical space, where walls have been removed, and replaced with seating. Noise as part of a coup de théâtre and the noise making of the audience, then, are both used in unusual ways, but carefully organised to marshal the audience's attention on the performance material, rather than to facilitate convivial encounters.

In the aspects of their work described here, Shunt and Punchdrunk organise actual noise so that it doesn't become noise in the sense of interference: they maintain their control over the signal. There is still the potential, untapped in much of the interactive and immersive theatre that is capturing the imagination of theatre-goers, and makers, to give up control of the signal. There is something reciprocal about the invitation of noise—unsettling the audience through participation also brings chaos into the work itself, and potentially de-territorialises it—and this goes against the instincts of most theatre makers, who if they want to unsettle an aspect of their practice, want it to be securely managed, not at the whim of a stranger.

References

Attali, Jacques. 1985 (trans. Brian Massumi). *Noise: the Political Economy of Music*. Manchester: University of Manchester Press.

Blackadder, Neil. 2003. *Performing Opposition: Modern Theatre and the Scandalised Audience*. Westport: Praeger Publishers.

Bourriaud, Nicolas. 1998. *Relational Aesthetics*. London: Les Presse du Reel.

Darlington, W. A. 1949. *The Actor and his Audience*. London: Phoenix House.

Deleuze, Gilles, and Félix Guattari (trans. Brian Massumi). 1988. *A Thousand Plateaus: Capitalism and Schizophrenia*. London: Athlone Press.

Kattwinkel, Susan. (ed.) 2003. *Audience Participation: Essays on Inclusion in Performance*. Westport: Praeger Publishers.

Kostelanetz, Richard. 1994. *On Innovative Performance(s): Three decades of recollections on alternative theatre*. New York: McFarland.

Lehmann, Hans-Thies. 2006. *Postdramatic Theatre*. London: Routledge.

Machon, Josephine, 2009. *(Syn)Aesthetics*. London: Palgrave Macmillan

Ridout, Nicholas. 2006. *Stage Fright, Animals and Other Theatrical Problems*. Cambridge: Cambridge University Press.

Wilkinson, Chris. 'Edinburgh festival: Holocaust show's theatre of violence spills offstage' in *The Guardian* 22/8/2008: http://www.guardian.co.uk/culture/theatreblog/2008/aug/22/edinburghf estivalholocausts (accessed October 4, 2010).

White, Gareth. 2009. Odd Anonymized Needs: Punchdrunk's Masked Spectator. In *Modes of Spectating*. Ed. Alison Oddey and Christine White, 219-230. Bristol: Intellect.

CHAPTER XVIII

ALL AROUND THE PLACE:
SOUND IMMERSION AND THE THEATRE

JEANNE BOVET

Being a listening place as well as a seeing place, the theatre is a place where sounds and images coexist and interact. Although in Western theatre both sound and image are mostly frontal phenomena due to the use of the frontal stage, other combinations have occurred throughout history, and have been made seemingly boundless with the technological and digital development of stage and sound design. Drawing on Jonathan Sterne (2003) and Walter Ong's (1981 [1967]) very different theories of sound, this chapter attempts to discuss the apparently obvious and somewhat overused concept of sound immersion as it may (or may not) apply to the theatrical experience, namely by confronting it with the so-called visual notion of focus. The use of sound immersion processes in internationally renowned Québécois stage director Denis Marleau's 'technological phantasmagory' *Les Aveugles* (2002) will serve as an illustration to underline the sensorial and perceptual shifts induced in the theatrical relationship between the visual and the aural experience.

What is sound immersion?

The concept of immersion is often used to define sound phenomena and their sensorial perception. Such a definition pertains to what Jonathan Sterne calls the "audiovisual litany" (Sterne 2003, 15), a series of assertions about the difference between hearing and seeing that establishes a clear-cut axiology of the senses, hearing being—among other characteristics—spherical, immersing the subject in the world, and vision being directional, offering a remote perspective on the world.

Indeed, while the eye can never literally achieve peripheral vision, the ear simultaneously perceives all the surrounding sounds:

> At a given instant I hear not merely what is in front of me or behind me or
> at either side, but all these things simultaneously, and what is above and
> below as well. (Ong 1981, 129)

Moreover, however specific its source, sound is an omnidirectional, intrusively invasive natural phenomenon, because sound waves propagate and resonate through the entire available space. Immersion would thus be our mode of existing in sound. As it plunges us into sound, it situates us "in the midst of a world" (Ong 1981, 129). Such an embracing, inclusive position is not necessarily a comfortable one. As stage director Matthias Langhoff remarks, it is impossible to distance oneself from sound. Ong explains: sound immersion makes the hearer,

> intimately aware of a great many goings-on which it lets [him/her] know
> are simultaneous but which [s/he] cannot possibly view simultaneously
> and thus [has] difficulty in dissecting or analyzing, and consequently of
> managing. (Ong 1981, 129-30)

Being so beyond the hearer's control, sound immersion therefore also poses the threat of auditory indistinction. At best, it allows the hearer a global prehension of the sonic environment, a process which Ong calls "auditory synthesis" (Ong 1981, 130). At worst, it gives way to the anxiety-inducing feeling of submersion.

This at least is Ong's thesis, as he reflects in ontotheological terms on sound as the manifestation of the sacred in oral cultures. Since its first publication in 1967, the work of Ong has of course been criticised, notably by Sterne, precisely because of this ontotheological bias. But such criticism does not invalidate the main notion of sound immersion itself. Regardless of the ideological issues at stake in Ong's work—as well as that of many other heralds of the 'audiovisual litany'—it is this very notion of sound immersion that I wish to question in this chapter.

Selective listening

While immersion can indeed be considered a given fact of 'natural' auditory perception, the same cannot be said of the auditory synthesis described by Ong. Empirical experience proves quite the reverse, i.e. that even in a noisy soundscape, the ear is capable of discrimination. This is not merely a matter of distinguishing between the 'natural' non-discriminating state of hearing, and the 'cultural,' discriminating practice of listening—as Sterne rightly urges us to do. In animals as well as in humans, there are natural, neurophysiological mechanisms that favour auditory discrimination. A good example of this is the phenomenon of sleep. When we are asleep, all surrounding sounds continue to access our inner ear, while the brain filters them out, blocking or minimising some (such as background noises), staying in alert for others (such as loud, sudden, or high-pitched sounds).

The same applies to many cultural situations, including theatre-going. Not because one sleeps in the theatre (even though one might, of course!), but because the theatre audience's attention is channelled and directed towards a certain type of listening. Evidently, the overall context of the theatrical experience remains that of sound immersion, as much because of the physical, acoustic nature of sound itself, as well as because the listener is surrounded by more or less noisy fellow spectators in a common space, more often than not indoors. But at the same time, the listener is also engaged in the process of focusing his/her attention towards the sounds of the stage, whatever that stage's particular scenography might be (frontal, bi-frontal, or in the round). This type of selective listening is clearly a cultural activity, one that has to be acquired and practiced. It might even be deemed what Sterne calls an "audile technique," even though, contrary to the listening skills described by Sterne in *The Audible Past,* it is not related to a private, individuated acoustic space—such as that of the stethoscope, telephone, or headphone (Sterne 2003, 23-4)—but rather to the collective, communal space of the theatre.

Immersed in the theatrical sound event, the audience member hears everything, but listens selectively. In that respect, the World Soundscape Project categories[1] might provide useful methodological tools for theatre research, as they could help describe both the sonic theatrical event and its listening process. These categories distinguish:

1. the key note, i.e. the ubiquitous and prevailing sonic background of the event
2. the signals, i.e. the foreground sounds that are listened to consciously, as they usually encode messages or information
3. the soundmarks, i.e. unique and specific sound objects that are unique and specific to a certain place (here the theatre)
4. the sound symbols, that trigger collective and cultural associations.

---

[1] Developed by Raymond Murray Schafer and his Simon Fraser University fellow researchers to analyse the soundscape, or sonic environment, which is the sum total of all sounds within a defined area (Schafer 1977).

All these categories of sounds can be heard in the theatre. But what the theatre listener focuses on is usually not the background (keynote). To various extents, s/he will rather pay attention to the signals, soundmarks, and symbols, as s/he perceives them in a more or less balanced relationship, coming either from the stage, or from the audience—such as the nerve-wrecking unwrapping of candy in the third seat of the second to last row. Therefore, if the concept of sound immersion does apply to the theatrical event as well as to any sonic experience, the audience's sonic perception process does not seem to take the global form of auditory synthesis, but would be more adequately defined by the concept of focus.

Auditory focus, a cultural construct

In the audiovisual litany's clear-cut axiology, the concept of focus is, of course, related to vision and not to hearing. However, considering what has just been stated, the use of the notion of focus to describe the listening process is by no means metaphorical. It pertains to the epistemological and theoretical move advocated by Sterne, that is, to refuse to narrow the field of research by assuming that there are special, ontological qualities to each one of the human senses, "that certain configurations of activity belong to certain senses or faculties by right of origin" (Sterne 2003, 345). As Sterne points out, some of the qualities supposedly special or unique to sound are not. He gives the example of the ephemeral, which, far from being specific to sound, is "a quality endemic to any form of perceptible motion or event in time" (Sterne 2003, 18), and thus can be perceived by the eye as well as by the ear. In the same way, one could argue that, as a perception mode, focus is not specific to vision, but can be applied to listening, as well as to touching, perhaps even to tasting and smelling, as wine tasters and perfumers could demonstrate.[2]

This broadening of operational terms has nothing to do with synaesthesia, but rather with an attempt to re-describe the senses by opening the field of research to their historical and cultural dynamics rather than restricting it to their supposedly static nature. Since "phenomenology always presupposes culture" (Sterne 2003, 13), "even phenomenologies can change" (Sterne 2003, 19). Hence, since the definition of sound is necessarily "based on the understood possibilities of the faculty of hearing" (Sterne 2003, 12), sound should be considered as a historical "variable rather than a constant" (Sterne 2003, 13), and the experience of sound as a social and cultural

---

[2] For instance, Sterne uses the word focus to describe audile techniques such as the "directional and directed" listening skills of sound telegraphers (Sterne 2003, 24).

construct. This makes the audile technique of focusing part of the cultural history of the theatre.

Indeed, directing one's attention to the sounds of the stage has not always been as obvious as it seems now. In contrast with our twenty-first century habits, attending a play in seventeenth century France, for instance, was a much more immersive sensorial experience, since the participatory noise of the (talking, applauding, booing) audience accompanied and often matched or challenged the actor's declamation, while the lights stayed on in the room, and members of the audience were even seated on stage among the actors, facing the stalls. This is not to say that the skill of focusing on the sounds of the stage was unknown to French seventeenth century theatre-goers. But one must admit that auditory focus has been drastically reinforced by the gradual silencing of the audience, just as the visual focus on the stage has been reinforced by plunging the audience in the dark. Pertaining to the aesthetics of the fourth wall, these historical transformations in the spectatorial function have turned the acoustic space of the theatre into a stage oriented one, favouring directional, directed and distanced listening over the global immersive acoustic experience.

In this perspective, the ways in which contemporary theatre attempts to disrupt auditory focus by constructing immersive sound effects are obviously worth investigating. Apart from understanding how these immersive effects are technically produced, one should also wonder what they stand for in our day and age. In that respect, the work of Québécois stage director Denis Marleau proves to be particularly interesting.

Back to nature? Sound immersion in *Les Aveugles*

One of Marleau's most famous productions is his 2002 staging of Maurice Maeterlinck's 1890 play *Les Aveugles*. The first of three 'technological phantasmagoria' using the same audio-visual devices,[3] *Les Aveugles* features no live actors. What the audience sees in front of them are the multiplied images of a male and a female actor's faces, which are projected in a frontal way on three-dimensional, disembodied mask-like structures, hanging over a pitch-black stage (see figure 18-1). We gradually come to understand that they represent a group of twelve blind men and women lost on an island. As the video begins, the faces come to life; their eyes start to move, and their mouths to utter the pre-recorded

---

[3] The two others being Samuel Beckett's *Comédie,* and Jon Fosse's *Dors mon petit enfant,* both created by Marleau two years later, in 2004, and since then having toured with *Les Aveugles* as a triptych. Excerpts are available on Denis Marleau's "Ubu, compagnie de création" website (www.ubucc.ca).

lines of Maeterlinck's play. Sound designer Nancy Tobin has placed the speakers for each individual character's voice next to each mask, making the sound setting match the frontal setting of the faces, the difference being however that, contrary to the visible masks, the speakers stay hidden from the view of the audience.

Figure 18-1: *Les Aveugles* all images of actor Paul Savoie. Photograph by Richard-Max Tremblay.

Apart from this frontal sound device, *Les Aveugles* also makes a selective and very effective use of peripheral speakers. Also invisible to the audience, these serve to disperse another type of sound—what Maeterlinck's stage directions call "les rumeurs étouffées et inquiètes de l'Île" (Maeterlinck 2006, 116), which could be translated as "the muffled and worried rumours of the island" on which the characters are lost. The sounds created for that purpose by Nancy Tobin evoke the surrounding presence of the sea, the forest or the wind. In contrast with the frontal, articulate speech of the characters, these immersive sound effects let us hear, every now and then, the underlying, ubiquitous voice of nature. As the audience is thus immersed in the ambient sound as well as in the dark, it finds itself both visually and audibly in the midst of the blind men and women's world, as though it were part of it.[4] The sense of the invisible threat on the characters is definitely heightened by these inclusive processes. So is the sense of the sacred which, in Maeterlinck's work, is to be found in the invisible, and is described by the playwright as "the idea of the Christian God, mingled with the idea of Antic fatality, forced back into the impenetrable night of nature" (Maeterlinck 1999, 496).[5]

There is one immersive effect, however, that does not come from the sounds of the surrounding nature, and thus particularly stands out against them. It occurs towards the end of the play, as the approaching menace grows closer to the terrified, helpless group. A wailing sound arises on the right side of the audience, the voice of a character who we know is among the blind, but who we do not see any more than they do, as it is not represented by a mask or any other visual device. Throughout the play, a child has been sitting within the group, the baby of one of the women—the *infans,* incapable of speech but, unlike his mother and her fellow companions, very capable of seeing. And what he sees is precisely whatever is approaching them, hence his sudden, alarmed reaction.

Against all expectation, the infant's voice does not come from where he is located, which would be in front of the audience, on his mother's lap. Instead, it starts out on the side speaker, and, as it gets louder, it is progressively transmitted through all the peripheral speakers in a simultaneous, circular movement, as an overwhelming burst of uncontrolled anxiety. Beyond just signalling the infant's fear of the unknown, the spherical diffusion of his wailing, running all around the place, transforms the audience into the echo chamber of the twelve blind character's panicked thoughts, bouncing uncontrollably off the walls of the closed space of their minds.

Be it the voice of the elements or the voice of the child, the peripheral sound effects in *Les Aveugles* are all the more potent because they not only break, but ultimately blur all boundaries, as they immerse both the stage into the auditorium, and the auditorium into the stage. As the spatial setup of the infant's voice well shows, they definitely play against focus, both visual and auditory. If only for a moment, they bring us back to the

---

[4] Although being in the dark is a common theatre-goer's experience, here it takes on special meaning, as it replicates the character's condition—which the blackening of the stage space around them also leads us to understand.

[5] "L'idée du Dieu chrétien, mêlée à celle de la fatalité antique, refoulée dans la nuit impénétrable de la nature" (Maeterlinck 1999, 496). For further consideration on the presence of the invisible in Maeterlinck's plays, see Gérard Dessons 2005.

primitive, indistinct, unmanageable state of sound immersion, or rather, they force us into it, which is even more uncomfortable. However, there is nothing natural about these immersive effects. Well hidden, well mastered, they remain a technological construct, a *'trompe-l'oreille'* similar to the three-dimensional *'trompe-l'œil'* use of video on the masks. As such, they are an undeniable, creative experience, opening the field of the senses to unusual, literally unheard-of, artistic modes of perception.

References

Dessons, Gérard. 2005. *Maeterlinck, le théâtre du poème*. Paris: Laurence Teper.

Maeterlinck, Maurice. 1999. *Œuvres I: le réveil de l'âme, poésie et essais*. Ed. Paul Gorceix. Brussels: Éditions Complexe.

Maeterlinck, Maurice. 2006 [1890]. *Les Aveugles*. Ed. Paul Gorceix. Paris: Eurédit.

Ong, Walter J. 1981 [1967]. *The Presence of the Word: Some Prolegomena for Cultural and Religious History*. Minneapolis: University of Minnesota Press.

—. 1982. *Orality and Literacy: the Technologizing of the Word*. London/New York: Methuen.

Schafer, Raymond Murray. 1977. *The Tuning of the World*. Toronto: McClelland & Stewart.

Sterne, Jonathan. 2003. *The Audible Past: Cultural Origins of Sound Reproduction*. Durham: Duke University Press.

CONTRIBUTORS

ROSS BROWN is Dean of Studies and Professor of Sound at the Central School of Speech and Drama. He has created and performed live scores for over twenty silent films at festivals from Rome to Lapland, and performed in music theatre productions for the Glasgow Citizens, Lancaster Dukes and Derby Playhouse theatres. Ross has composed music for BBC Radio Drama and has been a regular composer and performer for Red Shift Theatre Company since the mid-1980s. Publications include; 'Sound Design: the Scenography of Engagement and Distraction' in *Theatre and Performance Design: a Reader in Scenography*, (eds J. Collins and A. Nisbett. London: Routledge 2010), and *Sound* (Basingstoke: Palgrave Macmillan 2010) and 'Noise, Memory, Gesture: the Theatre in a Minute's Silence' in *Performance, Embodiment & Cultural Memory*, (eds R. Mock and C. Counsell, Cambridge Scholars Publishing 2009). For more information see www.noisegarden.net.

JEANNE BOVET is Associate Professor in French literature at University of Montreal, where she teaches the history and aesthetics of theatre. A founding member of the international CNRS/CRI research program on Theatre Sound, she mainly researches the aesthetics of voice, both on stage and within the dramatic text. She has published several essays and book chapters on the topic, and is co-editor with Marie-Madeleine Mervant-Roux and Jean-Marc Larrue of *Le son du théâtre. 3 Voix Words Words Words*, *Théâtre/Public*, n° 201 (*Théâtre/Public,* Fall 2011). Thanks to funding from the Social Sciences and Humanities Research Council of Canada (SSHRC) and the Fonds québécois de recherche sur la société et la culture (FQRSC), she has recently completed a book on the oratorical inscription of declamation in seventeenth century French drama (to be published in 2011), and is currently investigating the relations between voice, text and media in twentieth century theatre.

JOHN COLLINS is the Artistic Director of Elevator Repair Service Theater (ERS). John founded ERS in 1991 and has since directed or co-directed all of the company's shows. From 1993 to 2006 he also worked for The Wooster Group as a sound designer where he was the recipient of two Drama Desk nominations and two Bessie Awards. Also a lighting designer, he won a Bessie Award for his design of ERS' *Room Tone* in 2003. John is a 2010 Guggenheim Fellow in Drama and Performance Art and recently received the Elliot Norton Award for Outstanding Director for *Gatz* at The American Repertory Theatre. John holds a B.A. in English and Theater Studies from Yale University.

ADRIAN CURTIN Ph.D. is a Lecturer in Theatre at the School of Performing Arts at the University of Lincoln, UK, and a graduate of the Interdisciplinary Ph.D. Program in Theatre and Drama at Northwestern University. His research interests include theatre sound, avant-garde theatre, theatrical modernism, music-as-theatre, cultural thanatology, and contemporary British and Irish theatre. He has written journal articles on works by Antonin Artaud, Peter Maxwell Davies, James Joyce, Ben Jonson, and W.G. Sebald. He is a recipient of a Presidential Fellowship from Northwestern University and the 2010 winner of the New Scholar's Prize, awarded by the International Federation of Theatre Research (IFTR).

ZACHARY DUNBAR Ph.D. is a Lecturer on the MA Music Theatre and MA Acting at the Central School of Speech and Drama. A career as a concert pianist (Yale University; Fulbright scholar at the Royal College of Music) eventually converged with drama and he has since developed a freelance career spanning different genres including Beijing Opera, soundscape drama, dance theatre, radio drama (BBC 4), stage plays, and mainstream musical theatre. Original works have been staged at Camden People's Theatre, Pleasance Theatre, Bloomsbury Theatre, Brighton Underbelly and several Edinburgh-fringe productions (Fringe-First nominated), and the Junge Hunde festival (Denmark). He also gives performance workshops internationally that explore musicality as a function of actor and ensemble training. He has academic publications in the field of Greek tragedy and also in music theatre and holds a Ph.D. from the University of London.

GEORGE HOME-COOK read Theology at the University of St. Andrews and trained as an actor at East 15 Acting School before completing an MA in Performance at Queen Mary, University of London. Since 2006 he has been working towards a Ph.D. at Queen Mary, for which he was awarded a Westfield Trust studentship. His thesis, *Stretching Ourselves: The Phenomenology of Sound, Listening and Attention in Contemporary Theatre* investigates the phenomenal experience of listening in performance, the co-option of the senses and the theatricality of auditory attention. As well as working as a professional actor and director, George is an experienced teacher/lecturer and has taught drama and performance studies at both undergraduate and secondary school level.

LYNNE KENDRICK Ph.D. is a Lecturer in Drama at the Central School of Speech and Drama and she also works as a director/producer. She is a founding member and director of Camden People's Theatre, a north London venue that produces contemporary theatre and has a history of exploring experimental and applied theatre practices including verbatim theatre, intergenerational, intercultural and interdisciplinary practices. Lynne was a fellow of CSSD's Centre for Excellence in Training for Theatre exploring emergent graduate training and production opportunities and she managed the School's graduate company residency scheme. Lynne has published articles on disability arts, cultural policy and national and international touring, and more recently on theorising actor training including in 2011 "A Paidic aesthetic: an analysis of games in Philippe Gaulier's ludic pedagogy" in *Theatre, Dance and Performance Training*, Vol 2 (1), 2011.

DANIJELA KULEZIC-WILSON Ph.D. studied musicology at the University of Belgrade and received her doctorate from the University of Ulster. Her research interests include approaches to film that emphasise its inherent musical properties, the musicality of sound design and the use of silence in film and musical aspects of Beckett's plays. Danijela's work has been published in journals such as *Music and the Moving Image, Film and Film Culture, Musicology, Journal of Music, New Sound* and *Music, Sound and the Moving Image*. Her publications include essays on film rhythm, musical and film time, the musical use of silence in film, Darren Aronofsky's *Pi*, P.T. Anderson's *Magnolia*, Peter Strickland's *Katalin Varga*, Prokofiev's music for Eisenstein's films and Jim Jarmusch's *Dead Man*. She teaches at University College Cork in Ireland.

ALICE LAGAAY, Ph.D. is a researcher at the philosophy department of Freie Universität Berlin where she was employed from 2002 to 2010 at the collaborative research centre "Performing Cultures". Since completing her doctoral thesis in 2007 entitled *Towards a Philosophy of Voice. Reflections on the Sound—and Silence—of Human Language*, her work has focused on the performativity of silence, secrets and *not*-doing as well as on the relationship between theatre and philosophy. Book publications include: *Metaphysics of Performance* (Logos 2001); *Medientheorien. Eine philosophische Einführung* (ed. with D. Lauer, Campus 2004); *Nicht(s) Sagen* (ed. with E. Alloa, Transcript 2008), and *Performanzen des Nichttuns* (ed. with B. Gronau, Passagen 2008); *Ökonomien der Zurückhaltung* (ed.

with B. Gronau, Transcript 2010). Articles include: "Between Sound and Silence: Voice in the History of Psychoanalysis" in *E-pisteme*, vol. 1 (1), 2008; and "Passivity at Work. A Conversation on an Element in the Philosophy of Giorgio Agamben" (with J. Schiffers) in: *Law and Critique* 20, 2009. Alice Lagaay is currently working on an anthology with Laura Cull entitled *Performance and Philosophy*.

JEAN-MARC LARRUE is Co-Director of the Research Center on Intermediality (CRI) at Université de Montréal (Canada) and is Professor of theatre history and theory at Collège de Valleyfield. His research mainly focuses on theatre, modernism and media. He is the author or co-author of several works: *Yiddish theatre in Montreal* (Lansman-Jeu 1996); *Les Nuits de la "Main"* (VLB with André-G. Bourassa 1993): *Le Monument inattendu* (HMH-Hurtubise 1993), *Le Théâtre à Montréal à la fin du XIXe siècle* (Fides 1981), *Théâtre au Québec—repères et perspectives* (VLB, with André-G. Bourassa and Gilbert David 1988). More recent publications include: *Lives and Deaths of Collective Creation* with Jane Baldwin and Christiane Page (Vox Theatri 2008), *Mettre en scène* (*Intermédialités* 12, 2008) and the series *Le son au théâtre* (*Théâtre/Public* 2010-11). He is the recipient of grants from the Social Sciences and Humanities Research Council of Canada (SSHRC) and the Fonds québécois de recherche sur la société et la culture (FQRSC).

MARIE-MADELEINE MERVANT-ROUX is Senior Researcher at the Centre national de la recherche scientifique CNRS (Atelier de recherche sur l'intermédialité et les arts du spectacle [ARIAS]) and Associate Professor in Theatre Studies at Université Sorbonne Nouvelle-Paris 3. Her research is mainly concerned with the figure of the spectator: *L'Assise du théâtre. Pour une étude du spectateur* (CNRS Éditions 1998); *Figurations du spectateur* (L'Harmattan 2006) and *Du théâtre amateur.* (CNRS Éditions 2004). Recent publications include: *Art et frontalité. Scène, peinture, performance*, in: *Ligéia, Dossiers sur l'art*, n° 81-84; 2008; *Claude Régy*, book and DVD-rom (CNRS Éditions 2008), *Genèses théâtrales* (CNRS Éditions 2010), and *Le Théâtre des amateurs et l'expérience de l'art* (L'Entretemps 2011). As the French Co-ordinator of the international Project "Sound Technologies and the Theater (19th-21st centuries)", she published (with J.-M. Larrue, C. Guinebault-Szlamowicz and J. Bovet): in October 2010 *Le son du théâtre. Vol. 1. Le passé audible*, *Théâtre/Public*, n° 197; in March 2011 *Vol. 2. Dire l'acoustique*, *Théâtre/Public*, n° 199, and in September 2011 *Vol. 3 Voix Words Words Words*, *Théâtre/Public*, n° 201. For more information see www.lesonduthéatre.com.

MISHA MYERS Ph.D., is an artist and researcher who creates socially engaged, dialogic and propositional events activated through collective acts of walking, singing, writing or other performance mechanisms that invite participants to reflect on and articulate their experience and inhabitation of particular places and landscapes. Her work often engages with particular social groups or inhabitants of places, such as her recent work *way from home* involving collaboration with refugees and asylum seekers across the UK. Recent publications and research considers the dramaturgy, narrative choreography and new technologies of walking tours, new aesthetics of spatial mobility, conviviality and modes of participation in peripatetic performance, and new forms of collaboration, self-organisation and social interaction in participatory choral performance. She is the Programme Leader of Theatre at University College Falmouth incorporating Dartington College of Arts.

PATRICE PAVIS was Professor of Theatre Studies at the University of Paris (1976 – 2007). He is currently a Professor in the Department of Theatre at the University of Kent, Canterbury. He has published a *Dictionary of the Theatre* (translated into thirty languages) and books on performance analysis, contemporary French dramatists and contemporary theatre. His most recent publication is *Las mise en scène contemporaine* (Armand Colin, 2007) an English translation of this book is forthcoming, published by Routledge.

DAVID ROESNER Ph.D. is a Senior Lecturer in Drama at the University of Exeter. In 2002 he finished his Ph.D. thesis at the University of Hildesheim, Germany, on *Theatre as Music* analysing principles and strategies of musicalisation in productions by Christoph Marthaler, Einar Schleef and Robert Wilson. He taught at the Universities of Hildesheim, Bern and Mainz and given workshops in Kristiansand, Reykjavik, Bern and Kassel. Recently, he has won the Thurnau Award for Music Theatre Studies, 2007 for his article "The politics of the polyphony of performance", published with *Contemporary Theatre Review* (1, 2008). In 2009 he conducted an AHRC funded project on *Composed Theatre* together with Matthias Rebstock (Hildesheim). David Roesner also works as a theatre-musician and director. For traces of his work and a full list of publications see: http://humanities.exeter.ac.uk/drama/staff/roesner.

KATHARINA ROST is currently working as a research assistant at the Theatre Studies department of the Freie Universität Berlin. She is writing a dissertation on the topic of auditory attention in contemporary theatre performance. Her research interests include the sound design in theatre, listening, attention, participation and spectatorship. From 2008 to 2010, she was a member of the research group "Voices as Paradigms of the Performative" in the research project *Cultures of the Performative* at Freie Universität Berlin. She has studied Theatre Studies, Philosophy and German Literature and assisted in the public relations and press department of several international dance and theatre festivals.

ERIC VAUTRIN is Associate Professor (maître de conférences) in performing arts at the University of Caen Basse-Normandie, member of LASLAR, UCBN Langage and Arts laboratory, and of ARIAS, CNRS laboratory on intermediality and the performing arts. After a Ph.D. on contemporary European theatre entitled *Fashion and pace of the myth in the contemporary theatre, an anthropological approach of the representation*, his research focuses on theatrical scenes and analysis methods of performance, including the anthropological dimensions of artistic and cultural practices.

PIETER VERSTRAETE Ph.D. is a Lecturer in the Drama Department of the University of Exeter. He was previously researching at the Amsterdam School for Cultural Analysis whilst teaching at the Theatre Department of the University of Amsterdam and the Cultural Studies Department at the Radboud University in Nijmegen. In 2009, he completed a Ph.D. dissertation, entitled *The Frequency of Imagination: Auditory Distress and Aurality in Contemporary Music Theatre*. In 2009 he co-edited a book, entitled *Inside Knowledge* (Cambridge Scholars Publishing), and published chapters in books, such as *Performing the Matrix* (Epodium 2007), and *Sonic Mediations* (Cambridge Scholars Publishing 2008), *Cathy Berberian: Matchless Mistress of Vocal Art* (Amsterdam University Press 2012). He published articles on music theatre, opera and interactive installation art in, among others, *Urbanmag, De Theatermaker, Etcetera, Courant, nY, Forum Modernes Theater* and *Performance Research*.

GARETH WHITE Ph.D. is a Lecturer in Applied Theatre and the Central School of Speech and Drama. He was an actor, director and facilitator before gaining a doctorate from Goldsmiths College, University of London. As a practitioner Gareth White has specialised in work with community groups and in educational settings. He is formerly a director of Armadillo Theatre, a company producing issue-based workshops, performances and creative residencies, and an actor with Box Clever Theatre Company. Publications include "Odd, Anonymised Needs: the masked spectator in Punchdrunk's theatre environments", in *Modes of Spectating*, (eds A. Oddey and C. White, Intellect 2009) and "Navigating the Ethics of Audience Participation", *Applied Theatre Researcher* (2007) online.

TIM WHITE is Associate Professor in Theatre and Performance Studies at Warwick. After several years working as a stage technician at Birmingham Repertory Theatre he completed a Ph.D. at Warwick concerning the use of the performative to disrupt form in the work of artists since 1960. He teaches modules on practical video, experimental music, the American Avant-Garde and performing online. Publications include, *Diaghilev to the Pet Shop Boys* (Lund Humphries Publishers 1996) as well as articles for *Contemporary Theatre Review* and *Dance Theatre Journal* and, most recently for the September 2010 issue of *Performance Research* concerning *Listening*. He is currently researching a book on the theatricality of restaurants.

INDEX

70, 71, 74, 76-80, 82, 84, 86, 92,
139-145, 147, 151-155, 157,
159-161, 174, 175, 187, 219,
220
theatrophone, 19
timbre, xxii, 47, 49, 50, 52, 84, 85,
159, 167, 170
utterance, xv, xviii, xix, xxii, xxiii,
41, 44, 48, 58-60, 66, 82, 89, 90,
132, 150, 164, 171, 172
vision, x, xix, xxvi, xxvii, xxxi-
xxxiii, 5, 7, 8, 34, 35, 41, 90,
103, 106, 107, 150, 166, 189,
208, 211
vocality, vi, xv, xviii, xxii-xxxii, 57-
61, 66, 67, 82, 83, 86, 87, 89,
94, 176, 184, 186
Voegelin, Salomé, xv, xxxv, 13, 67,

69, 177, 180-183, 188
voice, v, vi, x, xiv, xviii, xix, xxii-
xxiv, xxvii, xxx, xxxi, xxxiii, 1,
3, 14, 15, 20, 21, 34- 36, 39, 45,
48-50, 53, 57-77, 79-94, 102,
104, 105, 109, 120, 130, 136,
141, 144, 151, 160, 164-172,
176, 180, 182-184, 186, 187,
190, 194, 213, 214, 216, 218,
219
atopic voice, xxiv, 73, 74, 90
authoritative voice, xxiv, 74, 86-
90
Warner, Daniel, xiv, xxiii, xxxiv, 12
Wilson, Robert, 45, 165, 196, 197,
220
Wooster Group, The, vi, viii, xxi,
xxvii, 24-29, 82, 83, 91, 216